# NOT WELCOME HERE

"Luke...," George said, her voice alarmed, which made Trinity look up just as Lucas Jensen grabbed him by the front of his shirt and hauled him from the booth. Trinity had little time to react before the larger man punched him hard in the stomach and threw him to the floor.

"Luke, stop it!" George yelled and grabbed Jensen's arm. He shook her off angrily, then backhanded Trinity across the face as the smaller man struggled upright. Trinity sprawled facedown on the slick tiled floor, his hands slipping in the spray of blood from his nose. Jensen kicked him, missing his head, but his boot slamming into his shoulder. Searing pain shot through Trinity as he curled into a ball. He gasped for breath, his arm numbed.

Trinity steeled himself for another blow as George threw herself at Jensen, knocking him off balance. "Stop it!" he heard George screaming in anger. "Stop it right this minute, or I'll call Sheriff Holbrook!"

"Go right ahead," Jensen shouted, his voice thick with rage. "See how much support you get for harboring a terrorist!"

# LEE JACKSON

# REDEMPTION

LEISURE BOOKS  NEW YORK CITY

*In memory of my father and best friend, C.J., who was
instrumental in the genesis of this story, and who will
never see this result of our impassioned debates about
the nature of justice, freedom and love.*

*I miss you so much, Old Fart.*

A LEISURE BOOK®

October 2008

Published by

Dorchester Publishing Co., Inc.
200 Madison Avenue
New York, NY 10016

ISBN 10: 0-8439-6158-9
ISBN 13: 978-0-8439-6158-4

The name "Leisure Books" and the stylized "L" with design are
trademarks of Dorchester Publishing Co., Inc.

Printed in the United States of America.

10 9 8 7 6 5 4 3 2 1

Visit us on the web at www.dorchesterpub.com.

# ACKNOWLEDGMENTS

The town of Redemption, Montana, is fictitious, as are all the characters in the novel. With the exception of historical or political personages and occurrences, any similarity to actual events or real people is coincidental and unintended.

Novels are not written in the vacuum of some ivory tower. I am grateful to everyone who helped me do the research that a novel like this needs to breathe the illusion of reality into it and to those who bring it to fruition. I quite literally could not have done it without you.

Thank you to the absolutely invaluable Jacki Riffey, who has been the backbone of this novel, and to her student, M. Terra "Badger Woman" Chamberlin in Columbia Falls, Montana. Thanks to Long Standing Bear Chief, publisher of the *Piikani Sun* in Browning, in the Blackfoot Nation. Thank you to Betty Erbetta of Great Falls; to Sheriff Glenn Huestis of Blaine County; and to the Havre Chief of Police, Mike Barthel. A very special thank you to Officer Catherine A. Huston of the Havre City Police Department, and to Patrick D. Sheehy in St. Paul, Minneapolis, former city editor of the *Havre Daily News*.

Thanks to Chuck Hawks of Gunsandshootingonline.com for his guidance on weapons. Thanks also to my dear friend, retired County Sheriff Mev Camozzi, a superwoman in her own right. Thanks to Nathan Wheeler for catching my all too frequent "techie-type" mistakes. Thanks also to the rest of the gang at C&L: Nicole Belle, Mr. E., Gregory Mast, and "Alvin"—you guys rock. Thanks to my literary agent, John Silbersack, and his former assistant, Kate Scherler, and my wonderful editor, Kelley Ragland. In Britain, with love to my ever-faithful fount of arcane linguistic wisdom, Andrew Plant, and to my Geordie guardian angel, Jon Barron. Also thanks to John Hughes-Wilson of Kent for his advice on security and terrorism. In New Zealand, much thanks to the Jackson clan, especially Simon, Georgina, and Isabella. Much love and thanks goes to my vastly smarter kid sister, Kathryn.

And of course, as always, for my best mate, Robinson the cat.

I would also like to show my appreciation and deep respect for those people who I've never met, who aren't famous or powerful, but who have made a difference in a difficult world: Yulie Cohen Gerstel of Israel; the late Tarek Ayyoub of al-Jazeera; Sibel Edmonds, former translator for the FBI; Arcelia Lopez and retired FBI agent Jim Wedick in Sacramento; FBI Investigator James Wynne in New York; and Purna Raj Bajracharya, a Nepalese Buddhist mistakenly suspected of terrorist activities.

Unhappy the land that needs heroes.

We have made clear the doctrine which says if you harbor a terrorist, if you feed a terrorist, if you hide a terrorist, you're just as guilty as the terrorist.

—GEORGE W. BUSH

Necessity is the plea for every infringement of human freedom. It is the argument of tyrants; it is the creed of slaves.

—WILLIAM PITT THE YOUNGER

The war on terrorism is a war of ideas. The greatest restraint on human behavior is not a police officer or a fence—it's a community and a culture.

—THOMAS L. FRIEDMAN

# REDEMPTION

# CHAPTER ONE

Trinity's breath puffed through the knit wool of his scarf in little white clouds, crusting into ice on the outside and clinging uncomfortably to his face like sweat. The snow crunched underneath his boots, loud in the quiet, as he trudged along the empty road. He could hear the engine in the distance long before he turned with his thumb out and walked backward as he waited for it to appear over the gentle swell of hills. His thumb wavered when he saw the drab olive green, his throat tightening. But in spite of the military-style camouflage and a gun rack in the back window supporting two hunting rifles, he immediately realized it was nothing more than a battered Chevy pickup. As it rolled past him, oversized studded tires churning up snow, Trinity expected it to keep on going. But the truck slowed to a stop several hundred feet on, one red brakelight glowing, the other covered in duct tape.

Trinity ran, awkward in the deep snow, with his backpack slapping his shoulders. The driver had leaned over to roll the passenger-side window down a few inches, an old man with bright blue eyes and a beard like Santa Claus—if Santa Claus was partial to Army jackets and deerstalker hats and had an NRA sticker on the back of his sleigh.

"What on earth you doing way out in the middle of nowhere, son?"

"Freezing, mostly."

The man chuckled. "Where ya headin'?"

"Spokane."

The old man's eyebrows raised in incredulity. "I can take ya as far as the Hi-Line. Head toward Havre, y'kin get U.S. 87 down to Interstate 15."

"That'd be fine, thanks," Trinity said, aware his own accent had modified to mimic the old man's. He slung his backpack into the back of the pickup between stacked bales of hay and climbed up into the passenger seat, grateful for the heat blowing gustily out the air vents.

Neither spoke for several miles, Trinity content to simply watch the bleak scenery roll past from the comfort of the warm cab. Steel-gray clouds slid between the crags and ridges of nearby mountains, the line between ground and sky blurred.

"Don't get much traffic out on these back roads," the old man said. "'Specially this time of year. Been out there long?"

"Awhile."

The old man nodded, and didn't speak again until they came up behind a snowplow blowing a fan of white powder up onto a bank already over six feet high. The truck crawled behind for miles, the only two vehicles on the deserted road.

"Hope y're not in any hurry," the old man said laconically.

"No, sir."

The old man laughed. "'Sir.'" He glanced at Trinity in amusement. "You a military man or just polite?"

"Just polite."

"Well, you ain't young enough and I ain't old enough for 'sir.' You just call me Jack."

"Ben."

They nodded at each other in acknowledgment and slipped back into silence. Whatever concoction the old man was mixing with his diesel to eke it out stank like burning fat, pungent even inside the cab, but Trinity was warm, and didn't care. Clotted snowflakes began to spin against the windshield, white puffs melting instantly against the warm glass. A few flakes soon became many, and many became a flurry so thick even the snowplow in front of them was nearly obscured. Jack grunted.

"Sorry, son. I got cattle to get feed to before this gets too bad. Don't look like you'll be makin' it to Havre today. There's a little place just a few more miles, I kin drop ya off there to wait for this to let up. Better chance a' catching a ride there than freezing your butt off out here."

The wind had picked up, gusting frenzied eddies of snow into the air, eerie in the headlights as the sun set. Jack pulled into a deserted parking lot in front of a clapboard diner. The peeling hand-painted GRINNIN' BEAR CAFÉ sign was barely visible while the neon Coors logo over the door glowed garishly through the haze of blowing snow. The only other vehicles were an elderly four-wheel drive Jeep and a Peterbilt tractor-trailer rig, with stylized horses and half-naked women airbrushed on the sides. Trinity got out and retrieved his backpack from the truck bed.

"Good luck," Jack said cheerfully and drove off, eager to catch up with the snowplow now totally vanished into the storm.

Trinity stamped as much snow from his boots as he could on the wooden steps before pushing open the door into the café porch. Enough melting snow still clung to his jeans to soak him clear to the knees. He peeled off his knit cap now crusted white, static electricity making his hair stand on end, and shook his arms out of the down jacket. Inside the café, a woman wearing a quilted vest over her waitress's uniform stood behind the counter watching the Weather Channel on an overhead television bolted to the wall. The weatherman gestured at a brightly colored weather front sweeping a blizzard down through Alberta and Saskatchewan to engulf the northern states as far as Salt Lake City in the west to Sioux Falls in the east. The scene cut to a reporter in a fashionable camel-hair coat far too light for the wind he was having trouble keeping his balance in, hundreds of cars behind him stalled on a major highway. A lone customer at the far end of the counter nursed a beer and picked at the remains of a sandwich while watching the weather report morosely. He lifted his Cenex baseball cap to run a hand over a balding head and said to the waitress, "Might as well gimme another, Carlene, I ain't goin' nowhere real quick. Global warming, my ass."

The waitress looked up as Trinity draped his jacket over one of the counter stools. She was in her late fifties but when she smiled, even as a perfunctory greeting for a stranger, it softened her face with a wistfulness of lost youth.

"Just coffee, please," Trinity said as she reached for a stack of menus squeezed in between napkin holders. He shook from his damp hair the water dripping into his eyes. "Is there a pay phone here I could use?"

"Through there," she said indifferently. "By the men's room."

The adjoining room was deserted and dark, the security shutters over the bar closed and locked, the blackjack and keno machines switched off. Two huge speakers bracketed a raised corner platform, microphone stands lined up beside the wall. Between racks of pool cues, he found an old-fashioned coin-operated box with a rotary dial rather than push buttons, lovingly restored and polished. He didn't need any coins, dialing the unlisted number he knew by heart.

"Hello?"

"Four seven five, eight three two, zero five," he said, keeping his voice low.

"One moment." He didn't recognize the tinny classical music playing while he waited on hold. They'd finally gotten around to changing the tune. *About time*, he thought; he was sick of Vivaldi.

A woman's voice cut off the music. "McGraff."

"Four seven five, eight three two, zero five," Trinity repeated quietly.

"You're cutting it pretty damned fine, Ben. You were forty minutes from being in violation, you know that?" Her cigarette-and-whiskey voice might have been sexy, if he didn't know what Mrs. Clarice McGraff looked like. Or feared her.

"Yes, ma'am. Sorry."

He heard the tapping of computer keys over the line, imagining the inaudible signals bouncing off satellites thousands of miles above his head pinning him to a map like an insect on a specimen card. It took several seconds before McGraff said sharply, "You're not in Spokane."

"No, ma'am. I'm not."

"You've drifted way off your authorized route, Benedictus. A few more miles, and you'd be setting off alarms all over the country. Where the hell are you?"

He looked around the café, searching for a clue. "I'm not sure."

"They aren't going to hold that job for you much longer. You don't show up in the next twenty-four hours, you've lost it, gone."

"I understand, ma'am."

"You're not going to make it." Her irritation carried well over the line.

"No, ma'am. I'm not going to make it." No excuses, he knew, but couldn't help adding, "Bismarck's Cognident kicked my ticket. By the time they got their security system updated, my bus had gone. The cops took me as far as the Montana side of the border, so I've been trying to hitchhike to make up the time. But I won't get much farther now anyway, not in this weather."

"God damn it." He didn't expect any leniency regardless of circumstances. And some hapless minimum-wage ticket clerk at a remote North Dakota Greyhound bus station was about to receive an unpleasant phone call from Washington. "Why didn't you call in immediately?"

"This is the first landline I could find."

"Right." He could tell she didn't believe him. "So what the hell are you doing coming so close to the Canadian border?"

"I got turned around after Glendive; ended up near Medicine Lake before I figured out where I was. Only ride I could get was headed toward Glasgow."

She said nothing for several moments. "Don't even think about it, Trinity," she said ominously.

He didn't pretend not to understand. "I'm not, ma'am, I give you my word."

"Your *word*?" Her voice dripped disdain. "Let's run a spot check instead, okay?"

He glanced around, but the waitress and her customer were still engrossed in scenes of jackknifed eighteen-wheeler rigs, people shoveling snow from sidewalks in Rapid City and kids in Boulder building snowmen. He stripped off a fingerless glove, revealing a small circular tattoo in his palm no bigger than a quarter, and held the phone in his left hand, then responded to the familiar interrogation in a monotone of "yes" or "no" until she ran out of questions.

He listened to the hiss of the telephone line as he waited, certain she could read his mind as well as his biometrics through the microchip implanted in his palm. "You can take your hand off the phone now." He did, shifting it back into his untattooed right.

"You listen to me, Trinity. I don't give a shit about you, or those idiots in Homeland Security who foisted you off on me. I've had to sweat blood to keep this program operational, and so far, it's a statistical success. It had damned well better stay that way. The departmental budget review is next month. You fuck my program up, I'll fuck you over nine ways from Sunday, I give you *my* word, you got that?"

"Yes, ma'am, loud and clear."

He heard her exhale in impatience. "Right. Seems you're in some godforsaken shithole called Redemption, population less than two hundred, not counting the cows. And since it looks like you're going to be stuck there at least a few more days, I suggest you keep your head down and stay put until you're told otherwise. I'll talk to the DSD head office and see what I can reorganize in the meantime."

An odd wave of relief made his legs feel weak. He wasn't going back to prison. *Yet.* "Thank you."

"And Benny . . . ?"

"Yes, ma'am?"

"Be a good boy and don't *ever* push your contact deadline this close again." She hung up before he could say anything. He replaced the phone back on the hook and thrust his hand back into his glove, ignoring how much he was shaking. Even from hundreds of miles away, McGraff could still scare him.

By the time he sat down at the counter, his coffee was tepid. He emptied a small bowl with a dozen half-and-half containers, poured them all into the remainder of the coffee and drank it. The waitress picked up the round pot of coffee from the machine behind her.

"Need your cream warmed up?"

"Please," he said, not looking up as she refilled his cup. "And could I have a cup of hot water?"

"Just hot water?"

"Yes, please."

When she placed it in front of him, he ignored her bemused interest as he squeezed ketchup from the red plastic condiment bottle and stirred it into a makeshift soup. She set a basket of plastic-wrapped crackers beside his cup. "It tastes better if you crumble a few of these into it," she said with a wry smile.

"Thank you."

"Don't mention it." She glanced at the man in the Cenex hat. "We all got our problems." She started to move away.

"Miss ? . . ?" When she glanced back over her shoulder, he said, "Do you know if there're any motels around here? In walking distance?"

She laughed. "You have money enough for a motel?"

He smiled back. "If I give up such luxuries as eating."

She shook her head, poured the last of the coffee into his cup and took the now-empty coffeepot into the kitchen. When she returned, she slid a plate piled with steaming vegetables, mashed potatoes, and turkey slices swimming in watery brown gravy in front of him. He looked at her in surprise. She shrugged.

"Like he said, none of us is going anywhere in a hurry. Don't expect there's gonna be much of a dinner rush, so you might as well have it as me throwing it out."

"If you're passing out freebies, Carlene," the Cenex hat said, "how 'bout a slice of that blueberry pie?"

"If you're still hungry, Harry, I've got some nice mashed turnips and calf liver just going to waste." But she cut three slices of pie, handing one to Harry, and setting the other two in front of Trinity. "Mind if I join you?"

"Please."

She cut the tip off her pie and ate it slowly while he tried not to wolf down the first hot meal he'd had in days. "Where you from?"

He looked up warily, swallowing a mouthful of turkey and carrots before he said cautiously, "Florida."

She snorted her incredulity. "Why on earth would you want to leave the beaches and sunshine to come all the way out here in the dead of winter?"

"I had a job offer in Spokane."

"Had."

"Mmm." He washed down the mashed potatoes and gravy with another gulp of coffee. "I should have been there yesterday. It's gone now."

"You don't seem too broken up over it."

He shrugged. "There'll be another."

Pushing a mop in a Spokane jail was pretty much like pushing a mop in a Tallahassee jail, hardly what his grandfather had envisioned for him when he'd invested in Trinity's Ph.D. degree from Stanford. The old man still hadn't forgiven him for choosing liberal arts over medicine and rejecting the family's surgical practice, when he'd suddenly died of a heart attack from an overdose of too much foie gras, Cognac, and unfeasible demands from narcissistic film stars. Thank God his grandfather was already dead, Trinity thought. *This* would have killed him.

"Half the country out of work, and there'll be another, just like that? You're an optimist for someone living off ketchup Cup-a-Soup." When he didn't answer, she said, "Look, you're welcome to crash here. It's free at least." She followed his glance at Harry. "He's got a sleeper in his rig, color TV, frig, coffeemaker, all the comforts of home, which for Harry, it is. I live here, upstairs. I keep my doors locked and I sleep with a loaded shotgun." She smiled at his startled blink. "So you'll be safe from any grizzlies."

"Grizzlies . . . right," he said.

She chuckled, finished her pie, and took the empty plates to the kitchen to run them through the dishwasher. Outside, the wind continued to rattle the window glass and throw down a steady blanket of snow, glowing in the darkness. His stomach now comfortably full, he sat in a booth with his backpack wedged behind his back. He'd removed his boots, his socks damp, and had draped his jacket over his knees for warmth. He stared idly out into the night, listening to roof tiles groan under the weight of the snow. Harry and Carlene sat companionably drinking beer and watching an old rerun sitcom, canned laughter tinny and shrill.

The television made a loud pop as the lights went out, the picture vanishing to a white pinprick.

"Ah, shit, there they go again," he heard Carlene say. His eyes not adjusted, he listened to her shuffling in the dark, then held his hand to shield his eyes as a flashlight shone in his eyes. "You okay over there?"

"Yeah, fine."

"I'll go kick up the generator for ya, Carlene," Harry said, his words slurred with too much beer.

"Nah, I wouldn't send a dog out there when it's like this. You leave it for the morning, it'll keep. The Grinnin' Bear is now officially closed, boys. You go on home, Harry, I'll see you for breakfast."

She handed him a couple more bottles of beer and held the door open for him as he staggered out into the snow-storm, closing it as the freezing blast of snow blew into the café. They both watched Harry wade through the hip-deep bank, falling facedown once, the snow cushioning the bottles to keep them from breaking. Harry clambered up into his cab, struggling to close the door in the wind. He managed, a small reddish light in the cab making it seem warmer than Trinity was sure it was.

"Safe and sound," Carlene said. "You wait here a minute."

He wondered where she expected he was likely to go as she clumped upstairs, flashlight casting wavering shadows on the walls. He could hear the floorboards creaking as she walked overhead, and when she returned she handed him a pillow and a worn patchwork quilt, the fabric soft with age. It smelled like lilacs.

"You can sleep here or on the pool table, take your pick. No hot water in the gent's, but the sink in the lady's leaks, your choice," she said, and handed him the flashlight. "You shouldn't be too cold down here tonight."

"I'm very grateful, ma'am, thank you."

She smiled, her teeth reflecting the light off the snow. "Nice to see good manners still exist. Your mother must be proud of you."

*She wasn't*, he didn't say. His mother had died in self-imposed exile two years ago, politely shunned by neighbors and ostracized by society friends afraid of the taint by association. He hadn't been allowed to say good-bye to her, didn't even know where she was buried. No, it hadn't been his mother who taught him how to behave himself. If she had, she might have lived longer and been happier.

# CHAPTER TWO

*Dear Diary,*
*Mom made me get dressed for school this morning anyways,*
*just in case, then we listened to the radio while I ate break-*
*fast and it said every school in the tri-county area would be*
*closed today so I was real happy I get to miss the math test,*
*yay! Dad phoned Mom to tell her the storm coming in*
*looked real bad, a lot of roads already closing and he didn't*
*know if they'd have enuff snowplows to keep us from getting*
*snowed in before dark. So she phoned Nana to tell her she*
*wouldn't be in at the café today on a count of the snow, cuz*
*that would leave me here on my own, like I'm some little*
*baby. Then they got in a argument about Mom's new car—*
*new to Mom, not new like brand-new—Nana going on*
*about how Mom should get a four-wheel-drive Jeep like what*
*she drives, like it makes any diffrence when the roads are*
*closed.*

*And her old Jeep isn't that good anyways, Uncle Lonny left*
*it when he went to Iraq and she won't get rid a it just cuz it*
*was Lonny's. If it were me, I wouldn't never want to keep it,*
*cuz sometimes I imagine his ghost is sitting there with all the*
*bulletholes in him with blood and guts and stuff and it creeps*
*me out.*

Then while I was watching Missy Mystic on *Fox Kids*, all the electricity went out just as it got to the good part. The telephones were still working so I called Sophie and asked if she wanted to come over and she said she would but her brother Craig would have to bring her on his Dad's snowmobile. I don't like Craig, he's so stuck up bragging bout his Dad is a bigshot consoltant for the state so we all gotta do whatever he says. Just cuz he's got these three little hairs sticking out a his top lip he thinks he's the man. Mattie told me that Cindy told her Craig is always trying to stick his hand inside girls panties and cop a feel, and I didn't believe it till me and him were study partners in math class and he started horsing around trying to sneak his nasty hand under my skirt so I jabbed him real hard in the arm with a pencil and made him yell the F word so loud Ms. Dickinson kicked his pervert butt out. He got real mad and told me in the hall I better watch my ass and I got right up in his butt-face and said real loud so everybody could here me that if he didn't leave me alone I'd tell my dad he was a pedafile so he better watch his own pervert ass, so there. Mattie said that she and Cindy thought I was real brave standing up to him, but I wasn't really cuz I was so scared I felt sick to my stomack. Anyway, Sophie made us make up cuz if me and Craig are fighting then Sophie can't hang out with me so were all supposed to be freinds again, but I still don't like him. Pervert.

Sophie and Craig came over right at lunchtime so Mom made us all grilled cheese and tomatoe sandwiches and Craig was being all smarmy kissy-face with her, but she still wouldn't give him a beer with his sandwich. Then after, Sophie said he had to take us both for rides on the snowmobile and Craig said he could only take one of us at a time and took me first but he was going real fast and making sharp turns trying to make me fall off but I wouldn't cuz I've been

riding on back of Dad's police motorcycle since I was a fee-
tus, that's what Dad always sez, and can hang on like a
limpet. Dad told me a limpet is some kind of shellfish looks
sorta like a hat but I've never been to the ocean so I don't
know. But if limpets can ride snowmobiles, then I'm the
world champion of all limpets.

Craig got tired trying to make me fall off and it started snowing really hard anyway so we went back inside. The electricity was still out, so I asked Mom if Sophie could sleep over
and she called Sophie's mom who said she could so Craig
took his pervert butt-face back home by himself. I hope he
runs into a great big grizzly and dies a horrible screaming
death, but I wouldn't never say that to Sophie.

Mom called Mrs. Tearle Sandra's mom cuz Mr. Tearle
works for the electric company, and Mrs. Tearle said it was
something to do with this grid up in Canada or something.
The electricity goes off a lot even when it doesn't snow, cuz
the Canadians are always taking more power than they should
away from us, that's what Dad says. Sophie's dad got a big
fancy generator so Bakkers never ever have problems with
brownouts like everyone else does. The electricity was still
off at suppertime so Mom let me and Sophie cook wieners in
the fireplace and toasted marshmellows like we were camp-
ing out. It was dead cool, and Sophie said she wished the
electricity would go off at her house too sometimes.

Then Mom let me light all the candles in my room, even the
fancy aromatherapy ones Nana gave me for my birthday, it
was so romantic and me and Sophie lay on my bed and
talked about who we'd want to give our cherry away to. She
said she was in love with the red-haired guy on the tv show
about lost kids, but when I said I liked the other guy who
plays his boss she said he was too old and besides I'm too fat.
Like Little Miss Tubby-Pants can point fingers at anyone

*herself and nobody is ever going to want her cherry even if it came on top of a ice cream sunday.*

*So we had a fight but it didn't last too long cuz Sophie started bawling and at first I said good, she deserved to get her feelings hurt calling me fat but then she said shut up it wasn't me anyway. Her dad walked out on her mom but its a big secret cuz Sophie's mom said its such a horrible cleeshay and degrading cuz he's run off with his big-boob secratary and now he wants a devorce. I said so what, my mom and dad are devorced, its not the end of the world, and Sophie said I'd feel different if my dad was going to burn in Hell for running off with his secratary, and I started laughing because the idea that Dad would run off with the secratary at work is totally stupid, she's like a zillion years old and butt-face ugly. Even Sophie started laughing even tho she was trying to keep crying so I'd feel sorry for her.*

*Then Sophie said it was statisticle fact that kids who's parents are devorced don't get good grades in school or good jobs, and are more likely to get devorced when they get married too, and commit suicide like seventy percent more times, everybody knows its a fact. I said that she was making that up, my grades were okay and I was happier now than when my mom and dad were still together because now they don't fight or break stuff and he's nicer to her and spends more time with me, I perfer my parents being devorced. Sophie said she didn't believe I didn't want my parents to get back together cuz its always on tv how kids do all sorts of things just to get there parents back together, like lock them up in a barn for a month or strand them on a dessert island. I said that was stupid cuz they'd run out of food and die if you locked them in a barn for a month, and where are you going to find a dessert island in Montana? Sophie started blubbering all over again cuz she wasn't as smart as the kids on tv and couldn't think of a clever way to get her parents back together again.*

So I told her not to be such a woo-woo crybaby and started tickling her and the lights came back on so we went downstairs and played Renegade Rally on the Playstation. I had her nearly beat first time ever when the lights went out again, which was so not fair. Then Mom found an old pack of cards so we had to play gin rummy instead, totally lame.

Mom made up the sofa for Sophie to sleep on and said we had to go to bed the same time as if it was a school day in the morning, just in case the busses can get threw tomorrow even tho we know there not going to.

Mom said Bojangles could sleep in my room tonight and he's sitting in my lap purring and bumping my hand with his head which makes it hard to write. I feel sorry for Sophie, cuz she's like my best friend ever and I'd never ever in a zillion years tell anyone this, but sometimes I do secretly wish my mom and dad could be like two totally different people and make up and get back together but without all the yelling and hitting each other and breaking stuff again.

So that was what happened today. I'll write again tomorrow.

                                        Love, Amy.

# CHAPTER THREE

George woke as soon she heard the central heating boiler kick on, air in the old pipes complaining like elderly gremlins in the walls. At least that's what George told Amy they were when her daughter had been little and terrified of the mysterious noises in the dark, shadows in the closets, monsters under the bed. There were no such things as monsters, Lucas had scolded her angrily, his temper frightening the poor child all the more. His rational explanation of steam and air bubbles and expanding metal meant nothing to an eight-year-old.

So one night, when Lucas had been out on duty and they were all alone in the house, when the wind had been blowing and making curtains stir and the chimney whistle, when the pipes were chortling maniacally to themselves, when Amy had crawled into her mother's bed clutching her tattered Velveteen rabbit and shivering with dread, George had invented an elaborate story about a family of gremlins who'd been evicted from their cave in the woods by a mean old bear. The gremlins had tramped and tramped for weeks through the woods, cold and hungry, until they came across Amy's house. And way up in a window, they could see her sleeping and because she was so beautiful and sweet, they knew she would be their friend and that they had found a place where they would be safe, so they'd decided to move in.

Amy had still been sucking her thumb then, another trait Lucas had tried hard to shame her out of. She wasn't a baby anymore, take that goddamn thumb out of her yap before it makes her teeth go funny. But as George spun her magic, her little girl sat mesmerized with her jaw slack, thumb barely hanging from her mouth. The curtains moving? Why, that was only the little gremlin children playing hide-and-seek; you had to be very quick to catch sight of them. The noises in the pipes? That was Grandma and Grampa Gremlin in their creaky rocking chairs complaining about the cold. And the scary shadow Amy insisted she'd seen lurking under her bed? That was just the gremlin guard dog who slept there to keep Amy safe and sound from any bad monsters who might even think about bothering her.

Lucas had been livid, naturally, when Amy began talking about the gremlins who lived in the pipes, even more so when he discovered bits of peanut butter sandwiches and moldy cookies left in odd corners to feed these imaginary gremlin friends. But the night terrors subsided after that—at least for Amy.

Now Grandma and Grampa Gremlin were reminding George that the heating oil had nearly run out. Lucas was late on the child support again, and she couldn't afford to bounce another check. He enjoyed making her wait, seeing how long her pride could hold out before she had to ask him for it. One more time, she'd warned him, and she'd take it up with his boss, get his wages attached. Sheriff Holbrook wouldn't take kindly to an officer not providing for his family properly. But that's all it was, they both knew—empty threats. She was still too frightened of Lucas to test how far she could push him.

Her bedroom was still dark, the room bitterly cold. At least the electricity was back on, the alarm clock flashing the wrong time at her. She squirmed down under the quilts until she could grab her jeans and sweatshirt off the chair and drag them into bed with her, the cold cloth making her shiver. She dozed off for another half hour, her clothes warmed by the time she woke again. She wriggled into her jeans and pulled on her sweatshirt before throwing the quilts back.

Amy's room was cold as well. "Time to get up, sweetpea," she murmured in her daughter's ear, breathing in the smell of her hair. Amy whined sullenly and rolled over, dragging her quilt over her head. George sat on the edge of her bed, rocking Amy's hip gently until Amy violently spasmed her protest, trying to shake her off.

"Go 'way," Amy griped, muffled under the covers.

It was their ritual, as comforting and predictable as the sunrise. Bojangles yawned, stretched, and followed George down the stairs happily, his stomach more important than sleeping late. In the living room, Sophie huddled under a mound of blankets on the sofa, her head popping out as soon as she heard George on the stairs.

"Morning, Ms. Jensen," she said politely.

"Good morning, Sophie. Would you like oatmeal for breakfast?"

"Yes, please."

George wondered if Sophie was as grouchy in the morning with her own mother as Amy was with her. Probably. Everybody's child was the model of civility when at someone else's house.

Sophie's mother called George as she was stirring the oatmeal while sipping her first cup of coffee, enjoying the caffeine rush. Alison Bakker was still a loyal Pioneer fundraiser for the Republican Party and a Brownie leader who taught Bible studies to preschoolers every Sunday at the Baptist church, baked literally thousands of chocolate chip cookies and blueberry muffins for charity bake sales— a devout, high-strung, high-maintenance woman who not once had done anything to make George feel slighted. But George had never warmed to her, preferring to remain friendly neighbors rather than neighborly friends. Her husband Justin was away at an important business conference, Alison told her haughtily, so his brother Jack would be by as soon as he could to pick up Sophie. If the school was still closed and George would like the favor returned, Amy was more than welcome to stay over at their house. Their big, expensive house with the nice furniture and the fancy toys.

Sophie and Amy both came to the kitchen table, Sophie wearing a pair of Amy's pajamas and an old bathrobe of Luke's, hem dragging on the floor. On a school day, they would both have had to be dressed in their uniforms by now. They ate their oatmeal while listening to KOJM on the little portable radio calmly listing the school closures for Liberty, Chouteau, Blain, Hill, and Phillips counties. When it reached St. Mary Magdalene, the girls grinned and high-fived each other triumphantly like ice hockey players celebrating a goal.

"School's out for-ever!" the girls sang, a tune old when George was their age.

"That's that," George conceded and switched off the radio. "I talked to your mom, Sophie, and she said your uncle Jack will try to get here as soon as he can."

"Okay, Ms. Jensen."

"Your mom sounds likes she's got a bad cold, she all right?" George's concern was more about germs she didn't want Amy picking up, but the furtive glance exchanged between the girls told her far more than they realized. *Aha, business trip my ass—there was trouble in paradise.* Happened even to the best people, George gloated, then felt guilty over her satisfaction. Envy was not an emotion she was proud of. And while she couldn't help begrudging Alison her enormous wealth while so many others around her struggled to make ends meet, George wouldn't want to have to sleep with Justin Bakker for the privilege.

"She's fine, Ms. Jensen."

"Well, if you want to spend the day at Sophie's house, Amy, you girls go get dressed and be ready when Jack comes. Remember that it's your dad's weekend, so pack some clean pajamas and underwear. He'll come pick you up tomorrow morning at Sophie's. Don't forget anything this time. I'm not going to be driving over to his place because you've left your toothbrush behind."

"Okay, Mom," Amy said around a mouthful of oatmeal, not paying the slightest bit of attention.

"Take your schoolbooks and do your homework; school isn't cancelled permanently."

"Okay, Mom."

"If Sophie's uncle Jack can take me as far as the junction, I'll be at the café today. If you need to get hold of me for any reason and you can't reach your dad—"

"Okay, Mom!" Amy protested, an act put on for Sophie's benefit. "Like, *duh*, I got it already."

Without raising her voice, George added, "And if you take that tone with me again, you can forget about staying over at Sophie's. You can come work at the café with me and Nana instead."

"Okay, Mom," Amy said, this time penitently.

"Good. Now if you're done, wash up your dishes and get ready to go."

They had to walk down to the road from the house; even with his oversized snow tires Jack was unwilling to risk the long driveway obscured in several feet of snow. But the main road had been plowed during the night. He was happy to drop George off at the Grinnin' Bear, the four of them squashed into the cab of his old pickup, Amy half-sitting on George's lap. The girls didn't seem to mind, too busy arguing over who was cooler, SpongeBob SquarePants or Daggett and Norbert. By the time they reached the junction, George's leg was asleep, all pins and needles as she climbed down and waved good-bye to the girls.

"You be good," George admonished.

"I'm *always* good!" Amy shouted as Jack pulled out carefully, studded tires crunching in the snow. "And when I'm bad, I'm better . . ."

"Oh, ha, ha," George joked back, but they were far enough away not to hear her, waving bright mittens at her through the back window of the cab.

Someone had shoveled a neat path from the road to the front door of the café, George saw. Harry, probably, since his rig was still here, buried up to his wheel wells and not going anywhere soon. Poor Harry, she thought. Bad enough he'd had to sell his house trying to keep body and soul afloat. One more hike in diesel prices, and he'd likely lose the rig as well. She sighed to herself: Ma and Harry were pretty much in the same boat financially, with the boat getting more crowded every day.

The CLOSED sign was up on the door, the lights off. But the door was unlocked, and she could hear sounds of life inside as well as smell the bacon. "Ma," she called out. "It's me. You need any help back there?"

"No," Carlene called out from the kitchen. "I'm doing fine. You hungry?"

George shook off her snow boots, slipped into a pair of flat pumps she kept by the door and hung her jacket on the rack. "I had breakfast already. Jesus Christ, Ma, it's freezing in here!"

Carlene emerged from the kitchen to catch George waggling light switches futilely, the café's electricity still out. She set two plates with bacon and eggs on the counter. "Generator's on the blink again. Where's Amy?"

"At Sophie's house for a sleepover. Are you out of firewood?" George scolded, knowing she wasn't.

"If you're cold, wear a sweater. I'm not wasting firewood when the café's closed." She went back into the kitchen, returning with a third plate.

"I said I've had breakfast, Ma."

"As much as I do my best to ignore you, sweetheart,"

Carlene said tartly, "I did hear you the first time. *Boys!* Come and eat it while it's hot!" She sat down on the other side of the counter. "And take your grubby little fingers off my bacon," she admonished George.

George smiled, stealing a strip anyway.

Harry stomped the snow off his boots at the kitchen back door, wincing with his usual hangover. A dark-haired man followed him in, carrying the café's toolbox.

"It's gonna take a bit more persuasion, Carlene," Harry said grumpily. "You can't let maintenance on these things slide, then expect it to work when you need it."

George exchanged a look with her mother but said nothing. Lucas had taken over the café's maintenance after Lonny died, but his initial generosity had petered out as quickly as all his other well-meaning intentions seemed to do. And while Harry was a sweet guy, his drinking made his mechanical competence erratic at best.

George poured herself a cup of lukewarm coffee and swiped a three-day-old doughnut from under the glass dome on the countertop before she headed for the stairs. "I'll be up doing the books, Ma," she said, taking no notice of whatever muffled reply came from the kitchen.

Luckily, the power outage hadn't crashed her mother's dilapidated computer, a hodgepodge of units Lonny had umbilicalled together, and cobbled to an emergency car battery for backup power. Not so many years ago, her brother had been slated to take over the café when Ma retired, handling the thriving business's finances as well as the property upkeep while George had been happily married with a toddler. The future had seemed so bright and safe.

Then Lonny was killed in Iraq and Lucas walked out. The economy worsening by the day, the two women struggled to stay afloat in a starkly different reality. Sometimes George wondered if life had always been this hard, more fear than hope, but she could only see it now with the benefit of hindsight and harsh experience. This wasn't how she'd been promised the world was supposed to be.

Bookkeeping certainly wasn't anything George enjoyed, but her mother enjoyed it even less, tending to let things slide after Lonny died until George had reluctantly taken on the chore of getting the books up to date. She spent months trying to figure out Lonny's byzantine accounting system on a cantankerous computer before she gave up, threw everything out, and started over from scratch.

It hadn't been easy, having no experience with book-keeping. But it was at least better than dealing with customers, in George's opinion—quiet work in peace and solitude. She methodically sorted receipts and order forms into little piles, organizing them by type. Then she separated credit card slips by month and card companies, as well as far too many handwritten IOU slips of paper Carlene accepted from those too broke to afford a coffee and slice of pie, who likely would never repay in cash but bring in a dozen eggs from their hens or a haunch of antelope instead—welcome intangibles but hard to calculate on the books.

She heard the faint grumble of the generator, and the lights went on, the computer beeping happily. *Good, Harry's finally managed to fix it,* she thought with relief. She had never quite trusted her brother's jerry-rigged backup system. She began entering the numbers into her off-the-shelf bookkeeping program, trying to make the numbers even out.

"Excuse me." She looked up at the dark-haired stranger holding a steaming cup of coffee and a plate with a sandwich cut into triangles. "Ms. Ryton asked me to bring your lunch up."

George glanced at her watch, surprised how much time had slipped by. "Thanks," she said as he set the plate and coffee cup down on her desk and turned to leave. "Who are you anyway?"

"Ben Trinity. Just passing through. Got caught in the snowstorm, hitchhiking. Your mother was kind enough to put me up for the night."

"Ma's like that, always a soft spot for strays and waifs." Which was how she'd ended up with Bojangles, a homeless ginger tomcat who had wandered into the café begging for scraps six years ago, skinny, tattereared, and flea-ridden. He'd become a pampered mascot, beloved by everyone who came into the café . . . everyone except the health inspector. Faced with a two-thousand-dollar fine, Carlene's practical side kicked in and if it hadn't been for Amy bawling her eyes out, the cat would have been dumped off unceremoniously at the nearest pound to be gassed. Lucas hadn't allowed animals in the house, even those bathed and neutered, so poor Bojangles was banished to sleep in the old cowshed. But the day Lucas moved out, the cat moved in. *Fair trade*, George thought bitterly.

George smiled as she bit into the sandwich. Ham and cheese with a hint of mustard, just the way she liked it. "Where you headed?"

Trinity shrugged. "I was going to Spokane, had a job offer there. Too late now, so I'm not sure yet."

His voice was soft, but with an educated accent that didn't match his appearance. He was skinny to the point of near gaunt, his hair needing a trim but his face clean-shaven, his clothes worn but not scruffy. His deep tan spoke of someone who had spent time in the outdoors rather than in a tanning salon. She studied him as he stood without fidgeting, his hands by his side rather than shoved into his pockets, his eyes averted slightly rather than looking straight at her, not out of nervousness but habit. She knew what she was seeing.

She nodded, chewing on her sandwich. "Not a lot of jobs going round here. Redemption is pretty damned small. You might have better luck further south, someplace bigger like Great Falls or Billings."

He smiled, understanding. "You could be right," was all he said, and left.

She was aware of muted voices from the café below—Carlene open up for the lunch crowd, such as it was. "George," she heard her mother shout. "Lucas on the phone for you."

George winced, then picked up the extension. "Hello, Luke."

"I tried to call you at home, you weren't there. I figured you'd be at your mother's place. The roads are still shit. You didn't drive to the café, did you?"

"No, Lucas," she said patiently. "I got a ride with Jack."

"Amy with you?"

"She's spending the night over at Sophie's." She listened to the long silence, able to see his sour expression in her memory. "She knows it's your weekend. She's got everything she needs packed and ready to go."

"And I'm supposed to pick her up at the Bakkers', that it? When did you plan on telling me? After I wasted a trip all the way out to the house first? Or when I came looking for her at the café?"

"I was going to call you later after you got off work," George said calmly, although she felt anything but. "I didn't forget, but even if I had, I'm sure Amy would have called you to let you know as well."

"Oh, right. You're leaving it up to a twelve-year-old now?"

George shut her eyes, willing herself not to rise to the bait. "Of course not. And she's thirteen, old enough to take some responsibility for herself."

"I don't give a shit if she's thirty, she's still my little girl and you damned well better start remembering I'm still her dad, regardless of whatever you and your mother think of me. I have a right to know where my daughter is at all times, not just whenever you figure it's convenient for you to tell me."

She let the silence drag on for several moments. "Having a bad day at the office, dear?" she said lightly.

"Fuck you," he snapped before slamming the phone down.

She exhaled, and hung up gently. Thank God for the buffer of telephones. If she'd said anything like that to his face, he'd have slapped her silly. Still, she shivered, her hands shaking as badly as if he had.

Within minutes, her mother had come upstairs with a hot mug of cocoa and a plate of fudge brownies. "And how is our Lucas today?"

"Mean as ever."

"Don't let him get to you, honey."

George smiled, holding the mug under her nose to breathe in the warm smell of chocolate. "Just the medicine I needed. Thanks, Ma." She began picking the walnuts out of a brownie square. Outside the window, fat snowflakes began to fall silently from a sky nearly as white. "Damn. It's snowing again."

"You want Harry to run you back up to the house?" At George's wry look, Carlene added, "He's sober."

George considered a moment. "Nah. Amy's not coming home tonight, and Lucas is picking her up in the morning at Sophie's. I haven't caught up the books yet anyway. That is, if the office sofa bed isn't already spoken for."

"You mean the hitchhiker, Ben." Her mother leaned against the desk and chose a brownie for herself. "He's a nice young man. I feel bad for him. Came all the way from Florida for this job in Spokane and lost it, all because of a blizzard. Will you stop picking the nuts out of your brownies?"

"Then don't make them with walnuts."

"My customers like them with walnuts. I've been thinking . . ."

Alarm bells rang faintly in George's head. "Ma, don't."

"What, think?"

"I know what you're thinking. Don't."

George and her mother had always been close, the kind of familial bond that bordered on ESP, able to speak in a shorthand sometimes unintelligible to outsiders. Lucas had resented that intimacy, and had felt excluded, his ire only increasing when it became obvious Amy had inherited the Ryton women's intuitive nature.

And George knew, without her mother having to spell it out, what was passing through her mind. "Ma, you know nothing about him. He's not a stray cat."

"I know one thing about him: He's smart enough to have fixed the generator. Took him all of fifteen minutes after Harry gave up fiddling with it. And he's pitched in with the café—didn't even ask him to—clearing tables and washing up."

"If you needed help downstairs, Ma, you should have told me."

Carlene frowned. "I didn't *need* the help. It was a nice gesture to thank me for letting him crash here for awhile."

George widened her eyes in suspicion. " 'Awhile'? How long is 'awhile'?"

Carlene tsked her irritation. "I'm hardly going to throw anyone out in this weather, now am I?"

"Ma, he's a hitchhiker. The Hi-Line is obviously plowed and open, or we wouldn't be getting any customers. He can find a ride."

"He lost that job in Spokane. He's got nowhere to go."

"That's not our problem."

This was escalating into a heated argument, George could see.

"I don't know what your trouble with him is, George," Carlene snapped. "You know we could use a decent handyman . . ."

"We've got Harry . . ."

"Oh, *Harry*," her mother scoffed. "Half the time he's away, and when he is here, he's drunk the other half."

George grabbed a handful of receipts and shook them at

her mother. "We can't afford another employee! We're hanging on by a thread as it is."

"What else can we do? I'm sure Ben would work for minimum; that's all he would have been making in Spokane. Even less if I throw in room and board."

"Room and board . . . ?"

"He could stay in one of the cabins," Carlene said stubbornly.

George dropped the receipts, holding her forehead as if fighting a sudden headache. "Oh, for godsake, Ma."

"What do you have against this boy, George? So he's not Lonny . . ."

George glared up at her. "That's not it, you know better. And he's not a 'boy.' He's not that much younger than me, so why are you going all Oliver Twist over him?"

Carlene backed off, her cheeks red. "You know we need the help, or sooner rather than later we're going to have to admit defeat and throw in the towel. We can't keep the place up, just the two of us. And you know it sure won't break Luke's heart to see you fail."

"Don't play that card," George warned. But the low blow had found its mark, her stomach tightening in dread. That's all she needed, the café to turn belly up and Lucas to be back in court pressing for primary custody of Amy. She fought down another flash of irrational resentment at her brother for getting himself killed, a feeling just as swiftly followed by deep sadness.

"I know you miss him, sweetheart," her mother said with that sensitive instinct, reading her emotions. "I do, too. But we both have to face it: Your brother isn't coming back and we *need* the help."

"And there's a hell of a lot of people who need jobs. If we're that desperate, find someone local. Just not this guy."

"Why not? He's clean, he's polite, he's willing to work . . ."

"Exactly. Open your eyes, Ma. He's too clean, he's too polite, he's too willing to work."

"And this is a *bad* thing?"

George sighed. "Ma, he's an ex-con."

She watched as the pieces suddenly fit together behind her mother's eyes. Carlene crossed her arms and frowned. "Oh." George's told-you-so shrug and Carlene's expression of defeat said more than words could.

A gentle knock made them both turn. Trinity stood in the doorway. "Harry asked me to tell you we've got customers."

Carlene straightened up and smoothed her hair uneasily. "Thank you, Ben," she said as she brushed past him.

As Trinity turned to follow, George said, "Hold on a moment, will you?" He looked back at her evenly. "I can assume you heard all that."

"Yes, ma'am."

"Am I right?"

He nodded, hesitated, then said, "May I say something?"

"You're not going to change my mind."

"That's not my intention. I just want you to know I wasn't trying to ingratiate myself with your mother."

George raised an eyebrow. "'Ingratiate'?" she repeated. That was an awfully big word for the average felon.

"I wasn't expecting anything in return for helping out," he clarified, mistaking her cynicism for ignorance. "I didn't know she was thinking of offering me a job. As much as I appreciate the offer, I don't think I'd be allowed to take it anyway."

"Okay. That it?"

"Yes, ma'am. That's all I wanted to say."

"Out of curiosity, would you mind if I asked what you were convicted for?"

She couldn't decipher his fleeting amusement. "Credit card fraud." At least it wasn't anything sexual, violent, or drug-related. If he was telling the truth, she reminded herself. "How soon would you like me to leave?"

"That," she said, "is up to my mother. It's her café. I'm just the hired help."

He nodded and left.

George spent the next hour and a half crunching numbers, the income versus the outgo appallingly unequal. She knew the debt from the Iraq war was bad, but she couldn't grasp the difference between a trade deficit and a budget deficit, unaware when the Federal Reserve stopped publishing their M3 reports on exactly how much money it printed, oblivious to the flood of new currency being churned out—she only understood that her money didn't seem to go as far as it once did. The collapse of the dollar hadn't seemed a major disaster, not at first. So what if the Asians weren't buying dollars anymore, a concept George didn't quite follow anyway. It was Europe's problem, and Japan's, and Russia's, places George knew she would never see in her life, or cared to.

Petroleum prices, already high, skyrocketed after the Saudi Gharwar oil fields crashed, irreparably damaged from overproduction. George had watched the television specials with a sinking feeling, but all the loud and fancy computer graphics in bright primary colors illustrating imploded geological layers deep underground did not help her to understand terms like "rate sensitivity" or "peak oil" or how extracting a few more million barrels a day could possibly cause the biggest oil field in the world to collapse almost overnight, the subterranean geology beyond repair.

Two major hikes in gas prices had cars lining up at pumps for miles while Congress bickered over who was to blame for the oil shortage: greedy Arab states or the previous Republican administration's corruption. Where antiwar or global warming protests had failed to spur public outrage, an overnight forty-cents-per-gallon rise in gas prices galvanized a nationwide protest organized by Internet bloggers, mobilizing eighteen-wheelers draped with banners and farmers on tractors and grannies in Volvos and even kids on bicycles into one huge alliance that had blocked major highways from Washington D.C. to Washington state, the entire country honking horns at a standstill for weeks.

The cheerful carnival air didn't last—riots broke out in San Francisco, SUVs and Hummers were torched in New York, gas stations looted in Chicago, Philadelphia blazing under a pall of smoke, Muslims and anyone seeming even vaguely Arabic anywhere beaten with bricks and pipes and pieces of lumber. George had never been so glad that she and Amy lived in Montana where it was safe, far away from such madness. Then cold weather set in and people who couldn't afford the limited supply of heating oil froze to death—like old Enid Garcia and her little dog, both found stiff as boards in bed. Ominous talk of rationing—not just heating oil and gasoline but even food and electricity, maybe even water—was something George associated with old black-and-white movies about England during the Second World War and despondent stockbrokers jumping from Wall Street rooftops in the 1930s, a long-extinct specter rising from the ashes of history.

Then the Amtrak bombing in California revived the stagnating fear of Islamic terrorism, and the crisis over oil took a backseat. A small earthquake had shuddered up the length of the San Andreas fault line, causing minimal damage, but sending signal failures all along the Pacific Coast rail lines. Rail traffic ground to a standstill, the bottleneck worsening. Amtrak trains only allowed on Union Pacific track by permission of commercial freighters waited while two more trains, one a Burlington Northern carrying several tankers of liquefied ammonia gas, were being shunted to a siding on the opposite track to wait their turn. As the sky darkened toward a cloudless sunset, a Santa Fe freight train crawled past the Amtrak Starlight along the rails on the heels of three Union Pacific trains carrying several tank cars, each filled with ninety tons of chlorine.

Endlessly flashing red lights at train crossings had frustrated motorists who increasingly chose to ignore the warning lights to cross congested rail tracks as trains hooted in protest. One of the motorists in a brand-new Ford SUV with the price sticker still in the windshield barreled his way past more cautious drivers, mounted the tracks, and trundled along the railway toward the Amtrak Coast Starlight train. The SUV stopped beside the Union Pacific tankers, its tinted windows blurring the figure inside. A pair of conductors who had been scuffing their feet and griping about the wait began to walk toward the SUV, puzzled unease on their faces. A few of the Amtrak passengers crowded the windows of the train, grateful for any distraction in their boredom.

The massive explosion vaporized them and the SUV, rupturing all three chlorine tanks as well as several of the liquefied ammonia gas tanks. The Amtrak cars were hurled over by the force of the explosion, tossed like a model train set off the tracks, blowing out every window in a hailstorm of glass. The pressurized rail tank cars containing the liquefied ammonia were one of tens of thousands scattered throughout the country long past due to be upgraded or replaced, substandard cars well below the industry safety standards. Their brittle steel shells broke like eggs in the blast, spewing out their poisonous cargo to mix with the chlorine gas and form a super-toxic gas rolling in huge waves into a crystal-blue summer sky. Those passengers who weren't killed instantly died in the next gasp of breath, green clouds of toxic gas billowing out of shattered tankers.

It was only capricious luck that a gentle breeze changed direction to carry the poison gas east into the desert badlands, away from the heavily populated outskirts of Sacramento, asphyxiating millions of horned toads and rattlesnakes and roadrunners instead, killing jackrabbits and scrub deer, birds falling out of the sky like feathered hailstones. The immediate human death toll was miraculously low, only ninety-seven casualties, counting a family of three who were unlucky enough to live in a rusting Econoline trailer twelve miles downwind.

The suicide bomber in the SUV was identified some days later as twenty-two-year-old Joel Allan Rodrigues of Bakersfield. In a rambling eight-page suicide note he'd left for his mother in his cockroach-infested student apartment, he had taken full responsibility for the bombing, proclaiming himself a proud member of al-Jawasis freedom fighters, railing against the arrogance of the West and atrocities committed around the world by the American government, praising the glory of Allah. He'd signed it "Muhammed Youssef," something that came as a shock to his friends and relatives, with their recollections of a quiet young man who at most maybe smoked a little pot and listened to classic heavy metal. Even the nearest mosque had never heard of him, anxious to disavow any involvement with the bombing.

But the aftershock was felt clear to Washington, where disgruntled Republicans blamed their Democratic successors for being soft on terror, and Democrats scrambled to prove them wrong. The renewal of fear balanced against economic disappointment, blame and finger-pointing, and the usual injudicious use of Diebold machines was fractionally enough to swing an election, with both government and people bitterly divided.

The reality had moved closer to home: Nowhere was safe anymore. The café's business started falling off, Americans increasingly unable to afford vacations while the foreign tourists—afraid of the escalating violence and put off by intrusive security procedures—stopped coming. George stared at plumbing bills, invoices for roof repairs, receipts from electricians, and demands for payment from gasfitters—all for things Lonny could do but wasn't there to do anymore. Harry's last attempt at fixing squeaky hinges on the back door ended up with a hefty bill for a locksmith and a new doorframe. George and Carlene did their best on their own, buying dozens of fix-it-yourself manuals and *Do Your Own Upholstery*, the *Handyman's E-Z Guide to Bricklaying*, and the *ABC of Appliance Repairs*. The pictures made it look simple, but the results were far from satisfactory.

Her mother was right: The café was falling apart at the seams. No matter how George rearranged the numbers, she couldn't make them add up to anything that would stop her heart from beating so rapidly or the panicky ache in her chest go away. The dregs of cocoa congealed, the last of the brownie crumbs mopped up with her thumb, she gave up and went downstairs.

Harry sat in the corner booth with a couple of buddies, the three of them laughing as they drank beer straight from the bottle, quite a few bottles from the count on the table. Carlene was spraying rinse water to flush any remaining foam from the dishes coming out of the dishwasher, steam rising in wisps from the crockery.

"Where's whatsisname, Ben?" George asked sullenly.

Carlene looked at her, and again, the Ryton women's intuitive rapport said far more than words. Her mother smiled and nodded toward the toilets. "Ladies' room."

She found him lying on his back, head under the washroom sinks, bits of plumbing arranged neatly around him. He looked up at her from over the pipe wrench with which he was busily taking the sink apart.

"You do plumbing as well?"

"Fixing a leaky washer isn't rocket science," he said wryly.

"At the rates plumbers charge, you'd think it was." She nibbled her bottom lip fretfully. "You want to come out from under there a minute, please?"

He wriggled out and stood up, wiping the back of his hand across a sweating forehead, grease smearing on one cheek like war paint. "Yes, ma'am?"

He waited patiently while she wrestled with the words, his unnatural calm making her all the more edgy.

"Just credit card fraud. That's all, nothing else?"

"Nothing else," he said warily.

"You ever use drugs—meth, crack, heroin—anything like that?"

"No."

"Do you want this job?" At his look of puzzlement, she said sharply, "Make no mistake about it, it's a crap job. We need more than just a handyman. You'd be cleaning toilets, scrubbing out grease traps, doing laundry, picking up trash—every nasty dirty job there is, you do it. If you wait tables, any tips go into the general kitty; you don't get to keep them. Friday and Saturday, you'll work 'til two in the morning, and half-days on Sundays from seven to noon. We close for one week between Christmas and New Year's—assuming you last that long—and you don't get paid holidays. We can only pay you basic minimum wage, forty hours a week regardless of how many hours you work. No overtime, no health benefits, that's it. Minus tax and room and board, that will leave you barely enough to buy beer and cigarettes at the end of the week."

"I don't drink or smoke," he said quietly.

"Even better. You want it or not?"

"It's not up to me. I'd have to talk to my parole officer—"

"No, I would have to talk to your parole officer. Believe me, I'll check you out thoroughly, and if you've lied about anything, your ass will be out of here so fast you won't have time to catch your breath. You got that?"

He glanced past her shoulder, and she knew without turning that her mother was standing in the doorway of the ladies' toilets. "Yes, ma'am."

"Okay. Give me your parole officer's name and phone number."

He wiped his hands on an old Army T-shirt that had

once been Lonny's, another small pang George ignored, and wrote down a name and number in a neat hand on Carlene's order pad. As he held it out to George, he said so quietly she nearly didn't hear him, "Thank you."

"Don't thank me yet," she said starkly as she took the pad from him. "While I check his references, Ma, why don't you show him around the presidential suite?"

# CHAPTER FOUR

In more prosperous times not so long ago, the Grinnin'
Bear had also boasted a small colony of fishing cabins, a
dozen small clapboard shacks tucked behind a grove of
pines nearly half a mile from the café. Now they had the
distinct look of forlorn neglect. Trinity followed Carlene,
wading awkwardly through waist-deep snow. As they neared
the cabins, he could hear the sound of rushing water.

"Fairfax Creek," Carlene said without his asking. "Runs
just past that bend. Has to get a lot colder than this for the
water to freeze up completely. Best warm-water fishing
anywhere in Montana—walleye, smallmouth bass, pike,
catfish, yellow perch. You like fishing?"

"Don't know. I've never done any."

She gave him a pitying look. "You stay around here any
length of time, you'd best learn how."

The largest cabin was scarcely larger than a toolshed,
and looked as if it had actually served as one in the past.
But someone had made an effort to do it up, rough-hewn
timber steps leading onto a screen porch sheltering the
front door. The snow had blown into a bank nearly to the
windows on the windward side, and covered the roof in a
thick cap, with only the tip of a conical stovepipe visible.

"This used to be the caretaker's lodge. It's the only one
with electricity and a proper woodstove," Carlene said as

she unlocked the front door. "The rest are just for summer use, tourists on fishing vacations."

The hinges complained as she pushed her shoulder against the door to persuade it open. Inside, the air was bitter cold and smelled of stale dust. She flipped on the light, a single naked lightbulb hanging from the ceiling and casting harsh shadows. Wooden shutters covered double-glazed windows, one on either side. A coatrack made of upturned deer hooves was nailed to the wall by the door as the only decoration, no pictures anywhere. A black Franklin stove squatted on flagstones set in the corner, an old cast-iron kettle on top.

It was one large room, a log slab counter serving as a dining table all that divided the kitchen from the living room. A minifridge, an elderly microwave, and a two-ring hot plate bolted to the counter crowded up to edges of a small sink.

"Microwave is broke. Hot plate is okay. You've got pots and pans under here," Carlene said, pulling back a checkered curtain on a doorless cabinet, "and room for plates and cups and things here." She opened a cupboard over the sink. "You can take what you need from the café. The water's been turned off for the winter so that the pipes don't freeze. We'll get that turned back on, not a problem. Toilet and shower in here . . ." She opened the door to what he had mistaken to be a broom closet—a shower curtain hanging on a circular rod and a drain in the floor shared the tiny space with the toilet. "The shower's one of those dual-type things: there's a boiler heats up the water off the woodstove, but it runs off a solar panel on the roof in the summer. My son Lonny put that in. It's supposed to be energy efficient, good for the environment. Alls I know is it saves on electricity."

A faded oval braided rug lay on painted floorboards. Carlene whipped off a dustsheet from a daybed that served as a couch, the thin mattress rolled and tied. "We'll get you set up with bedding, towels, whatever. There's plenty of logs stacked in back. You'll find the axe in the lean-to. Just chop what you need and use it, help yourself. Once you've got the stove going, it'll be warmer than you'd think in here. It's a cozy little place." She nodded at the only other bit of furniture in the room, a small dresser on top of which a coiled wire trailed to the wall. "We'll get you a TV and a CD player in here, if you want. We don't leave anything like that out in the wintertime. Kids get in, trash what they don't steal."

"You have much of a problem with vandalism?"

"Not really. It's a little too remote in the winter and there's usually people around most of the summer, a few regulars who still come for the fishing every year. Anyway, TV's not cable, just an aerial, I'm afraid. No phone, but you can use the one in the café." She gestured vaguely at the room. "Well, that's pretty much it. It's basic, but comfortable. Good enough for you?"

He smiled fleetingly. "It's fine. But like I said, I doubt my parole officer is going to give her permission."

Carlene snorted. "She will. We're offering you a job. Anyway, the last fellah we hired on was also an ex-con. Which is why my daughter isn't keen on the idea. He was some kid George went to high school with—big sob story, father ran off, mother was a drunk, hung out with the wrong crowd, and got caught shoplifting once too often. George felt sorry for him, thought all he needed was a second chance and a bit of faith." She chortled. "He turned out to be a meth-head, lasted all of six days before he took off with a month's worth of till money." She eyed him meaningfully. "Didn't get far. George's ex is a county sheriff's officer with a bad temper. Very bad temper."

He caught her drift. "I understand, ma'am."

"I hope you do, because this time it's me feeling sorry for someone and taking the chance. I'd hate to think we'd be wrong twice in a row." She led him back out to the porch and locked up. "It's too late in the day, and it's still snowing pretty hard. Dinner crowd should be coming in soon, if there is much of one in this weather. Let's go show you how to run the dishwasher."

The "dinner crowd" turned out to be Harry, a couple of snowplow operators stopping on a break, and a local rancher who came in for a meal of hot coffee and cold beer. Carlene had Trinity use clean dishes in order to show him how to stack them properly into the racks and operate the automatic dishwasher. The rack pulled into a metal box on a clanking conveyor belt to emerge from the other end, the resilient china steaming and hot enough to scald his fingers.

"I thought you said you were from Florida?" he heard George say.

She sounded angry, and his heart lurched with dread. He turned around, shaking soap foam from his hands. "Yes, ma'am," he said carefully. "That's where my last job was, Tallahassee."

She held up the bit of paper he'd written Clarice Mc-Graff's number on. "So why's your parole officer in D.C.?"

He stifled an exhalation of absurd relief, his secret still safe. He'd learned by rote the official explanation, able to it reel off without even thinking, which was just as well as he didn't like the lie he had to live. "Because I'm a convicted felon on conditional release. Crossing state lines requires authorization at a federal level."

"But they allow you to travel all on your own?"

"Yes, ma'am. Ms. McGraff is with the U.S. Parole Commission at the Department of Justice; she's in charge of a pilot reentry program. Once I got to Spokane, I'd have registered with their county parole office. I've lost my placement there, so I'm just waiting to see where they reassign me."

George shook her head with disbelief. "White-collar

criminals get white-collar treatment, I suppose." He didn't react. "Pending submission by the relevant official for the State of Montana of further evaluation to ensure our facilities pass cost-efficient and safety requirement needs, Ms. McGraff has extended provisional approval in the interim while she reviews our application to sponsor you in providing an appropriate employment opportunity consistent with the objectives of assisting offenders in a productive and law-abiding return to society."

Trinity suppressed a smile as Carlene laughed.

"Is that what she said?" Carlene said.

"Verbatim. Translated into English, she'll check us out to make sure we're cheap enough, and that you're not going to run off first chance you get." George turned to him in a funny little movement, and he realized she'd had to restrain herself from extending her hand. "Congratulations," she said. "You can start Monday."

# CHAPTER FIVE

Lucas Jensen sat alone in his county sheriff's patrol car, the big Chevy S10 Blazer parked on the side of the road with his engine idling to keep the heater blowing warm air against the windshield. From his vantage point on the ridge road above U.S. Highway 2, he looked down on the meager traffic slowly moving between thick snowbanks plowed up on the shoulders of the road. Gusts of wind blew fairy mists from the snowbanks into the air, swirling in a silent ballet. The sky was a nearly uniform steel gray, overhung with thick, sullen clouds threatening to dump more snow.

He kept the police radio tuned to an almost inaudible level, background crackles and deadpan voices muttering to themselves. He wasn't listening to the radio chatter; he didn't have to. After so many years in the job, it barely made any impact on his consciousness until a code number or the tone of someone's voice inexplicably triggered his attention. Winter was a slow season even without a blizzard, burglars and rapists and methamphetamine pushers preferring to stay home where it was cozy and warm, where any other halfway sensible person should be right now.

At the moment, he was supposed to be using the slack time to update the logbooks beside him on the passenger seat, but sat with his arms crossed on his chest, working a wad of by-now tasteless chewing gum between his molars as impassively as a cow with cud. He hadn't smoked in six years, but joked he spent as much on gum as he had on cigarettes, one addiction replacing another. He watched, bored, as a lone highway patrol car flashing blue lights passed by, on its way to assist some fucking idiot without enough sense to use chains or snow tires sliding off the road to hit a tree or a deer, or some other fucking idiot who shouldn't have been out wasting precious gas in weather like this either.

His cell phone rang, playing the tune from *The Lone Ranger*. He retrieved it from the passenger seat, looked at the caller ID and scowled. Debating for a moment whether or not just to turn the damned thing off, he finally hit the receive button.

"What," he said flatly into it.

"Hi, baby. It's Wendy." She had her cheerful voice on, the one she used when she was trying to avoid a quarrel, as if by pretending everything was fine she could make it that way. He hated that voice.

"I'm busy. What do you want?"

"Are you going to be near Albertsons anytime today?" When he didn't answer, she went on, her words coming out faster, anxious. "Because we're nearly out of milk and if Amy's staying the weekend, you know how she goes through milk. And bread, too. I'd go but the roads are so bad and seeing as you're out anyway—"

"That's because I work, Wendy. You remember work, right? That thing I do so you can spend all my fucking money?" He heard her gulp, and listened to her silence, knowing she was close to tears. "I've told you before not to call me when I'm on duty. I don't have time for this shit. If we need groceries, haul your fat ass off the sofa and get some."

"I'm almost out of gas . . ."

"Put fifty bucks in the tank, that's it. I want to see the receipt."

"But my car doesn't have snow tires on anyway," she said timidly. She had asked him last weekend to change the tires around for winter, he knew. But he also knew she wasn't about to lay a guilt trip on him for not having bothered with it; she was too smart to challenge him.

"Then go get the chains out of the garage and put them on the fucking car. You're not some helpless little girl, and I can't be at your beck and call every time you break a nail. Okay?" He didn't wait for her to answer, switching the cell phone off and tossing it back onto the seat.

"Lazy bitch," he muttered darkly. He worked his ass off stuck in this goddamned car day after day no matter what the weather was like so she could sit around on her butt doing nothing, watching daytime soap operas and running up the phone bill yapping with her other brainless girl-friends. All he asked in return was a clean house and a hot meal to come home to, not that unreasonable a thing to expect. But he was getting sick and tired of her whining, her calculated tears and recriminations, the relentless pressure for that phony romantic crap she got off the tube, demanding love and hugs and kisses and when were they going to get married until he felt as if he'd explode with the suffocation.

He felt cheated; they hadn't even had any decent sex in weeks. All her silk teddies were in a drawer while she wore flannel pajamas now to bed, blaming it on the cold. She'd been more than eager when they'd first met a year ago, a woman barely out of her teens, bleached blonde hair down to her ass, and legs up to her armpits, skimpy leather skirts no matter what the weather was like, her nipples standing out in relief in the cold against her tight little T-shirts, al-ways willing to do it with him anytime, anywhere, any way. She'd gone down on him regularly in the patrol car, parked behind the station, getting off on the danger they might be caught. But then he'd made the mistake of ask-ing her to move in with him, and the sexy nympho who couldn't get enough turned out to be the same sort of hard-nosed, scheming bitch all women were. If he'd wanted to come home to cold food and the cold shoulder, he could have stayed married to George.

He sighed, closed his eyes, and rubbed his fingers into the sockets, making red flecks dance behind the lids. God, he was tired. Why did everything always have to be such a friggin' battle? His chest ached, and he wondered bitterly, as he frequently did, if he would eventually die of a massive heart attack, the way his father had, the way his older brother had—nagged into early graves by selfish vindictive women.

He rolled down the window just far enough to spit out the wad of gum into the snow, and unwrapped a fresh stick. Popping it into his mouth, he savored the first rush of spearmint, put the Blazer into gear, and started down toward the Hi-Line.

# CHAPTER SIX

Snow completely covered the windows when Trinity woke, his heart pounding with irrational panic, the inside of the cabin still dark. The shattered residue of his nightmare faded quickly enough, but left his limbs feeling heavy with a persistent vague dread. He took several gasping breaths to calm his nerves.

No one was coming for him, no one would hurt him. He was alone.

His bladder was full and he wondered what time it was, trying to find an angle to read his watch in the dim light. Just after five.

The eerie quiet was a luxury but, ironically, that made it hard to sleep, with Trinity constantly roused by the alarming silence, every tiny sound too sharp. Three years in detention camps had inured him to too many voices, too many people screaming in pain or fear, too many dogs barking and guards shouting in anger or malevolence or simple boredom, too many engines and machinery and traffic, too many military helicopters constantly flying in and out of the compound, too much clanging and banging and slamming of metal doors day and night until it had become a solid wall of noise that made any one sound impossible to distinguish. Where a constant regime of sleep deprivation had once made it easier to nod off within moments, now that he had plenty of rest, he was plagued with bad dreams and insomnia.

The noise in the transitional accommodations after he'd been flown to Florida hadn't been much better, constant if not quite as loud. He'd shared a locked wing with a dozen other of McGraff's handpicked test cases, most of them murderers and sex offenders similarly implanted and tattooed. Unlike the others, however, he had his own locked room, sterile and isolated. They in turn ostracized him, more afraid of McGraff than him, with good reason. He'd been absurdly grateful for the graveyard shift on his own, mopping floors and emptying wastebaskets and scrubbing toilets in Tallahassee's medium-security federal penitentiary's administration complex, usually under the constant observation of a single armed guard, usually watching him with silent hostility. He'd worked hard, kept his mouth shut, and did exactly as he was told, never protesting the often illogical or contradictory regulations, not willing to even question why he was still alive, never mind why he was back in the States.

But he couldn't remember the last time he'd had one good night of solid dreamless sleep.

The cabin was ice cold, his breath making clouds, his nose and ears aching. Even with fresh linen and clean bedding, he could still smell the faint stale odor of the mattress on the creaking daybed. He didn't mind, burrowing further under the quilt to doze off again, unwilling yet to get up even for a piss. The light through the gaps of the shuttered, snow-blocked windows glowed wanly when he woke again an hour later. Teeth chattering, he dressed quickly, even wearing the down jacket. Like the stillness, after three years of enduring sweltering, bug-infested heat, the cold was a novelty he almost enjoyed. But not quite.

The water had indeed been turned on, pipes gurgling as he flushed the toilet. There was no hot water, however, at least not in the kitchen sink. Although he had nothing in the small fridge or the cupboard, no tea bags or instant coffee, he filled the kettle and heated enough on the electric hot plate to make a cup of boiled water, drinking it to warm himself.

When he opened the door, a small avalanche of snow fell inside from the bank blown up against the house during the night. The hinges on the shutters over the windows were badly in need of oiling, folding back grudgingly. The sky was still dark, dawn barely a smudge of pale rose along the horizon. The café wasn't visible from this distance, but he knew Carlene would be working an early-morning shift. She'd told him if she needed him for anything, she'd let him know. He could sleep late if he wanted; this might be his last Sunday off for a while, after all.

He wasn't the type to sleep late, not even on a Sunday, not anymore.

He found the axe in the lean-to shed, a heavy malevolent-looking wedge with a thick oak shaft. He tentatively hefted the solid weight in his hands and carried it out to a large tree stump that had obviously served as a chopping block for many years.

Selecting one of the smaller logs from the neat stack against the back wall of the cabin, he placed it on the tree stump, balanced on one end. Then he raised the axe above his head and brought the blade down as hard as he could.

Instead of splitting the log in two, the axe felt as if jerked by an invisible hand to one side as the log sprang in the other. Off-balance, Trinity stumbled, cracking his shin into the stump and nearly falling. He dropped the axe, his arms numbed, before he regained his footing.

"Ow," he commented quietly, and was glad no one was around to see his completely inept result.

His second try left Trinity with the axe imbedded solidly into the end of the log, thoroughly stuck. He struggled to wriggle the blade out, and ended up on his knees in the snow, log clamped between his thighs, and pried the blade out by leaning his weight on the handle. It gave way and he landed facedown in the snow, log and axe underneath him.

He stood, panting and sweating, no longer cold but determined. Again, he set the log on the stump, and again, the axe became stuck as he brought it down with all his strength. This time he managed to force the blade out without having to eat snow.

"You've never chopped wood in your life, have you?"

He turned around, startled. George stood at the edge of the tree line, holding a thermos and a plastic bag, grinning at him.

"Oh, shit," he said before he'd thought about it. Then, as her grin widened in surprise, "I beg your pardon, I didn't mean to swear."

"I'm glad you do. You're far too polite to be real." She held up the plastic bag. "Ma sent these down for you. Apple fritters. And hot coffee."

"Thanks."

"Can I give you a tip?" She nodded at the fallen log and the axe in his hands. "The weight of the axe will do half the work for you, if you're not trying to swing it around your head like it's Darth Vader's lightsaber."

"Okay."

"Keep your eye on where you want it to hit, not on the axe. Aim closer to the edge of the log, not the middle. Think of it like cutting wedges out of a cake. And try to avoid the knots, they don't split well."

"Thank you."

She waited a moment, and when he made no further attempt to chop wood, she laughed. "You want me to leave now?"

"Yes, ma'am." He smiled in return. "If you don't mind."

He waited until she had safely disappeared, not even her footsteps crunching in the snow audible, before he balanced the recalcitrant log on the stump, eyed it warily, and raised the axe. He swung the blade down, putting his weight behind it, and jumped in surprise as the log suddenly split apart, two clean halves tumbling to either side of the stump.

For the next few hours, Trinity split wood, until he was hot enough from the effort to take off his down jacket, then even unbuttoned his shirt. His lungs burned in the sharp cold air, sweat running into his eyes. But he found a curious peace in the drudgery, the rhythm of the work spreading euphoria through him like a strange drug.

When he finally stopped, his muscles trembled with fatigue instead of cold. Trinity panted, his breath tasting like acid, sweat sticking against his ribs. He was hungry, and he sat on the ragged stump to wolf down the pastry, the coffee in the thermos still hot. The illusion of warmth didn't last, and within minutes, the raw winter air made him shiver. Shrugging on his jacket, he hoisted as much firewood as he could carry in his arms, making several trips slogging through the snow back to the cabin to convey his newly split logs and a small collection of twigs from a stack at one end of the porch under a rotting canvas tarp.

He'd never chopped his own wood before, and he'd never made his own fire before, either. He crumpled up the few pages of yellowed newspaper lining from the shelf under the sink, carefully built a wigwam of twigs on top of the paper in the old Franklin stove in imitation of a vague memory of a Boy Scout handbook illustration, then lit it with a cigarette lighter he found in the cupboard. It burned merrily for a few minutes, but all too quickly, the paper had vanished, twigs smoldering, fire out. He tried relighting the twigs by holding the lighter to them, but quickly gave up on that attempt as he burnt his thumb.

As he sat back on his heels, frowning at the woodstove, a shadow passed across the floor from the window behind him, followed by a soft knock. When he opened the door, George looked past him at the woodstove and smiled wryly.

"You can fix plumbing, but you can't chop wood and you don't know how build a fire, either," she said, hefting a cardboard box in her arms. "You *must* be a city boy."

"I'm willing to learn."

She set the cardboard box down inside the door and left. He could hear her opening the door to the lean-to, then she returned a moment later holding an old tin box and another handful of sticks and twigs. "Us country girls cheat," she said.

He watched without comment as she opened the tin box and took out a chunk of white stuff—like crumbly cheese but smelling sharply of kerosene—broke off a small portion, and nestled it under a loose pile of kindling. It lit within seconds, and a few minutes later, when she shoved in a few pieces of firewood and shut the doors on the Franklin stove, the fire behind the glass flickered vigorously.

"You make it look easy," he said.

"Anything is easy when you know how." She retrieved the cardboard box she'd left by the door and carried it into the kitchen. "Ma sent along some stuff she thought you could use." She started unloading the box onto the counter: canned soup, bread, a tub of margarine, a box of sugar, carton of milk, jar of instant coffee, bag of apples, onions, potatoes, dish detergent, sponge, toilet paper, paper towels—the items quickly crowding the small space.

"Thank you, but I'm still not sure I'm staying."

"What, you planning on making a run for it already?"

He smiled. "No. The job in Spokane was vetted. Residential halfway house, secure unit, locked doors, CCTV cameras. You don't have those here."

"Yet they trust you to run around the country all by yourself?"

He shrugged. She snorted her contempt with bureaucracy.

When she sat down on his unmade daybed, he stayed standing, ill at ease. "So where you from, originally?" she said, seemingly unaware of his discomfort.

"Tallahassee," he said softly without looking at her.

"Right," she said, leaning back and crossing both her arms and legs in annoyance. "Let's not start off on the wrong foot here, okay? I can spot a liar a mile off. You aren't from Florida."

"It's where I served my time." He hoped she didn't spot that lie as shrewdly as she had the first.

"I'm assuming you did have a life before prison."

"Yes, ma'am." He shifted his weight, knowing he was assuming his habitual inmate stance, head down, hands clasped loosely in front of him. How much of the truth he could reveal he wasn't certain. "I grew up in Santa Monica. That's where we lived until three years ago."

That got George's interest. "'We'? Are you married?"

It took him a long moment before he said, his voice expressionless, "No."

She gazed at him thoughtfully, then stood up. He was thankful she wasn't going to press the issue.

"It's getting warmer in here already. I should get back; the after-church crowd starts coming in soon. If you want some supper later on, Ma says to come up to the café before six. She's working on a list of things you can do starting tomorrow morning."

# CHAPTER SEVEN

November 22nd

Dear Diary,

Dad came and picked me up early from Sophie's on Friday and we drove all the way to Malta for dinner in a real resteraunt instead of Pizza Hut even though the roads were still pretty bad. He still had his uniform on straight from work, because he wanted to get to Malta and back before it got too dark. I asked didn't he want Wendy to come with us too, but he said he didn't get enuff alone time just him and me. It was a Italian resteraunt, with cloth napkins and candles and everything. He knew the waitress and he asked her real nice if they'd let me have a little glass of white wine with my dinner and because he still had his uniform on she said yes, which was fun even if it didn't taste that nice.

It was still dark when we got back to Dad's house, and I felt kinda embarrassed for Wendy cuz she'd made a roast chicken, even though she said she'd already eaten when she found out Dad and I had gone out and said she'd just cooked a chicken to make cold cuts for his sandwichs tomorrow. She had on a big smile like everything was okay-dokay but she looked like she was gonna cry. I don't know why grown-ups think kids can't figure out when they're lying.

I sorta like Wendy, even when she's trying to be all like my mother half the time and my best friend the rest, and pretends she doesn't notice when Dad says mean things to her, just laughs like he's making a little joke. She never fights with him like Mom did, or says mean things back. Anyway, Wendy made her and Dad some wisky hi-balls while Dad watched the news and I read a Dr. Spineshiver Investigates book that Sophie lent me. Dad doesn't want me reading scary books, cuz he thinks they still give me nightmares, but they don't anymore. I told Dad it was for a book report for school even tho Ms. Clymer the school librarian doesn't like any of the Dr. Spineshiver Investigates books either, cuz she sez they promote idolitry and profanity, even though there's no real swearing in them at all. Besides, I don't actualy believe in ghosts or monsters or magic, it's just fiction.

Wendy got pretty sleepy after three wisky hi-balls and went to bed early, way before Dad made me go to bed. I heard them talking later on, and Dad sounded mad and Wendy was crying. I think they're gonna brake up, even tho she's way prettier than Mom, and lots younger. She wasn't there when I woke up, but Dad was making pancakes in the kitchen, so I didn't say anything about Wendy and neither did he.

Saturday there was still lots of snow but the sky was all blue and Dad got out the old saucers he got when I was little and we went sliding down the hill in back of his house. He looked really funny sitting on a little kid's saucer with his legs all folded up and holding on to the sides and it was too small so he kept falling over into the snow. Then we made some snow forts and had a big snowball battle until the neighbors dog came over so we threw snowballs at the dog and he tried to catch them in his mouth which made us laugh even more.

I thought cuz of all the snow maybe we didn't have to go to church, but he said the roads were clear enough and its important not to let my Sunday School slide. He pays the part of my tuition so I can go to St. Mary Magdalene. Most of the other kids live in the main house all the time cuz there parents live in places like New York and Washington where there's lots of criminals and its really dangerous and Camille's parents live in Geneeva and wanted her to learn better English but she doesn't like it here and cries a lot. All the rich kids like Sophie and Craig and Camryn go there, but a couple kids like me and Sydne got church scholarships and if Dad's church didn't donate a lot of the money he couldn't afford to send me either so we have to go to his church every Sunday like to show our appreciation.

Anyway, Dad says its got a better curriculam than Stone Child High but its also got like super security where you gotta walk through a metal detector and they scan your eyeballs and fingerprints like airports do so crazy people can't get inside like Columbine and Virginia Tech and that Amish school, and everyone's got an ID card that's got a special chip in it like Mom and Dad has in their drivers licences, and we're always having snap locker checks and drug tests and stuff so its way safer than going to a regular school. We all wear uniforms, and they make you take classes in stuff nobody else has to like Latin and Religious History, major yuk. But next year Dad said if I get my grades up to a B +average I can sign up for ecquestrian class.

Dad wasn't happy I forgot to bring my good shoes with me, but he didn't want to go by Mom's to pick them up so I wore my dirty old sneakers to church which looked pretty stupid with a dress but Dad said that I had only myself to blame for forgetting. Mom doesn't go to church with us anymore. Mom never talks about it, but she and Nana both stopped going after Uncle Lonny got himself killed. Mr. Dayton *from Dad's church comes sometimes and talks to us about the Bible and One Christain Nation, but I don't think she pays much attention to him.*

Dad took me to Nana's after church cuz Mom was there doing the books. Nana hired this new guy to work at the café helping out and stuff. His name is Ben, but he's got this funny last name, Trinity, like he's a priest or something, but he doesn't look anything like a priest. He's kinda quiet but nice, and he was real polite to Dad, called him "sir" and all, but Dad still didn't like him. Dad never likes anybody new, anyway, so its like no big deal.

Ben wears these leather gloves with no fingers all the time, and when I asked him why Mom told me I should keep my long nose out of other people's business but he didn't mind. He's got exhama (I don't think I spelled that right), it's some kind of itchy skin problem that gets worse in the cold so he wears them to keep his hands warm. He doesn't tolerate cold all that well, he said. Ben is from Telehassey, that's in Florida, and he's way skinny and got a really good tan, I'm like so jealous! I wish we could go to Florida and I would just lie on the beach all day till I was as brown as a Mexican. Nana sez that's just courting skin cancer, but I don't care, I hate being as white as a worm in the rain, my legs are so pale you can see the blood veins under the skin which is so gross I can't stand it. If I lived in Florida and had exhama, I wouldn't want to move to Montana, that's totally for sure.

Dad gave Mom and me a lift back home, and even though they weren't fighting at all, not even saying much of anything, I sat in the back with my iPod headphones on the whole way and texted Sophie on my phone until the battery went dead, I hate this crappy phone. But when we got out of the car, Dad told Mom she should be careful around that boy, you hear me? Dad would be keeping an eye out on them both so she'd better watch her step. Mom looked like she was going to say something nasty to him, but she just shut the car door and went in the house.

I don't know if Dad is really jealous or if he just says stuff like that to make Mom mad. Besides, he's got a girlfriend so why should he care if Mom goes out with other people, as if there were anyone in Redemption Mom would even want to date, which there isn't, this place sucks.

Bojangles has decided to sleep in Mom's room tonight, so I'm all alone and that was what happened this weekend. I'll write again tomorrow.

                                        Love, Amy.

# CHAPTER EIGHT

Trinity settled into life in rural Montana with amazing ease. Transient customers who came into the café simply saw him as just another anonymous waiter and couldn't care less who he was. The regulars—ranchers and farmers and townspeople who came at certain times and sat at the same tables or booths with clockwork consistency—had treated him with polite suspicion at first, but warmed to him surprisingly quickly. He knew most of them by name, and even accepted a few good-natured jokes about credit cards when he rang up their bills. The Spaight sisters, two plump women in their eighties who Trinity suspected weren't sisters at all, adopted him as a sort of mascot, knitting over-sized pullovers and hats for him, hideously bright affairs made from a medley of leftover knitting yarn. He wore them, much to the amusement of the locals.

The café had been in a shabby state for quite some time, maintained just well enough to pass health inspections by the barest of margins. When Trinity wasn't waiting tables, washing dishes, or scrubbing floors, he fixed leaking pipes, patched cracked walls, renovated broken tiles, mended rotting window frames, repaired the faulty microwave, replaced the spark plugs and oil filter in Carlene's Jeep, rebuilt the sagging stock shelves in the storage room, rewired the dance floor speakers to get the buzz out of the sound system, on and on—the chores seemingly endless.

If it was broke, he fixed it. Everything except the office computer, to George's bemusement: he refused her offer to even play solitaire on it.

As with anywhere unemployment was high and money tight, the barter system was alive and well in Redemption, and it wasn't long before Trinity realized the most valuable commodity he had to trade was himself. A couple days spent repairing cattle fencing along Jack Bakker's property in exchange for stocking Carlene Ryton's freezer with a side of beef extended to being drafted into the "volunteer" crew rebuilding the derelict back loading docks to Rousseau's Feed-n-Seed, the local livestock supplier, lumberyard, and hardware store. Taking advantage of a freak winter thaw, the morning was still dim when Jack Bakker drove around the back of the seed store, with his nephew Craig and Tom Mifflin in the cab. Trinity sat in the bed of the Chevy pickup, back against a bale of hay, legs wedged between tool chests and power tools and coils of extension cords. Two other men waited in the cold, stamping their feet for warmth, breath hanging in the air, gloved hands around thin plastic cups of vending machine coffee.

One of the waiting men began unloading the back of the pickup before Jack had even turned off the engine, muttering, "Mornin', Ben."

"Morning, Mr. Ingersoll."

Jared Ingersoll, the feed store's part-time assistant, paused just long enough to frown and shake his head. Trinity jumped over the side of the truck, toolbelt slung over his shoulder as Jack Bakker handed his nephew a roll of quarters. "How you take your coffee there, Ben?"

"Milk, no sugar, please."

Once Craig had gone into the feed store, out of earshot, the other man sidled up to Jack with a smirk to ask, "So how's that randy brother of yours doing, Jack?"

If Jack felt any irritation, his beard and the rim of his battered cowboy hat hid his face. "Still married to the richest gal in the county," he said laconically. "How's that brother of yours? Still a no-good thieving drunk?"

The other man laughed, unfazed. Craig reappeared around the corner, cutting off the man's amusement. Unaware of the banter, the boy had his concentration on gingerly holding a couple of obviously too-hot cups of coffee, the neck of a Coke sticking precariously out of his jacket pocket.

"C'mon, ladies. You can scratch each other's eyes out some other time," Tom Mifflin groused. "Let's just get this bastard built already. I want to get home before midnight."

The two-story feed depot had been built during the 1930s, in the popular square-edged Wild West frontier style. Although the store struggled with the same economic hard luck as every other commercial building in Redemption, effort had been put into maintaining the front facade. Numerous coats of red paint had been applied over the clapboard, with plenty of large advertisements for Vitovax300 seed treatment and Pro-Gold feed additives and Monsanto Maisoline biodiesel pasted over the siding. Less professional ads competed for space—handwritten placards selling stud bulls and patchwork quilts, posters touting rodeos and powwows in every small Montanan town along the Hi-Line. Smaller, sadder fliers were taped to the inside of windows for lost dogs and unwanted kittens and machinery auctions on farm foreclosures.

But around the back, where upholding the illusion of prosperity wasn't as crucial, the building was less looked after, functional if ugly. Faded paint peeled away from weathered siding. Rust bled down from bolts all along the grain elevator and the pipes feeding in and out of it. A small retaining pen for cattle had been dented into scrap metal by angry hooves. Dead weeds were frosted with rime, a dusting of snow clinging to the frozen ground. Dirt streaked the barely legible lettering REDEMPTION on the water tower, microwave relay dish bolted to the ladder, the underside of the tank covered in much cruder graffiti: *Go Grizzlies*, *Reece luvs Courtney* and *Trust in Jesus* superimposed over *Jimmy Maxwell is a Asswipe*, *Reece luvs Jody*, and *Class of '06 Rules!*

By mid-morning, the rotted boards had been stripped back to the concrete support pylons. Craig kept busy with pitching the debris onto the small bonfire. Although the crew worked without much conversation, it didn't take long for the others to notice Trinity's competence, his cuts precise, his hammering accurate and fast. Shortly after noon, a brown Ford pickup bounced over the ruts in the dirt road leading toward the back of the store, tires shattering puddles turned to hollowed sheets of ice. The blonde teenaged girl at the wheel got out with an armful of brown paper bags stamped with the Town Pump logo.

"Lunch," Jack called out to his nephew, who was still happily engrossed in incinerating offcuts of lumber and dead branches, tossing any other flammable scrap he could find into the blaze, including any unlucky shrubbery nearby he could manage to uproot.

The five men sat lined up on the half-built loading dock, eating squashed hamburgers and rubbery French fries while the blonde girl stood next to the bonfire with Craig, sharing his Coke. Now that the saws had been switched off, tools downed, Trinity could hear the crackle of burning wood in the silence, the distant low of cattle, crows cawing in the fields. The sun didn't rise that far in a winter sky, but the air was so clear the pale blue stretched above them like fine porcelain, seemingly fragile in the cold.

"Y're not too bad at this, Ben," Jared commented from around a mouthful of hamburger. "They teach you how to do construction work when you was down in Tallahassee?"

Before Trinity could answer, the man he didn't know snickered. "Hell, if I'd knowed they'd learn me a job that good in prison, I'da gone out and whacked a few little old ladies on the head to steal their purses myself."

The others stopped chewing to stare at him in silence. The man's smirk faded slightly, his face reddening.

"Just kidding."

"Not too funny, there, Shep," Jack commented acidly.

After an awkward moment, Shep stood and with a rebellious mutter of, "Some folks just cain't never take a fuckin' joke," he wandered over to insinuate himself into the gawky flirtation between Craig and the blonde girl.

"Don't pay him no mind, Ben," Jared said. "Shep was born with his foot in his mouth."

"It's okay," Trinity said, fishing in the bottom of the greasy bag for the last of the salt-encrusted fries. "You might want to warn him the only thing they teach in prison these days is Bible studies; there hasn't been any vocational training in years." Not since Congress had eliminated Pell Grants for cons working toward college degrees and the ambitions of a Texan senator to appear "tough on crime" had extended the ban to *any* sort of education, the subsequent upsurge in recidivism be damned. "But I hope no one thinks I've ever mugged old ladies."

"Just that useless dumbass," Tom Mifflin grumbled. "Why the hell do you keep him on anyways, Jer?"

Ingersoll grimaced. "I used to go out with his sister."

"What, and that obligates you for life?" Jack laughed.

The conversation steered off into the vagaries of familial responsibilities that kept small communities united, and away from Trinity's ambiguous past. At the end of the day, a sharp chill in the air as the sun faded, Jared Ingersoll distributed whatever supplies the men had bartered for, in Jack's case a large roll of barbed wire and, for Trinity, enough leftover lumber to fill the bed of the pickup.

"Y're a damned hard worker, Ben. Don't exactly seem right, payin' you in wood," Ingersoll said. "Not when I know you're just givin' it away to Carlene. Sure you cain't use something for yourself?"

"I'm happy with this," Trinity reassured him. "It's keeping a roof over my head. Literally."

Weekends were often the busiest time of the week for the café, so Trinity usually took his only day off on a Monday or Tuesday. Amtrak, as well as all other trains, trams, and subways, was off-limits to him, and Greyhound didn't serve this remote part of Montana. The only other public transport was the twice-daily Red Ace Bus Line, a fleet of two ex-yellow school buses run by the Confederation of Indian casinos to ferry gamblers, mostly retired grannies out en masse, on a continuous loop down to Great Falls and over to Lewistown, up to Fort Peck and west to Havre. So once a month, he got a ride from Jack Bakker into Havre, where he caught the early-morning bus to Great Falls. There, he went directly to a discreet office in the courthouse and reported to whatever DSD agent was on duty, submitted to the usual urine and blood tests, took his routine polygraph, and was out by lunchtime to rummage through secondhand bins in bookstores to fill his backpack.

Even here, he was cautious about his selections, eschewing the political or military history areas in favor of titles like *The Life and Death of Christopher Marlowe* or *The Translated Works of Aristotle, Horace and Longinus*. He had become such a familiar customer the clerks would sometimes set aside an obscure volume of Wordsworth or a biography of C. S. Lewis for him. Only once had he inadvertently got it wrong, the years spent in custody creating blind spots.

"I'm looking for Orwell's *1984*," he said to the clerk.

The young man had blinked, owl-like behind rimless glasses. "That book would be out of stock," he said blandly. "Do you want to order it?"

As soon as he heard the catchphrase "out of stock," Trinity's heart skipped a beat, his breath catching in his throat.

"No, thanks," he said hurriedly.

Censorship did not exist in the United States of America. The First Amendment was sacrosanct. But certain things had a way of quietly disappearing from public notice, library books that were checked out and never returned, CDs by particular musical artists that couldn't find distribution for "commercial" reasons, classic movies withdrawn from television broadcasting or dropped from video rental stores, even children's cartoons ruled as indecent by the Federal Communications Commission bowing to pressure from the Parents Media Council watchdog, the list growing longer, and the offending material more extensive. You could, of course, special-order anything you liked, which immediately alerted Homeland Security to assess your risk to public safety. Trinity didn't need his reading habits flagged and adding any additional complexity to an already difficult existence.

Once he'd bought his books, he'd catch the return bus back to Havre in the evening where someone would be waiting for him, Jack or George or sometimes anyone handy Carlene could talk into picking him up.

At the end of March, when the snow thawed to dirty patches clinging along the shoulders of roads, Tom Mifflin invited him to go rabbit shooting.

"Will Paterson tells me he's seen a whole load of white-tailed jacks up near Murphy Butte," Tom cajoled, "and there's still a few fine-looking snowshoe hares hopping around."

"Thanks anyway, but I can't."

Tom scowled in disgust. "Don't tell me you're one of them sensitive tree-hugger types can't bear to kill a cute little bunny."

Trinity smiled. "No, sir. I'm one of those convicted felon types who aren't allowed to handle guns."

"Oh. Oh, my. I clean forgot about that." The man's flustered embarrassment and apology both amused Trinity and made him feel guilty. "As if fiddling a bunch of credit cards has anything to do with hunting. Ridiculous, if you ask me."

And George's daughter Amy had developed a mild crush on him as well, Trinity noticed uncomfortably. Luckily, her desire to maintain her facade of cool kept her burgeoning hormones at bay, while he'd had plenty of experience side-stepping schoolgirl infatuations.

At the moment, however, Amy wasn't feeling as romantic toward him, slouched in the seat at a table in the café at such an acute angle Trinity feared for her spine. She stared at the paper two inches away from her nose, her head lying on the table as she irritably doodled amorphous squiggles on her math homework.

" 'The quotient of two numbers, or their product, with same sign is a positive number whose absolute value is the absolute value of the product or the quotient of the absolute values of the original numbers,' " Trinity read aloud from her textbook.

She stared up at him sullenly. "I don't understand a single word of that."

"All it means is that when you multiply two numbers with the same sign, the answer is always positive, even when both are negative numbers," Trinity said patiently. "So, minus three times minus two is?"

"Six."

"But three times minus two is?"

"Minus six."

"Exactly. It's that simple."

"Then why can't it just say that?" Amy complained. Trinity wondered himself.

He rubbed his forehead, an ache forming behind his eyes. He'd never been that good at math himself in high school, as he remembered.

The Sunday after-church crowd had come and gone, only an elderly pair of tourists murmuring in a corner while nursing coffees and Swiss rolls and poring over road maps. Carlene brought out another pie to cool on the counter, the aroma of apple and cinnamon making his mouth water.

"Let's try this again," Trinity said. "First thing you need to do is work out the greatest common factor for eighteen and eighty-four . . ."

"What's a greatest common thingy again?"

Trinity stifled an impulse to throw something at her. "Factor. It's the largest number that divides evenly into a set of other numbers."

Amy flung her pencil down, kicking the stand underneath the booth table hard enough to threaten toppling her Dr. Pepper. "I'm never going to remember all this stuff. I hate algebra," she declared. "I'm stupid."

"You're not stupid. I just haven't figured out how to explain it to you yet so you understand."

"Okay," Amy said grudgingly. "*You're* stupid."

"No argument there." He leaned back, exasperated, and quickly scanned through the textbook's convoluted method, an impenetrable explanation about prime numbers that caused more confusion than it clarified. He closed the book in disgust and shoved it off the edge of the table, where it made a quite satisfactory thump on the floor. Surprised, Amy sat up and stared at him, eyes round.

"Forget the book. Math is supposed to be easy."

"No, it's not . . ."

"It is, if you know the shortcuts. Let me show you a secret my mom taught me when I was about your age. It's called Euclid's algorithm. You don't have to remember that." He shoved her scrap paper and pencil at her. "Divide the bigger number by the smaller number."

"Eighty-four by eighteen?"

"Yeah."

He watched her laboriously work out the long division. "Uh, four and . . ."

"Just four is fine. What's the remainder?"

She glanced at her arithmetic. "Twelve."

"Divide the eighteen by twelve."

Again, he waited as she made her large, looping numbers. "One and . . ."

"What's the remainder?"

She glanced at him, dubious but intrigued. "Six."

"Divide the twelve by six."

"Two," she said promptly.

"What's the remainder?"

"There isn't one."

He made a bold circle around the six. "Then that's your greatest common factor."

"Really?"

"Yeah. It's a magic trick. But you can't tell anyone, it's a secret."

"Not even Sophie?" The idea of a secret magic trick intrigued her, as Trinity knew it would.

"Maybe just Sophie. You want to do another?"

"Cool, sure," Amy said, brightening.

Trinity breathed a sigh of relief. "Fantastic."

As Amy scribbled in her workbook, Trinity got up to pour himself another cup of coffee. "Clever, aren't you?" he heard George's voice behind him say. He turned, cup in hand. "You're good with her. You missed your calling; you should have been a teacher instead of a thief."

Startled, he laughed. "Maybe," he said, to her obvious puzzlement. He took a long drink of the coffee to hide his smile before going back to Amy's table.

An hour later, the elderly tourists had driven away in their equally ancient Winnebago, replaced by a trio of local farmers waiting for their steak and eggs. George had taken their order, happier for Trinity to sit and tutor her daughter in math than to bus tables. Soon, the Sunday lunch specials would be on and they'd both be busy. Trinity was so deep into explaining how to compute percentages he was only vaguely aware someone else had entered the café and walked up behind him.

"Luke . . . ," George said, her voice alarmed, which made Trinity look up just as Lucas Jensen grabbed him by the front of his shirt and hauled him from the booth. The dregs of Trinity's coffee spilled from his toppled mug onto Amy's math book. Trinity had little time to react before the larger man punched him hard in the stomach and threw him to the floor.

"Luke, stop it!" George yelled and grabbed Jensen's arm. He shook her off angrily, then backhanded Trinity across the face as the smaller man struggled upright. Trinity sprawled facedown on the slick tiled floor, his hands slipping in the spray of blood from his nose. Jensen kicked him, missing his head, but his boot slamming into his shoulder. Searing pain shot through Trinity as he curled into a ball. He gasped for breath, his arm numbed.

The three farmers had stood, uncertain. "Now, Lucas, don't go doing anything you're gonna regret . . . ," one of them started. Jensen raised his fist by his head, his aim tensed to strike.

"Daddy, don't . . . !" Amy yelped, her voice squeaky with fear.

Trinity steeled himself for another blow as George threw herself at Jensen, knocking him off-balance. "Stop it!" he heard George screaming in anger. "Stop it right this minute, or I'll call Sheriff Holbrook!"

"Go right ahead," Jensen shouted, his voice thick with rage, shaking her off. "See how much support you get for harboring a terrorist!"

For a stunned moment, the only sound was Trinity struggling for air.

"What?" George said finally, her voice dead.

Jensen's fury dissipated into something colder, but far more malevolent. "I've read more in-depth graffiti on a shithouse wall than on the rap sheet his P.O. sent over. So I ran his prints, just as a precaution, check out what sort of lowlife you've been allowing my daughter to associate with. *Stay down*," he said sharply to Trinity.

Trinity had managed to sit up; still winded, but he didn't attempt to stand. He didn't look at either George or Jensen, his head hanging as blood dripped from his nose. Amy scrambled out from the café booth to hug her mother, whimpering with fright and threatened tears.

"You took his prints?" George's voice shook, with fear or anger or something else, Trinity wasn't sure.

"Got 'em off a cup first week this jerk got here, took it back to the station, and pulled a clean right thumb and two fingers. Shoulda been just a run-of-the-mill check. Except AFIS pops up a big red flag; classified, no further information available. I send 'em down to a Department of Justice buddy in Helena, had him run it past his Major Case Section's internal Cognident. Same bullshit. So my buddy calls in a favor with this guy he knows at the NSA in D.C., takes him a few weeks of digging, but he finally sends along a whole pile of restricted records. The ones the government doesn't want Joe Public to see. Go ahead, tell her who you are, asshole."

Trinity said nothing, wiping away the blood still dripping down his chin. Jensen reached down to grab Trinity's hand, wrenching his arm painfully in the socket, and stripped off the fingerless leather glove to expose the tattooed palm.

"Meet Benedictus Xavier Trinity," Jensen said, scornfully. "Card-carrying member of the al-Jawasis terrorist group who blew up the Amtrak train in California, killed ninety-seven people. Isn't that right?"

He yanked Trinity hard enough by the arm to lift him from the floor, forcing him to kneel off-balance.

"Caught him trying to flee the country along with any other of his raghead buddies who weren't already long gone. Ninety-seven people die, women and children blown to bloody pieces, half the state choking on poison gas, and here you are walking around free. You see this, George? You know what that is?" Jensen jerked Trinity's arm harder, his grip around Trinity's wrist crushing as he held out Trinity's naked palm. "It's the mark of Cain."

Jensen didn't release his hold, his free hand unsnapping the holster to pull out his service pistol and press the barrel against Trinity's brow, the blue-black metal cold.

"Tell her who you are," Jensen nearly whispered, pushing Trinity's head back.

When Trinity didn't answer, Jensen snicked off the safety, the click loud in the silence. The blood rushing in his ears sang as Trinity slowly smiled, still staring up at Jensen beyond the Glock at his forehead. "I'm whoever you want me to be. You've got the gun."

"You smart-mouthed motherfucker . . ."

"Lucas," George said quietly, "this has gone far enough. You're not going to shoot him. In front of your own daughter?"

Trinity watched the muscles in the man's jaw work, his head amazingly clear, unafraid. He was almost disappointed when Jensen holstered his gun with contempt. He grunted in pain as Jensen hauled him to his feet, twisting his arm up behind his back hard enough to activate the microchips. For a moment, as his heart skipped hollowly, Trinity feared he'd black out, not even caring as Jensen handcuffed him.

"No, I'm not going to shoot him. I'm gonna arrest him."

The pain shot down Trinity's left arm, leaving him breathless. The fear he was having a heart attack triggered his dormant anger. "What for?" he demanded.

A mistake, he realized a second later as Jensen wrenched his cuffed hands upward behind his back, the pain searing into his already throbbing shoulder sockets. "We can start with creating a public nuisance and resisting arrest," Jensen growled in his ear. "Don't worry, I'll think up more by the time we get to the station."

Jensen dragged him stumbling out the door so quickly he fell to his knees twice in the graveled parking lot to be roughly jerked onto his feet each time. "You got the right to remain silent, I suggest you use it," Jensen monotoned as he opened the back door of the police cruiser and pitched his prisoner headlong onto the backseat. "You got the right to have an attorney present before questioning, if you don't have an attorney one will be appointed for you. Depending on whether or not we can scare one up willing to waste a perfectly fine Sunday afternoon to represent a piece of shit like you. Do you understand your rights as I have given them. . . ." Without waiting for an answer— even if Trinity had the breath to make one—Jensen slammed the car door shut, Trinity barely getting his feet clear in time.

He didn't bother trying to sit up for several minutes, lying facedown on the backseat struggling to get his heartbeat back into a normal rhythm.

The drive wasn't long, the town center of Redemption not much more than a motley collection of brick and clapboard buildings along a single street. They passed a gas station and hardware store, a long-defunct Dairy Queen, Rousseau's feed and grain depot, a library, clothing thrift store and post office combined in a single building, and pulled into the back lot the sheriff's office shared with the Redemption Volunteer Fire Department.

Jensen drove through the open gate of a chain-link fence and around the back of a squat cement building under multiple layers of peeling paint the color of split pea soup, parking in a space marked on the cracked tarmac with white paint and labeled SHERIFF. A burly police officer with long black braids leaned against the back door smoking a cigarette as Trinity was hauled out of the back of the cruiser. He watched with disinterest as Jensen frog-marched Trinity toward the station.

"Christ," the big man commented dryly as Jensen

slammed Trinity hard against the reinforced steel door. Fresh blood erupted from Trinity's nose to stream down onto his shirt. "You might want ease up there a little."

"Just get the door for me, will ya, Tonto?" Jensen said.

The Indian deputy's expression flickered with momentary annoyance, but he turned and punched in a code on a keypad. The door beeped.

Jensen jerked open the door and heaved Trinity into the passageway by his collar. The Indian deputy dropped the cigarette to grind it out under his heel, and followed Jensen into the station. At the end of the hallway, Jensen snagged a ring of keys from a hook and unlocked a steel cage, an exposed toilet in the middle between a pair of iron bunk beds on either side. On the bottom bunk, a drunk sprawled half on and half off the bed, snoring loudly. On the top bunk of the bed opposite, as far away from the reek of alcohol and unwashed body as he could get, a sullen boy of eighteen or nineteen lay reading a *Russell Country Fishing & Hunting* magazine several years out of date. He barely glanced up as Jensen kidney-punched Trinity before propelling him into the cell, still handcuffed. Off-balance, Trinity fell to his knees, his head narrowly missing the edge of the metal toilet. Twisting to sit on the floor, he struggled for breath against the pain as Jensen banged the cell door shut and locked with more force than necessary.

"I think maybe you oughta take them cuffs off him, Luke," the big deputy said dubiously.

Although Jensen stood a good six inches shorter and several pounds lighter, he crowded into the big man's face, inches from his nose.

"And I think you oughta mind your own fucking business," Jensen snarled.

The Indian shrugged laconically, unfazed. "Your funeral."

The two of them left, the connecting door between the holding cells and the station wheezing shut. Still winded,

Trinity tried to relax as much as he could, the steel cuffs biting into his wrists, shoulders aching, his abdomen throbbing. He didn't trust himself to try standing just yet.

Curious, the kid looked down at him, half-smile on his feral face. "Man, Jensen's got a hard-on for you, that's for sure. What the hell you do, anyways?"

"Killed ninety-seven people."

The sly smile vanished uncertainly. "No shit?"

Trinity didn't answer.

The kid resumed scrutinizing his magazine, but Trinity noticed he wasn't turning many pages. Trinity managed to find his feet and sat down on the bunk underneath the kid. After an hour, his neck and shoulders had coalesced into one sharp pain he couldn't find any position would alleviate when the Indian deputy returned to the holding cells, keys in his hand.

"Back on up here to the bars and I'll take them cuffs off."

As Trinity stood to comply, the kid said nervously, "Hey, Dennis. This guy says he killed ninety-seven people. He's just bullshittin' me, right, man?"

"Nope," Dennis said, jiggling the keys into the cuffs. "That was the official body count, ninety-seven."

"Well, mebbe you might want to just leave them cuffs on him a while longer, y'know, just in case?"

"Don't worry, Frankie." Dennis removed the cuffs and withdrew them through the bars as Trinity stifled a whimper of relief. "You just behave yourself and you got nothing to worry about."

"Excuse me," Trinity said quietly as he turned around and read the big man's nametag, "Officer Red Wolf, could I make a phone call?"

"You're entitled." Dennis Red Wolf glanced toward the front office, where Trinity could hear muffled voices. "Just chill out and hang on a bit longer."

A bit longer stretched for a couple more hours before Red Wolf came back to the holding cells, clearly unhappy.

"Local?" he asked without preamble.

"Toll-free."

Frowning, Red Wolf fished a small cell phone from his pocket. "Here, use mine," he said, holding it out to Trinity.

Trinity looked at it, but didn't take it. "I can't use a cell phone."

"What?"

"I can't use a cell phone. It's a condition of my parole. Landlines only."

Red Wolf looked incredulous. "Yer shittin' me."

"No, sir."

Red Wolf stared at him for a long moment, then scowled and shoved the cell phone back in his pocket. "The hell with this," he muttered and left.

Trinity sat back down on the bottom bunk, watching the peaceful rise and fall of the drunk's chest as he snored. He examined his face with tentative fingers, his nose painful but not broken, thankfully. A few minutes later, Frankie's head leaned down from above, his expression a mix of apprehension and curiosity. "You're really a bad-ass serial killer? That's like . . . wow. Are you famous?"

"I shouldn't think so."

"Dude, how can you not be famous? That's a shitload of bodies, you'd think I woulda heard of you. So, like, how long did it take you to kill all them people?"

"About five seconds."

"Man," Frankie breathed in awe. "That is so . . . *man*." He made a sign with his fist toward Trinity, the gesture reverent rather than obscene. "Respect."

Trinity lowered his head into his hands, ignoring his throbbing nose as he rubbed his eyes until an ominous sparkle shivered behind his lids, the hint of an impending migraine. "Frankie, would you do me a favor?"

"Sure, anything . . ."

"Shut up."

"Hey, cool, no problem, I hear you."

The quiet lasted less than ten minutes before Frankie's head popped back over the edge of the bunk. "You might wanna know, Dennis is okay. He's my cousin . . . well, sort of. His sister-in-law is married to my cousin. At least I think she's his sister-in-law. Anyway, he's from Rocky Boy, y'know, Chippewa-Cree. But he's cool. He and Jensen don't get on too well, though, cuzza that trouble over at the 4 C's a few years back, y'know?"

Trinity didn't know, and didn't care.

"That's why he don't work for the tribal police no more. He's real straight-arrow, not like a lot of 'em. Cops, I mean, not Injuns. Not that I got anything against Injuns, neither. But like this one time, me and my brother boosted this cherry Camero with all this coke in the trunk? We didn't know nuthin' about it, right, I'm like *so* not into drugs, no way, and Dennis, he chased us clear to Big Sandy afore he caught us . . ."

Trinity had little interest in the boy's chatter, tuning out the rest of a convoluted story of felonious woe. He removed his remaining glove and stuffed it into the pocket of his jeans, then gently massaged his hands and chafed wrists, trying to soothe the still agitated microchips buried deep under the skin.

Frankie was well into the third act of his personal operetta when Jensen and Red Wolf came back into the holding area.

"C'mon out, Frankie," Jensen said, unlocking the cell. "Deppity Dawg here is going to run you over to County, you're being extradited to Idaho. Do us all a favor; next time you decide to steal a car, don't drive it up here to visit your mama, okay?"

"Man, I hate fuckin' Idaho," the kid grumbled.

Red Wolf didn't meet Trinity's eyes, and Jensen appeared in far too good a humor, sending a thrill of dread through Trinity's gut. But all that happened after Red Wolf had gone was the drunk slowly regained consciousness, rolling to sit upright, head hanging as he muttered darkly to himself. When the drunk could stand, Jensen unlocked the cell to let him stagger out, leaving Trinity the sole occupant.

Trinity leaned back against the wall, sitting on the bottom bunk, the thin plastic-covered mattress without blanket or pillow to soften it, and closed his eyes. He was only aware he'd managed to doze when the sound of voices and laughter roused him.

"Suppertime," Jensen said cheerily, backing through the connecting door with a plate of food. Another man with crooked teeth in a mean grin followed him in. Jensen slid the plate through the slot in the bottom of the cage door.

Trinity looked down at the food impassively, refried beans and mashed potatoes and the crumbled remains of what he assumed had once masqueraded as meatloaf. In the middle of the plate, a cockroach lay on its back, greenish guts oozing from its burst sides, legs still waving feebly. Jensen hadn't supplied any cutlery, not so much as a plastic fork. Trinity picked up the plate without comment, and ate using his fingers, careful to avoid the doomed cockroach or tainted food. He finished, then cautiously placed the plate back on the floor on the other side of the slot in the door.

The two men still grinned, but Jensen's smile was forced while his companion appeared more perplexed. They left without retrieving the plate, and Trinity didn't see Jensen or Red Wolf again the rest of the night.

Sleep was hard, the air chilled and the naked lightbulb in the ceiling burning continuously. Trinity wrapped his arms around his chest, his hands tucked into his armpits, and drew his knees up for warmth, fear an all-too-familiar knot in his stomach. As he'd done for most of the three years he spent in the detention camp, he closed his eyes and began to recite, trying to focus his mind on the words. He hadn't even thought about the words in months, and now they came slowly, his memory rusty and his concentration hampered with worry.

"*Sigon Þā tō slǣpe,*" he murmured late into the night. "*Sum sāre angeald ǣfen-rœste, swā him ful-oft gelamp, siððan gold-sele Grendel warode, unriht ǣfnde, oðÞæt ende becwōm, swylt æfter synnum . . .*"

His eyes burned with fatigue, but thankfully the words still came, alleviating some of the soul-crushing dread, the boredom, the uncertainty.

"*Þœr him āglǣcaœt-grœpe wearð; hwæðre hē gemunde mægenes strenge, gim-fæste gife, Þē him god sealde, and him tō answaldan āre gelȳfde . . .*" He wasn't aware of when he had stopped whispering and fallen asleep, leaning against the wall.

Monday morning came early, the smell of fresh-brewed coffee almost painful in the air. He saw no one except for a female officer, a VILLE DU HAVRE POLICE patch on her blue uniform jacket, who walked through the holding area, pausing only to glance at him curiously, before she was gone through the opposite door. By midafternoon, he was thirsty and hungry and wondering if they were planning on detaining him indefinitely when Red Wolf walked in with a man in a suit and carrying a briefcase.

"Someone to see you," Red Wolf said as he unlocked the cage door. He looked down at the plate with the now-dead cockroach and pushed it out of the way of the door with the toe of his shoe.

Trinity stood as the man in the suit looked around the cell but made no motion to enter it. "Ben Trinity?"

"Yes, sir."

"I'm Special Agent Lloyd Shovar with the FBI out of Glasgow. Mr. Eastlake from Helena DSD asked us to make a courtesy call." Shovar glanced at Red Wolf. "You guys have an interview room?"

"You can talk in the office."

Wordlessly, Trinity followed Red Wolf into the front office, a tiny room made even more claustrophobic with four desks crammed into it. Jensen stood with a disgruntled scowl and his arms crossed as Shovar looked around with disdain. "We'll need some privacy. And a decent chair."

"Use the chief's office," Jensen said, and opened the door with the name "Undersheriff Larry Ensler" painted on the glass to an even tinier room. Shovar dragged the leather-bound executive's swivel chair out from behind the undersheriff's desk, a well-worn Navajo blanket folded on the seat.

"Make yourself comfortable, Mr. Trinity," Shovar said.

From the doorway, Jensen barked an incredulous laugh. "*He* gets the comfy chair?"

"No one ever expects the Spanish Inquisition," Trinity murmured, barely audible, as he settled into the desk chair gingerly, his bruised ribs still tender.

Shovar said nothing as he shut the door and closed the Venetian blinds to block out Jensen's disbelieving expression. But he was fighting back a smile when he turned and opened his briefcase to reveal equipment Trinity was all too familiar with.

As Shovar assembled the device, Trinity asked softly, "Are you really FBI?"

Shovar found this equally amusing, the ends of his lips twitching upward. "Yes, Mr. Trinity, you can relax. I really am FBI."

"How did you know I was here?"

Shovar looked up in mild surprise. "I assume someone made the usual phone call. Not you?"

When Trinity mutely shook his head, Shovar gave him a sharp appraisal, taking in his bloodstained shirt and grubby appearance. "That your lunch back there?" he asked, nodding to one side to denote the roach-infested plate he'd seen on the floor.

"Last night's dinner."

"You eaten anything today?"

When Trinity shook his head again, anger flickered over the agent's face before he jerked open the door. "Hey, you— big guy. You must have doughnuts around this dump some- where," he said to Red Wolf. "And coffee, *now*." When Red Wolf came back with a grease-stained Dunkin' Donuts box half-filled with maple-glazed rolls and chocolate éclairs, Shovar added, "And get this man something he can clean himself up with. What the fuck's the matter with you people?"

Red Wolf said nothing, his expression flat, but returned with a handful of wet brown paper towels and a small tub of baby wipes.

Once Trinity had washed down a couple doughnuts with the coffee and cleaned his face and hands as best he could, he sat back in the comfy chair and slid his fingers into the slots in the palm-readers, watching as Shovar strapped the Velcro fasteners around his fingertips and wrists. "Not too tight?"

"It's fine."

Shovar shoved the papers crowding the undersheriff's desk unceremoniously to one side and settled his hip up on the desk, the laptop computer in his open briefcase casting a blue tint onto his face. "Is your name Benedictus Xavier Trinity?"

"Yes," Trinity said placidly.

"Is your DSD registration code four seven five, eight three two, zero five?"

"Yes."

"Have you consumed any alcohol or illegal drugs in the past thirty days?"

"No."

And so the interrogation began, the usual routine he submitted to every month, with a few extra questions thrown in until Special Agent Shovar was certain he had extracted the truth, the whole truth, and nothing but the truth from Trinity. Once he was satisfied, he unclipped

Trinity's hands and repacked his equipment. "You're going to be released immediately," he said, snapping the briefcase shut. "Go home and wait. Mr. Eastlake will be in touch shortly to let you know their assessment of your situation."

"Thank you, sir."

"Don't thank me," Shovar said as he opened the door. Red Wolf and Jensen turned, a third man with them in a sheriff's uniform waiting impatiently. "I'm just doing my job. You Undersheriff Ensler?" He strode out into the man's office without a glance back at Trinity. "Get someone to take this man back to where he's staying."

"What!" Jensen objected. "Now hang on there a minute . . ."

"You've got no grounds to hold him on. Release him."

"That's up to the County Prosecutor, not the friggin' feds . . ."

Shovar didn't even look at Jensen, his attention focused directly on Undersheriff Ensler. "The County Prosecutor is going to tell you the same damned thing, except if he has to tell you, then it becomes a matter of public record. Get my meaning?"

Undersheriff Ensler frowned as Jensen continued to protest. "You *know* who that bastard is. What the hell is he doing in Redemption anyway? We're not a dumping ground for human garbage . . ."

Losing patience, Shovar turned on the deputy. "He's here because the United States government wants him here. I don't give a rat's ass if he's Adolf Hitler, Osama bin Laden, and Judas Iscariot rolled into one. This county has already had enough problems with corruption and abuse and I am sick to death of cleaning up after a bunch of *Dukes of Hazzard* jackasses. You are law enforcement officers, not vigilantes. Do you *get* me, chief?"

"Loud and clear," Ensler said quietly. "Dennis, take him home. Lucas, my office, now."

Without a word, Trinity followed Red Wolf out of the

sheriff's office, Shovar not giving him a glance, having completely dismissed him from his awareness. The ride back was quiet, neither Trinity nor the deputy exchanging a word until they were nearly to the crossroad leading to the café.

"I called the FBI," Red Wolf said. "Figured they'd know what to do with you." Trinity didn't respond. "Jensen is an asshole, but he isn't a crooked cop," Red Wolf added. In the back, separated by the secure cage barrier, Trinity looked at the reflection of the deputy's eyes in the rearview mirror. "He just gets overprotective when it comes to his family."

Trinity nodded. "Okay."

"Okay."

Nothing more was said. Red Wolf pulled into the café parking lot, gravel crunching under the tires, and let him out. The lot was half-full with pickup trucks, the dinner rush on. Guitar music twanged as an out-of-tune voice, not improved by beer or the amplifier, sang, "Whiskey don' make you crazeeee . . . ," the Grinnin' Bear Café's Monday night karaoke already starting up.

McGraff would be furious DSD security had been so easily cracked, Trinity thought as he avoided the café and walked back to his cabin. They'd have to pull him out now, his cover too compromised. He stopped as the cabin came into view, a thrill of alarm rushing through his ears. Word spread with the usual wildfire swiftness in a place as small as Redemption. But whoever had spray-painted graffiti on the walls had long gone, the only sound the velvety rustle of pine needles. MURDERER and BABY-KILLER nestled among other more obscene invective, standing out in stark white on the weathered redwood shingles, paint dribbling from the letters like tears. Although the windows were peppered with splattered eggs and flour and brown smears Trinity's nose had no trouble recognizing, the glass was thankfully intact.

He stripped off his bloodstained clothes as soon as he walked into the cabin, dropping them to the floor. Turning the heat up on the shower as hot as it would go, he gasped with shock as the water hit his face, his nose tender. He scrubbed away the remaining dried blood feverishly, nearly breathless in his frantic haste, then stood in the shower until his skin had turned red and the hot water had run out. He began to shake, knees buckling, and he sank to the bottom of the shower stall, letting the cold spray hit him on the back of the head. He was too drained, too numbed to weep.

Afterward, he dressed in clean jeans and a sweatshirt, then sat on the daybed with his bare feet up, arms around his knees, and stared out the window at the wind trembling in the trees. He didn't know how long he sat there, but it had been long enough for the sky to darken when a knock on the door startled him. He was chilled now, his hair still damp, and he shivered. When he ignored the knock a second time, the door opened anyway. He didn't look up as George came in uninvited.

"Lasagna," she said, and put a foil-wrapped plate on the dresser. She stood ill at ease, shoving her hands in her jacket pockets. "Jesus, it's cold in here."

When he still said nothing, she busied herself with making a fire in the old Franklin stove. He didn't watch, gazing down at his bare hands clasped around his knees, his remaining glove in the pile of discarded clothing. Once she had the fire going, she leaned against the dresser, nowhere other than the daybed to sit.

"Oh, and I found this. Thought you might want it back, what with your 'eczema.'" She pulled his other glove from her jacket pocket and placed it on the dresser beside the lasagna. "Don't you have anything to say?" she asked after an uncomfortable silence.

He shook his head lethargically.

Irritated, she pushed away from the dresser and paced

the small room. "Amy's upset. Ma, too." He still didn't respond. "Look," she said crossly, "I think you owe us an explanation."

He glanced up at her, his eyes feeling hot and dry. "An explanation," he repeated, his voice hoarse.

Her bravado withered. "Is what Lucas said . . . is it true?"

He exhaled in a silent, scornful laugh. "Sure, whatever," he said lifelessly, looking away again.

She sat down on the opposite end of the daybed, careful not to touch him. "No, not 'whatever,'" she said, annoyed. "That's not good enough. We have a right to know. Are you . . . were you really a terrorist?"

"Call me anything you like, it doesn't make a damned bit of difference," he snapped in sudden anger, then bit back his words, breathing shallowly in his effort to control the emotions welling up in him. "But please don't ask me questions I'm not allowed to answer," he said more impassively. "Not that it matters now."

She was quiet for a long moment. "Benedictus Xavier Trinity. Is that your real name? Or is that a state secret, too?"

He grimaced a small smile, the effort strained. "That's my real name. And it's pronounced *zah-vee-ay*, not *zay-vee-yer*." When she returned his smile tentatively, he added, "I was named after my grandfather. Could have been worse. His brother's name was Anastasius Celestine. But I'm not even sure I'm allowed to tell you that much."

"All in strictest confidence, cross my heart. No one will find out."

"Sure they will. I still have to go to confession once a month." His smile faded, the despair seeping back. "You're not in any danger, Ms. Jensen, you or Amy, if that's what you're worried about. Not from me."

She stood up to open the Franklin stove and placed another large piece of split wood into the fire. The little cabin had warmed quickly, the flickering glow peaceful as the window darkened. "Most people just call me George," she said to the fire, prodding the orange flames under the log with the poker.

"Yes, ma'am, I've noticed."

"I don't know what to think. You were doing so good," George said. "People 'round these parts really liked you, Amy likes you. She got a B-plus on her math test this morning. She was so excited, that's the best grade she's ever gotten in math. She wanted you to know."

He nodded, pleased in spite of himself. George shook her head regretfully.

"The café has been running so much better since you've been here. I kind of thought . . . I don't know . . . like we'd done something good, that maybe you had a future here."

"Not your fault you tried to rescue a stray dog and it turns out he's got rabies." His attempt at mollifying her obviously wasn't working. "I don't have a future anywhere, Ms. Jensen. All I have is *now*, and a long succession of nows stretching out until someday I run out of nows. I'm grateful to you and your mother, honestly." He smiled sadly. "This has been the best now I've had in a long time."

She nodded, setting the poker back on its hook by the fire. "I've got to go. Amy's waiting for me to pick her up at the Bakkers'."

He remained silent, to her obvious exasperation.

"Look, Ben. Maybe I'm an idiot and you're one hell of a con artist. But I don't think so. I think you're just a good person who did something bad."

"You don't know anything about me," he said in a low voice, "or what I've done."

"You're right, I don't. It seems what I did know was a lie. I can't even say everyone deserves a second chance, I'm not sure that everyone does. All I can judge you on is what I've seen so far. I've seen how hard you've worked for Ma, and I've seen how confident Amy's gotten in school, because of you. So whoever you were then, it's not who you are now. It's not who you can be."

This upbeat all-American pep talk was depressing him even further. "Thank you," he said softly. "I appreciate that. Could you please just leave me alone now?"

He stared into the fire for a long time after she'd gone, trying hard to stop the memories of when he'd been happy. He'd almost been happy again, and he wasn't sure he could bear losing it for a second time.

# CHAPTER NINE

Early the next morning, Trinity scrubbed the mess off the outside walls and windows as best he could, then found several containers of brown exterior paint in the tool shed and spent the next couple of hours painting over the graffiti. It didn't quite cover in one coat, the ghosts of accusation still discernible. The whole cabin needed repainting, he thought, but he wasn't likely to be the one to do it.

He put the paint away, washed, and walked up to the café. Standing outside the kitchen entrance, he had to take several deep breaths before he found enough courage to open the door and walk in. Carlene barely glanced at him, her expression impassive as she turned a row of bacon sizzling on the grill, adding a few crisp strips onto a plate of steaming food before sliding it under the heat lamps where three other plates were ready for serving.

"You're late," she snapped. "Two scrambled and one over easy with bacon, table four, pancakes and sausages for Tom. Put up another decaf while you're at it."

"Ms. Ryton . . ."

She turned sharply toward him, her hands flitting oddly as if trying to brush away invisible insects in frustration.

"Look, just . . . don't talk to me. Go do your job and don't talk to me today. You think you can do that?"

"Yes, ma'am."

"Good." She turned back to the grill, a muscle in her jaw working.

He pulled the red apron over his head, straightened the blue pin that read "Hello! My name is Ben," and walked through the swinging doors into the café with a sense of irreality. Tom Mifflin looked up from the counter, his face hardening. Trinity took the plate of pancakes from under the heat lamp and set it down in front of the rancher, not meeting his eyes.

" 'Morning, sir," he said quietly.

Tom said nothing, not even moving to pick up a fork to eat. Trinity refilled his nearly empty coffee cup before serving the couple and their young son seated at table four, they, like Tom, stone-faced and silent. Carlene had already served two other tables, the old Spaight sisters and the Patersons, regulars who normally would have greeted him with a smile and a friendly word but now watched him with mute hostility.

He had made up a fresh pot of decaf coffee when six teenaged girls wearing St. Mary Magdalene school uniforms under oversized parkas came in, chattering and giggling as they bounced into the corner booth, schoolbags and parkas shoved under the table and into the window ledge. They quieted as he walked over, fishing his notepad from the pocket of his apron.

"Good morning, ladies," he said, ignoring their gaping at him as they jostled elbows self-consciously. "May I take your order?"

The one he recognized as Sophie, Amy's friend, said, "Toast and coffee."

"White or whole wheat?"

"Whole wheat."

He repeated this five times, only one girl opting for a bran muffin. By the time he'd walked back around the counter, ripped off the sheet, and clipped it to the order ring in the serving hatch, Tom had bolted his breakfast down and was out the door, little bell jingling merrily in his wake. Trinity turned to clear the empty dishes and stared at a single penny dead center of the plate, soaking in a puddle of maple syrup. His chest feeling oddly empty, he looked up, holding Carlene's gaze. Without a word, he scraped the remnants off the plate, penny and all, into the slop can under the counter, and stacked it in the wash rack.

He took the girls their coffee and toast, setting out toast and muffin in the right places, and filled the last cup. "Is there anything else I can get for you ladies?"

After a moment of furtive shoving and pushing, one of the girls whispered urgently, "Go on, Sophie!"

"Can I see it?" Sophie blurted out.

He stared at her as her cheeks flushed bright red, then turned and walked away without a word.

"I told you he'd get mad at me," Sophie said from behind him crossly. "This is all your fault, Mattie."

"Oooo," the girl he assumed to be Mattie retorted in a high, nasally whine. "Nobody was twisting your arm, Sophie, so don't go blaming me."

The muted argument continued as he rang up the Patersons' bill, Will Paterson not looking at him when Trinity handed him the change, while his wife could barely keep from sneering. Once they had gone, he cleared the table, another penny left in the middle of the plate doused in red-eye gravy and biscuit crumbs. He scraped this one into the slop can with the other, put the plates in the rack, and stood for a moment, clenching the edge of the counter and swaying as if struggling to keep his balance, eyes shut. When he opened them again, Carlene was watching him, frowning.

He wrote out a bill for the girls and walked back, Sophie's eyes glistening and fearful as he placed it on the table. He peeled the fingerless glove from his left hand and held out his palm. The girls froze, then glanced at one another uneasily while Sophie gazed up unblinking, eyes wide. When he raised an eyebrow, she looked down at his hand without moving her head as if afraid he was holding something that might bite.

The café had gone eerily silent, and he was aware of the attention focused on him and the girls like a spotlight at a prison breakout.

After a long silence, she said softly, "It's a tattoo."

"Yes."

"It's a real one, right? It's not going to like wash off or fade or anything, is it?"

"It's real."

She ran the tip of her tongue over lips thickly coated with lipstick, the heavy makeup making her seem even younger, oddly enough, than she was.

"What's it mean?"

He traced the pattern with the forefinger of his right hand, the tattoo like a blue stigmata in his palm. "That's the seal of the U.S. Department of Justice, and the DSD stands for Domestic Surveillance Division; they're run by the Homeland Security Agency. That's my registration code here, four seven five, eight three two, zero five. It's the number I have to give whenever I talk to my parole officer."

"What's the 'T' for?" the girl he assumed was Mattie demanded with an air of forced bravado. "Treason?"

"No. Terrorism."

"Is that what you were convicted for?"

*You couldn't be convicted of anything if you never had a trial*, he didn't tell her. Such subtle legal distinctions were lost on most people, never mind a thirteen-year-old schoolgirl. "Yeah," he said, because it was easier.

"Were you?" one of the other girls asked, intrigued. "A terrorist?"

When he didn't respond, Sophie colored again. "Geez, Cindy, you are such a freakin' moron."

"Sorry, Mr. Trinity, I didn't mean to be rude . . . ," Cindy said hastily.

"That's okay, ask whatever you want. But there are some things I'm not permitted to talk about. That's one of them."

"Did it hurt?" the muffin girl asked, her voice timid.

"Did what hurt?"

"Getting a tattoo. On your hand like that?"

"No, it didn't hurt. I was asleep when they did it." At her confusion, he added, "On an operating table."

"Wow," Cindy said. "My brother has lots of tattoos but they never had to put him to sleep to do any of them."

"It's more than a tattoo." He flexed his thumb back as far as he could, and pointed out the faint outline of something imbedded deep under the skin. "Right there, can you see it?" The girls crowded over the top of the table to gawk at his hand. "That's a microchip. It's like a master circuit connected to all these little wires that go down to even smaller microchips just under the fingertips." He pulled the glove from his other hand. "Both of them."

"Can I feel it?" the muffin girl asked shyly.

"Sure, go ahead." He held out his hands to the girls. As they took turns prodding the lumps and bumps under the skin, a movement made him glance up at the couple and their son. The father pushed the boy back into his chair, restraining his obvious envy.

"But Dad, they get to . . . ," the boy whined.

"Be quiet."

"What does it do?" Sophie asked, fascinated.

Whatever apprehension the girls might have had about him had evaporated, their curiosity too intense. "A lot of things, they don't tell me all of it. Some of it is just data about me, blood type, medical history, where I was born, stuff like that. But mainly they use it to keep track of me so they know exactly where I am and what I'm doing."

"Even when you're in the bathroom?" Sophie asked, wrinkling her nose. "Eww, gross." The girls giggled.

"It's not a camera, it's more like . . ." He thought a moment, not wanting to equate it to the clunky electronic devices strapped to the ankles of prisoners on home release. "You know when they put those transmitter collars on moose and wolves to study how they move around in the wild? It's sort of like that."

"Cool," the muffin girl murmured, awed.

Mattie was studying his hand thoughtfully. "How do they get it out again?"

"They don't," he said quietly.

"Never ever?"

"Never ever." Suddenly, it wasn't quite so cool, the girls sobering. He smiled and pulled his hands away. Outside, the St. Mary Magdalene minivan stopped and honked impatiently. "Right, you ladies better finish up; you don't want to miss your ride," he said more cheerfully than he felt.

He walked back to replace the coffeepot on the burner, his gloves still in one hand. Knowing all eyes were on him, he deliberately opened the lid of waste bin beside the cash register and threw the gloves away. He rang up the charges for the family at table four, and took them the check.

"Thank you," he said, monotoned. "Come again."

"Can I, Dad, please? Can I?"

"No," the father said sharply, but before Trinity could move off he added belligerently, "but as long as you're answering questions, I've got one for you."

"Be my guest."

"So what's stopping you from yanking all of it out, just get rid of it?"

Trinity smiled without humor. "You mean, other than because it's wired into my cerebral cortex, any attempt to remove it will cause my heart to fibrillate and kill me?" The man's expression didn't change, although his wife bit back a small gasp. "Common sense. Where could I go? What would I do?" He snorted his suppressed anger and derision. "As long as I play by the rules and behave myself, I get by." He couldn't help adding, "Just like everyone else." He held up the tattooed hand. "Only some of us need a bit more persuasion than others." When the man didn't respond, he said, "Is there anything else? No? You folks have a nice day."

As he turned away, he heard the boy say, "Mom, what's 'fibbulate' mean?"

"Kevin, for godsake, shut up."

They didn't leave a tip, but at least there was no penny left on the empty plates either. He worked the rest of the breakfast shift, scraping a few more pennies into the slop bin. When Trinity handed Nick Gilman his change and receipt, an out-of-town trucker watched in bewilderment as Gilman hawked and spat on the counter before he walked out the door without a word.

"Lordy," the trucker said with sarcasm as thick as his Alabama accent, "y'all are a real friendly bunch out here, ain'cha?"

At eleven, the café finally empty of customers, Trinity shrugged into his down jacket, poured himself a cup of coffee, and took it out back on his break. Sitting on the porch bench with his coffee on the floor between his feet, his elbows on his knees and head in his hands, he didn't look up when he heard the kitchen door open. Carlene came out to lean against the railing, facing him.

"Is that why you don't ever use the computer?" she asked without preamble. "Those things in your hands?"

And the freak show must go on, he thought bitterly. "Bull's-eye, give the lady a kewpie doll."

"Don't get flippant with me, city boy."

"Begging your pardon, ma'am," he said, his eyes still shut.

After a moment, she said curiously, "So what does it do, read the movement of your fingers as you type or something? Records what you're writing?"

He sighed wearily. "No, nothing that sophisticated. The microchip reacts to the circuitry in the computer. It just hurts like hell. Same thing with cell phones, digital cameras, ATM machines. Then the next time I check in, they know about it."

A biting wind cut through pines, rustling branches making him feel colder.

"I got a phone call last night," she said tersely. "From a Mr. Ted Eastlake down in Helena."

He grunted, unsurprised, but didn't open his eyes.

"I take it you know who he is?"

"He's the DSD Assistant Director for Montana."

"Mm." Trinity couldn't tell if that were a comment or a question. "Well, he's on his way up here."

"I'm packed."

"I don't think he's coming here to take you into custody."

At that he did look up. "Why not?"

Carlene was holding a cup of steaming coffee, bare hands wrapped around it for warmth, her plaid scarf tucked into the neck of her sheepskin jacket. Her nose and cheeks had reddened with the cold, making her look as if she'd been crying. Perhaps she had, he thought. "He wasn't too happy with Lucas. Or his buddy in the Helena Department of Justice. And we had a long talk about you. About . . . things. Asked me if I'd still be willing to sponsor you. As your employer." She looked away, knocking crusts of old snow off the steps with the toe of her shoe. "I said I'd consider it."

He was surprised. "Why?"

She scowled her annoyance. "I don't know. Anyway, I haven't said yes yet."

He smiled bleakly. "Look, this was all just an improvised

situation until the DSD could figure out what to do with me, anyway. I appreciate all you and Ms. Jensen have done, but it's not working out. I should go."

"Go where?"

He shrugged. "Wherever they send me."

"Even if that means back to prison?"

He stood up, tossing the now cold coffee over the railing to splatter onto the weeds. "I don't have a lot of choice," he said flatly. "And three years of wearing orange jumpsuits and sleeping in leg chains tends to knock a lot of defiance out of a man, y'know? I go where they want, I do what they tell me."

"Are you sorry for what you've done?" she demanded.

He stared at her. "What?"

"My son died fighting to protect us from people like you. Tell me it wasn't for nothing and I'll tell this Mr. Eastlake whatever he needs to hear, you can stay."

For a brief moment, a surge of anger swept through him, and just as quickly, he pushed it down.

"Ms. Ryton, you tell Mr. Eastlake whatever you want. So right now, unless you intend to fire me, I've got dishes to wash."

Ted Eastlake pulled into the café parking lot an hour later. Trinity recognized him from the bureaucrat's suit and tie, as out of place in Redemption as a pig in a horse race, Carlene would remark later. Trinity was occupied with serving a small group of men in hunting jackets when the DSD agent walked in, all congenial smiles and handshakes. He watched cautiously as Carlene sat chatting with the man, waiting until they motioned him over to join them.

"Mr. Eastlake," Trinity said warily. Although the DSD agent was still smiling, he didn't shake Trinity's hand.

The agent gestured for him to sit down. "Ben," he said, immediately establishing their status. "How have things been here for you, on the whole?"

"Fine, sir."

Trinity didn't react to the agent's shrewd appraisal of his bruised face. "Mrs. Ryton here has given you an excellent evaluation, Ben. Impressive."

He risked a glance at Carlene, then stared back at his clasped hands resting on the table, feeling oddly exposed without his gloves. "Thank you, sir."

"Despite the unusual circumstances, reports from your parole officer have been favorable, and you've turned out to be one of the project's most promising subjects. Up until this weekend, the locals here have had nothing but good things to say about you. But . . ." Eastlake shrugged, still smiling. "The secret's out. No use shutting the barn door after the horse has bolted."

Trinity said nothing, but didn't miss Carlene's expression at the man's incongruous attempt at down-home aphorisms.

"Yeah, well, I've got a question about that," Carlene said, and waggled a finger in the direction of Trinity's hands. "I've seen this . . . this . . ." She seemed unable to find the right word, so let the gap stand in its place. "On the news. I thought it was only used on child molesters, special electronic tagging to make certain they stayed away from schools and playgrounds, to protect kids."

Eastlake stifled a laugh. "It's being used on a lot of high-risk parolees, not just pedophiles. Would you have been happier with him working for you if you thought he'd raped a child?"

Carlene frowned. "No, I guess I wouldn't."

Eastlake spread his hands with mock regret. "Well, there you go. Unfortunately, we've had a lapse in our computer system, but that does not excuse anyone hacking into our records, police or otherwise. We take security breaches very seriously. I've spoken with your Sheriff Holbrook, who assures me the sheriff's office will conduct a thorough investigation and if the deputy in question is found culpable, he will face disciplinary charges and possible dismissal."

For violating government security, Ben knew, not for any assault on him. Carlene shifted uneasily.

"The deputy is Ms. Ryton's son-in-law, sir," Trinity said quietly, knowing his input wasn't welcome, but risking it anyway.

Eastlake looked surprised, although Trinity had little doubt the man already knew this. "That a fact."

"*Ex*-son-in-law," Carlene corrected. "Lucas sometimes gets overly hot under the collar when it comes to his family. He was just looking after my granddaughter."

"Well, I'm not sure how I'd react if I thought my kids were in danger either, puts a different spin on things. It's not like he was involved in any sort of conspiracy to overthrow the government, just overstepped his authority a tad. Right, Ben?"

Trinity was sure Carlene wasn't any more taken in by the man's faked bonhomie than he was. He gazed back at Eastlake impassively, his face bruised and his body still aching. "Of course, sir." He managed to say it without a trace of sarcasm.

"Which leads us back to the question of what to do with you," Eastlake said. The agent's attention had shifted back to Trinity, Carlene once again merely a bystander. "Shall we go through the options? Option one would have been to minimize this little indiscretion, liaise with the local law enforcement, convince the local population that this was all a big misunderstanding, glitch in the system, computer error, whatever. Of course, now you've decided to put yourself on public display, that's pretty much out of the question."

Trinity swallowed. "Sorry."

"No, forget it," Eastlake waved this misconduct away casually. "Bound to happen sooner or later. Luckily, we happen to have another placement available in . . ." He set his briefcase on the table and opened it to shuffle through its files. "I have it somewhere, ah, here it is: Prudhoe Bay, Alaska. It's on an inlet in the Beaufort Sea, someplace with a little less contact with the public than you've had here. You'd be working on the Trans-Alaska Pipeline extension in the Arctic, with men who won't be as nosy about your past. They've got their own to worry about. It's perfect. How's that sound to you?"

It sounded like more punishment. Trinity had to take a quick breath to steady his voice before he answered, "Good, sir."

Carlene glanced between them, troubled. "What about him staying on here?"

Eastlake shrugged, closing his briefcase and snapping the locks. "If he's happy enough with Alaska, there's no point."

"Ben?"

Trinity kept his eyes lowered. "I go where they want, I do what they tell me," he said softly.

Carlene's mouth twisted in irritation. "Mr. Eastlake, let me ask you something. If he *had* been a pedophile, wouldn't Megan's Law let the public know who he was, where he lived, publish it in the paper?"

"That is correct."

"So how many more like him are there that nobody knows about? If he's so dangerous, why isn't he still in prison? And why wasn't the public told about him?"

"Glitch in the system, computer error, whatever," Eastlake said lightly. Then his attitude sobered. "Let's see if we can alleviate some of Mrs. Ryton's concerns, Trinity. Why don't you explain how you ended up in this mess?"

"Officially?" That hadn't been wise, Trinity realized, as the man shot him a dark look. "I married the wrong woman. I donated money to the wrong charities."

Carlene's eyes narrowed as she stared at him, baffled. After a moment, she said skeptically, "That's it?"

Eastlake chuckled unpleasantly. "You think if he was guilty of anything more than that he'd ever be allowed to see the light of day again?" As Carlene turned her disbelief toward Eastlake, he shrugged. "Figuratively speaking, of course."

"Of course," Carlene said, her tone hardening.

Eastlake turned his wry attention back on Trinity. "Nor is it quite as simplistic as that, is it, Ben?"

Trinity didn't meet her eyes. "My wife is . . . was . . ." He stopped to clear his throat. ". . . *is* a French citizen, but her parents were Iranian. We set up the Triad Trust, an aid organization providing auxiliary medical care for children in the Middle East—Iraq, Lebanon, Palestine, wherever it was needed—making sure organizations like Médecins sans Frontières and the Red Crescent had enough drugs and medical supplies, funding scholarships to train foreign doctors in the States on surgical techniques they wouldn't have learned in their own countries."

"Which then became an ideal front for funneling money to Islamic terrorists," Eastlake put in, and turned his cool smile back on Carlene. "Abdul bin Zahedan is the ringleader of a particularly nasty offshoot of the Zarqawi terrorist group, calling themselves al-Jawasis. Every Western security agency—CIA, MI6, Europol, you name it—has been after him for years." He shrugged. "We got Zarqawi, we'll get him. Zahedan's sister came to America just before 9/11 under a false passport, where she met and married our Mr. Trinity here, and settled down to live happily ever after with a rich plastic surgeon's son, despite the fact she already had a husband back in Iran. You see, Ben used to be quite a wealthy man, a trust fund baby. Big house, fancy yacht, expensive cars. A French name and an American husband provided Zahedan with the perfect sleeper. While she hosted champagne brunches for left-wing politicians and designed pretty Web sites for antiwar campaigns, Ben spent over five million a year on these so-called Islamic 'doctors,' the sort that wire explosives to cell phones and sixteen-year-old suicide bombers."

"Did you know about it?" Carlene asked Trinity.

He took a breath and exhaled against the ache, then looked up at Carlene unswervingly. "I loved my wife."

"Aiding and abetting a terrorist makes you just as guilty as the terrorist," Eastlake said. "Zero tolerance, no exceptions. The money used to pay for the SUV and the explosives Muhammed Youssef packed into it? That was all traced back to al-Jawasis bank accounts, with our Ben here making regular deposits, checks he'd personally signed. Ninety-seven people dead, half of them children. Tens of thousands hospitalized from breathing poison gas, a hundred square miles of open countryside contaminated." Eastlake let the silence drag on for several painful moments before he asked softly, "Still feeling charitable, Mrs. Ryton?"

Trinity looked up as the hunters signaled him for another round of coffee. "I'll take the job in Alaska," he said as he stood.

"You'll take what you're given," Eastlake snapped, all charade of civility gone.

"Ben, go pour those guys their coffee," Carlene said.

He did, as well as seat a road-weary couple with two sullen teenaged boys, passing out menus as Eastlake and Carlene stood up, shaking hands. Eastlake walked out the café door as Carlene passed Trinity on her way to the kitchen.

"You're staying," she said brusquely, without looking at him.

He hesitated, then said to the couple, "I'll be back in a minute to take your order," before loping out the door after Eastlake. He caught up with the man just as he opened his car door. Trinity grabbed the top of the door to stop Eastlake from getting in. Eastlake looked at him in surprise.

"What's going on?" Trinity demanded.

"Not a smart move, Trinity," Eastlake commented, glancing down at Trinity's hand on his car blocking him.

"You're right, it isn't. Why aren't you pulling me out of here?"

"Are you complaining?"

Trinity swallowed, his throat dry, but didn't reply.

Eastlake snorted his amusement. "Didn't think so. You willingly waived your rights, Trinity. You signed on the dotted line and agreed to abide by the regulations in order to be accepted into this program. You knew full well what you were getting into, so it's a bit late in the day to change your mind now."

Trinity had to force down the anger, his fingers curling into impotent fists. "'Willingly'?" he echoed acidly. "That's a joke, right? I'd still be in a detention camp if I hadn't. Or dead. Disappeared, 'never to see the light of day again,' isn't that how you put it? But this is not what I agreed to and you know it—"

Eastlake barked a hostile laugh. "Hang on a minute, let's just do the math here. Let's see, ninety-seven innocent victims blown to Kingdom Come . . ." He pretended to deliberate a moment, then leaned closer to Trinity to breathe in a low, ugly voice, "And we own your sorry ass. *That's* the 'agreement,' you got it?"

Trinity doggedly stood his ground. "Ms. Ryton means well, but she's not qualified to supervise my parole. Especially not now. You do what you want with me, but you're putting others at risk by keeping me here. This isn't the sort of community that's going to take too kindly to people who employ terrorists."

Eastlake sighed. "Look, part of the project's objective is to see how well we can eventually integrate people like you back into normal society."

"'People like me,'" Trinity repeated, his voice scornful. "You got a lot of people like me out on parole, Mr. Eastlake?"

Eastlake conceded the point with a raised eyebrow. "Obviously, we've had a serious hiccup with security. But the damage is done, your identity is already blown. Local law enforcement has instructions to assure your personal safety. If things start to get out of hand, we'll pull you. You don't worry about Ms. Ryton or her family. We'll be keeping a close eye out, they'll be protected. But we've decided to let things stand as they are for now, let's see how it pans out." He smiled humorlessly. "You're our guinea pig, Ben. Just remember, if you fail"—Eastlake shrugged meaningfully— "won't only be you who pays the price."

A rush of fear prickled Trinity's face, to Eastlake's obvious satisfaction.

"So don't go kicking up too much of a fuss, okay? Just lie back and try to enjoy it while it lasts."

As Eastlake drove away, Trinity stood in his venomous wake, his gut tense.

# CHAPTER TEN

Dear Diary,

My birthday was pretty okay, tho this year Mom didn't invite Dad over so I ended up with two birthdays instead of one. Dad picked me up from school and I spent the night before my official birthday with Dad and Wendy. Dad got me some new games for the Playstation and a complete hardback set of Dr. Spineshivers Investigates books, even the brand new one which is really hard to find cuz it's been sold out in the stores for like ages and you have to be on a waiting list and Dad had to pay extra to get one off the Internet. And he got me a new ten-speed mountain bike cuz my old one used to be Lonny's and its falling apart, this one has a tytanium frame and fancy spring shocks for going over rocks and stuff, its so cool.

Wendy got me a necklace with my birthstone and little diamonds around it, altho they aren't real diamonds but the chain is solid gold even if its just 9 carrots. She said the emerald is Indian, like from India, and its real too. Then me and Wendy played the new Dracoola Dragon game on the Playstation. She's seems a lot happier than she was before cuz Dad finally gave her a friendship ring like she wanted, which isn't an engagement ring, although Wendy acts like it is, but when she's not around Dad says that it's just to keep her from nagging him all the time, they aren't ever getting married. Anyway, she kept letting me win like I'm some poor-sport little kid and that's so boring but I didn't say anything cuz she was just trying to be nice.

Then the next day, Dad took me home after lunch and dropped me off with all my presents. Mom smiled real big when she saw the bike although I could tell that was her fake smile she puts on when she's pissed off. It makes me feel weird inside because I feel bad that Mom can't afford to buy me stuff like Dad can but I can't tell Dad he shouldn't buy me expensive stuff cuz then its like I'm taking sides or I'm not gratefull or something and I really wanted a new bike.

And Dad was pissed off, too, cuz Nana brought Ben with her and he and Dad hate each others guts. Or at least Dad hates him, but Ben is always super-polite to Dad and hardly ever says anything anyway. I think if Dad had beat me up and threw me in jail like he did Ben I'd be scared of him, but Ben never acts like he's scared of him at all which I think just makes Dad madder. He got in trouble with the County Sherrif who gave him an official rippromand so he's not allowed to beat up Ben again so maybe that's why Ben isn't scared of him. Sometimes I think about all those people that got killed, but even when I try real hard I can't imagine Ben being mean or violent, not like Dad. I try to pretend I don't like Ben when Dad is around but not too much cuz I really do like Ben and I don't want to hurt his feelings, either. Sometimes its hard trying to make everyone happy.

But its not like Ben is over here all the time anyway, I hardly ever see him anymore and Nana had to practically drag him with her and he only came cuz its my birthday. Nana baked a chocolate cake with fourteen roses for the candles with pink icing ribbons all along the side. She's so excellent at doing homemade cakes instead of the Betty Crocker ones from *a box that Mom makes. Anyway, while Mom was cooking dinner, Ben sat in a chair on the back porch so Nana could cut his hair cuz Mrs. McHenry at the Unisex who used to cut Ben's hair said she won't anymore cuz of what he done. Ben's hair is really dark and curly when it gets long and I think it looks nicer longer but Nana sez he has to keep it cut short for hygene reasons and Ben said he doesn't care what it looks like. Nana said that's good cuz she's not that practised at cutting hair, so she just cuts it all one length all over. Bojangles kept playing with the hair on the floor, and when nobody was looking, I took a little piece of Ben's hair to keep in my diary.*

*Mom made fried chicken and tatertots and creamed corn and salad, which is like my second all-time favorite meal, and she opened a bottle of sparkling cider and we all pretended it was champayne. Then after the cake I got my presents from Mom and Nana. Nana got me a bunch of boring stuff like socks and panties and pajamas and I pretended I liked them even if that's what I always get every year. Mom got me a couple movie DVDs and a new cell phone, not a fancy one, no Internet or TV or anything, but at least it takes pictures and text messages. Then she gave me the same new Dr. Spineshivers Investigates book as Dad, so that was embarrassing. She acted like it was no big deal, but I could tell it was. I think she thinks Dad did it on purpose, but she just said she'd take me into Havre and I could exchange it for something else.*

*Even Ben gave me a present, a board game he made himself that he said is a really old Chinese game called Go and it looks simple but its not. He said he used to play Go with his grandfather when he was my age, and its a good strategy game to excersize the brain. He's good at woodworking, even better than Dad, and he made it out of some old wood with brass hinges so it folds up and its got two drawers underneath* to hold the counters, which are like little pebbles except these are glass he bought in Great Falls and half are clear and half are dark blue and got air bubbles inside them. After dinner, Ben explained the rules, and then while Nana and Mom cleaned up in the kitchen we played the game. Ben said I did real good even though he beat me three times in a row, and showed me what I did wrong so I can do better next time. I wouldn't tell Mom or Dad, but that was my favorite present.

It was nice getting to talk to Ben all on my own without anyone else around, and I liked it when I made him laugh. Ben doesn't laugh much, but when he does he looks younger and his teeth are real straight and white like a movie stars. When I told him Craig said his dad said Will Paterson told him Ben was an alcoholick and wrecked a real expensive Italian sports car and had to go to A.A. meetings now and that's why he couldn't drink anymore, Ben just looked surprised and started laughing. He said all he told Will Paterson was that he didn't smoke by choice but he didn't drink by fiat. When I asked what that meant, he said I had to look it up, and I should always remember that even when everyone speaks English sometimes things get lost in translation. I don't understand what that means either.

Then we watched one of my new DVDs and Nana fell asleep on the sofa and Mom and me sat together on the other end of the sofa and Ben sat in the big armchair with Bojangles on his lap purring non-stop like a chainsaw while Ben rubbed his ears. Then when the movie was over we woke Nana up and she took Ben home. And when he left he wished me a happy birthday and kissed me on the cheek, and Mom laughed because it made my face go red, but Ben just smiled and said I looked lovely.

I can't tell anyone I think Ben is really cute and really nice, specially not Sophie who would blab it all over school, but I don't care what people say he's done, he's never been mean to anyone even when they've been mean to him, and he's kind to animals and he always treats me like I'm as grown up as he is, which is better than how a lot of people who think there so great act all the time.

And that was what happened on my birthday. Love, Amy.

PS: ♥ ♥ ♥ Ben+Amy 4-ever ♥ ♥ ♥

# CHAPTER ELEVEN

George hated the weekends without Amy, even though it meant it gave her time for herself and privacy she had so little of. It was too unsatisfying, she thought, as she lay in bed in the early-morning quiet, panting slightly as her pulse slowed, the tingling in her thighs dying away. Just like this thing. She held up the small vibrator she kept tucked away well at the back of her bedside drawer, never daring to use it when Amy was home. It did its job, and she'd had more orgasms by herself than she'd ever faked with Lucas, but it wasn't enough. This was just . . . maintenance, that's all. Making sure all the parts still worked, nothing more. She sat up and threw back the covers, disturbing Bojangles from where he curled up with his feet tucked under him, purring happily, totally oblivious. Opening the nightstand, she shoved the vibrator into the drawer, out of sight.

Not that weekends without Amy allowed her to lounge around and do nothing all day, either. But cleaning the house only took half the time when Amy wasn't there—dishes done, floors vacuumed, beds changed and made, laundry in the washer, ironing finished well before ten. Which gave her the morning to drive into Havre and get in the week's groceries.

She hated shopping on weekends, Gary & Leo's IGA always too crowded, the lines at the checkout taking forever, and her bad mood only increased as it seemed that the supermarket had more couples than usual, all young, all happy, holding hands, flirting behind the produce, kissing in the frozen food section. Or maybe she just saw them more when she was in a bad mood, she wasn't sure.

The regular lunch crowd was mostly over by the time she drove to her mother's café—only two nearly identical Harley-Davidson motorcycles with Oregon plates parked by the front door, painted flames along the black fuel tanks, oversized ape-hanger handlebars turned neatly in the same direction. Carlene was in the back running plates through the washer while a pair of unshaven bikers in dusty leathers lingered over pie and coffee before heading back out onto the road.

"Hi, Mizz Jensen," Holly Red Wolf said. The teenager had on Trinity's apron and had masking-taped her own name over his on his tag. "Can I take those for you?"

"That's okay, Holly." George set the paper bag of groceries on the counter, looking around. "Has it been busy this morning?"

"Oh, yeah," Holly said cheerfully. "We've had loads of people in for the specials, and Mizz Ryton said I've done so good she's letting me keep all my tips. I got nearly forty dollars already." Holly reddened as she showed George her handful of money tucked away in the apron pocket.

Only a month or so older than Amy, Holly Red Wolf had eagerly accepted the offer for a part-time job on weekends with a promise of a summer job if things worked out. Amy, on the other hand, had been enthusiastic about working after school, until she realized it wasn't a license to sit around and chat with her friends while customers waited impatiently for service. And with Trinity staying well behind the scenes and out of the way, much of the café's appeal quickly waned for Amy. But while Trinity's invisibility might make some of the customers feel better, George had to admit they were only able to afford part-time help outside the family owing to the improvements Trinity had brought to the café. The building gleamed in the sunlight with a new coat of paint, the Grinnin' Bear Café sign touched up and varnished. He'd even built massive timber planters by the doors, overflowing now with geraniums and impatiens and marigolds, a sweet pea creeper growing up a trellis just beginning to bloom, scenting the air. Some of the regulars teased Carlene about the place turning into some sort of faggot fern bar, but it didn't dissuade them from coming, and the new look certainly helped draw in the more family-oriented tourist traffic looking for somewhere with more rustic charm than the usual Denny's or IHOP.

"Hi, Ma. I brought Ben his groceries over, saved you the trip."

Carlene came out of the kitchen, wiping her hands on her apron. "Thanks, sweetheart. How much do I owe you?"

George wrinkled her nose and waved it away. "I'll just steal it out of the till when you're not looking, don't worry about it."

Carlene had a quick look in the bag, approvingly. "He's keeping busy down at the cabins. I'll take this to him later on when I get a moment."

George hesitated, then picked up the bag. "I'll do it," she said.

Her mother looked at her dubiously, and for once George was glad the Ryton women's famous sixth sense wasn't working. Not that she was sure herself why she was bothering.

Fishing season had been open since the third Saturday in May, but the summer vacationers wouldn't arrive in earnest until end of June, when the schools let out and city-weary families would load up their camper vans or hook up tent trailers to their station wagons and head out in search of the Great Outdoor Experience. Those with kids would find economy Holiday Inns or Best Westerns with swimming pools and pony trail rides, while those on an even tighter budget would opt for campgrounds and RV sites with running water and electricity. Hardy college students with mountain bikes and backpacks and kayaks would go for more photogenic parts of Montana, hiking in sociable troops. The one good thing you could say about a bad economic recession, George thought, is that it encouraged healthier outdoor vacations.

Only the more serious anglers sought out the rougher accommodations in quiet locations like Redemption, far away enough from other people's kids and dogs and communal RV barbecues to be secluded, but still within walking distance of a cold beer and a hot steak when the fish were uncooperative. Lonny had done his best to renovate a half-dozen of the cabins, primitive but comfortable enough. But Lonny's ambitions had died with him, and the remaining cabins had fallen into severe dilapidation not even the most die-hard sport fisherman would tolerate.

The man *had* been busy, George saw as she neared the cabins. Two roofs on the summer cabins had been completely replaced, the third stripped of its rotted shingles, new underfelt and batons nailed to the old joists gleaming in the sunshine. The power saw on the workbench had been unplugged, a mass of sawdust piled on the ground, extension cable coiled neatly. Recycled roof shingling had been stacked by the cabin, smelling of fresh-cut ceder.

Trinity was nowhere in sight, but a trickle of smoke wafted from the chimney of the caretaker's cabin, the aroma of bacon in the breeze. She knocked on his door before opening it and stuck her head in. He turned from the little stove, startled. His hair was covered in sawdust, his face and jeans grimy but his hands clean.

"Hi," she said, hoisting the bag on her hip. "I brought you some groceries."

"Thanks," he said, puzzled. "You didn't need to bring them all the way down here."

"I know," George said, setting the bag down on the slab table. She had to move his toolbelt from the single stool before she could sit down. "I haven't seen much of you lately, thought I'd see how things were going." She nodded toward the bacon sizzling in the pan. "You don't even eat at the café anymore?"

"I do, in the evenings after closing. It's just more convenient to make my lunch when I'm down here." When she didn't make any motion to leave, he glanced at the pan, then back at her curiously. "Are you hungry? There's enough for two."

She craned her neck toward the stove. "What are you making?"

"Leftover chili and cheese on Fritos, with bacon bits."

"Sounds yummilicious." She winced ruefully. "Amy-speak, sorry."

She waited as he poured chili on a mound of Fritos, sprinkled crumbled cheese and bacon over the top, and set the plate in front of her. Opening the minifridge, he said, "What would you like to drink? I've got orange juice, Mountain Dew, or Dasani water."

"Dasani's fine."

He poured her a glass, then sprinkled the last of the corn chips into the pan with the rest of the chili, and set the Dasani bottle beside it. "You only have the one plate?" George asked, realizing. And one glass, and one fork, she observed as he began eating with a spoon.

He shrugged. "It's the first time I've had a guest."

They ate in self-conscious silence, George aware he was watching her guardedly. She looked around the cabin, spotting one of Lonny's fishing poles leaning against the door next to his old waders and a box of lures, and a battered copy of *The Fly Fisherman's Handbook* opened on the daybed.

"You thinking of taking up fly-fishing?"

Trinity followed her glance, and shrugged. "Found the

gear in one of the sheds. Thought I'd give it try. Haven't quite got the hang of this bit yet," he said, mimicking casting. "I've only ever seen it done in the movies."

Nor would he find anyone willing to give him any pointers, either, she realized, embarrassed for him. As if he could read her mind, he smiled and added, "Not sure what I'd do with a fish if I caught it anyway. I just enjoy the quiet, being on my own."

"That's pretty much what Lonny liked about it."

The mention of her dead brother increased the awkwardness between them. The only other personal possessions she could see in the cabin were a neat row of paperback books on the dresser in a small pine book holder he'd made himself.

"You're really good at carpentry," she said, nodding at the carved bookshelf. "And plumbing and electricity and bricklaying."

"I worked a couple years in construction, building houses." She waited for him to elaborate, but he didn't.

The cabin was tidy and clean, yet somehow sterile. Like a hotel room rather than a home: austere, temporary. "You know, we could find you a few things to brighten up the place, some curtains and pictures or something. I've got a spare television you could use."

"Thank you, no," he said. "I'm fine."

"You don't even have a stereo. Don't you like music?"

"I like music."

This was like pulling teeth, George thought. "Jack's asked after you," George said, changing the subject again. "Wanted to know how you're getting along."

"That's kind of him."

"Not everybody hates your guts, you know." When he didn't react, she added, "Even Harry thinks you've done a lot to help out Ma, and that counts for something."

"I appreciate it."

She wished he would stop speaking in such clichéd civility. "Look, you have to understand. It's not like folks around here have ever had a lot of experience with . . . well, you know . . ."

"Terrorists?"

"Yeah. I mean, we get drug smuggling and cattle rustling and drunks fighting every Saturday night, but terrorism? You might as well have been a Martian, that's just something that doesn't happen out here. You don't even *look* like a terrorist."

He smiled, but still said nothing.

"And from the way Ma tells it, it's not like you ever intended to hurt anyone. You made a mistake, that's all, trusted the wrong people, made some bad choices. Folks around here can be pretty conservative, fixed in their ways, but you just gotta give them time to understand that."

He didn't respond, his detachment unnerving. She watched him eat his chili and chips with the same precision as had it been filet mignon in a fancy restaurant, realizing where Amy's sudden manifestation of good manners had sprung from.

After several minutes of silence as they ate, George said, "I Googled your name on the Internet." When he looked up, she added, "I couldn't find much."

He swallowed before he replied, "Doesn't surprise me. What were you looking for?"

"I don't know. Answers. The truth, I guess."

He chuckled. "You won't find it there."

"Ma says you used to be rich."

He shrugged one shoulder indifferently. "I suppose."

She pretended she didn't notice his reticence, stubbornly pressing him. "How rich? Kennedy rich? Bill Gates rich?"

"Not even close." He exhaled in defeat, then drank from the Dasani bottle, draining most of it, studying her. "I received around twelve million a year from a family trust fund."

"Twelve million?" George blinked with astonishment. "Every *year?*"

"Give or take, after taxes. Most of my income was annual profits from the company but I also had a private investment portfolio that did okay. The company was worth quite a lot more, we had shareholders to pay as well, naturally."

"And you don't consider that rich?" She shook her head in disbelief. Not even the Bakkers could boast that. "I can't even imagine having that much money. Jesus. Did you have horses and servants and stuff like that?"

He nearly laughed, she realized. "Servants? Well, let's see: there was a live-in housekeeper who was also the cook, and an au pair. The pool guy and the gardener. No horses, but we had a dog. I'm not sure the dog-walker counts. But nobody ever had to wear uniforms or curtsy."

Now he was making fun of her. "You must have had a hell of a big house," she said testily.

"The main one in Santa Monica was a pretty good size," he said lightly as if unaware of her pique. "We also had a holiday cottage with a couple hundred acres up near Big Sur, and a ski lodge in Colorado. I collected classic cars for a while as a hobby; I had a Porsche and a Jaguar, a Triumph and a couple MGs, a few others. Oh, and I had a yacht."

"A yacht?" she echoed, amazed.

"A small one. I inherited it from my grandfather, but I never used it. I get seasick."

"So what happened to it all?" George asked, still trying to imagine that amount of wealth.

"The government confiscated everything I owned," he said calmly, his humor fading.

George was baffled by his composure. "*Everything?* They can do that?"

"Right down to the Armani shirt on my back." He chased the last of the chili around the bottom of the pan with a Frito chip, seemingly oblivious to her disbelief. He finished his chili as she pushed the remains of her own around on the plate.

"That didn't make you angry?"

He stared down into the pan for a long moment. "They're just things," he said quietly.

Feeling like she was stepping into a minefield, she said as casually as she could, "I suppose your faith helps you. To accept it, I mean."

His brow wrinkled with confusion. "My faith?"

"Being a Muslim."

In the silence, she couldn't meet his eyes, her pulse in her throat.

"I'm not Muslim," he said finally.

"Your wife was."

He nodded slowly, watching her intently. "Yes, she was." His response sounded more like a question than a declaration.

"Lucas heard you praying. In Arabic. When you were in jail." She forced herself to look up at him directly. "It's not a problem, so please don't feel like you have to hide it. Ma and I are not bigots, we don't care, honest."

His expression cleared, his eyes amused but hard. "I'm not Muslim. I don't speak Arabic and I wasn't praying. What he heard was English, very old English. It's Beowulf. I memorized it when I wrote my master's thesis."

"Beowulf?"

"It's the name of the hero in an eighth-century Anglo-Saxon epic poem. I used to teach English Lit at Pepperdine University. Ms. Jensen, what are you doing here?"

"Trying to figure you out."

He picked up her plate and the pan and took them to the sink to run water over them, his back to her. "There's nothing to figure out."

She stood up and stepped around the table to stand next to him. "I don't get it. What really happened to you, Ben?

How on earth does an English teacher get himself mixed up with Islamic terrorists? How could you *not know?*"

He acted as if she wasn't there, filling the sink with hot water, squirting a bit of detergent to foam around the dishes.

"You can talk to me, you know."

His hands paused from sponging chili off her plate to stare at her, his face impassive but his eyes unblinking.

"I won't even tell Ma. Strictly between us, I promise."

His expression didn't change, but he raised an eyebrow. After a moment, she absorbed the unspoken message, her jaw dropping. She glanced around the small cabin, as if the sudden realization would make her perceptive enough to spot hidden microphones or cameras. "You don't think . . . ," she began, before his warning look cut her off.

*Really?* she mouthed silently, incredulous.

Then he smiled, a fleeting grin without humor. "I have no idea," he said in a normal voice. "It just seems like a sensible precaution."

He turned back to washing his dishes, rinsing the suds with cold water before stacking the little dishware he had on a dishtowel laid on the drainboard. She stood awkwardly, unsure of what to say, acutely self-conscious but unwilling to concede defeat.

"My great-uncle was a Catholic priest," he said, the change of subject throwing her. The statement hung between them as she struggled for an appropriate reply.

"So . . . you're Catholic?"

"Not anymore." He rinsed her glass, put it on the dishtowel and pulled the plug on the sink, wiping the sides of the stainless steel as the water drained.

"But you *are* still Christian, aren't you?"

"You want a coffee? I've only got instant."

"No, thanks."

Without a change in his tone, he added, "Uncle Stacey

died long before 9/11. Things were different then. Every year, on St. Patrick's Day, he would get all dressed up in his best cassock and stole and biretta and go to every Irish bar in whatever town he was in—Boston, New York, Philadelphia—walk along the crowds if there was a parade, shaking a big tin can soliciting donations. It always said 'For the orphans and widows of Northern Ireland' on the tin can, but everyone knew exactly what the money was for."

Trinity took a second dishtowel from the drawer to wipe his dishes dry, dropping the clean spoon and fork into a drawer. His voice was soft, nearly inaudible, but a muscle in his jaw twitched. "Women would kiss him on the cheek and men would buy him a beer, like what he was doing was noble, while they toasted Sinn Fein and spat at the mention of Ian Paisley's name."

George wasn't all that knowledgeable about Irish politics; the American news networks hardly ever mentioned anything political outside its own concerns. She had heard of Sinn Fein, but wasn't sure which side they were on, or who Ian Paisley was. As if he could read the ignorance in her face, Trinity smiled bleakly, which, for some reason, angered her.

"It's not the same thing," she insisted. "The IRA didn't fly planes into skyscrapers to kill thousands of Americans."

He nodded, and turned away, busily drying the saucepan. "And that makes all the difference, does it?"

She tried to soften her tone. "Anyway, he must have believed what he was doing was right . . ."

"So did I."

She watched as he continued wiping the saucepan, now completely dry, over and over. When he didn't look at her, she put her hand on his arm, and was startled by his trembling. He shut his eyes, resisting her as she tried to make him face her.

"Ms. Jensen . . ."

"You can call me George, you know."

"No, I can't. May I ask you to go now?"

"Ben . . ."

"Please. Just leave."

Baffled, George swallowed against the sudden ache in her chest. She let go of Trinity's arm and walked stiffly to the door, trying to keep her wounded pride from showing. But he never turned around to notice, still paying diligent attention to drying the saucepan as she left without a word.

# CHAPTER TWELVE

"Have you decided?" Trinity asked the lone customer sitting on his own in the corner, politely waiting with his pen poised over his order pad.

Trinity had finished repairs on the last of the cabins, all of them now occupied by die-hard fishermen who either didn't know or didn't care about the notoriety of the caretaker. But the extra clientele meant more business for the café, summer being the café's busiest season of year anyway. Even with Holly Red Wolf working nearly full-time and George coming in for evenings and weekend shifts, Carlene needed all the help she could get. A few days after the Fourth of July weekend, she had decided it was time for him to resume working in the café again, dealing directly with customers whether he—or they—liked it or not.

He resumed working weekdays, when it was slow, and left those people who still refused to have anything to do with him to either Holly or Carlene. Most of the regulars treated him with awkward embarrassment rather than hostility. No one left pennies anymore, but few smiled at him either, or spoke to him more than necessary. One of the old Spaight sisters became teary-eyed when he took their order while dressed in one of their multihued creations, the other sister admonishing her brusquely under her breath once he'd turned away. So he stopped wearing the sweaters.

But this was a stranger, a man in a casual suit too expensive to be casual, clean boots and clean nails, huge turquoise buckle on a pristine leather belt, Stetson hat still smelling of Scotchguard, fancy cowboy boots with shiny silver toetips; clear signs of the typical urban cowboy passing through.

"Yeah. Is it too late for the breakfast special?" The accent was definitely East Coast, Trinity thought, confirming his impression.

"No, sir, we can still do that for you. Hash browns or pancakes?"

"Hash browns."

"How would you like your eggs?"

"Scrambled."

"White or whole wheat?"

"Whole wheat."

"Coming right up."

Trinity turned away indifferently, tearing off the order sheet from the pad.

"Benedictus Xavier Trinity," Trinity heard the man say calmly, the words rolling out slowly, like a judge handing down a verdict. Trinity froze, a knot in his stomach tightening, then turned back warily. The man smiled slowly, knowingly. "That is you, isn't it?"

When Trinity didn't answer, the man pulled his wallet from his back pocket and opened it to a Press ID card. "Hugh Lowery, *New York Post*."

Trinity backed away, shaking his head. "I think you should go."

Lowery raised an eyebrow and smirked. "It's a free country." His smirk evaporated. "Or at least it used to be, remember? Back in the days when you were a respected college professor, happily married, the father of a handsome little boy. How old would Antoine be now, what, six? Seven? He's a hell of a cute kid, would you like to see a photo?"

Lowery unfolded a newspaper beside him, revealing half

a dozen photographs of a young boy playing soccer in a park with a couple of other children his own age. The boy seemed totally unaware of the camera, and Trinity suspected they must have been taken with a telephoto lens from some distance away. But they were clear, and left no doubt; it was Antoine. Trinity felt as if he'd been punched in the gut, bile stinging the back of his throat.

"Of course, he's not called Antoine anymore," Lowery said, watching Trinity's reaction. "You think he can still remember you calling him 'Ant'?"

"I can't talk to you," Trinity said, still mesmerized by the photos.

Lowery snorted his amusement. "It wasn't easy finding you, y'know. They've done a good job of expunging the records, and officially, you don't exist, just like someone in witness protection. Except no one *is* protecting you, are they? They didn't even bother with changing your name. Why is that, do you think?"

Trinity looked up from Antoine's photos to stare at Lowery, his eyes burning. "Leave," Trinity retorted, his voice hoarse. "Now."

Lowery took a card from his jacket and slid it across the table. "Sooner or later," he said in a low voice, "I won't be the only one who figures it out. But I can help you. So ask yourself this: How badly do you want to see your son again?"

Trinity's breath quickened as the anger surged. "*Ms. Ryton!*" he bellowed.

"Talk to me, Trinity, or wait until the TV crews start hammering on the door, it's your choice."

Startled, Carlene hurried out of the kitchen toward them with alarm turning to confusion. "What's the matter, Ben?"

"I can't serve this gentleman," he said heatedly. "Would you mind?" He handed her the pad and nearly ran out of the dining room, bolting through the kitchen to stand panting on the back porch. He wrenched the apron off over his head, flung it in a crumpled ball onto the chair, and paced the length of the porch like a neurotic cougar. Behind him, he could hear only the muted tones of their voices, Lowery's apologetic, and Carlene's scaling up into indignation.

"Get out," he heard her shout. "Get the hell out of my café right now!"

The front door slammed, and a car rumbled to life. He ducked back as a dark Ford sports car pulled out of the parking lot back onto the road, heading toward the main highway. He sank slowly onto the steps and was still shaking when Carlene came to stand beside him, looking down at him with concern.

"You want this?"

He looked at the card she held out to him. "No. I'm not allowed to talk to journalists," Trinity said softly, fighting down the fear.

Carlene sat next to him on the steps, looking into his face, troubled. "What are you going to do? Shouldn't you call Mr. Eastlake?"

Trinity gulped down a huge breath before his could speak, but his voice was still unsteady. "I don't know yet. If I don't, are you?"

She said nothing for a long moment before she pulled a photograph of Antoine from her own apron pocket and set it on the wooden floor between them. "You didn't tell me you had a son."

"Why would I have?" A deep sorrow Trinity wasn't even aware he'd buried threatened to engulf him. He buried his face in his arms wrapped around his knees, fighting back the grief so hard his body shuddered violently, alarming Carlene. She shuffled closer to him, patting him awkwardly on the shoulder until the moment had subsided.

"He's a good-looking boy," she said gently. "What's his name?"

He suspected her interest was more to help him regain his self-control than in a photo of an anonymous child.

"Antoine," he finally managed to say, his eyes dry as dust, his voice hoarse but lifeless. "His name was Antoine."

" 'Was'?"

He heard the unease in her voice.

"He's not dead," he reassured her, or himself, he wasn't sure. "I haven't seen him since he was four."

"They took him away from you."

"No, I was taken away from him. We were in France when I had to make a trip to California, and I left my son behind with his mother. I was arrested, and for years I didn't know what had happened to my family. While I was in the detention camp, I was told that the Americans had snatched him while he was in nursery school, got him out of the country on a private jet before the French could prevent him from leaving. But my wife fled France before they could detain her; she just disappeared. I was shown a video to prove Antoine was back in American custody. Then they made me an offer: If I cooperated fully, signed a confession, did whatever they wanted, I was promised he'd be safe."

"Are you saying someone threatened your *child?*" Carlene's tone was incredulous.

Yes, he thought, that's exactly what he was saying. "I was promised he'd be safe from the al-Jawasis, from my wife. From having to grow up with the stigma of terrorists for parents. He'd be given a new name, new family, a fresh start, but I couldn't have any contact with him again. I don't know what his name is now, or where he is."

Carlene looked back at the business card she still held in her hand. "But this Hugh Lowery, he knows."

Trinity straightened and snatched the card from her so quickly she flinched away, then methodically tore it into shreds until there was nothing but a small pile of confetti on the ground.

"Joseph Myers, thirteen months," he said tightly. "Ellen Jane Donaldson, twenty-three. Courtney Donaldson, three years and five months. Jasyn Cooke, five. Annie Scudmore, eight. Juan Castille, nine. Ho Yook Chin, nine. Robert Maksudi, eleven. You want more? I've got ninety-seven names, forty-nine of them children. I know every single one, in alphabetical order, by age, any way you want. They were all somebody's child, and I will never risk adding Antoine's name to that list."

He stood and bolted from the back porch, running blindly. He ran down the path toward the cabins, passed them, and ran on, crashing furiously through the undergrowth, slashing at bushes until the Fairfax Creek stopped him. He splashed into the running water, stumbling over rocks and fell to his knees. His throat was raw and he realized he'd been howling, a low, unyielding scream of pain squeezing up from deep in his chest. He struck out futilely, beating his fists against the rocks until the microchips buried in his hands awakened, biting back with a searing warning shuddering through his heart. It was enough to make him gasp in shock, and sink slowly into waist-deep cold water, the rushing stream soaking him. He tasted blood in his mouth mixed with rising acid, making him nauseous. He sat in the water for several minutes, his breath in shallow pants, until the numbing cold seeped into his muscles shivering uncontrollably.

The slow walk back did little to warm him, his wet clothing sticking to him and his shoes squelching with each step. Carlene was waiting for him by his cabin, but he said nothing, simply glaring reproachfully as he brushed past her. She followed him inside and watched as he ran water over his bruised hands, washing away the blood, threads of bright red swirling down the drain.

"Let me help you," Carlene said, reaching toward his hands.

"No." He turned his shoulder toward her to block her from touching him, resisting as she pulled on his arm. "I'm all right."

"You're not all right," Carlene snapped, irritated, her strong hands prying his from the sink. She looked down at his battered knuckles in disbelief, his hands looking like raw hamburger. "Jesus, what have you done to yourself?"

The concern in her voice was unbearable. He wrestled to free himself from her grasp. "Please . . . just go . . . leave me alone . . . !" The struggle increased until Carlene threw her strong arms around him, pinning him to her tightly. The fight went out of him and they both sank to their knees onto the floor. He hugged her around the waist, weeping with his head lowered onto her shoulder, misery wracking his body.

He could have endured anything, anything but kindness.

# CHAPTER THIRTEEN

Dennis Red Wolf had grown up in this vast, remote part of northern Montana, and loved it with a quiet passion he wouldn't have known how to speak about, even if he'd wanted to. His half-blood mother had run off with a gypo trucker when he was only twelve, sending him postcards with pictures from all over the States for a few months before those, too, had petered out. It nearly broke his heart when his white grandmother insisted on pulling him out of the tribal school and sent him to a boarding school near Butte, far away from the reach of his alcoholic father. There, he and one other student were the only Indians in his class, the other being Anja Apanakhi, a shy eleven-year-old girl as much a fish out of water as himself.

The fact that he was Chippewa-Cree while she was Blackfoot didn't matter to the white kids; Indians were Indians, and often treated with jealousy by those who longed to be special or as pariahs by others with an ingrained bigotry years of political correctness could never totally eradicate. Either way, that loneliness drove them together. As he matured from a scrawny adolescent into a huge six-foot-five teenager with a physique like the Incredible Hulk and a face like a chiseled hawk, she blossomed into a delicate Buffy Sainte-Marie beauty that even now, after more than fifteen years of marriage, could still steal his breath from him when she turned around in the light of a warm summer evening and smiled.

Her shyness had transformed into a tranquil strength like steel cable under the softness of an eagle chick's down. Dennis Red Wolf was continually amazed that someone as beautiful, as caring, and as loyal as Apanakhi could possibly love a man like himself. She was the only one who had ever seen beyond the powerful body and the rough face to his vulnerable self-doubt. He adored her with an intensity that frightened him, and when she said jump, he was only too happy to ask how high.

His size, his calm demeanor, his total abstinence from the alcohol that had destroyed his father, the harsh features that hid a gentle heart preordained his eventual occupation. He'd tried other jobs—road construction, logging, oil rigs, timber mills and ranching, shopping mall security guard and mind-numbingly tedious factory work, even a very brief embarrassing stint as a rodeo clown. He longed for the open country of his boyhood, the wide skies so blue it hurt your eyes, bleak plains of rolling grass, a silence in the dry desolate badlands so profound you could hear the Creator whispering on the wind; he wanted to go home.

But when he returned to Box Elder with a young bride pregnant with their first child, he found very little in the way of job opportunities. As with so many other Indian nations, poverty has always been an omnipresent feature of life on the reservations, employment nearly nonexistent. The lure of quick money from legalized gambling or illegal drug trafficking was an irresistible temptation for too many. Red Wolf wasn't a natural croupier and turned down offers for jobs as a bouncer on the door, not fond of casinos or the drunken clientele it attracted. Joining the tribal police department became ever more inevitable.

His first few years on the tribal police had been mildly interesting, but nothing too exciting, just the way Apanakhi preferred it to stay. He dealt with the usual gamut of stabbings and shootings and car crashes inevitably fueled by booze and meth and stupidity, chased teenaged carjackers and drug-addicted burglars that cycled through the reservation with habitual routine. With Rocky Boy being a "dry" reservation, meaning no gambling or alcohol allowed on Indian land, certain residents drifted into Box Elder where they regularly overindulged in gambling, drinking, fighting, and causing a noisy ruckus necessitating frequent police attention. Red Wolf held no illusions he could change the world for the better, content with simply holding the line against the night.

He took his kids to the Rocky Boy powwows and local barbecues and coached his youngest son learning to become a grass dancer. He drove his family to his wife's reservation for their Indian Days where Holly, his first child and only daughter, earned her Blackfoot name, Leaping Deer, and studied with her maternal great-grandmother to become a medicine woman. When his Jessie and Cody were old enough, Red Wolf was invited along with his sons by his father-in-law, a stern, small-eyed man with white streaks in his braids, to walk with the elders into the mountains where teepees had been erected over fire pits. They chanted and sprinkled water onto glowing hot rocks to sweat in the steam and rid themselves of any bad spirits.

He lay in the darkness, his vision filled with the vast blackness of a midnight sky, stars shining in air so transparent they barely shimmered, and held his wife's hand as they listened to his daughter retelling old legends as if they'd never been heard before. Her young voice excited, she related how Running Bear loved a girl on the other side of a river, but when they tried to swim across to meet in the middle, the current pulled them under where they drowned, but would live together forever in the spirit world. He smiled when Holly primly informed him that *innoka* was an elk and *sipisttoo* was an owl, *skiniopa* meant friend and *spoppi* meant turtle, as equally proud of her mother's heritage as her father's, seeing no contradiction in her blood.

Every Sunday, they dressed in their best and picked up his grandmother, Hazel Mae Beecham, a tall, rigidly proper woman in her nineties with pallid skin and pallid eyes, and white hair tinted a faint blue that smelled of lavender and peroxide, and drove her into Havre to attend the Presbyterian Church, seeing no contradiction in their faith, either.

For over a decade, it had been an uncomplicated life, a quiet life. His ambitions were modest, his expectations ordinary. Then several murders suddenly occurred on the reservation, confiscated drugs and material evidence disappeared, and his comfortably humdrum life became more interesting.

Late one hot summer evening, he had driven out alone to question Orville Bouvier, who had complained about some horses that had gone missing after seeing strange lights in the sky. Bouvier was a bad-tempered recluse who lived in a tumbledown shack on the edge of the reservation, without running water or electricity. He devoted his entire existence to tending his herd of mangy swayback flyblown horses not even worth turning into dog food, and regularly walked the twenty-eight miles to the nearest phone to grumble incoherently about government conspiracies to steal his veteran's pension and kids rustling his horses just to piss him off. No one liked having to deal with old man Bouvier, and as one of the lowest-ranking officers on the force, Red Wolf often drew the short straw.

Expecting to waste his time listening to a load of crap about UFOs and alien abduction, Red Wolf had been surprised to see strange lights in the sky himself long before he reached the Bouvier place. But these weren't little green men from outer space, Red Wolf instantly knew. Even with the running lights darkened, the faint glow from the windows of the aircraft stood out in the dark as it flew close to the ground. He'd cut his headlights, not so much to avoid detection as it was to better his own night vision. Driving as far as he dared off-road in the direction the plane had gone, he then hiked in the dark, listening for sounds other than owl hoots or distant coyote wails. He followed the faint echoes of trucks rumbling over rough country tracks through the low hills, the whine of an aircraft engine idling, and men laughing loudly without a care they might be overheard in such a remote outback.

He watched through night binoculars as three men unloaded crates from the cargo hold of the plane into a dark-colored van, exhaling softly in dismay as he recognized a fourth man with them, another tribal police officer who stood and watched and smoked and accepted a small manila envelope when two of the men got into the van and drove off while the third, the pilot, bounced the plane along the uneven ground of the clandestine landing strip and flew away. The tribal cop mounted what Red Wolf suspected was one of old man Bouvier's missing horses and disappeared silently into the night.

Red Wolf made no attempt to arrest anyone that night, nor did he say anything to anyone except Apanakhi. She'd listened to his terse description of what had happened while they sat outside and watched sparks flutter from the barbecue grill as grease from hot dogs and T-bones dripped onto the coals. When he had finished, they both sat without speaking while the kids chased each other around in the yard, turning ungainly cartwheels and soaking one other with bright plastic water pistols.

Then she stood and placed her small hand on his massive chest, as light as a bird's wing.

"You'll do what's right," she said quietly. "Because your heart is good."

Doing what was right was easy, knowing what was right another thing altogether. Red Wolf sat in the canvas folding chair, aluminum tubing bending precariously under his weight, folded his arms over his chest, and sighed to himself. His wife turned the steaks on the barbecue and his kids now bounced on a little round trampoline Hazel Mae had bought for them last Christmas, springs creaking in harmony with cricket song.

The next day, Red Wolf had a quiet word with the tribal investigator, who pursed his lips and shook his head and creased his brow with consternation, then promised to look into the matter.

A week later, an Indian kid who had filched one of Bouvier's horses found the old man's body at the bottom of a ravine with his skull split open like a shattered melon. The official cause of death was injuries sustained in an accidental fall, but Red Wolf heard through the inevitable grapevine the old man had other injuries not so easily explained: bruises on his chest and stomach where he'd been repeatedly struck with something like a baton, red marks on his wrists where they'd chafed on something like handcuffs, a multitude of broken bones more consistent with a fall from an elevation slightly higher than any cliff on Bears Paw Mountain—say, from a plane, for example. When Red Wolf asked to see a copy of the coroner's report, his request went astray, phone calls were never returned, a stonewall of silence building up around him. Officers he'd been friendly with for years began avoiding him, baseless rumors whispered he found impossible to fight.

Then Jessie and Cody came home from school, bubbling with excitement because one of their father's colleagues had given them a ride, lights and sirens on, and driving as fast as a fairground ride. Red Wolf smiled, but his skin prickled with cold; the colleague had been the same man he'd seen over near old man Bouvier's place. It was a warning, as subtle and deadly as a rattler's scales sliding over rock.

After Red Wolf had briefly entertained the fantasy of blowing someone's brains out the back of their head, he mulled over his more rational options, and did the even more unthinkable: he sought help outside the tribal police.

Sheriff Holbrook had a reputation for running a clean county, a rare hard-nosed politician who cared more about his community than being reelected. He knew how far to bend rules without breaking them, and demanded results from his deputies rather than statistics. Unlike the tribal investigator, he listened to Red Wolf stoically without interrupting. When Red Wolf finished, he said nothing for a good minute.

"Shit," was his only comment.

Sheriff Holbrook told him to go home and wait. A few weeks later, Red Wolf got a phone call one evening inviting him over to Holbrook's home for an informal chat with a small number of other people, forming an ad hoc task force.

"Special Agent John Langdon with the FBI out of Billings," Holbrook introduced them. "Sam Delahue, CIA."

"Retired," Delahue said self-effacingly, his accent softly foreign. "But I still have a few friends in low places."

"Valery Kankowski, BIA, Internal Affairs Division." A serious-faced woman in her late thirties nodded her greeting. "I think you already know Undersheriff Ensler, County Sheriff's Office in Redemption."

"Yes, sir, I do," Red Wolf said, shaking his hand in turn.

"My deputies, Lucas Jensen," Ensler said. "And Sandy Gosden."

In the faintly musty rumpus room dominated by a pool table and surrounded by a multitude of football trophies and photos of Ensler's sons holding them, Holbrook delayed the meeting only long enough to pass out Bud Lights to the five other men and a Coke each for the woman and Red Wolf.

"There's been a drug trade on the reservations for decades," the FBI man began without preamble. "Most of our problem here is meth, being flown in from clandestine labs all over Montana. But in the last six months, we've seen a sudden rise in the volume of imported cocaine, a massive increase. The problem is southern borders with Mexico are pretty well covered by radar, and INS has tightened the net last few years. So on the West Coast, cocaine and marijuana are being hidden in double-walled shipping containers and sailed up the Pacific Coast into out-of-the-way Canadian fishing ports. On the eastern seaboard, we've got people flying in to Nova Scotia and Prince Edward Island from the Caribbean. They off-load onto smaller planes and fly into Saskatchewan, then back-flush the stuff into the U.S. across our border."

"What, we don't have radar in Montana?" Jensen asked.

"Yes and no. Most of the radar sets we use need a squawk box to pick up."

"A what?" the woman from the Bureau of Indian Affairs asked.

"An IFF tag, 'identification friend or foe,'" Delahue explained without condescension. Not everyone in the room would have the same expertise. "It's a radio transponder in a plane set on certain frequencies. That blip you see on air traffic control radar, that's a squawk. So unless you've got your IFF tag on, it's a fairly safe bet you're not going to show up on too many law enforcement radar sets."

"The bad guys also have some pretty sophisticated radar detectors now as well," Langdon added. "Tells you the signal strength, approximate distance between you and any AWACs, easy to avoid the radar if you know where it is. But we just don't have the money to upgrade all our equipment. We don't even have enough sets to go round as it is."

"Why not?"

Langdon sighed. "The Bureau is under pressure to divert money from other investigations deemed of minimal impact on national security to counterterrorism. My department supposedly handles health-care fraud." He chuckled acidly. "Try finding ways to link *that* to terrorism. Even the guys going after sturgeon caviar poachers have to claim it's funding Islamic militants in the Ukraine. In any case, it means Montana has a lot of black spots along the border—we're porous as hell."

"So much for our invincible doyens in Homeland Security," Delahue observed dryly, leaning back with his hands clasped behind his head, idly rolling his neck to pop the joints.

The national security obsession that had swept through the nation after 9/11 had had relatively little impact in northern Montana's isolated communities. Bigger cities with the right political connections could cut deals with the feds: new quarter-million-dollar rescue trucks in return for firefighters duly spending a couple weekends a year on "first-responder" training courses, or the latest emergency communications systems, new night-vision police helicopters, cutting-edge medical equipment for hospitals, even nifty toys like portable X-ray machines to scan mailboxes for suspicious contents, all things that had been badly needed to fight ordinary crime long before the Twin Towers came down and only now possible to obtain in the sacred name of counterterrorism.

But smaller towns like Redemption saw very little change, except for a Republican Congress approving legislation to shift even more money away from already poor rural areas to those states with bigger media hype and more strident politicians. The "war on drugs" had been superseded by the "war on terror." Which meant that while Red Wolf wasn't overly worried about any imminent incursion by al Qaeda into northern Montana, stemming the tide of drug trafficking had become like trying to nail Jell-O to a barn door.

"Our problem is a lot of this stuff is being flown into the reservations, where the county sheriff's office doesn't have jurisdiction," Sheriff Holbrook said. "Even when we know there's a shipment coming out, by the time I get hold of the FBI and get roadblocks up, it's too late."

"And now we've got another dead body," Kankowski said. "Orville Bouvier is the fourth unsolved murder we've had in the last six months we think is drug related. The man we think is behind the killings?" She glanced at Red Wolf meaningfully. "He's damned near fireproof. We can't even get him suspended pending an investigation, so he knows he's being watched while he still has full access to his own investigative files. Big surprise: things have gone missing. But cocaine and pot is largely regarded as an import for the rich elite; domestic meth tends to involve a different section of the population. Dead Indians are just not a high enough priority," the woman from the BIA said bitterly.

"And too many people are making a huge profit," Langdon added. "Drug smuggling has long been a venerable tradition raising money for covert activities that can be kept off Congressional ledgers, so a lot of the people you'd be going up against are wearing uniforms and badges indistinguishable from the real thing, mainly because they *are* the real thing. Telling friend from foe is going to get sticky."

"So what we need here, folks, is a little quiet interdepartmental cooperation," Delahue said.

Thus began a nightmarish, frustrating eighteen months fighting corrupt county officers, a rival FBI task force interfering with any investigation which might implicate any of their own colleagues, leaks from the U.S. Attorney's office, witnesses either terrorized or bribed into silence, or disappearing altogether, drug raids where impounded evidence vanished, on and on. Nor did the intimidation stop; Sandy Gosden was shot in the leg and his house burnt to the ground. When his wife was rear-ended, dragged out of her car, and assaulted by three men she either couldn't or wouldn't identify, Gosden quit and moved to Wyoming.

Dennis Red Wolf disliked drugs for the same reason he disliked alcohol; he'd seen the damage it had done to his people. The illicit whiskey peddlers of his grandmother's era had been replaced by cocaine pushers and methamphetamine factories springing up in every unlit corner of the state like poison mushrooms. It was easy to spot who was involved in the trade; in an area where most people drove whatever they could keep together with chewing gum and baling wire, a new expensive BMW stood out like a beacon, the money tearing families apart as much as any addiction. But Red Wolf was a realist; this was a war he knew was unwinnable, and he didn't take it personally.

Lucas Jensen, however, was a crusader. He viewed the world in black and white with the zeal of a traveling preacher heralding the end of civilization and the damnation of all mankind. His fanaticism nearly got them killed when the last raid finally did come down, charging into the fray like a suicidal doughboy going over the top. It was a miracle no one ended up dead. Several arrests were made, including the tribal officer involved in Bouvier's death. A few lower-ranking state officials were indicted for conspiracy as sacrificial scapegoats, while those higher up the food chain simply decided to take early retirement in the Bahamas.

Jensen was praised as the hero of the hour. He received a glowing write-up in the local paper and a commendation from the City Council. His church convinced the St. Mary Magdalene school board to offer him a partial grant for when his daughter entered high school.

Red Wolf, on the other hand, was ostracized by his own colleagues, furious one of their own had betrayed another while cooperating with outsiders as well. He came home from work one afternoon to find his wife consoling a sobbing Holly who had discovered a shoebox left on the doorstep with a dead pigeon inside, its throat cut and contorted body soaked in blood.

That Holly had been distressed by the fate of a dead bird while oblivious to the message it carried was of little relief for him. But Dennis Red Wolf had had enough. He resigned from the tribal police the next day, and moved his family out of Box Elder and into his grandmother's house in Redemption the following weekend. It took him nearly a year of pumping gas and fixing cars at Henderson's Garage before his meager take-home pay and injured pride convinced him to accept Sheriff Holbrook's job offer.

By then, most of the corruption had been eradicated, or at least squeezed out to become some other county's problem. Internal investigations had cleared out the rot inside the tribal police, veiled threats against his family stopped, and he'd been able to go back to his comfortably unexciting life, hoping it would stay that way. Then, on an early August weekend afternoon while he was working on the extension in back of his grandmother's house that would eventually become Holly's new and improved bedroom, he stopped long enough from hammering stub noggins onto the roofing joists to wipe away the sweat dripping into his eyes and spotted Trinity waiting patiently in the yard, fully laden toolbelt draped over one shoulder.

Startled, Red Wolf said simply, "Hey."

The man smiled and said, "Lend you a hand?"

Red Wolf thought it over for a moment, baffled. "Okay."

He knew Trinity had been conscripted into construction work for the upcoming annual Pioneer Days Festival, and had only narrowly wriggled out of it himself. But Jack Bakker hadn't been exaggerating: Trinity knew his way around a building site, Red Wolf observed, fixing joist hangers in place, nailing struts between the span of rafters, measuring and sawing with practiced ease, his butt cuts with a handsaw as precise as those Red Wolf made with the Skilsaw. Red Wolf noticed the bandages on the man's hands and the blue swollen knuckles, but asked no questions. They worked together without speaking, which was how

Red Wolf preferred it, until his grandmother appeared at the kitchen door with two glasses of iced tea on a tray.

"Y'all come down out of that sun and take a break," Hazel Mae said, the round vowels of long-extinct Georgia gentry in her voice. If she was aware of just who their visitor was, she didn't bat an eye. She set the tray down on the plastic garden table and went back into the cool interior of the house.

They stood together in the backyard in the shade, drinking iced tea.

"Amy's been talking about Holly's new bedroom for weeks," Trinity said finally, answering an unspoken question. "She's got a few grand design ideas of her own now."

"George Jensen give you a lift over?"

Trinity shook his head. "I walked." Red Wolf eyed him, incredulous; it was a good twelve-mile hike from the café to his house, most of it uphill, on a hot summer day carrying a load of tools. Trinity looked up at him directly, his eyes intense. "She doesn't know I'm here. No one does."

"I see," Red Wolf said, although he didn't see at all.

Trinity finished his tea, staring into the glass as he swirled the melting ice cubes around the bottom. "That kid, Frankie."

It took Red Wolf a moment to remember whom Trinity was talking about. "Frankie Hopkinson? What about him?"

"He told me you're a decent guy." He smiled. "For a cop."

"Well, Frankie's a decent kid, for a lowlife scumbag car thief."

Trinity laughed, a low chuckle that didn't last. He went back to studying the ice in his glass. "I've got a problem."

Inwardly, Red Wolf winced, loath to get embroiled any further with Lucas Jensen's crazy jealousy troubles. But, like the UFOs over old man Bouvier's place, the obvious sometimes disguised the factual.

"I think I'm being set up to violate my parole."

"Who by?"

Red Wolf waited as Trinity chewed on his lip, looked up at the cottonwood trees marking the boundary of Red Wolf's property, waved away a small cloud of gnats buzzing around their heads, cleared his throat, and looked back down into the empty glass before he could answer. "Homeland Security."

"Huh," Red Wolf grunted in surprise.

"Yeah."

Red Wolf listened without interrupting as Trinity outlined his dilemma. "This isn't how the re-entry program was supposed to work," he said. "Once that assignment in Spokane fell through, I should have been immediately recalled to Tallahassee, or at least held in custody until I could be transferred somewhere else. No offense to your law enforcement competence, but this just isn't an area set up to handle people like me. Then DSD security is breached, confidential files leaked." Trinity shook his head, a muscle in his jaw spasming. "And I'm *still* here." He looked down at his bandaged hands. "Right where they want me."

Red Wolf deliberated for a long, patient moment. "You don't think maybe you're being just a tad paranoid? As I remember it, you got stranded because of a blizzard. Not even the government controls the weather."

"I had a through bus ticket all the way to Spokane, no problem until we stopped in Bismarck and their security singled me out for a red flag, but didn't give an explanation why. I should have been held there until someone from DSD came to take over custody. Instead, North Dakota Highway Patrol drove me to the state line and dumped me on the other side with the suggestion I didn't even glance back over my shoulder. That very definitely was not supposed to happen. I was on my own with less than fifty dollars in my pocket, most of that in change, and twenty-four hours to find a way to get to Spokane. Blizzard or not, I wasn't going to get far."

"Why Redemption?"

Trinity shrugged. "I don't think anyone picked out Redemption specifically. Any remote little town in Montana would have done. But that red flag wasn't accidental. And I can't believe Luke Jensen or even the State Department of Justice could breach DSD security that easily, either; my files were leaked intentionally."

"What for? They hoping someone would decide to shoot you and solve the problem for them?"

Trinity glanced at him, his amusement sour. "The thought did occur to me."

He pulled a photograph out of his shirt pocket and handed it to Red Wolf. A dark-haired boy kicked a soccer ball around a park with a couple other boys in the background, the white stamped date along the bottom less than two months old. Red Wolf turned it over to the blank reverse, looking for the significance, then handed it back to Trinity.

"So?"

"That's my son."

Red Wolf raised an eyebrow questioningly. He listened as Trinity held the photograph carefully, staring down at the image of the boy while he described his encounter with Lowery, his voice low but unable to mask the anger seething underneath, making Red Wolf briefly wonder if he'd bruised his hands punching the journalist in the face. "Contact of any kind with anyone from the media is a specific violation of my parole, punishable by immediate revocation of my conditional release with no possibility of appeal," he finished, tucking the photograph of the boy back into his pocket.

"Lowery approached you, right? You didn't contact him."

"I don't think I'm allowed the luxury of that distinction," Trinity said wryly.

"So you gonna tell your P.O.?"

"I've got a couple weeks left yet, but yes. I'll have to."

Trinity held up his left hand, turning his palm up to expose the tattoo peeking out from dirty gauze. "They're going to know if I try to lie or hide it from them. This thing in me is very accurate." He dropped his hand.

"So you're worried you'll be taken back into custody."

"I'm worried I won't." At Red Wolf's raised eyebrow, he added, "I'm bait."

"For what?"

Trinity set his glass on the table and stared at the ground. "I like it here. I'm aware the feeling isn't universally mutual, but I like the people here. Folks in this town have been good to me, all things considered." He looked up at Red Wolf, his expression stony.

Red Wolf said nothing, waiting for the man to make himself clear in his own time, aware of his internal struggle.

"Everyone seems to think I know more than I do. But I don't. All I did was set up a medical charity."

"You telling me you're an innocent man?" Red Wolf said cynically.

Trinity snorted. "Something I'm sure you've heard from every convicted felon you've ever met. I don't expect you to believe me. But I'm not looking for exoneration. Or forgiveness. I got that hope knocked out of me a long time ago."

There was no anger in Trinity's voice, no emotion at all, just a soft lifelessness Red Wolf found jarring.

"My wife did have a brother called Abdul bin Zahedan, but he was supposedly killed along with her parents when he was thirteen, some twenty-odd years ago. Of course, that could have been a lie, too. Maybe she did use me and the trust to funnel money to Islamic extremists, I just don't know. But it was my signature on the checks; I wrote them out. Everyone working for Triad was arrested, everyone. Nurses, doctors, secretarial help, translators we hired from temp agencies, janitors, bus drivers—anyone who ever got paid out of the trust. Maybe some of them were terrorists, I don't know. They could have been. *Any* of them could have been. A few people did escape, including my wife. That's what I was told, anyway. I think I'm being used as a lure in the hope she or her al-Jawasis contacts will come looking for me."

"What, to rescue you?"

Trinity laughed quietly. "Rather unlikely. Maybe they think I still have access to Swiss bank accounts, or I know something that could compromise them. I don't, but who knows what kind of buzz is being put out about me."

They stood in silence, Red Wolf gazing up at the hot sky impassively, Trinity waiting with his head bowed, a posture Red Wolf had seen often enough before.

"You think she'd show up *here*?" Red Wolf asked finally.

Trinity studied the shrubbery, then sighed in frustration and glanced back at Red Wolf, his eyes intense. "I rather doubt it. But flapping me around like a big red flag is going to attract all kinds of attention, none of it good. Like Lowery, for one. The DSD doesn't give a damn about my safety, and they don't give a damn about anyone else's in Redemption, either. No one here deserves to get hurt because of me. I'm long past caring what happens to me, but Antoine is my *son*. I would do anything to protect him. Anything."

Red Wolf absorbed this, scratching the back of his neck idly. "Right. Bottom line: What do you want from me?"

Trinity shrugged helplessly. "Nothing, I guess. Just . . . be aware. I don't know who to trust in the DSD or FBI or police or what side anyone is playing for. I'm taking the chance you're one of the good guys on the say-so of a teenage car thief. But if the shit does hit the fan, I need someone to know the truth, because sure as hell no one is going to listen to anything I say."

Red Wolf studied him speculatively. "Okay."

Trinity exhaled, as if a huge weight had been lifted from him. "I'll be going now." He unbuckled his toolbelt from around his waist and hefted it over his shoulder. "Please thank Ms. Beecham for the tea."

"Sure."

He followed Trinity as far as the corner of the house and watched him walk down the dusty road until the man was out of sight.

"God damn," he said slowly, knowing his grandmother would have hauled off and smacked him for his blasphemy, even at her age, had she heard him utter the words. This doing-the-right-thing bullshit was getting to be a pain in the ass, he thought.

# CHAPTER FOURTEEN

Lucas Jensen ambled slowly through the crowd, sweating in the late August heat. Hordes of spotty teenaged boys pestered nubile girls in halter tops while their obese parents, huge haunches squeezed into spandex leggings, beer bellies slopping over Levi waistbands, milled around him while pretending not to see him, as if his uniform had somehow rendered him invisible. For his part, he helped the illusion along by wearing a pair of impenetrable mirrored sunglasses and a surly expression that didn't invite familiarity. The odor of burnt sugar, greasy hamburgers, and overcooked chili dogs wafted from a bank of food stands, the smell making him both hungry and revolted at the same time.

At the end of every summer, Redemption held its Pioneer Days Festival, ostensibly to celebrate the Reverend Ezekiel Washington Fairfax, the eccentric nineteenth-century founder of the town. Over the years, however, what had once been a subdued village fair had evolved into a full-scale rodeo and carnival. For such a sparsely populated town like Redemption, the fair regularly attracted a good-sized crowd of out-of-towners bringing in badly needed cash, this year no exception.

A parade with bearded drag queens on John Deere tractors, preschool cowboys and Indians on homemade floats, dueling high school marching bands playing enthusiastically bad theme tunes from various television shows, and a precision wheelchair team followed by the mayor and her husband waving to the crowd from a classic open-top Cadillac convertible launched the weekend festival, leading the way to the open fields at the end of the town temporarily transformed to a fairground. A small troop of mounted police clip-clopped along, smiling and waving to the crowd, just part of the entertainment, folks. Once at the fairground, however, they would fan out and patrol the parking areas and outskirts of the fair in earnest.

Sheriff Holbrook had duly consulted the most recent Homeland Security alert level, which both he and his officers secretly considered a joke, but one they were still federally mandated to follow. Neighborhoods caught in the cross fire of gunfights between rival drug gangs, disgruntled high school kids with semiautomatic weapons turning them on classmates, even unhinged postal clerks mailing anthrax were far more of a genuine threat than al Qaeda these days. But the alert level hadn't been below yellow in several years and since the arrival of Redemption's very own pet terrorist had been elevated into a permanent state of orange.

The public by and large ignored it all anyway, having been too many times scared witless with the apocalyptic threat of "imminent attacks" that never materialized, confused by paradoxical information, and finally inured to the relentless Chicken Little squawking of politicians less concerned with battling terrorism than with keeping a malleable electorate suitably cowed. The public could afford to be blasé, Jensen thought sourly. They weren't required to pull extra duty.

The fair had hired its own private security on the gate as well, which Jensen considered an even worse joke. The Cognident reader scanning the microchips imbedded in driver's licenses and student cards had crashed three times before noon, and the lines of people waiting to get in grew longer and more impatient before the machine was finally ditched. With the amount of heavy belt buckles and jewelry, brass-handled walking sticks and silver Navajo hat bands, a metal detector would have been more trouble than it was worth, and Jensen wondered if the minimum wage rent-a-cops even knew what they were doing as they waved bomb detectors like magic wands over people standing with their arms out, women allowing a dilatory glance inside handbags while men opened their jackets, more to prove they weren't sneaking in bottles of beer to prevent a monetary loss to vendors than anything else. The security measures had as many holes in it as chicken wire, a charade performed solely to intimidate the public and maintain an illusion of safety. Jensen shook his head in disgust and moved on, heading toward the outdoor stage.

Amy had landed a speaking part in the annual opening skit reenacting the good reverend's life, as "Village Woman # 2." While she only had three lines, she was thrilled, since the role of "Village Man # 2" was to be played by one David Brearley, otherwise known as Most Popular Boy in Sophomore Year. Consequently, George had been assigned the unenviable task of creating a gingham dress and bonnet that would be both historically accurate as well as glamorous enough to catch a fellow artiste's eye. Amy had shown off her costume the weekend before the fair, wanting Jensen's approval, whirling around his living room like a ballerina to make the skirt flair.

"You look gorgeous, honey," Jensen had assured his daughter.

"I could do your hair," Wendy had offered, "in a bun like the pioneer women used to wear?"

Amy shrugged her indifference. "It's too short and besides, who's gonna see it under the bonnet anyway?"

Wendy pretended Amy's perfectly reasonable logic didn't matter but didn't hide her hurt feelings well enough, irritating Jensen. The stupid woman should have gotten it through her thick skull by now that she wasn't Amy's mother, and stopped trying so damned hard—it was embarrassing both to him and his daughter.

He spotted George sitting on a blanket spread out on the grass, a Tupperware box of sandwiches and a cup of coffee from a Thermos beside her. She shaded her eyes with her hand to look up at him, squinting in the sun.

"Mind if I join you?"

George wasn't any more adept at hiding her feelings than Wendy, her smile strained. "Not at all," she said as she scooted over on the blanket to make room. He hesitated, preferring to stand, but levered himself down to set cross-legged on the blanket, shifting baton and holster out of the way. It felt undignified, and he sat with his back straight, his posture uncompromisingly rigid.

"When does it start?" he asked, more for something to say.

George checked her watch. "One o'clock, but they're a little late, as usual."

They waited in silence while other families claiming their own bits of territory with plaid horse blankets and shabby quilts spread out on the grass argued cheerfully over fried chicken and coleslaw and Cokes. Jensen glanced at the Tupperware box between him and his ex-wife, noting the number of sandwiches and packages of potato chips. "Your mother coming?"

"If she can get away. She's working her stand." She noticed his glance, opened the Tupperware box and extended it toward him. "Sandwich?"

"No, thanks," Jensen said, even though he was hungry. George opened a bag of Fritos and nibbled at a ham and cheese sandwich, ignoring him.

Every year for three decades, Carlene had press-ganged her family and friends into a marathon of mass pie-baking, the county fair a family tradition. Before his divorce, before Lonny had been killed, Jensen would have been included in the duty of collecting wild blackberries before daylight ran out. As much as he had pretended to dislike the work, he'd enjoyed the easy camaraderie he'd had with his younger brother-in-law, looked forward to time spent with Jack Bakker and even Harry talking endlessly about fishing and football while peeling bushels of apples for pies, the women in the kitchen stewing rhubarb and quartering strawberries for dozens of jars of homemade jams labeled with the café's logo. It was good for the community, Carlene insisted, as well as the pocketbook. What had once been just good fun had turned into economic necessity, every penny counting.

Business must have been good at her stand, Jensen thought after another twenty-minute's wait in tense silence with George. His legs were beginning to cramp by the time the mayor stepped onto the stage and tapped the microphone to see if it was on. She smiled brightly at the crowd on the grass and leaned into the microphone.

"Welcome everyone to the sixty-third Redemption Pioneer Days Festival!" the mayor said loudly through the feedback squeals, the microphone totally unnecessary.

Once the mayor had finished with the obligatory listing of credits thanking the sponsors while various local businessmen, members of the Rotary Club and the Junior Farmers of America each stood to take their bows in return for polite applause, the mayor was helped down from the stage by her husband.

Thankfully for Jensen, the schoolchildren from St. Mary Magdalene were the first in the day's lineup, in a skit depicting the story of Redemption's beginnings, a perversely camp production that Jensen wasn't completely sure was meant to be quite so funny.

"In 1841," a blond-haired boy with an unbroken voice as sweet as a girl's recited nervously, "St. Mary's Mission was established by Roman Catholic missionaries in Stevensville, which became the first permanent town in Montana."

Another boy walked nervously out onto the stage, blushing furiously at a smattering of applause from his proud parents and heckling from his siblings.

"But in 1887, Reverend Ezekiel Washington Fairfax and twenty-three of his followers left Stevensville to found a new settlement because he was opposed to Rome's doctrine of papal infallibility." Unfortunately, the actor's nerves got the better of him, and he stumbled over the pronunciation of the final word, chopping it into a stutter of unintelligible syllables. More hooting and applause from the audience only deepened his mortification.

Another child, this time a girl, entered stage left to recite her single line of dogmatic narration, the play carved up and spread out thinly to allow as many of the school's thirty-two attending students their chance in the limelight as possible. When Amy took her turn on the stage, Jensen grinned in spite of himself, watching her self-conscious recitation of her lines.

"The winter has been long and cold," Amy declaimed in a near yell. Above the actors, nearly hidden behind the canvas backdrop of unconvincing mountains, two boys on ladders each shook a cardboard box filled with popped corn to simulate snow. Amy held up a swaddled plastic doll with melodramatic despair. "Our babies are freezing and our horses are all dead. We have nothing left to eat so we must go back to Stevensville!"

"Never!" cried the Reverend Fairfax, a beard of cotton balls barely clinging to his acne-spotted face. "We shall live free and trust in God!"

The sorrowful band of travelers struggled on through a popcorn blizzard as three teepees with feet tottered on stage. Once settled, the feet disappeared from the fake teepees before two boys and a girl emerged, dressed in buckskin and face paint, wearing matted black wigs with braids. None of them looked remotely Indian, an incongruity loudly pointed out by native students from rival

Stone Child High sitting on the hill behind Lucas and George, jeering good-naturedly and throwing wads of candy wrappers and odd bits of fruit and stray popcorn in-effectually toward the stage.

"We must help these poor travelers," one of the ersatz Indians intoned.

"But they will steal our land and kill our buffalo," the synthetic squaw objected, her accent softly foreign. Jensen vaguely remembered Amy blathering on about some Swiss exchange student. Or was it Swedish?

"We come to these lands seeking only peace between our people," Reverend Fairfax assured the Indians, his beard now dangling off one ear precariously.

Any mention of the infamous battle and defeat of Chief Joseph and the massacre of the Nez Perce in the Bears Paw Mountains had been expediently overlooked. Instead, within seconds, the forlorn refugees and the noble Indians had become fast friends, with handshakes all round and a disorderly powwow joined in by imitation settlers and imitation Indians alike.

"Yeah, right," George murmured beside him. "Like *that* ever happened."

The ensuing script, a tortured fantasy of politically cor-rected history, lasted another toe-curling fifteen minutes, long enough for the town of Redemption to materialize on the northern hills of Montana and the Reverend Fairfax to establish his church advocating his radical doctrines of the vernacular in public worship and optional celibacy of the clergy as well as equality between the races, become Redemption's first mayor, run for (and lose) the election to the House of Representatives before dying in his bed sur-rounded by adoring followers, with theatrical gusto worthy of *Swan Lake*.

The overall farce was only enhanced when the canvas backdrop depicting the inside of the good Reverend's house came unstuck, crashing to the stage floor to reveal chagrined stagehands behind an unflappable Mrs. Mary Elizabeth Fairfax, the honorable Reverend's long-suffering wife doggedly proclaiming her intent to found St. Mary Magdalene's for Girls in her sainted husband's memory—an Old Catholic private boarding school which went coed in 1970 and became an accredited virtual high school enrolling over four hundred online students in 2002, according to the actor playing the role of "Footnote."

After the curtain call and obligatory encore bow demanded by enthusiastic parents, the St. Mary Magdalene Drama Club made way for the Stone Child High School Drummers and Dance Troupe, their outfits far more professional.

"And now, ladies and gentlemen, sit back and let the experts show you how it's *really* done," the leader of the group scoffed into the microphone, a young Chippewa music teacher who clearly enjoyed his work and his students.

As the Indian drummers began and a mix of both white and native students danced with considerably more expertise than had their competitors, Jensen hauled himself to his feet, his joints aching as George gathered the debris of their lunch. When she'd finished, she stood up, looking past him for a moment before averting her gaze too quickly to be casual. He turned and spotted Trinity. The two of them locked eyes for a brief moment before the man melted away into the crowd. Now Jensen understood why the number of sandwiches.

"I see you've invited Osama Ben Trinity along," he said irritably.

"Oh, for . . . ," he heard George mutter under her breath. "Luke, he works for Ma and Amy likes him. Just leave him alone, okay? He's not hurting anyone."

"Not hurting anyone?" Jensen laughed, an ugly bark that died abruptly. "What the fuck's the matter with you, George? The man's a murderer, or have you conveniently forgotten that?"

"I am not going to stand here and have this same old argument with you all over again," George said, her face tight with familiar stubbornness.

He felt his frustration and anger making his fingers twitch. He leaned in closer to her menacingly, relishing her alarm as she retreated. "I'm not arguing with you. I'm *telling* you. I don't like him so close to my daughter. I don't like you allowing him to spend more time with her than you do me. I don't like having my ass hauled over the coals just because I tell him to back off from my family."

"You *hit* him, Luke . . . ," George began.

"You disgust me," Jensen said, his voice low and quiet. "What is it about women who find killers so attractive? I swear to God, I don't understand." Her eyes reddened as if she were about to cry, the color high on her cheeks. "You get off on the bad boy thing, is that it? Does it get you hot?"

He'd managed to shock her, at least, her face draining white. "I don't believe this," she protested, her voice shaking. "You've got no right—"

"But *he* does? They should have locked that cocksucker up and thrown away the key." He glanced around, glowering as curious eyes turned away in discomfiture. "No, actually, they should have leaned him up against the nearest wall and put a bullet through his head."

He watched George struggle to keep her emotions in check, annoyed when she raised her chin, glaring with uncustomary bravado. "You volunteering?"

If they hadn't been standing in the middle in a crowd, Jensen thought, he'd have sorted out her attitude. As it was, he simply snarled, "You keep Amy away from him, do you hear?"

He walked off before she could answer, wrath singing in the pulse in his ears. He had only intended to come and see his daughter in her play, show his support as a good dad, trying his best to be civil with George. Until that bastard Trinity showed up and spoiled it all. He couldn't understand what was so wrong about wanting to protect his daughter from scum like that, why instead of making him feel good and strong and proud for doing what was righteous, George's defiance only infuriated him further, made him feel small, made him feel weak.

He'd wanted to kill people before, but he genuinely did respect the uniform too much to ever cross that line. Oh, he might have been a bit rougher on a suspect than the ACLU might have approved of, or bent the rules now and then when rules needed bending, but only to those who deserved it. How the hell else could anyone expect the job to ever get done? Life was hard enough with drug dealers pushing poison off on little kids, junkie whores and homosexuals spreading AIDS, thieves and sex perverts who preyed on the old and the vulnerable; who could really argue they would be any loss to society? He was all for the death penalty, but deemed the system far too ponderous. The streets would be safer without a bunch of spic gang members shooting each other along with innocent bystanders. Decent people could certainly breathe a sigh of relief if all the nigger welfare cheats draining the economy and breeding an endless succession of more lazy, ignorant mouths to feed were simply sterilized. Roads would be better off without every drunken buck in the county plowing their dilapidated heaps of junk head-on into each other and anyone else just trying to get home from an honest day's work. His hatred was a dispassionate, detached sort of hate, something more philosophical than personal. Like putting down rats and rabid coyotes, just something that should be done for the public good, that's all. He didn't lose sleep worrying about it.

Ben Trinity was different. Whenever he thought of Trinity, his gut tightened in revulsion, a consuming hatred that made him feel sick with helpless impotence. As if life wasn't shit enough, now he had to worry about terrorists lurking behind every tree. Nowhere was safe anymore. He could understand foreigners who despised freedom and democracy and the American way of life wanting to detonate car bombs and hijack planes, a bunch of ignorant Muslim sand niggers halfway around the world stupid enough to believe they'd go straight to heaven by blowing themselves up along with any Jews or Westerners within reach. But another American? An educated wealthy man who had had everything anyone could have asked for handed to him on a silver platter the day he was born? A betrayal that deep was unspeakable. There had to be a special place in Hell for someone like him.

That Jensen had actually been slapped down, a black mark put in his jacket over something as trivial as giving that asswipe a bloody nose, infuriated him. His hands ached with the desire to choke the life out of him, watch the fucker turn blue as he crushed his windpipe and spit in his face. A good man like Lonny gave his life for his country, while that bunch of brain-dead Democrats who had taken over Congress allowed dirtbags like Trinity to walk free. Jensen wondered what he was doing in this job anymore, what was the use of catching the bad guys if handwringing knee-jerk liberal politicians and gutless judges just let them all out again? They might as well install revolving doors on the jail cells. What the fuck had gone wrong with the world?

On the other side of the fairgrounds, Dennis Red Wolf wandered through the crowd, relishing the warmth of the sun on his shoulders, nodding in greeting at those who recognized him. He didn't particularly like working the fair, and would have preferred to enjoy it with his wife and kids like anyone else. But Holly was helping out on Ms. Ryton's stand while Apanakhi was busy with Cody at the Stone Child High dance demonstration. As it was, he was as content to draw overtime strolling around the fair, alone, in uniform, as have a day off to stroll around the fair, alone, out of uniform.

He managed to catch most of his son's performance from the edge of the crowd, proud of the boy, returning Cody's small wave from the stage when it finished. He'd also caught most of the altercation between Jensen and his ex-wife, not close enough to overhear the dispute, but he didn't need to be. He briefly considered stepping in before it escalated out of control and was relieved when Jensen stalked away with an expression as black as a thundercloud. If Jensen saw him standing there, he didn't give any indication.

Red Wolf watched as George clumsily folded the blanket, the muscles in her face stiffened into a blank expression while tears rolled down her cheeks. Amy and Sophie, still in costume, appeared with Alison Bakker and immediately surrounded the stricken woman with hugs and words of comfort. As if responding to the signal, other women in the crowd swarmed around George in support and sympathy, bees encircling the queen. He wasn't needed—women were usually best left to take care of their own problems—so he moved on.

The Redemption Pioneer Days Festival was a pretty standard event, the same Ferris wheels and bumper cars and harmless kiddie rides operated by the same bored, unshaven itinerant barkers everywhere, prizes from nearly unwinnable games all the invariable garish stuffed animals, half-dead goldfish in plastic bags, gigantic multihued lollipops. Kids squealed in pretend fright on the Wall of Death while littler kids squealed in real fright at a clown in a gorilla outfit passing out coupons. Tinny music from every kiosk clashed jarringly, painful on the ear.

He stopped by the Grinnin' Bear Café stand, the number of jars of homemade jams reduced since the fair had opened, slices of cakes and brownies selling out rapidly. Holly beamed, pleased to see him, eager to look more grown-up than he knew she was.

"Doing good," Red Wolf commented.

"Not too shabby," Carlene said, smiling. "Weather helps, thank God."

"Mm." He looked around. "You two holding down the fort on your own?"

Carlene knew what he was asking. "We're fine. Amy's with George and Ben's been helping Jack out with the litter patrol." She turned to serve a couple with two small boys begging for brownies.

During the day, the fair would be reasonably relaxed, moms and dads with kids in tow, adolescent couples wrapped up in puppy love, out-of-town tourists buying cheap souvenirs. It would be later when it would inevitably get ugly, when teenaged boys began to clot together to draw their boldness from too much beer and frustrated testosterone, overtired parents impatient to drag their hyperactive kids away, irate drivers quarrelling over right-of-way out of the parking lot.

But until then, Red Wolf was determined to amble along and enjoy the sunshine, appreciate the curves of healthy young mothers as they bent over goats and lambs in the petting zoo and encouraged their toddlers to feed peanuts to already overweight livestock, listen to the live bands, banjos and fiddles and whiskey-rasped voices belting out country songs, inhale the smell of hot earth and fresh-cut hay, diesel tractor fumes, and barbecued steaks sizzling on open grills, and savor what little peace he had left to the day.

So it was the change in timbre rather than any increase of noise that alerted Red Wolf. He scanned the crowd, eyes narrowed, studying the way people suddenly turned and retreated and stared to pinpoint where the problem came from. Someone else spotted him as well, as a boy's voice yelped in warning, "Cops!"

The plural seemed rather premature, he thought, not bothering to chase any of the half-dozen youths who scrambled through the crowd and ran. He didn't have to, their escape already pointless. Rog Conrad, Craig Bakker, Jamie Wilson, Dickie Allen, and Collie Thompson—Red Wolf mentally noted the names. And two other boys he didn't recognize but could be reasonably confident their collaborators would give up in a heartbeat once he'd rounded up those he knew.

He pushed his way into the ring of people encircling a man sitting on the ground, an older gentleman kneeling beside him in concern. The older man looked up anxiously at Red Wolf. "He's hurt bad," he said, his accent not local.

The identity of the injured man didn't surprise Red Wolf. Ben Trinity had his legs curled up close to his chest protectively, his hands pressed against his ribs covered in blood. A large bruise on his cheek had already begun to swell, turning a motley blue.

"I'm okay," Trinity kept repeating, his voice oddly subdued. "I'm okay."

Red Wolf squatted down and tried to move Trinity's hands away from his chest, gently at first, then more forcefully as Trinity resisted. "It's nothing, I'm okay," Trinity repeated, insistent. His face was bloodless and clammy, the greenish cast around his eyes like a woman's badly applied makeup.

"I don't think so," Red Wolf said. "Let's take a look."

As Trinity allowed his hands to be peeled back, a fresh spray of bright red blood spurted through the rip in his shirt. Behind him, someone murmured, "Oh, shit," and fainted, his companions grabbing hold of him to lower him to the ground.

Red Wolf quickly pressed the man's hands back onto the wound. "All right," he said firmly, "Keep pressure on it."

"That kid in the blue-check shirt had a knife . . . ," someone began.

Craig Bakker, Red Wolf instantly knew. "First things first," he said. He briefly considered radioing in for backup and an ambulance, but he knew getting Jensen involved with this would only make the situation far worse. He glanced up at a man in a NYC baseball cap. "Go get someone from the first-aid trailer over here, *now*."

The man who had fainted had already managed to stagger to his feet, mortified but unhurt. "Wimp," the woman with him sneered as she dragged him away.

Red Wolf looked at the man who had identified the Bakker boy. "You stay here. Anybody else seen what happened, stick around, I'll want statements. Rest of you, show's over, go on," Red Wolf said. The man who had identified the Bakker kid glanced at Vince Murphy, a mechanic Red Wolf had worked with from Henderson's gas station, who grimaced unhappily. A little old lady in a straw hat, her mouth pinched with indignation, primly stood her ground. Red Wolf didn't imagine anyone else would leave, witnesses or not, morbid curiosity being what it was.

The man in the NYC cap returned with a woman in a white lab coat so new it still had the creases from the package. He recognized Darcy Rousseau, nodding at her in greeting. Darcy ran the Prairie Gulch riding school and pony trekking out of her home on the east side of Redemption during the day, and worked every evening, weekend, and holiday as an EMT with the Havre Fire and Ambulance Service. Her husband owned the feed and grain depot on Main Street and spent his lonely evenings as a CPA helping the locals negotiate the financial mine-fields set by the IRS. They both were active members of the Kiwanis. They had no children, to no one's surprise.

Darcy set her EMT kit, a huge blue nylon trauma bag with a reflective Star of Life on the side, on the ground and unzipped it. "My name's Darcy," she said to Trinity.

"Can you tell me what happened to you?" She eyed the blood as she pulled on a pair of latex gloves.

"I'm okay," Trinity still protested. "Leave me alone."

"You're not okay, all right?" Red Wolf said. "We're trying to help you, so for right now just shut up and do what you're told."

"Yes, sir," Trinity murmured, the response automatic, ingrained. But he at least kept quiet as he sat supported between the two of them. This time, when Darcy pried his hands from the injury, the blood spurt wasn't as dramatic, more a pulsing dribble against the fabric of his shirt.

"That boy stabbed him," the little old lady reported indignantly. "Took out a big old hunting knife and stuck him with it. I saw him do it, too. He come up with a whole gang of his buddies, at least six of 'em, I think, and started pushing this poor fellow around, picking on him for no good reason . . ."

"Thank you, ma'am, I'll be taking a statement in a minute, one thing at a time."

Darcy reached into the trauma bag to retrieve a pair of suture scissors, and began cutting off Trinity's shirt. Trinity batted her hands away anxiously.

"It's ruined anyway," Darcy said. "It's in the way and I have to be able to look at the wound."

"No, don't take my shirt off," Trinity insisted, gripping the torn cloth with what seemed like absurd modesty. "Please. Not here. Not like this."

She looked over at Red Wolf for backing, exasperation in her frown. "Can you walk?" Red Wolf asked him. When Trinity nodded, Darcy placed a fresh gauze pad over the wound, and pressed her hand against it to hold it in place. "Vince, give me a hand, will ya?"

Darcy followed with her kit as Red Wolf and Murphy got him to his feet and, between them, slowly walked the few hundred yards to the first-aid trailer, trailed by a nosy following. Red, white, and blue pennants snapped in the breeze along the ropes anchoring an awning into the soft ground, and Northern Montana Hospital sponsor banners draped on the sides of the trailer advertising free blood pressure checks. At the far end, keeping under the shade of the awning, an obese black woman with the distinctive stamp of Down's syndrome sat behind a folding card table covered with brochures. "The doctor is in," she announced, listlessly fanning herself with a diabetes information pamphlet, her thick eyelids drowsy.

"Okay, you and you," Red Wolf said, pointing to his witnesses, "you stay right here, don't go nowhere."

Once Murphy and Red Wolf had helped him inside the trailer, they lowered Trinity into a plastic folding chair. Murphy shifted from one foot to the other uncertainly and kept trying to catch Red Wolf's eye in appeal, wanting to leave. Red Wolf ignored him.

"What have we got here?" another woman working in the first-aid trailer said, wiping her wet hands on a paper towel. Her name badge said: P. ERICKSON, M.D. She was younger than Darcy by at least a decade, a petite woman with elfin features making her seem even younger. She wore her hair back in a severe bun and granny glasses on a chain, too obviously trying to enhance an air of authority.

As the doctor bent over to examine Trinity, Darcy drew a curtain around them to block them from the prying eyes of people outside. "We need to take your shirt off to get a better look at you, will you let us do that now?" Darcy said as gently as if addressing a child.

Trinity kept his head down, his fingers slipping around the buttons, slick with blood, then attempted to pull his shirttail up instead.

"Trinity, you're gonna have to let us help you," Red Wolf said, and unbuttoned the shirt while trying to avoid getting his own fingers bloody. Trinity resisted for a moment before his hands dropped away, resigned.

But it wasn't modesty, Red Wolf realized the moment he

stripped the shirt off Trinity's shoulders. At first, he didn't grasp what he was looking at before it sank in. When he glanced at Darcy, he knew she had understood immediately.

"*Jesus,*" Murphy said, the word pronounced on an intake of breath. He stared at Red Wolf incredulously and asked, "What the hell did Jensen do to this guy, anyway?"

Trinity's torso was crisscrossed in ropy scars, a livid network of puckered tissue, lumps on his ribs from badly healed fractures, and what Red Wolf recognized as old cigarette burns, dozens of them, burned into his skin like craters on the moon. He hadn't seen anything quite as bad since they'd arrested the parents of a six-year-old girl subjected to years of abuse that had left similar marks on her pale little body.

"You guys want to wait outside?" Dr. Erickson said firmly.

By now, the crowd had become bored and trickled away, leaving the little old lady waiting for them, alone. Murphy's friend had gone. "The other man," the little old lady said apprehensively, "he said he'd rather not get involved. He didn't want to make any trouble for the boy's family."

"Me, neither," Murphy said, backing away, hands waving in front of him like an old-time jazz singer. "Unless he like dies or something, I want nuthin' to do with this, Dennis. Count me out, okay?" Without waiting for Red Wolf to respond, Murphy walked off, shaking his head.

He took a statement from the little old lady, a retired bank clerk from Kalispell, whose sense of civic duty had been shaken by her compatriots' desertion. The fat black woman had her eyes closed, snoring softly. Once he had taken down his notes, the little old lady's description of the attack getting hazier by the moment, she said, "I'm not sure if I can afford to come back if this goes to court, you know. It's also a long way for someone my age to be traveling."

"I shouldn't worry about it too much, Ms. Kirol," he said

tiredly, closing his book. Darcy Rousseau appeared in the open doorway of the trailer and gestured for him.

"But if it's important," she added, unwilling to appear unsympathetic.

"We'll let you know."

He slid the notebook back into the leather holder on his belt, blowing out a weary breath, and followed Darcy back into the trailer.

"It's not life-threatening," she said, keeping her voice low. Red Wolf glanced at the shadows barely visible behind the yellow curtain. "Deep enough to require quite a few stitches, but superficial. We really should have taken him into Havre, but he won't go. You know who cut him?"

"Yeah."

She didn't ask if he knew why.

"Dennis, those are old scars, at least one, maybe two years old. No way Jensen could have done that to him."

"I didn't think he had." They didn't speak for a moment. "So you know who that is, don't you?"

"Yeah," Darcy said. She shook her head in disbelief. "Still. Y'know?"

"Yeah."

Dr. Erickson's curtain drew back briskly. Trinity sat on the examining table with his hands holding a blue paper gown closed, his head bowed.

"He's refusing to take any pain medication," she said, her tone annoyed. She handed Red Wolf a small brown bottle. "But he may just change his mind when the local wears off. Don't let him drive for the rest of the day."

"I don't think he has a driver's license anyway."

"Just as well." Dr. Erickson was obviously unaware of her patient's identity. "He needs someone to watch him at least for the next twenty-four hours." She turned to Trinity. "No strenuous activity, don't be picking anything up. Just take it easy." When Trinity didn't reply, she shook her head in exasperation. "Has he got someone to take him home—wife, friend?" she asked Red Wolf.

Mentally, Red Wolf groaned. He was a cop, not a goddamned chauffeur, and certainly not this brother's keeper. But he said, "Yeah. Come on, Ben."

Trinity wordlessly stood up, still clutching the blue paper gown, then stood unmoving. Red Wolf frowned, and began to shrug out of his uniform jacket.

"Hold on," Darcy said, slipping off the white lab coat. She unpinned her name badge before holding out the coat to Trinity. "You can give it back when you come in to have the sutures removed."

Trinity blinked, still staring at the floor, then reluctantly took it from her. "Thank you," he whispered, barely audible. Darcy and Red Wolf both glanced away as Trinity removed the paper gown to change into the lab coat.

"Ten days, Outpatient Clinic, hours between nine thirty and five," Dr. Erickson said briskly, holding out a card. Trinity didn't look at her as he took it and dropped it into the coat pocket.

They had walked halfway across the fair toward the car park where Red Wolf had his cruiser before Red Wolf said, "I know it was the Bakker boy who cut you." Trinity said nothing. "You want to press charges?"

At that, Trinity glanced up at him, darkly amused. His expression was eloquent enough. Red Wolf said nothing else until they reached the car.

"You gonna have any problem getting into Havre to get them stitches out?"

"I can remove sutures, it's no big deal." Trinity said. "Not worth the trip."

At that, Red Wolf stopped, Trinity looking at him quizzically. "Look, if it's a question of money, most everyone else in this county can't afford medical insurance, either. You can go to the free clinic. Nobody's asking you to make yourself into some kinda martyr."

Trinity smiled. "Hospitals keep records," he said evenly. "Just like the police do. Records are stored on computers."

Red Wolf digested this, then helped Trinity into the backseat of the police Blazer. "You'll be okay here. Just chill out for a bit while I find someone to take you back, all right?"

Trinity nodded, leaned back on the seat and closed his eyes, looking haggard and exhausted. Red Wolf closed the cruiser door, locking Trinity in automatically, not that the man inside seemed to care. He stood for a moment, observing Trinity through the window thoughtfully before he shook his head and headed toward the Grinnin' Bear Café stand.

"Don't tell my mother," George said hastily after Dennis Red Wolf had taken her aside and told her what had happened. She glanced behind them at the Grinnin' Bear Café's stand where Holly and Amy bracketed Carlene, Amy still in her pioneer woman costume, all of them chattering and laughing, not a care in the world. "Not yet. Don't spoil their day."

"I got the man sitting in the back of my cruiser, George. I can't keep him there, I need my car back." Red Wolf scowled, making his harsh features even more intimidating. George had always been slightly afraid of Dennis Red Wolf, although he'd never given her any reason to be. "The doctor said he shouldn't be left on his own, he has to have someone watch him at least until tomorrow morning in case he starts bleeding again or passes out. Either your mother takes him or he spends the night in lock-up again. Ms. Ryton is his sponsor or guardian or whatever. Who else is there?"

"I'll take him with me, she doesn't have to know. Amy is sleeping over at Sophie's house. . . ." She stopped as his frown deepened. "What?"

"The Bakkers are gonna be real busy later on."

"You mean it was *Craig?*" she said in astonishment. Red Wolf said nothing, as good as an affirmation. "Why?"

"Why do kids that age do anything? I won't know until I've had a chance to talk to him." He sighed, his massive chest swelling. "Tell Anja I said Amy can stay over with Holly tonight, if that helps you out."

"Yes, thank you."

They stood together without speaking for an uncomfortable moment before Red Wolf said, "You maybe wanna . . . make your excuses to your mother, so we can go get this guy out of my car? Please?"

George's knees felt like sponge as she walked across the grass to her mother's booth, her smile as if cut out of a magazine and pasted on. Carlene's gaze slid past her, toward where Dennis Red Wolf waited, and back questioningly.

"Hey, Amy," George said brightly, "how would you like to spend the night over at Holly's house?"

Holly looked as surprised as Amy. "Really?"

"Your dad said it was okay with him, if that's okay with you."

The two girls exchanged a quick, uncertain look. "But Mom," Amy said, obviously trying not to sound disappointed, "Sophie's mom already invited me."

"I'm sorry, honey, but Sophie's mom has something she needs taking care of instead." She watched her mother's radar emerge, as visible as antennae quivering. "And you've never been to Holly's before, it'd be a nice change, wouldn't it?"

"Hey, it's okay with me," Holly said. "We can kick my brothers out of their room and make them sleep on the sofa. And you can come check out what my new bedroom is gonna look like."

"Yeah?" Amy still sounded uncertain.

"Yeah, it'll be cool. My mom got me all these sample books with fabrics and paints and stuff? You can help me pick out curtains and carpets. It'll be like that show on Fox Five, y'know? *Designer Divas?* You be Erika and I can be Nikki."

Amy's indecision slowly melted. "Okay. Cool," she said, although not too enthusiastically, reluctant to betray her loyalty to Sophie. But while Holly outlined her vision of a "muriel" painted on the wall over her new bed, George drew her mother discreetly to one side.

"What's going on?" Carlene asked.

"I'm going to take Ben back now."

"Damn. Trouble?"

George shrugged, unwilling to go into details. "He's a hard man to take out in public."

Carlene tsked, wincing. In the week before the fair opened, Jack Bakker had been determined Trinity would help out in erecting the outdoor stage, ignoring both Trinity's ineffectual attempt to beg off and the silent stares of other volunteers when they had arrived the first morning.

"You're a part of this community now, whether folks like it or not," Jack had said firmly. "And it's time they got used to the idea you ain't going away, neither."

So Trinity had kept his head down and his mouth shut, did whatever job he was allocated, kept himself on the periphery without seeming to turn his back on the rest, ate his packed lunches in silence, smiled at jokes but made no attempt to join in. Once the public stage had been finished, Jack and Trinity hammered together the booth where Carlene and George would sell homemade jam and home-baked pastries and painted it bright red, hanging red-checked fake curtains at the side posts. By the third day, George had been pleased when the others began to relax around him even if they excluded him from their Happy Hour beer-drinking camaraderie. It all had seemed so encouraging.

*Back to square one*, George thought as she followed Red Wolf across the crowded parking lot, weaving their way through rows of battered pickups and family station wagons, a scattering of new hybrid biodiesel SUVs and classic sports cars with out-of-state license plates here and there. George was shocked when she reached Red Wolf's police cruiser. Trinity was in the back seemingly asleep, but his eyes opened as soon as they'd reached the car. His face was ashen, his expression empty as he stared out the window.

"Ms. Jensen is gonna take you home," Red Wolf said as he opened the back door to let Trinity out. Trinity simply nodded and climbed out gingerly, his movements slow like an old man's.

He said nothing on the way back, until she had reached the crossroads for the café but didn't turn. He watched it pass, then glanced over at her questioningly.

"You don't have a television," was all she said.

He smiled weakly, then shut his eyes, keeping them closed until she had turned down her drive and parked in front of the house. He'd opened the door and got out before she'd had the chance to get around the car, grunting softly in pain with one hand on his side as he stood up. He raised his hand to block her from taking his arm to support him.

"It's a little tender," he said, chiding. "That's all. I'm perfectly capable of walking on my own."

His obstinacy irritated her. "Suit yourself," she said acidly. She walked away without looking back, unlocked the front door and went in, leaving the door open. She pretended not to notice as he shut the door, and followed her into the kitchen.

"I'm gonna have a cup of coffee. You want one?"

"Please."

She busied herself with lighting the gas ring on the old stove, and filled the kettle with water. As it boiled, she took down a couple side plates and placed a couple of chocolate chip cookies—misshapen rejects from her mother's baking marathon—onto each plate and set them on the table without a glance toward him, as if averting her eyes were a kind of rebuke. When the kettle whistled, she made two mugs of instant coffee and placed those beside the plates before she sat down. Only then did she look up at him.

He stood in the doorway of the kitchen, watching her with a faint smile.

"You want one or not?" she said, gesturing to the chair on the other side of the table.

He sat down across from her and took a sip of his coffee, his gaze roaming around the room.

"What?" she demanded.

He shrugged one shoulder. "I like your kitchen."

"You're kidding," she said, surprised. She looked around, trying to see the appeal. The dated splash tiles over the sink were cracked, one missing; the sink still contained unwashed breakfast dishes. The tap dripped, leaving a persistent rusty streak down the side of the basin. Pots of wilted herbs lined the windowsill, leaves drooping on a neglected avocado seedling Amy had insisted on growing from a stone balanced on toothpicks over a Mason jar, the water a slimy green. The window glass was streaked gray with dust, spider webs clinging like tattered lace curtains on the corners outside. The old gas stove had been an antique when her mother was born. The secondhand refrigerator in the corner wheezed and occasionally rattled as chunks of frost fell off the bottom of the freezer, the door covered in fridge magnets pinning Amy's dental appointments, school lunch vouchers, a long-outdated reminder from the vet for Bojangles's rabies booster. The countertops were crowded with an assortment of odd appliances, half of which George never used. The cheap vinyl floor tiles looked grubby, streaked with black scuff marks from Amy's school shoes and tracked with paw prints. Muddy boots lined up by the back door. Two of the four mismatched kitchen chairs served as repositories for old magazines and stacks of newspapers, most of them unread. "The place is falling to bits."

"It's got . . . personality."

After a moment, she snorted. "Yeah, right. Isn't that what people say about ugly girls? 'She's got a great personality'? You calling my kitchen ugly?"

At that, he did smile and started to laugh before his breath hissed and he grimaced, his hand gingerly pressing against his chest.

"You've got blood on that," she said, her irritation relenting as she nodded at the white lab coat. "Get it off and I'll put it through the wash before it sets."

"I don't have another shirt with me."

She took a quick sip of her coffee before pushing back from the table and standing up. "I've got plenty spare," she said. She opened the broom closet, shoved the ironing board to one side to reach a cardboard box on the top shelf, an assortment of men's shirts folded loosely inside. "Take your pick. They're clean," she said, holding out the box. "If you don't mind a few paint splatters." At his uncertainty, she added, "They were my brother's. You're about his size."

He stood and took it from her. "I'll just use your bathroom, if that's okay."

While he was changing, George quickly washed up the dirty breakfast dishes with a sense of embarrassed guilt. She had rinsed the last cup and was putting it in the drainer when she heard the downstairs toilet flush and Trinity came back into the kitchen. She turned, a smile already in place, then felt her breath catch.

"What?" he asked at her expression.

She had bought that shirt for Christmas ages ago for Lonny, faked batik fish on blue cotton softened and a little faded by so many washings. For a moment, the image of her brother wearing that shirt hit her with near physical pain. Then it was gone, and the shirt was just a shirt.

"Nothing. It fits you."

His eyes said he knew there was more to it than that, but he put the box on the table and sat down to finish his coffee, still moving carefully.

"Are you okay? They did give you some pain pills, right?"

"I flushed them."

"What did you do that for?"

"I didn't want them."

George let that statement hang in the air before she shook her head, sighing through her nose. "That boy is in so much trouble," she commented. "Alison Bakker is going to blow her top."

He looked at her evenly. "I didn't see who did it. It happened too fast. Can we change the subject?"

She leaned back in the chair and folded her arms. "Sure. What would you like to talk about? Pick a subject. Any subject." When he didn't answer, she said, "Grizzlies are doing well this season, aren't they?" At his confusion, she said, "Not a football fan, then? Well, how about this spotted knapweed? I don't know which is the bigger headache, the weeds or the Organic Farmer's Association complaining about pesticides being sprayed next to their fields . . . no?"

He had dropped his gaze to his hands clasped around the empty cup, and didn't respond.

"Right," she said tartly. "That's what I thought." She pushed back her chair, legs scraping the floor like fingernails on a blackboard. "You don't mind leftovers, do you? I'll go put this in the washer and start on supper. If you want to watch some television, you know where it is."

She got as far as the kitchen door when he spoke. "Ms. Jensen . . ." When she looked back, he was still staring into the depths of his empty cup. "I'm sorry. I don't want to be here any more than you want me here."

"Oh, Ben," she said, regretfully, "that's not true. Everyone needs a little help now and then . . ."

He looked up, his eyes hard. "Spare me the Hallmark moment."

She felt her face flame, and the anger went out of his expression as quickly as it had come. "Damn you. Why do you make it so hard to let anyone care about you?"

He went back to studying his cup. "Because people who care about me tend to end up getting hurt," he said softly, his voice dispassionate. "And I'm pretty much maxed out on how much guilt I can live with."

After a moment, she said quietly, "I'm going to go put clean sheets on Amy's bed. It'll be more comfortable than the sofa."

# CHAPTER FIFTEEN

Maybe the nightmares surfaced again because he was sleeping in Amy's bedroom, surrounded by all the trappings of childhood, he wondered later. Or maybe it was the grating pain in his side that kept his mind drifting just underneath consciousness with a feverish lucidity. In any case, he was back in his house in Santa Monica, wandering from room to room searching for something unnamed, elusive, everything overly large but still achingly familiar. The glass doors in the conservatory leading out to the pool were open, gossamer curtains stirring on the breeze that carried the heavy scent of eucalyptus and overheated dust and chlorine. The portrait of his grandfather over the fireplace mantle seemed nearly animate, the line blurred between paint and person. The Steinway grand piano gleamed with ebony brilliance, but when he touched the keys, they made no sound. He heard a dog barking with joyous exuberance, and called out.

"Chorizo! Here, boy! Where are you?"

But the dog wouldn't come. He kept searching, opening doors, climbing stairs twisting like an Escher drawing, until he found Antoine's room with an odd sense of relief. But when he entered his son's bedroom, instead of the loft bed shaped like castle battlements he had made himself, instead of shelves crammed with children's books, instead of the carpet nearly obscured by toys scattered everywhere, the room was barren, empty. He heard the clacking sound of someone typing on a keyboard, and looked back over his shoulder.

And he was in the south of France, the light streaming through the window of the little cottage overlooking the sea, pots of wild lavender on the balcony. A dark-haired woman sat at the desk with her back to him, concentrating on lines scrolling down a computer screen.

"Marie-Claude . . . *ç'est toi? Qu'est-ce que tu fais, chérie?*"

She turned around, a cigarette hanging from her heavily lipsticked mouth, and his heart lurched with a sudden jolt of fear.

"You missed your contact deadline," Clarice McGraff said, her whiskey voice husky with distaste. "You are in such deep shit, buddy. You're trying to escape again, aren't you?"

"No, ma'am," he said quickly, and wondered if it was the truth. A mist of sharp ocean brine wafted through the louvered French doors, chilling him to the bone although he could feel sweat trickling down his ribs. McGraff glanced past him, nodding at someone who had walked up behind him. But before he could see who it was, a black bag was shoved over his head, his arms jerked painfully behind him, plastic straps cutting into his wrists.

And he was in the camp, naked, chained and blindfolded, the stifling heat sucking the life out of the air. He was blind, writhing helplessly as steel-toed boots slammed into his ribs, cracking bones, bamboo sticks whipping down onto his body. He smelled cigarette smoke and the harsh odor of burning flesh as pain seared through him like some small, vicious animal gnawing its way into his body. Through distant screams and mosquitoes whining, harsh commands barked out in a language he couldn't understand, ringing in his ears. He heard the chorus of zippers and knew what would happen next, could already smell the urine as heavy boots pinned him down onto the concrete floor and a rough hand clamped over his nose until he had to open his mouth to breathe, only to gag on the stream of hot liquid flooding down his throat, choking him, scalding his skin, pouring over his chest in a torrent that wouldn't stop.

*I'm dreaming,* he suddenly realized. *I can wake up. I can wake up. I can . . .*

He gulped in a huge rasping lungful of air, like a drowning man breaking through the surface from an inky depth. His eyes shot open, the vivid dream popping in the sharp reality, fragile as a soap bubble. He lay curled on his side, still trembling with dread, his clenched fists spasming into the pillow. The tangled sheets were soaking wet. It was only sweat, he knew, his skin clammy. But he could still taste it on the back of his tongue, in his nose, still feel it burning on his face, his skin, the sense of utter contamination indelible.

"Jesus," he exhaled in a shaky whisper into the pillow, "Jesus fucking Christ . . ."

"You okay?"

He started violently, then rolled over.

"Sorry," George said from where she leaned against the doorjamb, arms crossed, her hair in disarray as it fell over the shoulders of a terrycloth bathrobe. "Didn't mean to scare you." She looked tired, the skin under her eyes dark.

"It's nothing," he managed to say, his voice thick. "Just a bad dream."

"I know. Mother's radar. Have a kid, and you end up developing bat ears. I can sleep through anything, except the sound of someone having a nightmare."

He glanced around, the room cast in the pearlescence of early morning light. "What time is it?"

"Going on six thirty."

"Sorry to wake you."

She shrugged. "I get up this time most mornings." She pointed with her chin at him, indicating his injury. "How're you feeling?"

"Sore," he admitted.

"You shouldn't have flushed the pain pills, then, should you?" She observed him for a moment longer, unsmiling, before she turned and left. He heard a door along the hall shut and a moment later listened to water gurgling noisily through pipes as she showered.

He dressed and went downstairs barefoot, filled the kettle, and lit the gas ring on the stove. Outside the window, delicate mare's-tail clouds, burnished gold and pink in the sunrise, speckled across a pale blue sky, moving leisurely east on a high wind. A thick flock of distant starlings, like undulating black specks, rippled just over the treeline, then disappeared altogether. The kettle sang and he switched off the gas. Bojangles thumped down the stairs and ran into the kitchen, slithering around his ankles in entreaty.

"Sorry there, cat. No idea where they keep your food."

"On top of the frig by the Cheerios," George said as she walked into the kitchen. She had her hair wrapped in a towel, and wore a pair of faded jeans and a gray Montana U sweatshirt. She took down both the box of Cheerios and dry cat food and three bowls from the cupboard. He made the instant coffee while she poured milk over the cereal and put the cat's bowl on the floor.

They ate in silence, Bojangles crunching happily through fish-shaped tidbits.

"I didn't know you could speak French," she said when she'd finished her cereal. Obviously, he'd been talking in his sleep as well. He didn't respond, chasing the last of the garish yellow O's floating in the milk with his spoon. "Who's Marie?"

"My wife. Marie-Claude."

"You told me you weren't married."

He took a long drink of his coffee before he spoke. "I don't know if I am or not."

"You don't know if you're divorced or not?"

"I'm not sure I was ever legally married." At her confusion, he added, "Marie-Claude may not even be her real name. And there's some question she might have already been married to someone else." He wasn't sure she was even still alive, he didn't want to add.

"Did you know that when you married her?"

"No."

George snorted a laugh. "Must have come as a shock when you found out."

"At the time," he said, deadpan, "it was the least of my worries." The cat had finished its breakfast, back to winding itself around Trinity's legs. He winced against the pain as he leaned over and scooped the cat up onto his lap. "How long have you been divorced?" he said, more to shift the attention away from himself.

George got up to pour two glasses of orange juice, and put a bottle of Excedrin next him. "Two years October," she said. "He walked out, withdrew every cent from our joint account, and took both cars, all the furniture, the stereo, the television, the DVD player, the computer, the washer, the dryer, the refrigerator, the dishwasher, the microwave, the lawn mower, and anything else that wasn't bolted down. I got to keep the house, which was generous of him, considering it was mine to begin with."

"Not bitter, are you?" Trinity said with mild amusement.

"They're just things," she said, returning his smile. "You know how that one goes. Besides, I got Amy. As long as I have her, nothing else matters."

He looked away, the sudden ache in his chest crushing. To hide it, he busied himself opening the Excedrin bottle and shaking out a couple of tablets. It was easy enough to palm the pills, pretending to swallow them with a sip of orange juice. The next time she looked away, he shoved them into the pocket of his jeans.

"How long have you lived here, then?" he asked.

"Most of my life. My grandfather built this house. He'd joined the Army and fought in Korea, came home missing a leg, and married his high-school sweetheart. His father helped him build this house as a wedding present. There used to be a little farm here; my great-grandparents lived a couple miles back along the coulee, in the prettiest part of the valley. They mostly raised beef cattle, but small ranchers just couldn't survive competition with big business. After his parents died, my grandfather sold their house to the Bakkers along with most of the land, like a lot of people around this area. The Bakkers tore that house one down and built their own where it used to be. Justin Bakker owns over fifty thousand acres, mostly agricultural land. He grows GM canola and soy beans for the government's biodeisel program now, less work, more money. Jack's the only one in the family still raising cattle, even if it's fancy purebred Black Angus."

She swallowed the last of her orange juice and laced her fingers around the empty glass.

"My grandfather kept this house and a hundred acres, mostly woodland, and my mother and her sister were both born here, upstairs in my bedroom. Aunt Rosie was fourteen years older than her sister. Ma was sort of a last hurrah surprise. Rosie got married when Ma was only eight and moved away to West Virginia. I've got a few cousins, but I never see them much. They've got kids, a couple of their kids have kids, and we all exchange Christmas cards every year, y'know, the kind with the generic Xeroxed newsletter keeping everybody updated on extended relations nobody can ever keep straight anyway. Don't let him eat off the table."

Bojangles had become overly interested in whatever goodies were still on the table, so Trinity set him back on the floor. The cat meowed a plaintive protest before an itch at the base of his tail suddenly required urgent attention.

"Anyway, Ma met my dad when she started working at the Grinnin' Bear Café. He owned the café, they fell in love and got married, big fairy-tale wedding, the works. They'd been married about four or five years when my grandfather died. Grandma decided to retire in Arizona; Montana winters were too hard on her. So she sold the house to my parents and bought herself a little bungalow next to a golf course. She remarried some retired golf pro when she was in her eighties and they're still out there, playing golf every day. The year my parents moved in, I was born in the same room as Ma and Rosie. Then my brother almost exactly ten months after that. We grew up in this house, never lived anywhere else. I left home when I was eighteen, big girl wanting to make my own way in the wide world. Lonny was supposed to get the house and the café. He was the boy, that was always understood."

She took the damp towel off her head, draping it over her shoulders, and raked her fingers through her wet, uncombed hair. He could smell the clean fragrance of shampoo, something herbal and fruity.

"I met Lucas when I moved down to Billings as a college freshman. I was a biology student, he was a campus security cop. I was young, he was cute, I got pregnant, we got married. So that was the end of college. Sheriff Holbrook was a friend of my dad's, Luke was offered a job so we could move back closer to home. Amy was the first one in three generations to be born in a hospital. Dad was almost twenty years older than Ma, and smoked like a damned chimney. He died of a stroke when Amy was two. Lonny joined the National Guard when he was eighteen, to make a little extra money, but mostly just as a way to get away from here for a few weeks out of the year. He never expected he'd ever fight in a war. He was only supposed to go to Iraq for six months, but they kept him there over three years under the 'stop loss' program. Ma was having to send food packages because he only got two meals a day, always hungry. Anyway, about a month before Lonny was finally supposed to come home, his unit was ambushed just outside of al-Mahmudiya. Nobody had had a break in six weeks; they were tired, eating speed because they were pulling twenty-hour patrols every day. Nobody had on the right body armor because there was a shortage. They'd reinforced their Humvee with scrap metal; might as well have been cardboard. They tried to call for backup, but their radios didn't work, out of range or something. My brother had bitched about it in his letters home, but nobody in the military ever paid much attention." She shrugged. "They told him you go to war with the army you got; even if that means sticks and stones, I guess. They were all killed."

George had recited this litany in a near monotone, no emotion behind any of the words. She placed her empty bowl with a half-inch of milk still in it on the floor for the cat. Bojangles lapped it up eagerly while purring nonstop.

"Lucas and I were living in an apartment in Havre, but the commute was too long, and Ma decided it would be easier if she moved into the café and let Lucas and me live here after Lonny died. Luke offered to buy the house off her, but Ma was smart; we lived here rent-free but she kept the title in her name. So when Luke left, he wasn't able take half the house away from me. I bought it from her the day after my divorce was final, for a dollar, which was about a dollar more than I could really afford. I'm praying that we find a way to get Amy through college so she can get a good job and move as far away from Redemption as she can get and never look back. So there you go, my entire family history in a nutshell." She crossed her arms in front of her and cocked her head at him. "Your turn."

"It's not a quid pro quo," he said.

She smiled cynically. "I didn't get far enough in college to know what the hell that means. Give me the *Reader's Digest* version. C'mon, Richie Rich, I already know you're a bigamist."

"Ah, no," he corrected. "My wife was the bigamist. I'm just a terrorist."

That at least got an honest laugh, the tension lessening. Oh well, he thought. If Ted Eastlake wasn't going to play by the rules, why should he bother?

"Okay, let's see. My grandfather was a plastic surgeon in Los Angeles. His father had been an old-fashioned family doctor in Louisiana, made his first fortune on medical instrument patents, then started up the Triad Medical Supply Company. Every hospital in the country still uses them. That's where the money all came from. Sent his eldest son to California back in the days when plastic surgery wasn't so trendy and people like John Wayne and Tony Curtis and Elizabeth Taylor had to sneak in back doors for facelifts and tummy tucks."

Trinity grinned fleetingly at the memory. "Grandfather used to say the secret to his success was the louder he denied doing anything, the more celebrities would flock to his clinic. Anyway, my father was still in medical school when he was killed in a car accident. I never knew him; my mother was still pregnant with me. My grandfather's only brother . . ."

"Anna something . . ."

"Anastasius Celestine, that's the one. He was a devout Catholic who turned out to be gay, so the family decided it would be best if he became a priest. It was just what you did in those days."

"What about your mother's family?"

"She was *Québécoise*," he said, pronouncing it the way his mother had. At George's incomprehension, he added, "French-Canadian. She went back to Quebec after my father died. I was born in Canada, spoke French before I learned English. Anyway, they were Calvinist Protestants and unhappy she had married a Catholic. Not that anyone in my father's family other than Great-uncle Stacy had seen the inside of a church in decades. I think the last time I ever went to Mass was my confirmation. Eight years old in a white suit with a pink cummerbund and a pink buttonhole carnation while my gay great-uncle stood there in front of God and everyone in his frilly dress and told me I looked like a sweet little ice cream cone. Absolutely mortifying. Put me off religion for life."

She laughed with him, both of them relaxed. He hadn't felt quite this comfortable with anyone in years, the pleasure almost narcotic. She got up to reheat the water in the kettle.

"My mother wasn't happy in Quebec, and I was my grandfather's only heir. He offered to send her through medical school so she could become the plastic surgeon my father was supposed to have been and carry on the family tradition, on the condition that she and I would come back to California. I was about four or five when we moved in with my grandfather, that big mansion in Santa Monica with all the servants." George rolled her eyes at him. "My mother's family never spoke to her again after that. So no cousins. No brothers, no sisters. Just my grandfather, my mother, and me. Mostly just me and the nanny a lot of the time, to be honest."

"Must have been lonely for you."

He shrugged. "A little. But kids consider whatever they grow up with as being normal, it's all they know. I never missed what I never had."

"So why didn't you become a doctor?"

"Medicine didn't appeal to me, especially not plastic surgery. I did a couple years of premed out of a sense of duty, didn't enjoy any of it. Then I took an elective English course with a brilliant professor who got me hooked on the history of language, the written word, novels and poetry. It was the first time anything had fired my imagination like that. Beowulf, Chaucer, Shakespeare, Bacon, Marlowe. Voltaire, Victor Hugo, Jean de la Fontaine, I loved it all. I dropped out of medical school and decided to become a teacher. Which was *not* what my grandfather wanted to hear. I was supposed to follow in the footsteps, but my mother was doing a far better job of running the company than I ever could, I didn't see the point. We had some pretty intense arguments. At one point, he cut me off without a dime."

She paused from pouring boiling water over instant coffee. "You're kidding? So what happened?"

"Richie Rich told him to stuff his money and got a job with a college buddy whose father ran a construction company in East L.A. Ramon and I lived in a run-down squat with hot and cold running cockroaches and slept on army cots in sleeping bags. We cooked refried beans and tortillas on a butane camp stove and drank cheap beer and smoked truly awful weed. Ramon and his father Esteban taught me how to build houses and renovate apartment blocks for low-income Hispanic families, and in the evenings I taught English as a second language to immigrant Mexican kids and sometimes their parents. I was mugged three times before the local gang members decided the idiot white boy needed bodyguards. Then rather than just getting mugged, we got shot at instead. Scared the shit out of me, but it was the most fun I ever had."

"And that's where you learned to do plumbing."

"Yes, ma'am. Grandfather finally relented, and sent me back to Stanford, although I still spent every summer building houses with Ramon. Then after I'd earned my Ph.D., I got a job teaching at Pepperdine. Six years later, I was one of the youngest professors ever to get tenure."

"Is that where you met Marie-Claude? Was she a student?"

Suddenly, the enjoyment of the moment dimmed, like a cloud passing across the sun. He held up his tattooed palm toward her.

"That's off-limits."

She smiled ruefully, and stood up to collect the dirty breakfast dishes. "Fair enough."

He rested his chin on his hands, the unshaven stubble on his cheeks rough under his fingers, and studied her back as she washed the dishes. She stacked the bowls and glasses into a drainer already full of dishes. Finally, he said, "She wasn't a student. I met her at an antiwar protest."

George leaned back against the sink, drying her hands on the towel still draped on her shoulders. "Are you allowed to be telling me this?"

"Probably not. Should I stop?" When she didn't answer, he said, "I was a privileged rich boy who helped build houses for poor Chicanos in East L.A. so that people would think of me as a good person. But the truth is, I just enjoyed building houses. Rich people, poor people, I didn't care who lived in them. I gave money to charity because that's what you do when you're rich, that's the burden of noblesse oblige." If George heard the sarcasm in his tone, she didn't react. "My mother and my grandfather spent their working lives trying to make the beautiful people perfect. Once in a while, they'd do pro bono surgery on orphans from some third world country who'd been maimed by war, get their picture in the paper with the kids. Good publicity for the clinic."

He could feel his anger churning within, like a dormant snake roused in his head. It made him feel reckless rather than afraid.

"It was never about having a conscience, any more than why I built houses. They would both still vote for the same bastards who dropped bombs on these kids in the first place, the kind of right-wing mentality that thinks the way to defuse a landmine is to hit it with a sledgehammer. So while your brother was busy dying in Iraq, my family was making money off the bloodshed and I was safe and sound teaching poetry written by dead white men to snotty rich students who mostly didn't give a shit, either."

"Okay, that's enough," George said suddenly. "I don't want to hear any more."

"I'm sorry about your brother." His voice came out harsh, unapologetic.

"I don't care if you're sorry or not. Just shut up."

"You wanted to know," he pressed ruthlessly.

"You're going to get yourself into trouble . . ."

He laughed without humor. "What can they do to me, put me back in jail?"

"*Yes!*" George looked as if she were about to burst into tears. "So stop, okay? Just stop now."

He lowered his head, staring down at hands laced together so tightly his knuckles were bloodless. "Too late. You opened the door."

George tossed the damp towel onto the back of her chair, shaking her head. "I'm not listening to any more of this," she said and walked out of the kitchen.

He pushed back his chair forcefully enough to make himself inhale sharply against the shooting pain in his side, and stalked after her into the living room. "I got dragged to an antiwar demonstration by one of those snotty rich students," he said heatedly to George's back, following her. "I didn't even want to go. I thought it pointless; the government was going to do whatever it damned well wanted no matter how loud a bunch of scruffy dope-smoking dropouts in tie-dye shirts and dreadlocks chanted their silly slogans. I had nothing in common with those people, they made me uncomfortable.

"Then I met Marie-Claude, this elegant French émigré whose entire family had been massacred in Iran by the Ayatollah's fanatics. You should have seen her, so dignified and fragile, surrounded by photographs of Iraqi civilians killed in the war, those tens of thousands of anonymous people you never saw on television—old men blown up in cars, women cut in half, babies with their skulls split apart . . ."

George covered her ears with her hands, still walking away from him. Cornered, she tried to brush past him to escape. "I don't want to hear any more!"

Trinity grabbed her arm and yanked her back, shoving

her against a wall so hard picture frames rattled. "Too bad," he said ruthlessly. His heart pounded in his ears, as if he was running, making him lightheaded. "I want you to know about her, the other side of her no one else will ever tell you about. If she was a terrorist, then she was the most talented actress on God's earth. She was the bravest, most beautiful, most passionate woman I'd ever seen. Everyone she'd loved had been murdered, the Iranians hated the Iraqis and *still* she was there campaigning for peace. You know what happened? People *spit* on her."

His face was close enough to George's that his breath made her turn away, her eyes squeezed shut. His hands gripped her wrists so tightly he could feel the bones, her body trembling against his.

"They knocked down her posters and stomped on the pictures of dead children," he said, his voice a hoarse whisper. "They shoved her around while the police watched and did nothing. They called her a traitor and a bitch and a liar and a whore and told her that Jesus would send her to hell along with the rest of her kind."

George's chin trembled, and he watched a single tear tumble down her cheek. He blinked, as if coming out of a trance. His hands loosened, but she made no effort to pull away. When he released her, she opened her eyes, watching him warily, lips compressed into a thin angry line, her face blotchy with fear. Gently, he brushed the wetness from her face with the backs of his fingers.

"They made her cry," he said softly, ashamed, his own anger exhausted, a dry husk blown away in the wind. "While I stood there and did nothing. Except fall in love with her."

Her expression softened and her mouth parted as if she wanted to say something but couldn't find the words. Although he still leaned over her, her back pressed to the wall, he suddenly felt powerless, unable even to move away.

She traced her fingertips carefully along his jaw, her touch making his skin dance with electricity. His breath caught in his throat as he lowered his face into her cupped palm and closed his eyes, like a man praying, the storm in his chest breaking on the detritus of his past, its power already spent. She slipped her hand around his neck to pull him toward her, and kissed him, her mouth tasting of coffee and hot milk and tears.

[illegible faded text from previous page]

# CHAPTER SIXTEEN

Red Wolf was going through Monday morning's logs and catching up on the usual routine paperwork he started off every working day with, when Jensen slammed through the rear door of the office like he was on a vice bust. He slammed his fist down on the desk and leaned over it, his face bloated and red with fury.

"Just what the fuck is that asshole saying about me!" he demanded, close enough for Red Wolf to feel the heat of his breath brush his skin.

"Luke," Red Wolf said softly, his words calmer than he felt, "you got about two seconds to back on out of my face."

Jensen's breath whistled through his nose, distending his nostrils like a winded horse. His entire body quivered in the effort to restrain his anger before he pushed away from the desk and stepped back. "What did he say to you?" he insisted, every word spaced. "I want to know *exactly* what that lying piece of shit says I did."

"I assume you're referring to Ben Trinity." Red Wolf leaned back in his chair, wood creaking under his weight in protest, and laced his fingers together across his chest. "Ben Trinity didn't say one damned thing about you."

"Then why am I hearing bullshit rumors about how I tortured him while he was in custody?"

Red Wolf smiled lazily. "Gee, Lucas, damned if I know."

"I never laid a finger on him," Jensen snarled. When Red Wolf raised an eyebrow, he said, "You know what I mean. One little nosebleed and suddenly we're running Abu Ghraib here?"

Red Wolf regarded him speculatively. "Y'know, you oughta think about taking up meditation or yoga or something. This can't be good for your blood pressure."

"Fuck you."

Red Wolf shrugged and went back to the paperwork on his desk. "Whatever."

As Jensen stood in the middle of the tiny office, shoulders hunched and head lowered like a bull looking for a target, Red Wolf got up, crossed to the filing cabinet to rifle through the files.

"You remind me of a dog I used to know," Red Wolf remarked. Although he had his concentration focused on the files in front of him, he was acutely aware of the man standing barely an arm's length away. "One of those skinny African plains dogs, call 'em basenjis, I think. They're weird little dogs, like they're built outta coat hangers and springs. They're not supposed to able to bark, either, but they do make this god-awful yodeling noise, worse than a coyote in heat."

He pulled out the file he was looking for, shut the cabinet drawer, and sat back down. Jensen hadn't moved, but at least he was listening.

"Anyway, this neighbor lady bought herself one—pretty expensive dog, too—but it kept getting out of her yard and killing chickens belonged to a man down the road. He complained, so I helped her put up an electric fence to try to keep the dog from getting out the backyard.

"We turned it on, the dog goes over for a sniff and gets his nose zapped. Bowls him over like a hedgehog. Dog gets up, growling, mad as hell, runs back, and bites the fence. Gets another jolt of electricity sends him ass over teakettle." He chuckled at the memory. "Damned dog gets back up, teeth bared, hair standing up, runs back over, and bites the fence. No matter how many times he gets zapped, he just gets up and goes back for more. We finally had to turn the fence off before he electrocuted himself."

"I'm sure you got a moral to this story, Aesop. I'm persistent, so what? That's what makes me good at my job."

"You think?" Red Wolf scratched behind one ear serenely. "Couple days after we turned the fence off, dog gets out and goes after the chickens again. This time, guy down the road got out his twelve-gauge and shot that dog full of double-aught, put an abrupt end to his yodel-ay-hee-hooin' days."

"And what's that supposed to mean?"

"Means any sensible dog learns not to bite electric fences. You keep this up, and somebody's gonna hand you your ass."

"You know what?" Jensen snapped. "You can take that inscrutable Indian crap and shove it."

Red Wolf shook his head, and turned his attention back to the file on his desk. But as Jensen started toward the door, Red Wolf added without looking up, "You go anywhere near the man in the next forty-eight hours, Luke, and I'll lock you up."

"Bullshit."

"Try me."

As they locked eyes, Red Wolf was certain Luke Jensen was going to have a heart attack, the man's face so livid he was purple. But instead, Jensen whirled around and barged out the front office door, nearly knocking over Jack and Craig Bakker as they came up the step. A moment later, they heard the sound of Jensen's car door slam, the engine roar and tires screaming against the tarmac as he drove away.

"Everything okay here?" Jack Bakker asked as Red Wolf stood.

"Yeah, no problem." He nodded at Craig. "Been looking for you, son. Where you been?"

The boy shrugged morosely with his hands shoved deep into his pockets, head down to stare at his feet, rubbing the toe of one shoe against a crack in the floor tiles. Jack popped the flat of his hand against the back of the boy's head.

"Answer the man."

"Nowhere." Jack smacked him again. *"Ow."* Craig shot his uncle a poisonous look before he resumed scuffing his shoes.

"Uh-huh." Red Wolf motioned Jack toward a chair beside his desk and dragged another over for the boy. "Why don't you have a seat and tell me what happened at the fair."

"Nuthin'," the boy mumbled sullenly. He sat down and began fiddling with a collection of paper clips Red Wolf kept in a handleless coffee mug. "I didn't do nuthin', can't prove I did."

"We got witnesses saw you do it. You're busted, Craig, okay? So don't waste my time here."

Craig squirmed on the chair. "It was an accident."

Red Wolf raised his eyebrows. " 'An accident'?"

"I wasn't trying to hurt him. We were just messin' around." He looked up, his eyes reddened with barely repressed fear and anger. "All I wanted was to scare him a little, y'know?"

"You cut the man with a hunting knife, took fourteen stitches to get him closed. I think that kinda rules it out as an accident, Craig. What did Ben Trinity ever do to you to make you want to hurt him so bad?"

"Nuthin'." The boy fidgeted uneasily, his attention still focused on the paper clips. "But nobody wants him 'round here anyway, so like what's the big deal?"

"The big deal is you used a weapon during the commission of a crime. That's a felony all by itself, not to mention assault and battery, maybe even attempted murder. If he presses charges, you could be looking at a heap of trouble."

Craig looked astonished. "No way. He can't do that, can he?"

"Yeah, believe it or not, he could. Whatever Ben Trinity has done in the past don't give you the right to stick a knife in him. And your friends Rog and Jamie and Dickie Allen and that other one, Collie, they can all be charged as accessories."

"But my dad . . . ," Craig started stubbornly, cut off by another smack to the back of the head. "*Ow*."

"Don't you dare play that card," his uncle warned him, "or I'll drive you down to the jailhouse myself, you got that, boy? Stand up and take responsibility for what you done like a man."

Now the boy looked genuinely worried, his lower lip trembling, but still he said nothing.

"Did Ben Trinity say or do something to you at the fair to piss you off? Did he threaten you?" Red Wolf pressed him.

"No."

"You just walked up to him out of the blue and stabbed him for no particular reason? You gotta give me something better than that."

The surly obstinate teenager was back, still toying idly with the paper clips. Craig shrugged, eyes averted. "Dunno. To get even, I guess."

"For what? The Amtrak train bombing in California?"

Craig glanced sidelong at him, brow furrowed in skeptical confusion. "No. It's just that . . ." He heaved a forlorn sigh and abandoned his paper-clip fixation. "I got sick and tired of listening to Amy going on about him all the time." His voice shifted to a mean contralto in imitation. " 'Ben did this' and 'Ben said that,' like he's some sort of fucking movie star or something."

"Language," Jack warned.

"Sorry," Craig muttered. "I just thought . . . y'know, if I stood up to a terrorist and showed Amy what a wuss he is, maybe she'd like, sorta . . . I don't know . . ." His voice trailed off, his objectives ambiguous.

Inwardly, Red Wolf sighed. A girl. Ben Trinity nearly got his ticket punched over some kid trying to impress a girl.

National security and international politics meant nothing to a fifteen-year-old boy suffering from unrequited lust egged on by his equally dimwitted buddies, insecurity shored up by bigotry and beer, taking out his adolescent angst on a man who couldn't afford to fight back. How pathetic.

Just another ordinary day in Redemption.

He sent Craig home with his uncle, advising the boy to think hard about proffering an apology, without revealing Trinity was very unlikely to file any complaint. Then he stepped outside to smoke the first of the only four cigarettes he allowed himself to smoke in a day, surveying the little morning traffic along Main Street as he deliberated.

The harder Ben Trinity tried to blend into the woodwork and become invisible, the more discord he stirred up. Whatever tenuous merit the man's conspiracy theories had, his simple presence was enough to provoke trouble all by itself. He didn't want to see the man become a target for anyone with a grudge to settle or points to score, or just out of simple-minded vengeance. They'd all been lucky. Next time, instead of a vindictive kid with a knife it could be a vindictive kid with a gun, with more victims than just Trinity ending up dead.

And this just wasn't going to go away on its own, Red Wolf knew. Unwilling as Red Wolf was to see anyone, even Trinity, turned into a scapegoat, the man would have to go. For his own safety as much as for keeping the peace in Redemption.

Doing the right thing just seemed to get harder and harder every damned day.

He exhaled the smoke, dropped the cigarette with barely half an inch burned away, crushed it under his shoe before he went back inside, and picked up the phone.

# CHAPTER SEVENTEEN

"Buying you new shoes and schoolbooks should be top of the agenda, Amy," George said firmly. She glanced in the rearview mirror at her daughter in the backseat of the car. "You need to think about notebooks, paper, pens, all the rest of that boring stuff first. After lunch, we'll drop Ben off at the courthouse, and if there's still time after his appointment, *then* we'll worry about getting this . . . what is it again?"

In the passenger seat, Trinity gazed out the window, preoccupied with his own worries. This might be the last lunch in relative freedom he would have in a while, he didn't want to say, his mood bleak. There was every good chance he might not return from his meeting with the DSD parole officer, not after he'd confessed his latest indiscretions.

"It's a Splat-O-Meter," Amy said. She unclipped her seat belt to lean over the back of the driver's seat, holding out a well-crumpled photocopy, a list of required Back-to-School supplies St. Mary Magdalene had mailed out to parents the week before classes resumed. "You put it over your license plate, see? And each week you count the number of bugs that get splatted on the grid. Then every school in the science project enters their data into the Web site to calculate how many bugs there are in different places in Montana for the birds to eat."

"Uh-huh," George said, her eyes on the road. "Now sit back and put your seat belt on, sweetie."

"But, Mom," Amy protested, "you didn't even look at it."

Trinity roused himself enough to turn, reaching toward the paper. "I'll have a look, if you want."

Amy snatched the paper out of his reach and flung herself back into her seat, her arms crossed rebelliously. "Don't bother," she snapped. She sulked silently, then heaved several petulant sighs when the conciliatory response she obviously had been hoping for didn't occur. "Dad would get it for me," she muttered darkly.

"Seat belt, Amy," George reminded her mildly, not rising to the bait.

"Duh. I'm not a baby," Amy retorted, making a production of redoing her seat belt.

George exhaled tiredly. "Looks like it's going to be one of those days," she said quietly to Trinity with an apologetic glance.

He smiled at her wanly. "I hope not."

She put her hand over his knee reassuringly. When she didn't remove it after a few moments, he covered it with his own, just long enough to acknowledge its presence. When he slid his hand from hers, she put hers back on the steering wheel as casually as if it hadn't happened, leaving a lingering warmth on his thigh.

Amy had sensed the change in the rapport between her mother and Trinity in the few days since the fair, her jealousy confused and resentful. She and Sophie had had a furious quarrel over a trivial matter after Craig's attack on Trinity, the two girls now declaring themselves mortal enemies for all eternity times infinity. Alison Bakker, already suffering the humiliation and scandal of her husband running off to Missoula with his lover, had completely shut herself off from the outside world after her son's debacle, leaving her brother-in-law Jack to handle the fallout.

Barely two days after the fair, Jack had dragged the boy

into the café in the middle of serving breakfast customers, to Trinity's dismay, for Craig to proffer a shamefaced public apology without once meeting his eyes. The dining room had only been half full, most of them locals watching in startled silence. Trinity had hastily interrupted Craig's nearly incoherent stuttering with, "I'm not pressing any charges. Just forget it ever happened."

Craig glared at the floor until a nudge from his uncle prompted him to reluctantly extend his hand. Trinity immediately shook it, anything to end this, Craig's clammy palm limp. As soon as Trinity's grip relaxed, Craig pulled away as if scalded.

"Thanks," Jack Bakker had said gruffly. "We owe you one."

"No," Trinity said quickly. "You don't."

He watched them leave before turning back to find Tom Mifflin gaping up at him open-mouthed. "I'm sorry," Trinity said, his throat dry. But it wasn't fear causing the pencil he held over the order pad to shake so badly he could barely write. "Was that steak or ham you wanted?"

Tom blinked with owlish uncertainty. "Uh . . . ham."

When Trinity returned to set Tom's ham and eggs on the table, Tom said softly without looking at him, "Whenever you need a ride into Havre, you let me know."

For a moment, Trinity couldn't speak, swallowing hard. "Yes, sir, I will."

And as rapidly as word of his identity had once spread throughout Redemption, the attitude toward him shifted just as mercurially. There were many whose hatred would never relent; those customers who didn't boycott Carlene's café in favor of driving miles out of their way for Town Pump coffee and vending machine sandwiches still ignored him with stony hostility. But a few, like Will Paterson and Jared Ingersoll, thawed enough to be polite if distant. The next Sunday, the Spaight sisters shyly presented him with another of their ugly pullovers. The colors changed drastically a good six inches from the bottom, unmistakable evidence of the interlude between his downfall and return to provisional grace.

Despite the last of the summer heat, he'd decided to wear it when George and Amy picked him up to take him to Great Falls. If his parole was to be revoked, this was one of the few good things he wanted to hang on to for as long as he was able.

Amy's mood lifted after an hour of retail therapy, to George's obvious relief. St. Mary Magdalene's European-style uniform code specified generic black trousers or skirts, white cotton shirts, and sensible black shoes bought anywhere parents chose. The compulsory ties, jackets, and sweatshirts with the school's embroidered logo, however, the school sold themselves, at an outrageous profit. Since there was little variety to select from, Amy's shoes, skirt, trousers and blouses were tried on for size and bought within minutes. It was the after-school ensembles that entailed exhaustive debate between mother and daughter, requiring much more deliberation and time.

"You could use some new clothes, too, Ben," George remarked, testing the corduroy fabric of a pair of men's trousers between her fingers.

"I have enough, thanks," he said.

"Besides, Ben prefers the thrift store," Amy sneered. "It's more his style."

"Amy!" George admonished. "What on earth has gotten into you?"

Amy shot a bad-tempered look between them, eyes narrowed. "Well, it's true," she grumbled under her breath at him the moment her mother had shaken her head with annoyance and turned away.

Trinity leaned toward her conspiratorially, and whispered back, "You're right. Thanks. I hate corduroy."

That wasn't what Amy had expected, her brow creased with bewilderment. But her antagonism lessened noticeably after that, even granting him the occasional fleeting smile before she would remember her pique.

By lunchtime, Trinity had been ambling a few steps behind George and Amy, one hand tucked in his jeans pocket, the other laden with shopping bags while Amy chattered away at top speed to her mother in a not quite subtle enough attempt to persuade George into parting with the better part of sixty dollars for a blouse that—in Trinity's judgment—looked like it could have been made for a fraction of the cost by stapling a few gingham handkerchiefs together with rhinestones. Distracted by her daughter's blitz campaign, neither of them noticed when Trinity slowed, alert, or the dark-suited men striding purposely toward them, mirrored sunglasses and short haircuts as obvious as military uniforms.

Trinity twisted to look over his shoulder, spotting another pair of identical dark-suited men. One of them casually brushed open his suit coat to momentarily expose the gold badge clipped to his belt just as a dark plain Ford pulled to the curb beside him. Trinity stopped to cautiously place the bags on the sidewalk, and pulled his other hand free of his pocket. He held his hands out, down and away from his body, empty palms facing forward. One of the dark-suited men smiled at him, nodding in approval while his partner neatly separated him from George and Amy.

"Excuse me, ma'am?" Trinity heard him say to George, who belatedly realized something was wrong. "Would you mind coming with me for a moment?"

"Step over to the curb," the man said to Trinity, "and put your hands on the car."

Trinity offered no resistance as he walked to the side of the car and placed his hands on the roof.

"What's going on?" George demanded.

"Sorry to bother you, ma'am, but could I see some identification, please?" his partner asked George.

The man efficiently, but impersonally pushed Trinity against the car, arms splayed across the roof, the metal hot against his face. Holding Trinity in place with one hand pressed on his back, the man expertly kicked Trinity's legs apart to frisk him.

"Hey!" he heard Amy protest.

"Miss, please don't interfere."

"But we haven't done anything," George said.

His partner's voice changed slightly, the tone still pleasant but colder. "I'm going to ask you one more time, ma'am. You are required to produce proof of identification on demand by a federal officer at all times. I need to see your driver's license, now."

"You can't do this," Amy said, her voice cracking with anger and alarm. "Leave him alone!"

"Amy, don't worry about me. You just do what they say," Trinity said, trying to sound reassuring, knowing he was risking retribution.

"But, Ben . . ."

He twisted as far as he could against the man's grasp to glare at her. *"Do it, Amy!"* He was instantly slammed hard against the car, knocking his breath from him.

"We're going to have to ask you to come with us," the man pinning him down said politely. It wasn't a request. Although Trinity made no attempt to resist, the man kept his hold on him as he opened the back passenger door.

He placed his hand on top of Trinity's head as Trinity got into the backseat. It had always looked like a courtesy when he'd seen it on the news or in a movie, a polite gesture to keep a prisoner from banging his head against the car. Experience had taught him there was nothing considerate about it. The hand on his head pressed down hard, forcing him into the car, a way to control his movement.

He smiled with a confidence he didn't feel and, before the door shut, mouthed *I'm okay* to Amy and George still standing with one of the dark-suited men waiting for

George to fumble her ID out of her purse while his colleague probed the contents of the bags Trinity had dropped onto the sidewalk. In that fraction of a moment, George stared back in distress while Amy scowled, red-faced in anger—with him or with the men in the dark suits, Trinity couldn't tell. Then they were gone.

From the outside, the car looked unexceptional, only the smoked glass windows a little unusual. It obscured a more ominous interior, thick Plexiglas barrier between the front seats and the back. In the back, the controls for the door had been removed, no way to open the doors or wind down the windows from the inside.

Trinity said nothing as the car rolled with near-silent smoothness along the road, watching buildings pass by, other drivers beside them oblivious to his existence. He had thought they would go directly toward the city courthouse. His heart felt hollow as they turned right off Central instead. They crossed the river at Fifteenth onto the Old Havre Highway, the 87 North, the familiar road heading back toward Redemption. Buildings and houses quickly fell away behind them. Once outside the city limits, the two men in the front relaxed, the passenger stretching languidly, cracking his knuckles over his head. "You seen that new Kevin Spacey movie?" he asked the driver, offhanded.

"Wife won't let me go. We're still in the kiddie stage, can't see anything not suitable for anyone under eight. Any good?"

Trinity watched the passenger's shoulders lift slightly in a shrug. "It's all right, I guess. We're the bad guys again, of course."

"Yeah, right. Like Hollywood would know sweet FA about the FBI. Anyway, you say 'FBI' these days, freakin' morons still think Mulder and Scully, not J. Edgar."

"Hey, watch it. *X-Files* weren't that bad."

"You're jokin'. What, you were some sort of teenage nerd into aliens and all that spooky sci-fi shit?"

"Nah. I just used to watch it for the chick. Y'gotta admit, Scully was definitely a walking wet dream."

"You do know she's not even American. She's British."

"No way!"

"I'm not shittin' you, man, she's a Brit. And y'know that other one? Anthony LaPaglia?" He pronounced it with a hard *g*. "He's Australian."

"Now I know you're lying through your teeth. What sort of fuckin' Australian name is Anthony LaPaglia?"

"Look it up, you don't believe me." The agent leaned back, his profile silhouetted against the windshield as he turned toward the back of the car. "Hey, you. What do *you* think of *The X-Files?*" His voice seemed oddly flattened through the Plexiglas.

"I don't watch much television," Trinity said quietly.

They rode in silence for several more miles, the only sound being the muted hum of the engine and tires droning on the road. A few miles past Fort Benton, the driver turned off the main road, crossed the Missouri River and headed out into the empty patchwork of agricultural fields and arid brown grassland, low hills sharp on the horizon.

"But Jodie Foster, she's American, right?" one of them said suddenly.

"Yeah, she's American."

"Well, that's okay, then. One for our side." The two agents glanced at each other, and burst out laughing.

Trinity stared out the window unseeingly. Whoever these guys were, and wherever they were taking him, he was certain they intended to kill him.

"Up here, on the left," the passenger said a few minutes later.

The driver turned the car into the parking lot of a motel, gravel crunching under the tires. The motel looked abandoned, the low stucco building having an air of despondent neglect about it, a CLOSED sign in what would have been the diner, a NO VACANCY in the window of the shuttered office. But there were three other cars parked in front of the doors of three consecutive rooms, all plain American models two or three years old. Two had Montana plates, the other Nevada.

The driver parked beside the car from Nevada and turned off the engine as his colleague got out and opened the back door.

"Get out."

Trinity didn't deliberately refuse, his fear holding him immobile. The man removed his sunglasses and bent over to stare at him directly.

"Now," he said, his tone menacing.

Trinity got out, his legs feeling watery. They walked him to the middle door of the three, and knocked.

A large man answered the door, his body soft but still carrying the signs of military conditioning, the rigidity in his posture, the hardness in his expression, the attitude of someone used to being obeyed.

"Ben Trinity," he said, not so much a question as an affirmation of what he already knew. Trinity nodded anyway. "Thanks, you two can take off."

"Right, boss," the driver said. The two men left without looking back as Trinity entered the motel room, the door shutting behind him.

Inside, the curtains had been drawn, flecks of daylight through the fabric casting the room a wan yellow. Over the bed, a print of a wolf howling with the Rocky Mountains behind him had faded to only tints of blue and green. The king-sized bed was still made, with a little machine attached to it into which adventurous couples could feed quarters to vibrate the mattress. At the moment, it was being utilized as a desk, covered with piles of folders and papers, several open briefcases, a couple of laptop computers, and empty fast-food debris.

A young blonde woman sat by the window at the only table in the room, her attention focused on a laptop connected to a hodgepodge of miscellaneous equipment, some recognizable computer components, and various electronic apparatus Trinity was familiar with, some he was not. A cable ran from the laptop across the floor and out a gap in the window. She glanced at him neutrally, no expression in her pale blue eyes, before returning her concentration to her computer screen. A toilet flushed and a door opened, admitting another man wiping his hands on a small towel who looked at him curiously but without surprise. Beefy and well over six feet tall with body-building muscles straining the fabric of his shirt, he wore a gold badge clipped to his belt.

The man who had let Trinity in said, "My name is Sam Delahue. Kenneth Jones, Special Agent, FBI. Jackie McGuire, IT security consultant with DARPA—Defense Advanced Research Projects Agency for the Department of Defense."

They all waited, as if expecting him to respond. "Okay."

Sam Delahue smiled slowly. "You don't believe me." Again, it wasn't so much a question as a statement. "You want to see some proof?"

"Not really."

"Can we get you anything? Soft drink?"

"No, thank you."

Delahue nodded appraisingly, then turned to the woman. "How we doing on time, Jackie?"

"Twenty-seven minutes."

Delahue extracted a cell phone from his jacket pocket and pressed a speed dial button. When whoever was on the other end answered, he said, "Half an hour, guys. Get a move on." He hung up without waiting for a response, and eyed Trinity speculatively. "Nice sweater." Trinity didn't answer. "You mind taking it off?"

As Trinity pulled the sweater off over his head, the other

agent dragged one of the two chairs from the table under the window and placed it beside the bed. Trinity folded the sweater uncertainly, his hands shaking. Delahue took it from him and set it on the edge of the paper-strewn bed.

"Sit down, Mr. Trinity," he said, indicating the chair.

Trinity did, saying nothing.

Delahue pushed aside a pile of folders to make room on the bed and sat down across from Trinity. The FBI agent picked up the bedside cabinet and positioned it next to Trinity. The woman opened a briefcase on it and plugged the familiar lie detector into a laptop. She moved the other chair to his opposite side and briskly, without even acknowledging him, picked up his left hand and slid it into one of a pair of black plastic palm readers, fixing the Velcro around his wrist and fingers, wires trailing to her computer. Then, alarmingly, she fastened another Velcro strap around his forearm, binding him securely to the chair.

"You used to be some sort of schoolteacher, so I hear," Delahue said, as if oblivious to what the woman was doing. She moved around the back of Trinity's chair to attach the other palm reader to his right hand, and bound his arm to the chair.

"Professor of English Literature, Pepperdine University," Trinity said, rankled by the man's offhand tone despite his fear.

"Really." Delahue seemed singularly unimpressed, and Trinity felt foolish as well as frightened. "Tenured?"

"Yes." Just answer the question asked, he reminded himself. Never volunteer anything, ever; it only gets you into trouble.

"You any good?"

"At teaching?" Trinity swallowed, his mouth dry. "You'd have to ask my students."

The conversation, such as it was, paused while the woman unbuttoned his shirt. She didn't react to the scars, although Delahue raised an eyebrow. She stuck a half-dozen EKG pads to his chest, wires trailing to one of her machines, before pushing his head forward far enough to attach several more to the base of his neck and between his shoulder blades. Two more thick Velcro straps wrapped around his chest bound him securely to the back of the chair.

The woman finished hooking him up to the monitor, paying no more attention to him than had he been a laboratory rat, then began linking other instruments Trinity didn't recognize, plugging several leads into her computer. She settled behind the screen, rapidly tapping the keyboard. She grunted softly to herself.

"Problem?" Delahue asked.

"The biometrics is erratic. Heart rate is way up, BP in the red zone. Some endorphin spikes in the CGC wave." She looked up at Trinity, pale blue eyes as lifeless as marbles. On the other side of the bed, the FBI agent rooted through the clutter to retrieve a slightly flattened pack of potato chips. He opened it, stirring his fingers doubtfully in the chips in the bag.

"Translation: He's scared shitless," Delahue clarified. She grimaced as if the layman's description affronted her sense of precision. Delahue didn't seem overly concerned with Trinity's health. "Is that going to affect the programming?"

She shook her head. "Not significantly. I can make a few adjustments." After a few more minutes of tapping on her keyboard, she said, "That's as good as I can tweak it for the moment."

Delahue glanced as his watch. "Let's do it, then. We're running out of time here." He turned to Trinity and smiled wryly. "You know the drill."

"Yes, sir."

He tried to relax as Delahue watched him, waiting.

"So state your name," Delahue prompted.

Puzzled, Trinity hesitated, glancing between Delahue and the woman. Behind Delahue, the FBI agent apathetically munched his potato chips.

"Benedictus Xavier Trinity."

"And your DSD registration code is . . ." Delahue opened a file, skimmed through a few papers before shrugging and closing the file. "Whatever the hell it is," he finished.

"Four seven five, eight three two, zero five."

"I'll take your word for it." He turned back to the woman. "Is that enough?"

"Not yet," she said, still typing rapidly.

"Okay. Let's see. You currently reside in Redemption, correct?"

"Yes, sir."

"You're supposed to ask him if he's had any alcohol or drugs in the last month," the FBI agent suggested around a mouthful of potato chips.

Delahue nodded over his shoulder. "Yeah, that's good." He turned back to Trinity. "Have you?"

"No, sir," Trinity said slowly. This man's laid-back joviality didn't square with the shrewd coldness in his face. "Who are you people?"

Delahue laughed. "*Now* he wants to know," he said to the woman. She barely glanced at him. Delahue's smile withered under her indifference.

"I used to be a teacher, just like you," Delahue said amiably, although his eyes were hard. "My students were a little more unusual than the sort you're used to, but the job was essentially the same, educating gullible kids in concepts they'd never imagined existed and hoping a few might actually learn something. Spending a little extracurricular time tutoring the ones with any spark of promise." He nodded his head over one shoulder, his eyes still on Trinity, to indicate the other two people in the room. "These are a couple of my former students, my best and brightest."

Trinity glanced at the glacial IT woman and the agent

more preoccupied with chasing crumbs around the bottom
of the bag of chips. Delahue chuckled at his visible mis-
trust.

"And, like you, our school had a board of directors that
knew nothing about what I was teaching but didn't like
the way I went about teaching it. Any digression from the
approved curriculum was frowned upon. Any inconve-
nient facts that didn't support official reality were, at best,
ignored. Those of us who dared question the wisdom of
our fearless leaders found ourselves branded as disloyal and
casualties of purges masked as 'reform.' After I was forcibly
retired, I started up my own little independent consulting
business, so to speak."

"You were in Homeland Security?" Trinity asked cautiously.

"Hell, no," Delahue snorted, one hand flicking the idea
away derisively. "I predate that bunch of wackos by a couple decades. CIA. Back in the good old days when those
few of us who cared more about real national security than
bureaucratic turf wars were still tolerated."

"Sam?" Jackie interrupted, her voice weary. She'd probably heard this lecture before, many times, Trinity thought.
"We're on a schedule, remember. So can we get back to
what we're supposed to be doing here?"

"No problem," Delahue acquiesced with a faint mocking smile, as if this were all a hilarious practical joke to
him. Perhaps it was, Trinity thought grimly. "Do you need
him to answer any more questions?"

"Actually, what I need now is for him to lie, for contrast
comparison."

"Well, now, that's something you haven't done in a
while, isn't it?" Delahue raised a mocking eyebrow. "Hope
you haven't forgotten how."

Trinity didn't answer for a long moment, fear and anger
clenched in his gut, making him feel ill. Then he said
softly, "I'm a terrorist."

Delahue's expression didn't change, but the FBI agent behind him gaped at him in surprise, his hand frozen inside the potato chip bag. The only noise in the room was the computer bleeping as Jackie tapped the keyboard.

"I'm going to need a little more than that," she said.

Delahue gestured with exaggerated manners. "Mr. Trinity?"

He swallowed against the bile rising in the back of his mouth, his palms sweating against the pads of the palm readers. "I am an enemy of the American people and guilty of conspiracy to commit terrorist acts against the United States and her allies," he said, his voice shaking. "The Triad Trust was established as a front for al-Jawasis Islamic extremists. Every time I went to the Middle East it was solely to plot with terrorists, not to help doctors treat sick kids. I knowingly helped to plan and finance the Amtrak train bombing with the intention of killing ninety-seven people. And in all the years I spent in a detention camp, tortured and starved and interrogated about crimes I didn't commit, I never gave up hope that someone would believe me, that whatever my wife was involved with I was never a part of, and that justice would prevail."

He stopped, his throat painfully constricted, his gaze locked with Delahue's.

"Jackie?" Delahue said without looking away from Trinity.

"What?" Delahue turned to raise an eyebrow at her in exasperation. She looked up and said irritably, "Yes, that's plenty. I got enough, thank you."

His hand still in the bag of chips, Jones muttered, "You're kidding."

She scowled, either unaware or uninterested in the significance of Trinity's declaration. "You want to check it yourself, Einstein?"

The agent ignored her. "This guy didn't do anything?" he demanded of Delahue, incredulous.

"Oh, he's guilty as sin, all right."

Trinity exhaled, lowering his head in defeat.

"You see, that's the problem with intelligence these days," Delahue continued, still addressing Trinity. "Too much reliance on technology. That's our real enemy, this naïve belief in the infallibility of machines, the emphasis on collecting information and nothing on interpretation. All these fancy security gizmos and computer programs; it's not a substitute for old-fashioned common sense. This either-or mentality that can't see the subtleties, misses all the nuances, the double entendres. It stifles creativity, discourages lateral thinking."

The agent crumpled the empty bag and tossed it toward the wastebasket, missing. "So he *is* a terrorist?" he complained, mystified.

"I don't know," Delahue said, amused. "Maybe. Maybe not."

"But . . ."

"See what I mean?" He twisted on the bed toward the agent. "All that machine is capable of telling you is what this man believes. It doesn't have the power to distinguish truth." He leaned closer to Trinity, speaking quietly. "*Cela ne fournit qu'une fenêtre poussiéreuse sur l'âme d'un homme, pas un rayon de lumière éclatant sur l'esprit de Dieu.*" His accent was peculiar, more colonial Africa than Sorbonne.

"Huh?" Jones said after a moment of confusion.

Trinity didn't look up. "It only provides a dusty window into a man's soul," he translated dully, "not a bright light shining on the mind of God."

Outside, he heard the sound of tires crunching on gravel as another vehicle drove up, then the slamming of doors.

"Whatever," Jones said, twitching the curtains aside to look outside. He squinted in the intense sunlight. "His taxi's here."

Trinity raised his head just far enough to gaze back at

Delahue. The man studied him without moving, chewing pensively on his lower lip. Behind them, the motel door opened, Lloyd Shovar and Dennis Red Wolf entering.

"About time," Jackie commented. "Eight minutes, Sam."

Dennis Red Wolf barely glanced at Trinity, as if uncomfortable with the sight of him strapped to the chair. "We're all set at Willow Creek," he said to Delahue.

When Delahue didn't answer, still staring at Trinity, Lloyd Shovar tilted his head. "Sam? Is it a go?" He exchanged a baffled glance with the woman. "Sam?"

Delahue straightened and clapped his hands together to rub them briskly. "In a minute," he said, stepping across to open another laptop.

"You've only got seven left," Jackie warned him.

"Plenty of time," he said offhand, slipping a pair of reading glasses from his shirt pocket onto his nose. The others watched Delahue uneasily as he hunched over the laptop, and began typing rapidly, light from the screen reflecting on his glasses.

"Six minutes," the woman murmured.

Even though he had no idea what they were counting down to, Trinity felt his own chest tighten with the tension. Jones shifted his massive weight from foot to foot while Shovar watched Delahue with anxious skepticism. Red Wolf had crossed his arms, his expression unreadable.

"Five minutes."

"Sam?"

The printer hissed to life, paper slowly feeding from it. Delahue snatched it as soon as it had finished and barely glanced at it as he folded it in half. He held it out toward Trinity, a passport photograph of a man's head in grainy colors.

"Do you know this man?" he demanded.

"No . . ."

"Look at it carefully. Are you sure you've never seen him before?"

Trinity's certainty wavered. "He could have been a customer, but I don't recognize him." He glanced past Delahue at Red Wolf, who seemed as mystified as himself. "I
swear I don't know who he is!"

Delahue's face split into a huge grin. "Well, fuck me,
laddies," he chortled. "This is exactly what I meant about
lateral thinking. It never occurred to anyone to ask *you*,
did it?" He unfolded the page to reveal the print underneath. "Hugh Lowery, *New York Post*."

The man in the photograph bore no resemblance to the
journalist who had spoken to Trinity.

"Someone's been playing silly buggers with your head,"
Delahue said. "Question is, *why?*"

"Four minutes, Sam," the woman said, a hint of urgency
in her voice.

Delahue squatted in front of Trinity, their eyes level.
"Here's the deal," he said seriously for the first time. "Certain elements in our government have been taking anyone
they feel like into custody under the counterterrorist special interest pretext for years. But then you end up holding
a few thousand enemy combatants in custody in Guantá-
namo and Diego Garcia and Abu Ghraib and Bagram—
there are records and photographs, people know their
names, they've got families and lawyers. You can't prose-
cute the guilty because you've tortured them, and you
can't release the innocent because they'll kick up a hell of
a fuss. The real bad guys are too valuable to kill; the rest became too big a liability. Amnesty International, the European Courts of Human Rights, bleeding-heart ACLU lawyers
ad nauseum, they just wouldn't shut up—that embarrassed a
lot of folks, cost a few elections. Once the Democrats took
back Congress, things got even more embarrassing. It was
time for some heavy-duty housecleaning. A lot of evidence
got shredded and buried, literally. They'll be cleaning up
that mess for decades."

This wasn't anything Trinity didn't already know.

"But that was just a slight setback, nothing more. Doesn't mean it ever stopped; it just got a whole lot more covert. Once habeas corpus was suspended, *anyone* could be held indefinitely, even American citizens—without charge, without trial, without contact with the outside world. Special Removal Units kept right on snatching you and a whole lot of other people under confidential extraordinary rendition programs. You became more than just another ghost prisoner: your arrest, your case number, your name—wiped from the record. You never had any records in the first place, you and hundreds of others simply vanished, sent to new and improved undisclosed prisons around the world, hidden well away from American borders, while every trace of your existence was expunged. And this time, no embarrassing evidence was left behind when they were done with you."

He exhaled a silent, wry laugh. "I know, because I've been there, and I've seen it for myself. Innocent or otherwise, you're damned lucky to even be alive."

"Three minutes," the woman murmured. Shovar grimaced.

"Canada, however, still has records of you as a Canadian citizen," Delahue said, ignoring her. "You're one on a long list of Canadian and Commonwealth nationals who've disappeared under similar circumstances. They're pissed as hell, and they want their people back, they don't want any more Maher Arar fuck-ups, thank you very much. Our secret treehouse club here has worked out a reasonable business transaction; the Canadians have a few things we want, and in return we give them you. There's nothing we can do about removing the implants, not at the moment. But we can adjust the settings enough to give us a small window of opportunity."

"No," Trinity protested, his throat tightening. "Please. It'll kill me."

"Oh, believe me, it's gonna hurt like hell, but Jackie here knows what she's doing. Right, Jackie?"

"Two minutes," she said blandly.

Delahue nodded toward the ceiling. "There's a five-second delay every twenty-four hours in the satellite system. We plan to temporarily fry your implants and the tracking device without setting off alarms, just long enough for you to cross the border into Canada. They're waiting to take you into custody at the Port of Willow Creek. For your cooperation, testifying to everything you know—what you and your wife were involved in, who your contacts were in the Middle East, where you were held after you were arrested, who you saw there, how you were treated—you're being offered complete protection. They'll be able to remove the implants safely. If you are innocent, you'll get a new life, a new name. A new face, if you want it. You'll be a free man again."

"What about my son?"

"I have no idea where he is. The real Hugh Lowery is a rent-a-hack who'd pimp his grandmother for a nickel, and the *New York Post* isn't worth lining a cat box with. I seriously doubt he would know anything either."

"One minute and counting," the woman said.

"On the other hand, you want to know I'm thinking?" Delahue continued, ignoring her. "I think it's pretty fucking strange you're not in an unmarked grave in some third world shithole. I'm guessing here, but I think you were half-right; you *are* bait; why else would you still be alive and walking around Montana? They're not even making a token effort to hide you. When no one expressed much interest, they manufactured a fake journalist to stir the mix. They're taking a hell of a gamble, but they're not after your wife or her mysterious brother or any al-Jawasis boogeymen. They're after *me*."

Delahue grinned broadly, aware of the consternation behind him.

"'They' who, exactly?" Shovar demanded.

"Good question. See, I'm not very popular with my former bosses; turncoats and whistleblowers usually aren't.

When I was fired, I didn't go write a book, do the talk show circuit. I went underground, too. I use unorthodox methods to fix the unfixable, and that irritates officials in high places." His mouth turned down in a self-deprecating grin and he briefly glanced up at Red Wolf meaningfully. "Quite a few now in low places, thanks to me. I know where too many bodies are buried, and right about now I'm sure there are people who want to make damned sure I become one of them before they do. We could be walking straight into a big fat bear trap and end up with our arse bit off."

"Thirty seconds."

"So do we abort?" Shovar said.

Delahue kept his attention focused on Trinity. "Of course, I could be dead wrong. We could be throwing away your one chance at freedom on the paranoid fantasies of just another bitter ex-spook past his prime, desperate to keep a hand in the game, seeing conspiracies where there aren't any."

"*Sam!*" Shovar said urgently.

Delahue leaned in close to Trinity. "I can't guarantee you a damned thing, and I won't make any promises I can't keep. It's entirely up to you, stay or go? You've got about fifteen seconds to decide the rest of your life."

"More like ten. Nine . . ."

Trinity's mind was spinning, unable to organize his thoughts in any coherent order. His throat ached, breath squeezing his chest. He desperately tried to decipher the expression in Delahue's face, not wanting to see the madman's smile.

"*Oh, God,*" he whispered.

"Seven. Six . . ."

"I'll stay," he blurted, without even knowing why.

For an agonizing moment, Delahue simply grinned at him, as if enjoying the theatricality of running it down to the wire. "What the hell," he said in a calm voice. "Shut it down."

"Aborting mission now," Jackie said, her fingers hammering the keyboard.

"Jesus fucking Mary and Joseph," Jones breathed out, "Now what?"

"Now we clean up *our* mess and get to work," Delahue said cheerfully, standing up. "Welcome to the wild side, Mr. Trinity."

# CHAPTER EIGHTEEN

The two officers seemed to lose interest in George and Amy once Trinity had been snatched off the street. Amy's new clothes lay in a heap on the sidewalk, empty bags on top of the pile. Passersby slowed down to eye them curiously, and speeded up again once prompted by the officers' glacial expression.

After a cursory glance at George's driver's license, the shorter of the two men smiled at her, his eyes still masked behind dark glasses, and handed it back. "Your daughter is over twelve years old, ma'am. She should be carrying her Cognident ID with her at all times," he chided. "You might not be around next time she needs it."

The vague threat caught in George's chest, her lungs not working.

"Yeah?" Amy retorted, unaware of the implication. She squatted to shove the clothing back into the shopping bags, close to crying; George could hear the tears in her voice. "So can we see yours?"

The other man snickered as the pair turned and started to walk toward a car identical to the one that had spirited Trinity away.

"That's not such a bad idea," George called out to their backs, going after them. "Who the hell do you think you are to treat my daughter and me like this? I'd like to see *your* ID, if you don't mind . . ."

The shorter man turned around, his head canted aggressively. "And I'd like a condo in Maui and a full head of hair," he said, his voice hard. Any pretense at civility had vanished. It sent chills along George's neck. "Looks like we're both going to be disappointed."

"Hey," the other man said softly, his tone disapproving. Then he glanced at George. "You should take your daughter home now, Mrs. Jensen. Sorry for the inconvenience."

They got into their car, pulled out into traffic and were gone, before George even thought to make a note of the license plate number. Not that it would do them much good, she thought sourly. She helped her daughter shove her crumpled school clothes back into the bags, studiously ignoring Amy's red eyes or the way her face had scrunched in the effort to control her tears. As much as she wanted to comfort her daughter, any gesture of sympathy would break that dam, and Amy wouldn't thank her for it.

Instead, George said as bravely as she could manage, "Well, do you want to have lunch first, or just go home now?"

"We can't go home," Amy said stubbornly. "We promised Ben we'd pick him up from the courthouse after his appointment."

George's heart sank. "Honey . . ."

Amy glared at her, shoving the last of her clothing into a bag and stood up. "We *promised*," she insisted darkly, and walked away with long angry strides, her pace determined although George suspected she had no idea where she was headed.

They found a Subway café and ate their sandwiches in silence, Amy glancing at her watch every few minutes. George barely tasted her food, leaving most of it, her stomach too tense.

At two, they walked up the wide courthouse steps on Second Avenue, the white stone building gleaming in the sunlight. A flock of pigeons circled the tall dome and figure of Blind Justice, the copper patina as soft as pool table velvet. Under the canopy of an ancient tree, men and women in business suits ate packed lunches on the lawn while listening to a man wearing only dirty jeans and a crumpled cowboy hat play a guitar and harmonica at the same time. The American flag hung limply from the flagpole. An elderly man tossed a Frisbee for an elderly dog.

George's eyes took a moment to adjust to the abrupt change from sunlight to the shade as they passed the huge granite columns and into the foyer of the courthouse. There, all illusion of a bygone tranquil era vanished, security as tight and high-tech as any airport. George removed her ID from her purse to be scanned before their bags were searched, and compliantly held out her arms while an unsmiling woman waved a bomb wand over her body.

"She's my daughter," she said, when Amy failed to produce her card.

The security guard frowned, but responded only with, "You'll have to leave all shopping bags and cell phones here."

They were issued visitor's badges clipped to their clothing and directed toward the stairway leading up to the third floor; elevators, it seemed, reserved for less significant security risks than a single mother and a fourteen-year-old schoolgirl.

They passed the DSD office before retracing their steps to a nondescript door with only the room number and a small insignia of Homeland Security in faded gilt on the glass showing it existed at all. The door was unlocked, leading into a tiny waiting room with a leather sofa and glass coffee table, half a dozen magazines stacked neatly on the polished surface, facing an empty receptionist's cubicle. Bland Muzak whispered from hidden speakers, playing lackluster instrumental medleys of old Bee Gees songs.

George pushed the button by the window, hearing the faint ringing of a bell somewhere out of sight. A security camera in the corner of the room glared down at her, a small malevolent red light evidence that they were being watched.

Or possibly not, since no one answered George's bell. "We may have to wait awhile," George told Amy, and sat down on the black sofa, leather creaking as she reached to rifle through the selection of magazines. She picked up an old *Architectural Digest* and turned the pages. Too distracted to read any articles, she instead stared at the photos of expensive antiques and gorgeous houses with English cottage gardens much like Alison Bakker's, dreams well out of George's reach.

Amy scrunched down on the sofa beside her, her head nearly level with her knees, arms folded belligerently. It made George's neck ache just to look at her.

"Please sit up straight, Amy," she said quietly.

Amy glanced at her sideways, her expression sullen, then stood up to ring the bell again. A barely audible buzzer sounded under a violin and oboe chorus of "How Deep is Your Love." Amy pushed the button again impatiently.

"They know we're here, you don't need to keep ringing the bell."

"Really?" Amy stepped back to scowl angrily up at the camera and waved her arms at it as if trying to attract the attention of an overhead helicopter. "Hello? Anyone watching? You got people waiting, do you even care?"

"Sit down and behave yourself," George said in a low voice, although she felt a similar irritation. "Or we can go home now."

After half an hour, George sighed and stood up, ready to give up. She looked down at Amy still stubbornly slouched on the sofa, her daughter's eyes reddened with resentment.

They both started as a door opened on the far end of the receptionist's cubicle, admitting a stocky man in a severe blue business suit. He leaned over without sitting down and pressed his intercom.

"Can I help you?" he said unsmilingly, his tone flat.

"We're here to pick up Ben Trinity," Amy announced firmly before her mother could speak.

The man gazed back at them silently with eyes as dead as a fish, his expression unchanged.

"He had an appointment with his parole officer this morning," George explained, trying to sound more reasonable than nervous. "My mother is his sponsor, Mrs. Carlene Ryton? We must have gotten the time wrong because your people picked him up early. I'm sorry if we've caused anyone any inconvenience." George had to stop herself from babbling.

The man stared at her unblinkingly. "Mr. Trinity is not here."

George's heart sank, but for Amy's benefit, she asked, "Then could you tell me where we can find him?"

After a moment, the man leaned over the intercom again. "Mr. Trinity is not here," he repeated. Before George could say another word, he exited the cubicle, shutting the door behind him firmly.

George stood staring at the empty cubicle, hot frustration in her throat.

"Mom?"

"Let's go, sweetpea. We're done."

They went back down to the foyer, collected their bags without speaking, and walked out of the artificial chill of the courthouse into the bright light of a late summer day, the smell of bedding flowers and warmed earth heavy in the air.

"Are they sending him back to prison?" Amy finally said, her small voice shaking with threatened tears.

*Probably,* George thought. "I don't know, Amy."

Amy loaded their shopping into the trunk of the car, and got into the passenger seat beside her mother, subdued as she fastened her seat belt. Neither of them spoke, nor did Amy even bother to fiddle with the radio trying to find something suitable for the taste of a teenager, a sure method of annoying her mother.

On the way home, George spotted a thick pillar of smoke rising into the still air in the distance somewhere near Citadel Rock. *Someone burning scrap rather than paying to haul it to the dump,* she thought. *Probably hadn't even bothered getting a permit, risking burning trash during the dry season, the idiot.* Then, for some inexplicable reason, a surge of anger swept over her, an irrational bitterness with having to ask official permission for every aspect of their lives like naughty children; permits and licenses and ID cards and certificates and registrations needed for everything imaginable. Montana, Big Sky country, wide-open ranges as far as the eye could see and she couldn't even breathe anymore.

"Assholes," George whispered. "Goddamned *assholes!*"

"Mom! Mom, stop it, you're scaring me!"

George hadn't realized she was shouting, or pounding her fist against the steering wheel, Amy's frightened voice calling her back to sanity. She pulled the car over to the side of the road and stopped, weeping as her daughter, still buckled into her seat, hugged her awkwardly.

"I'm sorry, Mom, I'm really sorry," Amy was sobbing, hiccupping her tears.

"Oh, baby . . ." George hugged her daughter back fiercely, feeling guilty. "I'm not mad at you. You've done nothing wrong, I swear."

They rocked together gently for a moment, George's anger deflating into sadness.

"It's my fault," Amy mumbled, her face warm pressed against George's sweater. "They're going to put Ben back in jail, and it's all my fault."

George pushed Amy back gently and smiled, wiping her hand over her daughter's wet cheeks. "You can't blame yourself, Amy. It has nothing to do with you."

"It does, too," Amy insisted reluctantly. "Ben's in trouble now because of what Craig did. And Craig wouldn't have done it if I hadn't made him mad." Once Amy had started her confession, it poured out of her in a jumbled mess. "He's always picking on me at school and saying mean stuff, acting the big man always going on about he's so tough and how he's going to make Ben pay for what he's done and that Nana is a lefty liberal lover and she should move away to New England where all the other lefty liberal lovers are, and that you and Ben . . ." She blushed as the flood slowed, reaching dangerous territory. "He's said some really nasty things about you in front of Mattie and Cindy and everybody, and I said it wasn't so, he's a liar and making it up, but Dickie Allen and Jamie said it was, too, and they called you and Nana all kinds of disgusting names so I said Ben was more of a real man than he'd ever be, and he got real mad and said he'd show me." Amy sniffed wetly, and waited while George dug out a pack of Kleenex from her purse. She blew her nose and mumbled into the tissue. "I told Craig he didn't have the guts and I double-dared him. But I wouldn't have said it if I thought he'd ever do anything, I swear!"

"Amy . . ." George struggled to find the words. "You're not responsible for anything Craig did."

"But I double-dared him."

"And if Craig double-dared you to jump off a cliff, would you do it?"

Amy smiled wanly at an old defense she'd heard many times before. "No."

"You're not a lemming; you can think for yourself, and so can Craig. You're both old enough to know the difference between right and wrong. It wasn't your fault, honey."

"So how come Ben is in trouble?"

George started up the car again, checked the empty road behind her and pulled out onto the road. "I don't know," she said finally. "But I promise, just as soon as we get home, I'll call Mr. Eastlake and see if there's anything we can do to help Ben."

There was no need to phone anyone when they got back, they both realized as soon as they reached the access road leading to their house. Several men and women wearing FBI and DHS windbreakers milled around half a dozen unmarked sedans parked at awkward angles along the drive. In their midst was Luke's lone County Sheriff's patrol car, lights still flashing, the crackle of unintelligible radio chatter in the air. Lucas was nowhere to be seen. A man in a dark suit and mirrored sunglasses, shiny brass badge clipped on his belt, turned to stare unsmiling as George drove up.

She rolled down the window, anger making her face hot. "You're blocking my drive."

The man strolled unhurriedly toward her, followed by a woman in an FBI jacket. "Ms. Jensen?"

"And you are?"

He didn't answer her question. "Would you mind getting out of the car, please? You, too, miss?" he added for Amy.

George spotted strangers opening the front door of her house, walking out with cardboard file boxes in their arms, and felt suddenly breathless with disbelief. "You're in my house!" She opened the car door, struggling with her seat belt, and got out clumsily. "What are you doing in my house?"

"Ms. Jensen, where is Ben Trinity?"

She stared at him incredulously. "I have no idea, but he sure as hell isn't in there! So why are *you*?"

"He was last seen this morning when you drove him into Great Falls for his appointment with his parole officer. But he never made it."

" 'Last seen'?" George repeated. "Last seen by who? Your people arrested him just before noon and took him away. I haven't seen him since, so if you don't know where he is, how should I?"

Amy had got out of the car, but shrank behind the open door as the FBI woman smiled at her with false reassurance. "Hello there. You must be Amy," she said soothingly, reaching out a hand. "You want to come with me for a minute so your mother can have a little talk with my boss?"

"Mom!" Amy called out in alarm, darting around the back of the car to escape and clung to her mother, her body quivering.

"Ms. Jensen . . . ," the man began, his tone one of weary reasonableness that didn't fool George in the slightest.

"You leave my daughter alone," George said shakily, her arms around Amy's shoulders protectively. The woman glanced at him, and shrugged when he pursed his lips with disapproval, but shook his head. It was a small enough victory, but enough to bolster George's indignant courage. Still firmly holding on to Amy, she headed toward the house.

"You can't go in there at the moment," the man said, following behind.

"Have you got a warrant?" George said tightly.

He stepped in front of her to block her way, and held up his gold Homeland Security badge in a black leather wallet. "We don't need a warrant, Ms. Jensen."

The front door was open far enough for Amy to catch sight of her father walking across the room inside. "Daddy!" she cried out, and bolted into the house.

George tried to brush past the man to follow her daughter, and found herself struggling with him awkwardly, batting away his hands clutching at her arms. "Let go of me, you *bastard!*" she growled through clenched teeth, tears taut in her throat. "This is *my* house!" She broke free and nearly knocked down another DHS agent coming out of the house with a cardboard box in his arms, Amy's computer monitor poking out from the top.

"Get the hell out of my way!" she screamed in his face, and shoved past him. Startled, the man nearly dropped the box, then chuckled in her wake, infuriating George even further as she stormed through her front door.

Inside, it looked like a small hurricane had ripped through the rooms. The living room furniture had been shuffled around, books and DVDs and CDs pulled off shelves into jumbled piles, pictures and framed photos taken down and their backing peeled off. Her stereo and television had been disassembled, phone jacks and electrical outlets unscrewed leaving bare wires trailing from the sockets. A couple of men with large toolbox kits were probing the mess with strange electronic devices that beeped and buzzed now and again. A few more agents dusted for fingerprints, leaving smudgy black dots scattered everywhere.

Through the doorway into the kitchen, George spotted Amy standing next to her father, his face flushed with anger, his daughter's expression a mirrored image. The mess in the kitchen was, if anything, worse, every cupboard open, cans and jars and packages scattered chaotically. The contents of her flour canister had been spilled into the sink, followed by Cheerios and Raisin Bran, coffee grounds, and bags of sugar. Pots and pans littered the floor, and the stove was pulled out from the wall. The doors of the refrigerator and freezer stood open and the contents examined with no concern for neatness, a jar of raspberry jam on its side leaking clots of sticky goo.

"But, Dad!" Amy protested, attempting to seize something from her father's hands only to have him snatch it out of reach. "It's mine!"

As George reached the kitchen, she recognized Amy's little diary, pink roses on the cover with a brass catch to keep it closed. She'd seen it often enough tucked under Amy's pillows, the catch always fastened to safeguard against snooping eyes although the cheap lock could have been picked with a decent hairpin. Or a Swiss Army knife, which was apparently what Lucas had used to pry open the little book.

"What are you doing here?" George demanded.

Without taking his eyes off his daughter's writing, Lucas said stonily, "Assisting in a counterterrorist investigation," his voice bland, although George had had enough experience with him to hear the violence lurking just below the surface. He turned another page, again lifting the book out of Amy's reach when she made another attempt to grab her diary.

"Daddy," Amy objected, her face red with humiliation and her eyes wet, "that's my diary. You're not supposed to be reading it."

"Lucas, give the kid back her book."

"Sorry," he said, flipping another page. "It's been confiscated as material evidence."

"Oh, for God's sake . . . ," George began, before the man who had tried to prevent her from entering her own house cleared his throat beside her to attract her attention. "What? What? *What?*" she shouted at him. "What are you looking for? I don't know where Ben Trinity is. Why are you doing this to us?"

"He spent the night here three days ago," Lucas said, still not looking at her. "How long have you been sleeping with him, George?"

She stared at him, unable to speak for several moments, the fury stabbing through her throat. "Is that was this is about?" she finally managed to say. "You and your stupid jealousy again? You're *insane*, you know that?"

Luke's jowls had flushed a dark red, but he tried to keep up his charade of indifference, turning another page in Amy's diary. George made a snatch at it, tussling with him briefly before he wrested it away, all his pretense of equanimity gone. Luke's breathing was hoarse, his eyes bloodshot, his hands trembling with repressed wrath. The man in the suit took a step back, not so much out of caution as curiosity. The woman agent and one of the techs, drawn by Luke's and George's increasingly heated argument, drifted into the kitchen warily, but said nothing.

"Give her back her book, God damn you!"

"Daddy, it's mine. Please can I have it back? It's my private stuff," Amy begged, weeping now in earnest, tears flooding down her face.

"You're a fourteen-year-old girl," Lucas barked at her, "you don't *need* any 'private' stuff!" He turned on George with righteous anger, shaking the diary at her. "Have you read the crap she's been writing in this thing? *Have* you?"

A cold sliver of hatred splintered through George, making her tremble. "No, Lucas. I haven't. Amy has as much right to her privacy as *I* do." Turning on the man in the suit still watching them with a slight smile, she said, "How dare you—"

"You lost any right to privacy the moment you let that scumbag into this house," Lucas said. He turned another page and glowered as a lock of dark hair tied with a small ribbon fell out and drifted onto the floor. When Amy lunged for it, Lucas stamped his boot on top, narrowly missing her fingers.

"If you'd taken more of an interest in your own daughter, you'd know she's been talking with that Sophie Bakker kid about having sex with men. She's *fourteen years old*. What the hell is she doing talking about *sex*? Do you even know that bastard kissed her?" he demanded, turning the diary around just far enough to expose the adolescent "♥ ♥ ♥ Ben+Amy 4-ever ♥ ♥ ♥" in Amy's looped handwriting. "How could you allow him to put his filthy hands on our daughter?"

Amy sank to the floor, wrapped her arms around her knees and rocked back and forth, murmuring, "Daddy, give it back, please, please, please . . ." in a wet hiccup. The woman agent exchanged a concerned glance with the man in the suit.

"Officer Jensen," the man said, "let's try not to let things escalate out of control here . . ."

Lucas barked a harsh laugh. "Oh, no," he snarled. "That's already happened. I'm going to see to it 'control' is exactly what we get back." He leaned in close enough to George that she could feel his breath on her face, spearmint sickly sweet, holding Amy's diary up under her nose. "This is all the proof I need that you're an unfit mother. I'm getting a lawyer tomorrow and filing for custody, and I *will* get Amy as far away from you and the filth you associate with as I can."

"Mom!" Amy shrieked, her voice spiraling rapidly into hysteria. "*No, no, no, no*, don't let him make me . . . !"

As George crouched down to comfort her daughter, the man in the suit said crossly, "We're not here to get involved in any domestic dispute, we just need to find Ben Trinity. So if everyone could just calm down . . ."

Another agent opened the back door to the kitchen, drawn toward the angry shouting, his face puzzled and cautious. Bojangles could not have chosen a worse moment to make a bid for freedom, the cat bursting out of his hiding place inside the ransacked cabinet under the sink, frantically heading for the opened door. Lucas lifted his foot as George sucked in a gasp of alarm. Before she could utter a sound, Luke's boot connected solidly with the animal, kicking Bojangles as hard as he could.

The cat crashed into the leg of the kitchen table, body twisting with a sharp sound like a tree branch cracked in two. Everything became still, the quiet of horrified suspense. For a dreadful moment, George stared at the cat as he opened his mouth in a soundless yowl, his eyes wide with astonishment and pain. Then Amy screamed, a wail of visceral anguish that made George's hair stand on end.

The cat's front legs scrabbled against the floor, but his back legs splayed at an unnatural angle, utterly limp, his back broken. His fur was wet where the animal's bladder had given way, urine pooling around his tail.

In the space of three heartbeats—and George felt each one in her chest thump as clearly as a clock chime—she saw the emotions flood across Luke's face: disbelief and shame at what he'd just done, and the terrible realization that he'd crossed the border into a dark and treacherous world where there could be no road back. Then, just as quickly, it was gone, the mask of righteous contempt sliding back into place.

Amy crawled toward Bojangles, sobbing distraughtly. "Honey, don't touch him, don't try to move him," George said quickly, "you might make it worse." She stood and faced Lucas, feeling oddly calm, beyond fury.

"Get out," she said quietly.

"I've warned you about this before," Lucas retorted. "You shouldn't allow vermin in the house."

Amy sprawled prostrate on the floor, stroking the injured cat tenderly on the head, but rolled over to glare at her father, fresh tears rolling down her face and snot running from her nose. "I hate you," she snarled and picked up the nearest object she could reach, a saucepan, and threw it at her father. He dodged it easily. "I hate you I hate you I *hate you* . . . !" A cake tin followed the saucepan then a bottle of Windex before George stooped down to hug her, to restrain her as much as to console her.

"Ms. Jensen," the FBI woman started to say apologetically.

"Just go." George eyed the small audience of officials still watching. "All of you. Just take what you want and get out."

The man in the suit shook his head disapprovingly as he took Amy's diary from Luke's hand and dropped it into a cardboard box on the table, then handed it to the FBI woman. Amy didn't notice, her attention focused on Bojangles, who was now shivering in shock. George didn't bother to acknowledge the FBI woman's mouthed *sorry* as she searched George's and Amy's handbags, removing both their cell phones. These, too, went into the box with the diary to be carried away.

George sat beside her daughter, her legs curled under her on the cold floor, and stroked Amy's head, ignoring the exodus of people from the kitchen and then her house. A few minutes later, she heard engines turning over, cars filing out of her drive, and the house was quiet once more.

# CHAPTER NINETEEN

It hurt like hell all right. An understatement, Trinity thought. He sagged in the chair, Velcro restraints all that was keeping him upright, the sheen of sweat on his skin clammy. The overwhelming waves of pain faded quickly enough but the microchips still vibrated intensely, like a bone-deep itch impossible to ease. You'd think—the disembodied part of his psyche was commenting to itself— that after all the torture he'd been through, he'd have had better resistance to pain, not less.

"It's not that simple, Sam," the IT woman complained, Delahue pacing impatiently behind her. "We don't have that window of opportunity anymore. I can't just fry the damned things, I have to find the right balance. If I don't alter the implant settings enough, it won't work. But if I overload them, they'll know the system had been tampered with regardless."

"Think you can find this balance sometime today?" Sam Delahue said dryly, "before you *do* kill him?"

Jackie McGuire shot an irritated glance at Trinity. "Try it again."

"Jesus," Trinity whimpered. Then, his voice hoarse, he said as steadily as he could, "This is a lot of fun, I'm really enjoying this."

Jackie grimaced. "Not . . . quite . . . yet," she murmured, tapping the keyboard. "Nearly there." The electric surge made him gasp, his back arched, teeth clenched in an already aching jaw. But this time it wasn't as intense; the agony fleeting.

"Ah, c'mon," he panted, "do it again, I want more." He stiffened, anticipating the excruciating rush that didn't come.

Jackie smiled, her small teeth incredibly even and white. "I got it, boss."

"Thank God," Trinity whispered to himself.

"Good," Jones groused from the corner, hunched uneasily over his crossed arms. "Cuz it was getting kinda kinky, y'know what I mean?"

Shovar had stood with his back to Trinity the entire time, staring out the window, while Red Wolf had watched without expression, although a small muscle in his jaw spasmed every time Trinity had tried to choke back a scream.

"Are we done?" Trinity pleaded.

"Yeah, we're done," Delahue said, and began loosening the Velcro restraints. "Congratulations, Mr. Trinity. Once again, you, too, can lie with as much impunity as the next man. Ken, get him a glass of water."

Trinity had to be helped to sit on the bed, every muscle in his body spasming. He wrapped both hands around the glass Jones handed him to keep from spilling it. All the same, he dribbled a little water down his chin as he gulped down the entire glassful. It didn't ease his throat.

"So what's the game plan?" Shovar asked Delahue, his tone sour.

"Don't exactly have one," Delahue admitted cheerfully. "It's rather hard winning a game when the other side cheats and changes the rules middle of the ninth inning. We're just gonna have to make it up as we go along." Trinity glanced up at the two men: Shovar's back stiff, Delahue standing with his hands in his pockets, head tilted as he watched Jackie's laptop monitor, his attitude relaxed. Only his eyes seemed hard, a line around his smile tautening. "Don't worry, Lloyd. They used to teach how to think on your feet way back when I was a wee lad in spy school. It may be a lost art these days, but I haven't forgotten how."

Shovar exchanged a quick glance with Jones, who raised his eyebrows and shrugged very slightly in resigned doubt. The IT woman sat with her fingers resting motionless on her keyboard, waiting impassively.

"First thing to do is buy some time. By now, his friends are no doubt aware something's gone wrong and are headed this way." He nodded at Trinity. "So we gotta hide him."

"*Hide* him?" Shovar barked a short laugh. "How? You didn't fry his tracker, Sam; he's easier to find than an elephant in a flea circus!"

"So we disguise the elephant as a flea." He pointed to something on Jackie's screen. "Can you get into this?"

"Not a problem." Her fingers clattered on the keys as Shovar moved to watch. "There you go."

"How did you do that?" Shovar demanded suspiciously.

Surprisingly, the IT woman flashed a grin, her soft chuckle deep in her well-endowed chest. "I'm sorry to be the one to tell you this, Agent Shovar, but the FBI computer network is total crap. It's so crap all it takes is one dingbat secretary using file-swapping shareware from Bloggers R Us to download the latest Dixie Chicks single, and you're left wide open. Fifteen-year-old nerds can hack into your e-mails. How many millions got wasted on your Trilogy project before you gave up? And now you're stuck with using off-the-shelf Microsoft crap. Every time the system crashes, the upgrade patches need upgrade patches." Her fingers kept tapping as she spoke. "I know, because I've helped write half of them. It's like a guy bleeding from a thousand cuts; you end up sticking so many Band-Aids on him you can't even tell if there's anyone underneath anymore. Which is why you guys have to hire people like me to keep propping it up so we all can keep on pretending everything's fine."

Shovar's jaw twitched in irritation.

"Now, now, children," Delahue said lightly. "We're all on the same side, remember. Play nice."

She glanced up at Delahue, still smiling. "So which of these fine upstanding gentlemen do you want, Sam?"

"What do we got?"

"Sex offenders, mostly. Rapists, pedophiles, the usual."

"What are you doing?" Trinity said, alarmed, his voice hoarse.

"To a surveillance program, you're just a dot on a map," Delahue said without looking up, his attention on Jackie's screen. "Switch the labels around, and voilà, some schmo in Bumfuck, Illinois, or Kansas or Outer Mongolia becomes you." He grinned. "Electronic three-card monte. The simple ideas are usually the best."

"So we're still taking him to Canada?" Red Wolf asked gruffly. Startled, the others turned to stare. He hadn't spoken in so long they had almost forgotten he was even in the room.

"No," Delahue said. "Any dot heading for the border will give the game away. We'll have to hide him a few days, give us time to cover our asses and get our own ducks lined up."

"Hide him where?" Shovar asked.

Delahue smiled, his ironic humor resurfacing. "Where else? Sorry, Ben. You're going back to jail for awhile."

Trinity got the gist his strategy. "No," he said quickly, his pulse quickening. "Not as a sex offender, I won't go along with that."

"Point taken," Delahue admitted. "What else we got, Jackie?"

"How much do you want me to scramble all this?"

Delahue raised his eyebrows, his lips pursed as he thought. "Three days?"

"Okay, I can shuffle a few of these files around, make it look like a cascade error. There won't be any trace to indicate this was anything more than the usual Microsoft fuck-up." She tapped the screen, her nails flawlessly manicured. "How 'bout this guy?"

Delahue snorted. "He's twenty-three, three hundred pounds, and black." When Jackie glanced at him witheringly, he shrugged. "Perfect," he said dryly. "Arson okay with you?" he asked Trinity. It was rhetorical, Delahue uninterested in Trinity's answer. "Congratulations, you're now LeRoy Mitchell Walker, Junior, aka 'Notorious Bic.'"

"If you're right, Sam, and someone is after you," Shovar said, his voice impassive, "they're going to very pissed off when they find him. If they start thinking he's now more of a liability . . ." His question trailed off. Trinity's heart seemed to lurch in his chest as he realized the implication.

"What's to stop him from being killed?" Sam finished for him. He glanced at Trinity, his expression hard. "Me. Dennis?"

The casual use of Red Wolf's name startled Trinity; it hadn't occurred to him the two men would know each other.

"I can't take him in." Red Wolf glanced at Shovar. "Neither can he. We both have prior association." He exhaled, frowning. "But I can make an anonymous call, get someone from Havre or Great Falls PD to pick him up."

"You need anything else from me?" Jackie asked.

"That's it. You can clear out now."

Jackie snapped her laptop closed and rapidly unplugged the spaghetti tangle of leads and wires, packing the electronic equipment away into the cases within minutes. Shovar left the room, and returned with a small collapsible satellite dish attached to a telescoping pole, then helped her to carry the cases outside. A moment later, Trinity heard a car pull away. Delahue gathered up the files and papers, tapping the edges together before cramming them back into his briefcase. Jones handed Trinity back his ugly pullover with a doubtful air, making his opinion of Trinity's attire clear. Their movements were brisk, but not hurried. Only Red Wolf and Trinity watched, idle.

"How clean do you want this place, boss?" Jones asked, snapping the cuffs of a pair of latex gloves as he pulled them over his meaty hands.

"Two birds, one stone," Delahue replied. "He's an arsonist, right? Fire is quick and covers a multitude of sins."

Jones grinned, as happy as a child. "*Cool.*"

Delahue walked with Trinity and Red Wolf as they left the hotel room, heading for Red Wolf's Jeep Wrangler, the utilitarian four-by-four having seen better days. "This is your story," Delahue said to Trinity. "You were picked up by two men in Great Falls. They didn't identify themselves; you'd never seen them before. They drove you out into the middle of nowhere and left you there. You had no idea why, or where you were, so you just started walking. You saw no one. That's it. Keep it simple, don't elaborate. When you're taken into custody, you give your real name. Don't phone anyone, but don't do anything that might violate your parole."

"Except lie."

Delahue grinned. "Except lie."

Shovar had tossed the last briefcase into the trunk of a dark blue Ford Crown Victoria and slammed it shut before he walked over to join the small group. "Five minutes, and this place goes up. Everybody ready?"

Delahue dug a set of rental car keys from his trouser pocket, metal jingling. "Good luck, Mr. Trinity. See you around." Trinity wasn't sure it was a promise or a threat. Delahue got into the dark blue car and drove away, leaving a thin streak of dust in his wake to hang in the still, hot air.

"I'll go with Jones once he's finished." Shovar nodded at Trinity, still speaking to Red Wolf, and took a cell phone from his pocket. "You take him, I'll make the call. I've got a secure line, you don't."

"Fine," Red Wolf said, obviously dissatisfied with the change in plans.

"Why are you doing this?" Trinity asked Shovar, his voice still hoarse. "Why are *you* trying to help me?"

Startled, Shovar glared at him, his mouth working as if trying to extract something stuck between his teeth. "Because we're the good guys, Mr. Trinity, whether you want to believe that or not." He shot an angry look at Red Wolf. "Get him out of here." He turned on his heel and went back into the hotel room, slamming the door behind him.

Red Wolf got in his Wrangler and started the engine. He put it in gear before Trinity had had a chance to do more than open the passenger side and hastily jump into his seat, still struggling with the seat belt as they pulled out of the parking lot. Red Wolf sped along the badly paved road, grinding up through the gears, the Wrangler bucking wildly over every crack and rock. A few miles past the motel, Red Wolf turned onto an even worse road, gravel pinging against the undercarriage like a hailstorm. At one point, the road disappeared completely, the four-by-four bouncing down and across the stony bed of a dry coulee, tossing them around like test-crash dummies. Trinity glanced at him, the man's jaw thrust forward into a scowl. Neither of them spoke during the bone-shaking ride. Nearly an hour later, Red Wolf stomped on the brakes, the tires skidding against the sun-beaten earth, dust roiling around them in a thick cloud.

"Get out."

Without a word, Trinity opened the door and stepped down onto the hard-packed ground. He waited warily while Red Wolf sat staring out the windshield, huge hands clenching the steering wheel. After a few moments, Red Wolf rolled down the window on his side, motioning for

Trinity to come around. When he did, he found Red Wolf holding out a large plastic bottle of water.

"Take this. It may be awhile." Red Wolf nodded at the road in front of him. "Head north, in that direction." Without waiting for an answer, Red Wolf put the car in gear and drove away. The khaki Wrangler blended into the parched grassland, hard to spot within a few miles, only the faint whine of the engine and a trace of dust as it disappeared over the swell of low hills. A few miles more and even that had gone.

The air was dry, what little wind there was doing more to suck the humidity out of Trinity's skin than cool him. Desiccated grass undulated in snake lines as a thin streak of black smoke rose in the far distance into a sky an otherwise unembellished blue. Trinity popped the spout on the water bottle, and squirted a small amount into his mouth, enough to wet his dry throat, his tongue rasping on the fur on his teeth. It was warm, with a chemical tang.

He started walking. There was nothing remarkable to see. A startled lizard sunning itself darted away in a scaly panic. A small herd of cows lifted their heads, muzzles idly working their cud as he passed, staring at him with liquid brown eyes, ears flicking at flies. He spooked a pair of half-grown deer nibbling rolled bales of alfalfa hay, white rumps flashing as they bolted into the cottonwoods. He walked for several hours and saw no one else, not a car, not a house, nothing. Eventually, the rutted dirt road turned to compacted gravel, then finally a worn and cracked paved surface, easier to walk on.

The light began to fade, a chill in the breeze and a diffuse stain of pink glowing on the outlying hills making him glad for the ugly pullover. The sky had darkened enough for Venus and a few brighter stars to be faintly visible when he heard a car approaching. He stopped and waited as a sleek, low Chevy Impala emerged from the dusk toward him, a bar of unlit blue and red top lights on the roof, a blue

stripe along the side stenciled with POLICE, the Ville du
Havre shield, and an American flag. It stopped a few yards
from him, and a young woman in uniform got out. Her body
partly shielded behind the open car door, she stood with
one hand resting on the butt of the gun against her hip.

"Evening," she called out casually. "You're a long way
from civilization."

"Yes, ma'am," he said, his voice sounding croaky even to
himself. The water in his bottle was nearly gone. His feet
were tired, hot in the secondhand Reeboks well past their
best. The calves of his legs twitched with fatigue.

"Where you headed?"

He shrugged. "Don't know." Which was true.

She nodded, as if his statement seemed perfectly logi-
cal. She glanced around as if wary of any hidden accom-
plices, then back at him. Wisps of blonde hair escaping
from a tight French braid curled against her forehead, the
pale skin marred by the faint red line from her patrol hat.
"Getting a bit chilly out, don't you think?"

"Yes, ma'am, it is."

She smiled without warmth. "You mind showing me
some identification?"

*And so it begins*, he thought. He raised his left hand and
turned the tattooed palm toward her.

# CHAPTER TWENTY

"Mom, can we take him to the vet, please?" Amy had calmed enough to plead.

Bojangles lay on his side, his body contorted. He panted shallowly, his glazed eyes dilated in distress. George's heart sank, not wanting to appear callous but unwilling to waste money they didn't have on an animal with no hope.

"Let's just try to get him comfortable, okay, sweetpea?"

Amy looked up, her lashes clotted with tears, the skin around her eyes swollen. "Please, Mom? *Please?*"

George stood up to rummage through the debris of her house, trying not to hear her daughter's desperate entreaties. She eventually uncovered the cardboard box in which she kept her worn-out paint shirts, the box crumpled where it had been stepped on by careless or uncaring feet. Towels in the bathroom had been pulled down from the linen closet, tossed into heaps on the floor. She stuffed a couple of them into the box, worrying briefly that the cat would pee on them before deciding she really didn't give a damn.

When she returned to the kitchen, she found Amy sprawled beside the cat, her head flat against the floor as she stroked Bojangles between his ears tentatively as if frightened the animal might shatter, like fragile china. Armed with the box and towels, George hesitated, feeling powerless, unsure how to move Bojangles without hurting him any further. The faint sound of a truck pulling up into the drive was almost as much a relief as irritation. She recognized Jack Bakker's truck by the sound of the piston knock of the old engine ticking as he shut it off.

"We're in the kitchen, Jack," she called as soon as she heard his voice calling out from the front porch. She knelt down beside Amy and the cat, tucking a towel around the animal, looking up when Jack appeared in the doorway and stopped. He'd removed his hat, a courteous gesture out of place in the midst of such disorder, his hands clenching the curled brim of the old Stetson with white-knuckled force.

"You two all right?" he asked. His clear blue eyes took in the mess, but he didn't seem surprised, not even asking what had happened.

"Bojangles is hurt real bad," Amy said, fresh tears starting. "We need to get him to the vet right now."

Jack exchanged a quick glance with George, the comprehension passing between them unspoken. George saw his throat move under the white beard as he swallowed before he smiled as encouragingly as he could manage.

"Well, now, let's just have a look at him first," he said quietly. He squatted down to run his hand lightly over the cat's broken body, lifting a limp back leg experimentally. George marveled at the gentleness of the old rancher's chapped and sunburned hands, his thick fingers stiffened by hard work. He grimaced, and exhaled regretfully.

Amy grabbed George by the arm, understanding. "I'll pay for it, Mom, honest. I'll sell my bike. And my phone, everything, I don't care . . ."

"Oh, baby," George started, and astonished herself as she burst into tears herself, unable to hold them back.

Stunned, Amy stared at her, as if this confirmed her worst fears. She turned to Jack desperately. "A vet could fix him. Please don't let him die!"

"I won't lie to you, sugar," Jack said kindly. "If money

were all it took to save him, I'd pay for it myself. But this poor critter is past that sort of help."

Defeated, Amy face crumpled, still unwilling to accept the verdict. "But, Jack . . ."

"Now we gotta do the kind thing by him, Amy," he said firmly. "Even when that hurts us." He looked up at George. "I'll do it."

"*No!*" Amy screamed, but it wasn't a refusal, simply a howl of distress. She pushed up from the floor, and ran out of the kitchen and up the stairs, her feet pounding on the steps, a door slamming in protest.

Between them, George and Jack managed to maneuver the cat into the towel-lined box, Bojangles already limp and shivering, barely reacting. Jack stood up with the box in his arms and waited as George stroked the cat tenderly, trying to fight back her tears.

"You go on up and take care of Amy," Jack said.

"Good-bye, little guy," she whispered to the cat, the words coming out weirdly past her clotted throat. She wiped her nose on the back of her hand, then smeared the trail of snot on the seat of her jeans for want of a tissue.

After Jack had left by the kitchen door, George walked up the stairs and knocked softly on Amy's door. When Amy didn't respond, George tried the door. It was unlocked. Amy lay curled on her bed, her back to her mother, sobbing disconsolately. George sat down beside her, the bedspring creaking, and placed a hand on Amy's hip, rocking her gently. After a moment, Amy twisted around so quickly it startled George, flinging her arms around her mother's waist and burying her head in George's lap. The weeping subsided, but it wasn't grief lessening its hold; rather they both were holding their breath, waiting.

The sound was muffled, barely a pop. But Amy spasmed as if she had been shot as well, with a fresh wail of anguish.

George sat stroking her daughter's hair, neither of them speaking, letting Amy cry herself out. The bedroom window was opened a crack, just far enough for her to hear a shovel stabbing into the hard-packed dirt of the backyard. She looked down as Amy didn't react, expecting her to be asleep, the girl's breathing even. But Amy's eyes were open, staring at nothing, her hands tucked between her head and her mother's thighs. When Jack finished burying the cat, he came back into the house; George could hear him as he moved chairs around downstairs, pots and pans clanking, the smell of coffee eventually drifting up. Amy's eyes finally closed in exhaustion, her protest dulled by sleep as George extracted herself. George tucked her grandmother's patchwork quilt around her daughter before going downstairs.

The sky outside had faded to cobalt, the air cooling rapidly. Small gray moths and tiny gnats circled the bulb in the kitchen light. Jack's eyes were red, but dry, as he sat at the table nursing a mug of coffee. A second cup sat across from him, an empty chair set for her.

"That'll be cold by now," Jack said as she settled gratefully into the chair and picked up the mug.

"Don't care." She drank most of the lukewarm coffee in one huge gulp. It did little to ease the ache in her throat. "Thank you," she said, meaning for Bojangles.

Jack understood, nodding. "Your mother was worried, asked me to come check on you two," he said.

"Ma?" There were so many questions in that single word.

Jack raised an eyebrow and looked around pointedly at the mess, then back at her meaningfully. "Yeah." And so many answers in that single reply.

Overwhelmed, George slumped over the table, resting on her elbows, her hair spiked between her fingers clutching her forehead. "*Why?* Why did they do this to us? How could they be so . . . so . . ." She couldn't find a suitable word. "Awful."

Jack shrugged. "The government psychosis is a fearsome and desolate wilderness I have no wish to trespass upon." Her head still in her hands, she glowered at him. "Kinda feel a little guilty, it being me brought that boy into your lives in the first place. No good deed, and all that. You sure you got no idea where he's gone?"

"No. And even if I did, what gives anyone the right to come into my house and trash the place and steal our things?"

"The law, such as it is." Jack stood up, collected her cup, and poured the dregs down the sink. He had scooped the spilled cereal and sugar and flour out of the sink and into a garbage bag while she'd been with Amy, she noted gratefully. That he'd salvaged any of the instant coffee seemed a small miracle. The stove was still at an angle to the wall, but Jack had managed to get it working again—at least the gas hadn't been left spewing into the house for the whole place to go up in a ball of fire. The kettle whistled almost immediately, still hot. Jack poured them fresh cups and sat down again, smiling ruefully. "There's evildoers lurking under every rock wanting to do us harm, doncha know. If we're not fightin' terrorists over there, we gotta fight 'em over here. We need tough laws to defend our security." He grinned, his lips twisted sardonically. "Don't you feel more secure now?"

She snorted her disgust. "Better not let Alison hear you talking like that. She'll suspect you of being a Democrat next."

Jack chuckled. The humor was short-lived. "Still, stomping a defenseless animal to death seems just a touch too diligent, even for federal goons."

Reluctantly, she said, "It was an accident." Not knowing why, she added, "Lucas didn't mean to, he just overreacted."

"Uh-huh." Jack said, unimpressed. "That the same reasoning you used to excuse him whenever he left bruises all over your body?" When George looked away, embarrassed, he said softly, "Come on, girl, you weren't never foolin' anyone."

"He's still Amy's father. And he *has* gotten better since the divorce."

"This is 'better'?"

"It's not that simple," George muttered.

"It never is."

# CHAPTER TWENTY-ONE

To call Redemption a town was slightly misleading. The single road north out of Redemption toward the Hi-Line split in two after several miles, one road headed into Havre, the other to Chinook. Small crosses decorated with plastic flowers, stuffed toys, and tattered greeting cards occasionally dotted the side of the roadway, makeshift cenotaphs of tragic road accidents. South, the road wound through empty hills and cattle pastures before rising steadily into the Bears Paw Mountains, passing junctions east to the even smaller rural settlements of Lloyd and Cleveland or west into the Rocky Boy Reservation, before dead-ending farther up the summit. Those few thousand feet of elevation were enough to cool the land and encourage the growth of thick stands of pines and Douglas fir. Clear cold streams in dappled shade sheltered rainbow trout. Trails little more than deer tracks provided pony trekking through the woodland and meadows. There was even a small ski lift nearby for those who liked their winter sports uncrowded, if basic.

The town itself nestled into a wide, crooked valley enclosed by the Baldy, Corrigan, and Sawtooth peaks. What downtown it could boast of were mainly businesses, the only inhabitants being those owners who chose to live in the apartments above their shops. A stucco and tin roof double garage housed the town's only fire engine, a single small emergency truck their only defense against periodic brush fires during the drought season. A few dilapidated mobile homes, most of them rented rather than owned and none of them mobile, huddled together at the far end of the road, not in sufficient number or organized enough to call themselves a trailer park.

The vast majority of Redemption's population lived spread out for several miles in all directions along the valley, hard-pack dirt roads unmarked on any map leading to individual ranch houses, a few of them working farms, most not. Some posted signs advertising FARM FRESH EGGS or built makeshift stands of wooden crates with garden veggies on offer, if they were close enough to the main road to attract any passing tourist dollars.

The Grinnin' Bear Café dominated the northern fork, the first sanctuary the unwary traveler would see coming into the town from the Hi-Line. It might not be situated in the most lucrative area to attract passing custom, but it had little competition locally, and the backdrop of a pink and golden sunset glowing on the low mountains more often than not made up for any downside in location.

Farther along, St. Mary Magdalene's crowned a small knoll overlooking the Fairfax Creek. A small complex of neat port-a-cabins serving as classrooms adjoined the Victorian main house, the boarding school run much like an old-fashioned hotel for a young clientele. During school term, students in blue shorts and white T-shirts would pour out with clockwork regularity to play soccer or softball on the grass in front of the main house, squealing with childish laughter, while women in severe skirts and jackets supervised with formidable gusto.

On the prettiest side of the valley, the Bakkers had built their sizeable rancho-style mansion—pristine whitewashed walls, huge Gothic arched windows threaded with delicate stained glass, matching stables and a tidy paddock where an Appaloosa mare and two bay geldings with immaculate white stockings nibbled the grass. Massive curved columns of river-polished rock shaped the main chimney, the huge inglenook fireplace visible through French windows if the brocade curtains were pulled back. The thick-planked cedar front door opened on black iron hinges, metal twisted into curlicues of ivy leaves and vines. Bougainvillea and wisteria draped from pillars surrounding a cool veranda, clipped lawns kept a uniform emerald green with hidden sprinklers.

The front entrance to the Bakker property enclosed wrought-iron gates set into a European-style faux gatehouse rolling on electric tracks to allow selected access. As the walls disappeared into the wooded grounds, brick gave way to utilitarian electrified barbed wire adorned every hundred yards or so with signs that read KEEP OUT and PRIVATE PROPERTY and GUARD DOGS ON DUTY with the image of a snarling Doberman for those lacking in literacy skills. The Bakkers didn't own any Dobermans, but a motley crew of German Shepard mongrels was unfriendly enough to keep most intruders at bay. Less visible but higher-tech security defended against the more determined visitor, with armed security guards disguised as ranch hands, the Bakkers' concern with vigilance bordering on paranoia.

Just over the hill and prudently removed from her more refined neighbors' eyesight by a line of tall pines, George's house shared the barbed-wire fence-line with the Bakkers. Her gate at the top of the access road was an old rusted cattle guard left perpetually open, the weathered split-log fence facing the main road decorated only by bright red plastic tubes for newspapers and a U.S. mailbox pocked with .22 dimples.

A dozen miles away at the opposite end of the valley, Hazel Mae Beecham's modest bungalow was slowly being transformed into a pleasant two-story family home, still bedecked with scaffolding and untidy piles of lumber. Red

Wolf shared this end of the town with five other unexceptional houses spaced far enough apart to maintain a cordial seclusion, as close to a "suburb" as Redemption got. Although he exchanged waves with anyone out mowing a lawn or walking their dog, he didn't choose to socialize much with his neighbors. If it weren't for his kids playing with theirs, he wouldn't have even known anyone's name. He didn't particularly care for this area—too white and insular for his liking—and he resented the occasional well-meaning but forced efforts his neighbors made to prove their open-mindedness, making him feel more like the token Indian, not less. But it was a good place for the kids to grow up, as safe and quiet as anywhere could be, so he'd tolerated it. For now.

Lucas Jensen didn't live in Redemption. He chose instead to rent a small house in a new housing development on the outskirts of Havre, on a cul-de-sac off Twenty-fourth Avenue near Saddle Butte. He hated Redemption. He'd always felt like the outsider, like the people there judged him by standards he couldn't quite grasp. He was resentful of being beholden to the Ryton family for the connections that had gotten him the job with Sheriff Holbrook in the first place. And he was even more annoyed by the suspicion that whispers going on behind his back had kept him from getting a job with the Havre City Police, a necessary stepping stone in his career plans to head on to bigger and better places.

He had even toyed with the notion of possibly joining up with the ATF or Homeland Security, trying hard to hide his pleasure at being included in tossing his ex-wife's house, while angry with himself for feeling like the fat kid pathetically grateful to be picked for the team. Any illusion of camaraderie had been all too easily shattered by the disapproving glances and the cold brush-off after he'd kicked the cat.

It was just a friggin' alley cat, he thought darkly on the

drive back to Havre. He must have shot and killed hundreds of the damned pests growing up, what the hell was the big deal? It's not like he'd bombed a train.

The lights were off in the house by the time he got home, Wendy's car missing. He parked in the drive intentionally at an angle to prevent her from pulling her car up next to his and making it difficult to get his own car door open every goddamned morning. She'd just have to park that heap of scrap metal on the curb next to the garbage can, where it belonged.

The house was cold, the stale smell of last night's dinner clinging in the air: burnt onions and pork chops. He turned up the thermostat, taking no notice to what temperature—it could turn the place into a fucking sauna for all he cared. He got a Bud out of the fridge and popped the cap off with his thumb, letting it bounce on the kitchen floor and stay there. He drained the bottle in one go, popped the cap off a second, and took it into the living room.

Sprawling on the sofa, he picked up the remote and switched on the television, channel-surfing until he found a sports program, basketball. He didn't recognize either of the teams and didn't give a shit. As the evening grew darker, he didn't bother turning on the lights, the television casting flickering blue shadows on the walls. After the fourth beer, he got the bourbon out of the breakfront cabinet and poured himself a tumblerful without ice. He sat and knocked back half the bottle inside an hour, annoyed that it seemed to be having no effect on him at all. He glared balefully at two sportscasters, beefy has-beens past their prime blathering into the camera while grinning like idiots. They might as well have been speaking in Swahili, for all the attentiveness he was giving them, when he heard Wendy's car drive up.

She came in the door, her cheap perfume wafting before her like a tear gas assault, and turned on the lights. Without looking at her, Lucas lifted his wrist and pointedly gazed at his watch. "Where you been?"

She came around the sofa into his line of sight, her handbag balanced precariously on her shoulder as she juggled a pizza box and a cellophane-wrapped bouquet of flowers. His eyes narrowed, but she smiled, oblivious. "Sorry, it ran on a little longer than we expected." When he didn't respond, she added, "Kristel's birthday party? I told you about it this morning? You said I should pick up something on my way home." She lifted the pizza box, as if it were an exhibit in a court trial. "I got your favorite."

He vaguely remembered something about a girls' night out, but he hadn't been paying much attention. Unless she had her clothes off, she wasn't the sort of woman he ever paid much attention to. "Flowers?" he growled.

"Yeah," she said, brightening. Her eyes glistened and her cheeks were flushed. He realized she'd had a few too many herself, resenting that she had reached that pleasant stage of anesthesia he desperately craved. "I thought they'd look nice, cheer the place up a little, y'know?"

He drained what was left in his tumbler before pouring another drink, the bottle now almost empty.

"Flowers," he repeated, his tone dangerous.

This time she heard it. She froze, her head lifting unblinkingly, like a deer caught in the headlight. "They're really pretty, they're carnations," she said. "They smell like cinnamon." She started to hold the bouquet out toward him, then stopped, her entire body quivering.

"You're spending money on flowers."

"They weren't very much—"

"You're wasting my fucking money on a bunch of fucking flowers." He lifted the tumbler and threw the bourbon back into his throat, the harsh liquid burning, the fumes scouring his sinuses clean.

"I'm sorry, baby," Wendy said in that little-girl voice he hated. She dropped her handbag and put the pizza and the flowers on the coffee table before squatting down beside the sofa, running the palm of her hand along his thigh tentatively. He felt a muscle in his jaw twitch. "I'm really, really sorry. You've had a bad day, haven't you? Wan' me to try making you feel better?" She leaned in close, her mouth open for an expectant kiss, the sour reek of beer on her breath.

He pushed her away hard enough for her ass to thump onto the floor gracelessly, and studied the emotions flooding across her face: fear, self-pity, and a cunning animal instinct for self-preservation, but not anger. *Not anger.* God, how he so wished she'd just get mad, just retaliate the way George had in the early days of their marriage, give him a good reason. This childlike helplessness of hers was like being smothered to death in cotton candy, he couldn't bear it any longer.

He lifted his foot and carefully placed the sole of his boot against her cheek, watching her hands flittering uncertainly but not daring to push him away. He waited a moment, hoping she would react, then shoved her hard, knocking her down.

She collapsed onto the floor and started to cry big, weepy drunken tears. He despised her. He poured the last of the bourbon into his tumbler and stood up, stepping over her as if avoiding a pile of dog shit on the sidewalk.

"Get out," he said calmly.

She lifted her head far enough off the floor to gaze at him, mascara running, her expression bewildered. "What?"

He picked her handbag up off the floor, rooting in it for her keys. They were on a keychain attached to a fuzzy cartoon bunny with floppy ears and goggly eyes. The saccharine cuteness of it made him want to tear its head off. Instead, he sorted through her meager collection of keys—her car, her mother's front door, her gym locker, her bike lock—until he found his house key and pried it off the ring.

"I want you gone. Now." He pocketed the key and tossed her handbag at her.

"Baby, you don't mean that—"

He bent over her, his lips pulled back into a feral smile, and bellowed into her face. *"Get the fuck out of my house!"*

Shocked, she blanched, blinking at him stupidly but not moving. He reached down and grabbed her by both arms, hauling her roughly to her feet. He nearly laughed as—*finally!*—the bitch began to struggle, her efforts halfhearted and feeble, but enough to trigger the welcome rage welling up in him. He smacked her across the head, her hair whipping around. She gasped, more in disbelief than pain, her arms raised defensively as he slapped her again, this time with more force. Then he dug his fingers into her scalp, his nails scraping against skin, and dragged her to the front door by her hair.

He managed to open the door and tried to maneuver her through the doorway, not so easy with her twisting around in his grip like a sack of snakes, whimpering as she pleaded with him. He couldn't make out her words, wasn't listening anyway, intent only on getting her out of his house. It wasn't much of a scuffle, the fight unequal, but her tenacity surprised him as she clung to the frame, grunting as she refused to budge, resisting his attempts to pry her fingers off. Her face had contorted with the effort, a livid handprint stenciling her cheek where he'd struck her. He leaned back and stared at her, then punched her hard in the face.

That made her let go. She covered her head with both hands protectively as he heaved her out onto the lawn. She fell clumsily, arms and legs akimbo, and scrabbled in the grass toward him as he slammed the door closed and locked it.

"Lucas! *Lucas!*" He tried to shut out her strident howling as she sat crumpled on the front yard, bawling her head off like a three-year-old. *"Lucas!"* The hysterics were chopping his name into wet syllables.

He found a roll of plastic garbage bags under the sink and went from room to room, gathering her things and shoving them into the bags. There wasn't much; he hadn't ever allowed her to clutter up his home with her belongings, but it was amazing how much junk she'd managed to sneak in anyway: ceramic animals and kitschy souvenirs, trashy romance novels, and her endless, endless fashion magazines cluttering up his living room shelves. Exercise videos and CDs of whiny women singing sad love songs. He tossed in the potted plants off his kitchen windowsill, her herbal teas, her organic meusli.

He dumped her clothes straight from the drawers, her undies and bras, jeans and T-shirts. He jerked her dresses out of the closet, stuffing them into the bag hangers and all, along with all her shoes. He swept her jewelry box and trinkets off the top of the bureau with one arm, and shoved the ludicrous assortment of frilly lace throw pillows from the bed after them. He tossed in the framed photo of the two of them together—the only one in existence, to his knowledge—hearing the glass break as he banged the plastic bag against the bedpost. The bathroom was the biggest headache: all her jars and bottles and tubes and potions and makeup and a hodgepodge of mysterious electrical gadgets, her brushes and combs and hairpins and shampoos and moisturizers and toners and fingernail polish and fluffy little hand towels with more cutesy-poo rabbits on them—all of it, into the bags, wiping her existence out of his life.

Her possessions filled three large garbage bags, and as he dragged them to the front door he glanced around to make sure he hadn't missed anything, then shoved in the pizza and the flowers just for good measure.

She'd managed to get to her feet, wobbling with her arms hanging loosely by her side and her head lolling back as she sobbed brokenly. Neighbors had wandered out to watch the show, porch lights casting zombie shadows as they stood at a careful distance with arms crossed and faces puckered in disapproval like bulldogs sucking on a lemon.

He flung the bags at her one at a time. "Here! Take your shit and fuck off!" One of the bags burst on impact, spewing her belongings across the grass. He didn't wait for an answer, not caring if she gave one, before slamming the door and locking it.

Breathing heavily, he rummaged around in the breakfront for another bottle of something strong enough, finding a bottle of mescal, stiff worm floating on the bottom. That would do. He sat back down on the sofa, the television still yammering away, and felt pins and needles drift up his left arm. For a moment, he shuddered, certain this was a sign of the heart attack he'd always feared.

Goddamned women, he thought. He knew they'd be the death of him.

He welcomed it. *Take me. Just do it and get it over with.*

But the pain subsided, to his disappointment. He gulped the mescal, barely aware of Wendy's car doors banging, or the engine roaring as she drove away.

It was nearly three A.M. when he opened his eyes, not sure what had woken him, unaware he'd even been asleep. Wendy's car. The sound of her shrill voice outside, shouting.

"You fucking bastard!"

*What?* He stirred and groaned as the beginning of a vicious hangover gripped him by the forehead in a vise-like intensity.

"You're an asshole, you know that? You're a fucking goddamned asshole!"

Wearily, he got up and wandered over to the front window, watching indifferently as Wendy stood screaming abuse, her fists clenched stiffly by her sides. Even from this distance, he could see she had a beaut of a black eye, her left eyelid purple and swollen nearly shut. A few bedroom lights flicked on, curtains twitching across the street.

"You treat people like shit and expect everyone to kiss your ass, you . . . you . . . *asshole!*" Her ranting spiraled into incoherent gibberish as she danced in frustration. She tugged at her finger, yanking off the small ring he'd given her and threw it at him. It tinked against the window glass and fell into the bushes outside. "I wouldn't marry you if you were the last man on earth!"

*Now* she was angry, he thought cynically. Her timing always did suck.

Her pathetic attempt to salvage her self-esteem over and done with, she stomped back to the curb, pausing to kick over his garbage can—a pointless gesture since the can was empty—before she got into her car and slammed the door as hard as she could. She'd obviously been drinking, and drinking a lot, judging by the way she lurched all over the road as she drove off, nearly ramming into parked cars. He debated briefly whether or not to call the Havre PD and report her, let them toss her freaking butt in jail before she killed someone.

Then he decided he didn't care enough what happened to her, or to anyone else, drew the curtains, and headed for bed.

# CHAPTER TWENTY-TWO

As jails went, Trinity had certainly spent time in worse.

On a dusty, remote road, he'd turned and knelt as he'd been instructed, hands laced on his head, and allowed the female officer to handcuff him before she locked him in the back of her Impala cruiser. He'd tried to relax as much as he could on the ride into town, not an easy task as the back of the car had been designed more for the convenience of police officers rather than the comfort of their passengers. Plexiglas completely enclosing the back of the car muffled the chatter of her police radio, as well as cut off any access to the driver or door handles. The windows were barred, and the seat itself was unupholstered, simply a hard gray plastic shell with slip-proof strips and a drain hole on the floor. It smelled faintly of vomit and disinfectant.

It was dark by the time they'd arrived at the Hill County Detention Center. He'd been led in as meekly as a slaughterhouse calf where he was processed politely enough, if efficiently. They'd asked him the usual questions, which he answered truthfully, and waited patiently as computers hummed and pencils scratched and officers yawned. It took a while at that time of the night to find someone who knew how to use the specialized Cognident reader needed to decipher the implants in his tattooed palm.

"What'd you say your name was again?" the custody officer asked him.

"Ben Trinity."

"Uh-huh. This here says your name is LeRoy Mitchell Walker. Junior, like one of you wasn't enough. Eleven convictions for arson." The man raised an eyebrow at Trinity. "You saying that's not you?"

Trinity paused for a moment, his mind slow with fatigue, trying to puzzle out the correct answer. Yes, he was saying that, no, that wasn't him. "Yes, sir," he decided.

"Thought so."

He didn't demur, whatever conclusion the officer had reached.

"You picked a bad time to go burning down a motel there, LeRoy. This being a Friday night, you won't even be posting bond until you see the judge at nine A.M. Monday morning, at the earliest. We're a full house; you might have to stand in line."

Delahue would have his three days.

Trinity stood against the wall marking his height for his booking photo—front, left, right, a number and his alias spelled out with white letters on the computer image—then had his fingerprints digitally recorded. He submitted to a strip search, pissed in a plastic cup, and had the inside of his mouth explored with a wooden tongue depressor and a Q-tip. They handed him back his clothing, minus his belt, his shoelaces, the contents of his pockets and—he was unhappy to see—the ugly sweater. Perhaps they thought he could unravel the yarn and fashion a noose from it. It was chilly in the holding cells, and he could have used the extra warmth.

The holding cells lined the walls like cages in an Eastern European zoo, small and cramped and barren. He walked into the cell without resistance, went to the back wall and sat down on the metal bench, legs stretched in front of him, hands clasped in his lap. A barrel-chested man with baked leather skin and a neck like a tree trunk leered at him from the adjacent cage. He flexed steroid-thickened

arms covered in tattooed sleeves of naked women and motorcycles and swastikas and an American bald eagle with
the Confederate flag clutched in its talons. Sweat-plastered
strands of thinning hair stuck to his scalp, and a ripe odor
radiated in waves from him, as if his body thermostat had
gone haywire. Both his front teeth were missing and he
waggled his tongue at Trinity through the gap.

"Nice little ass you got there for a skinny white boy," he
said with a bad lisp. "Like a sweet Georgia peach, why don'
you scoot on over heah a little closer . . ."

Trinity turned his head and stared at him without expression, until the man's twisted smile faltered and he
blinked watery blue eyes in discomfort before glancing
away, muttering darkly to himself.

If the Hill County jail was cleaner and less sadistic than
environments Trinity had spent too many years surviving,
life inside the detention center was still oddly familiar:
harsh lighting, regardless of day or night. Footsteps echo-
ing as night-shift guards strolled along the corridors, bored
and sleepy. Drunks and crazies shouted nonsense and were
ignored, spitters and biters screamed abuse through spit-
hoods tied over their heads while prisoners who had obviously been guests of the facility several times in the past
laughed and joked and cursed and jeered and snored and
banged the cages just for the hell of it.

And that was pretty much how it was for next two days,
long empty hours punctuated with bad food three times a
day to keep track of the time.

"Hey, LeRoy. Sarge says you don't want to phone anyone,"
one of the guards said on what Trinity calculated had to be
Sunday evening, judging by the cuisine in the Styrofoam
box. "You sure? A friend, bondsman, lawyer, anybody?"

"Don't need to," Trinity said quietly. "They'll know I'm
here."

"Who will?" When Trinity didn't answer, the guard
shrugged. "Suit yourself."

On Monday afternoon, Trinity had just finished the bag lunch handed to him through the food slot of the door—a thin smear of peanut butter between slices of white bread and a bruised banana—and was sitting with his eyes closed, head leaned back against the wall, when he heard the clang of the outer steel doors, purposeful footsteps, and loud voices. He recognized one voice before he opened his eyes.

"Hello, Mr. Eastlake."

Eastlake glowered, mouthing *son of a bitch* silently before rounding on the prison guard. "He did give you his correct name, didn't he?" he said accusingly.

The guard's expression had set into one of polite resentment. "Sir, he could have told us he was Elvis Presley, and it wouldn't have made no difference. My guys processed him by the book, checked and double-checked—AFIS, NCIC, and Cognident all came back the same. There's nothing wrong with our system, not on this end. You got a problem with that, you take it out on someone else."

A young man behind them carrying the familiar large black suitcase blinked anxiously behind his glasses, swallowing and lifting his neck as if the collar of his shirt was too tight. The way his eyes kept darting at Eastlake made it clear on whom he feared his superior was likely to take out his anger.

Eastlake exhaled noisily in disgust. "Get him out of there."

They escorted Trinity to an interrogation room where the man in the glasses hooked him up to the Cognident microchip reader, not bothering with finding a comfy chair, the hard plastic seat cold through the fabric of Trinity's trousers. The uniformed guard stood in the corner, legs braced, and arms crossed over his chest, watching as Trinity's fingers were fastened into the palm-reader slots and wires plugged into the computer in the briefcase. It beeped and the technician nodded at his boss. Eastlake sat down across the table from him and leaned in aggressively.

"I think we can dispense with the introductions and just cut to the chase—"

"Um," the young technician said tentatively. "Actually, it is for the record, sir, we kinda need it . . . ?"

Behind Eastlake, Trinity watched a tiny smile flicker across the guard's face, barely more than a twitch at the corners of his mouth.

"Fine," Eastlake spat out. "Is your name Benedictus Xavier Trinity?"

"Yes."

"Is your DSD registration code four seven five, eight three two, zero five?"

"Yes."

By the time the usual questions had been dispensed with, Eastlake's anger had receded into something more controlled and malevolent.

"And you're sure you didn't recognize any of these men, they never showed you any identification?"

"No." Trinity tried to relax, but his pulse was racing, unconvinced that whatever Jackie had done to his implants had actually worked. The technician kept staring at the screen and fiddling with the keyboard, his brows drawn together doubtfully.

"So what made you think they were DSD agents?"

"Who else would they be?" Trinity responded mildly.

"Um, he shouldn't answer a question with a question," the technician objected. He flushed as Eastlake bared his teeth.

"Did either of them speak to you?"

Trinity paused, as if thinking. "One of them asked me if I liked *The X-Files*."

Eastlake stared. "*The X-Files?*"

"Yes, sir."

"It's a television show—," the technician offered.

"Shut up." Eastlake spread his hands on the table and studied them, as if searching for answers in the veins and network of skin. "So let me get this straight: these two men—they picked you up off the street, drove you out into the middle of nowhere, and just dumped you there, with no explanation, is that right?"

"Yes, sir."

"You didn't stop anywhere along the way?"

Now they were drifting onto hazardous ground. "No, sir," Trinity said, keeping his voice as steady as he could manage.

"And you have no idea whatsoever where you were."

"That is correct."

"You saw *nothing* at all, that entire time? No buildings, no people, no cars, no trees, nothing. What are you, fucking *blind?*"

"I thought I was being taken somewhere out-of-the-way where they intended to execute me," Trinity said quietly. "So I wasn't really into doing that much sightseeing."

Eastlake slammed his fist on the table, his face red. "Don't get smart with me," he said sharply.

Behind Eastlake, the uniformed officer tilted his head, his half-smile quizzical. When Trinity's eyes flicked up toward him past Eastlake's shoulder, the DSD agent followed his gaze, turning in his chair. The guard returned his look innocently.

"What?" Eastlake barked. The technician beside him blanched. "You want to get some input on this?"

"No, siree, not me," the guard said serenely. "Just real grateful you gentlemen are allowing me this rare opportunity to observe professionals at work."

Eastlake had clenched his teeth so tightly a tic along his jawline spasmed. He glowered at the young technician who looked up from his screen and shrugged, eyes round behind the glasses, which obviously was not the reaction Eastlake wanted.

"Son of a bitch," Eastlake said, this time audibly. "And you saw nothing else between the time these men left you on the road until the time you were picked up by the Havre Police. You're absolutely sure?"

Trinity squinted slightly. "A lizard, some cows, a couple deer—"

"Shut up," Eastlake snapped, and stood up abruptly, his chair scraping back. "We're done."

As the young technician disentangled Trinity from the Cognident device, Eastlake and the uniformed officer stood outside the open door of the interrogation room, their voices too low to make out words, but the tone all too evident. As soon as the technician had packed up, the two DSD agents left without another word to Trinity. But he remained seated, waiting patiently as the uniformed guard chatted with another officer, conferring over a clipboard before he signed it. Once the other officer had left, the guard stepped back into the room but didn't shut the door. He looked at Trinity with the same curious smile, as if amused by a private joke.

"Y'know," the officer said finally. "I been doing prisoner interviews now for over twenty years. I'd like to think I'm pretty good at it. It's sort of a skill you develop over time— reading body language, listening for meanings behind the words, seeing how a person cuts his eyes left or right when he's thinking, that sort of thing. Tells you a lot more than just a bunch of 'yes' or 'no' answers. So I can usually spot a load of bullshit when I see it."

Trinity kept his eyes down, his heartbeat whooshing in his ears, and swallowed a bubble of acid rising in the back of his throat.

"But, hey. I'm just some second-rate cop in the middle of Hicksville, USA. Who am I to question our fearless leaders with their highfalutin' electronical doohickeys? I'm just supposed to kick you loose and provide you with a taxi home."

Trinity followed the guard, his feet slapping in the undone running shoes, to where his belt and socks and shoelaces and the meager loose change he'd had in his pockets were returned to him, along with the ugly sweater. He signed the receipt, his hands shaking so badly his signature looked like a spider's web. Then he laced up his running shoes and pulled on the ugly sweater, smelling cigarette smoke in the wool.

"I think Officer Bedford's shift starts in about half an hour, if you don't mind waiting," the guard said to Trinity, still amused. "That's the young lady who picked you up hiking over near Studhorse Butte, which, in case you were wondering, was where you were at. I'm sure she wouldn't mind at all chauffeuring you on back to Redemption. But just as a suggestion here? It'd be a real good idea if you avoided making any unnecessary visits to our fair town in the future, if you get my drift."

"Yes, sir," Trinity said softly, paying meticulous attention to doing up his belt.

The guard started to walk away, then turned and snapped his fingers as if remembering something. "Oh, and you might ask her if she still has that bottle of water you were carrying when she picked you up, just in case you wanted that back."

Trinity's head jerked up, the breath punched out of him. The guard's smile widened knowingly.

"Then again, she's probably chucked it out by now anyways."

# CHAPTER TWENTY-THREE

Jack Bakker didn't stay the night, but he stayed until nearly two in the morning helping George try to put her house back into some semblance of order as quietly as possible as not to wake Amy. Finally, he made her stop, his hands on her shoulders.

"Go to bed, George. Before you fall down," he said before he left.

But she couldn't, not immediately; her bedroom had also been thoroughly ransacked, clothes strewn on the floor, her mattress stripped and turned over. But it was when she was picking up the scattered contents of her bedside table that she suddenly realized what was missing, feeling the prickles of dismay heating her face. It took a few more minutes of searching before she was certain; her little vibrator was gone. That, she had no doubt, had been Luke's doing—something to blackmail her with, something he could hold up in a court to humiliate her in his effort to wrest custody of Amy away from her. Finally, she simply wrapped her quilt around her like a mummy and fell asleep on the bare mattress.

"Mom?"

George started awake. It seemed like she had been asleep only minutes when she opened her eyes, sunlight cold against the windows. Amy huddled in the doorway in her bathrobe, her hands tucked under her armpits for warmth. George tried to smile, the skin of her face feeling as dry as paper.

"What is it, sweetpea?"

"Someone's at the door."

A small thrill of fear shot through her, and she pushed it down. "Who is it?"

Amy shrugged listlessly, then went back into her bedroom and shut the door.

George pulled on her jeans, her shirt wrinkled from having been slept in all night, and ran her fingers through her hair. She checked her wristwatch, amazed to see it was well after nine.

When she opened the front door, Dennis Red Wolf turned from where he'd been gazing out over the Bears Paw Mountains while he waited. Deep shadows crept down the sides of the mountain as the sun rose. Birds sang and the air was clean and crisp, as if all was still right with the world. Red Wolf held his deputy's hat in his hands in front of him, his manners seeming incongruous in the midst of chaos.

"How are you, Ms. Jensen?"

"I've had better days." She softened her tone, trying not to appear quite so bad-tempered. "Have they found Ben yet?"

"No, not yet." He shifted his weight, the wooden floorboards on the porch creaking under him. "I'm real sorry for all that's happened here."

George tried to shrug it away. "It's not your fault," she said, and was puzzled by the brief look of annoyance that crossed his features. "Have you been down to the café? Is my mother okay?"

"Yeah, she's fine. Mad as hell, but okay." He juggled his hat to reach inside his uniform jacket and extract a small book, holding it out to her. Amy's diary. "Thought you might want to have this."

George took it, then looked up into his face. It was enigmatic again. "Thank you. How'd you get it back?"

"Someone dropped it off this morning." Red Wolf shrugged. "Guess even the feds have a conscience." He shifted his weight again, obviously ill at ease.

"I'm sorry, I should invite you in for a coffee . . ." Her voice trailed off as she smiled wryly. They both recognized how absurd normal civility seemed under the circumstances, and yet just how important.

"No, thank you. I'm on duty." He hesitated. "I heard about your cat. That was uncalled for. It might be too soon, but I got this neighbor. Her cat just had kittens. She's looking for good homes for them, if you're interested."

"Thanks," George said. "I'll see what Amy thinks about it first."

"Of course." He settled his hat back on his head, brushing his braids over his shoulders, and nodded at her. "I'll be going now." He walked back to the dusty Blazer and gave her a little wave before he drove back down her drive and away on the main road. She waved back, liking Dennis Red Wolf more at that moment than ever, suspecting that underneath that formidable exterior was a real softy.

Amy still hadn't come out of her bedroom by noon, and George, assuming she was sleeping, didn't disturb her. Cleaning up the mess in the house took up the rest of the morning: washing and scrubbing and jotting notes onto a list of things she would need to replace. At half past one, she made chicken salad sandwiches for lunch and carried a plate with potato chips and a pickle upstairs, knocking on Amy's bedroom door.

"Amy? Are you hungry?"

Her daughter's face was wan and tired when she opened the door, but she was up and dressed, the bed behind her already made.

More than made, George realized as she stepped inside, amazed. "Wow." It was immaculately tidy. George started to smile with admiration before it hit her, something not quite right. Then she deciphered what was amiss.

The walls were bare, all the movie star and boy band posters and pictures of puppies and horses taken down. The tops of Amy's pair of dressers held her jewelry box on one and her television on the other. But the little curio cabinet of china cats, her collection of glass flower paper-weights, her Winnie the Pooh miniature cottage, all the dolls in their costumes—the cowgirl and the Victorian lady, the Japanese geisha doll and Cleopatra the Egyptian Queen—were gone. The antique Shoo Fly patchwork quilt was tucked neatly around the pillows, but there were no teddy bears propped up against them, no stuffed lions and tigers, no shabby Velveteen rabbit. Half the books in her bookcase were missing, and her study desk seemed re-markably uncluttered, even with the confiscated computer absent.

Then she spotted all the missing bits and pieces, even the Go game Trinity had made for her, piled into a corner by the closet itself in the process of being culled.

"What's going on, Amy?"

Amy shrugged, apathetic. "Nothing."

"So what's this about?" George nodded at the pile of dis-carded things. When Amy didn't answer, she pressed, "What are you planning to do with all these?"

Amy shrugged again. "I don't want it anymore." She glared up, her eyes puffy and bloodshot from crying. "It's all baby stuff anyway. Throw it out or give it to Mizz Bas-sett for her thrift store, I don't care."

George's heart hurt, her stomach hollow with a sadness for her daughter she had no idea how to counter. She sim-ply handed Amy the plate of sandwiches and tried to smile reassuringly. "You'll feel better when you've had some-thing to eat. Bring down the plate when you're done."

George had set the diary on the kitchen table when

Amy brought her empty plate down. Saying nothing, George pushed the book an inch just to attract her daughter's attention. Amy stared at it for a moment, then picked it up and walked away without a word. A little while later, as George stood at the sink washing dishes, her nose wrinkled: she smelled smoke. Vaguely apprehensive, she wandered through the rooms, sniffing, then out into the front and followed her nose around the side of the house.

Amy had a small fire going in the barbecue pit, methodically tearing pages out of the diary and feeding them to the flames one at a time. Tentatively, George stood next to her and returned Amy's glare of defiance with what she hoped was understanding. She put her arm around her daughter's shoulders, watching as the paper curled and blackened. Amy settled the cover onto the fire, the plastic giving off an acrid stink as it melted. The flimsy metal lock turned from brass to a pale pink glow in the heat.

"Do you want me to get you another one?"

"No." Amy shrugged off her mother's arm, rebuffing her embrace. "And I don't want a kitten, either."

George wasn't surprised Amy had been eavesdropping. "That's fine, you give it all the time you want. Whenever you feel ready—"

"No," Amy said sharply. "Not now, not ever." She started to walk away, toward the edge of the trees where she spent hours on end, hiding in the same fortresses of hollow logs and tiny meadows George and Lonny had played in so many years ago, a secret haven where they had felt safe, far away from all the cares of the world and the adults who ran their lives. Amy stopped and looked back over her shoulder at her mother, the expression on her young face far too grim. "Maybe Dad did us a favor, Mom."

Feeling like she was stepping into a minefield, George asked cautiously, "How's that?"

"That's the only way people can ever hurt you, you know. If you let them figure out what it is you care about."

"Oh, honey—"

But Amy glowered, and turned away, her slender back stiff and hostile.

George sat down heavily on the back porch, her arms across her knees, then put her head down against her arms and cried.

# CHAPTER TWENTY-FOUR

Trinity said nothing on the ride back to Redemption. The back of the cruiser was only slightly more comfortable without wearing handcuffs, and when the female officer opened the back to let him out, all his joints ached like an old man's.

"You stay out of trouble, now," was all she said as she got back into the driver's side.

"Yes, ma'am."

He waited until the Impala cruiser had vanished around the curve past the junction before walking toward the Grinnin' Bear Café. The sign read CLOSED but the parking lot was half filled, all cars and pickups he recognized as belonging to locals. He hoped to escape notice, heading for the path leading down to the cabins.

Trinity slowed as he got closer, eyeing the overturned timber planters, compost spilling out, uprooted flowers wilted. A sheet of plywood had been nailed over one window of the building, broken shards rimming the frame, remains of glass glittering in the sunlight on the ground. He could hear loud voices inside, arguing heatedly. He stopped, his head bowed as he listened.

"All I'm sayin' is that I seen the pichurs, absolute proof 9/11 was an inside job setup by our own gov'ment. Just no way buildings fall down that fast on their own, they gotta be blown up—"

"They *were* blown up, asshole. By a couple 747s flying into them—"

"Oh, no," Shep retorted. "Airplane fuel don' work like that. I seen this video where a guy 'splains it all, like how come if it were so hot to melt all them metal girders the heat didn't blow out all the glass windows, huh? And how come if it were so hot them people in the Pentagon got totally incinerated did they just happen to find them so-called hijackers' passports, huh? Same thing with that Amtrak train. How could anyone jess happen to know it'd be sitting right next to them chemical tankers at that exact moment, huh? 'Less the bombs was already *on* that train and not that SUV, waiting 'til it reached them tankers, bet you hadn't thought a that, didja? Yeah, maybe ol' Shep's not so stupid after all, huh?"

"Why in the hell would anyone want to—"

"Jesus, Nick, don't encourage him!"

"So's they could keep on scarin' the shit out of everybody, that's why! First they declare war and send our military boys and all the National Guard off to Eye-rac, so's they'd be distracted somewhere's else when martial law gets declared."

"Except nobody declared martial law . . ."

"Only cuzza Katrina. Didn't have to then. Look at N'Orleens, why you think nobody's ever done nuthin' there? Cuz they *wanted* all the blacks and poor people all scattered like the Israelites. Then they cut a deal with the Ay-rabs to drive our economy into the toilet on purpose, make it so people everywhere had to take out loans and credit cards just to keep the roof from falling in. And when we all don't got no more money to pay nothin' back, they make bankruptcy illegal and repossess everthing they got—just like Harry lost his truck—take everbody's houses and buy up their property for pennies 'til they own the whole damned country. That's why it's too late, it don't matter who's in Congress now an' no one can do fuck all about it."

"Shep, will you please shut the hell up?" Trinity heard Tom Mifflin say in a weary voice. "You're startin' to sound as conspiracy-crazy as those damned Hollywood nut jobs."

"Well, nobody gets it wrong all the time," Shep retorted. "And I find it just a bit s'picious all this shit started round here just when *he* showed up. Then he conveniently disappears? Rescued by his gov'ment pals, more like it, jess before they come down on us like a ton a bricks. I'm telling you, he's no terrist, he's one of them NSA secret agents. And all that 'lectronic stuff in him? They're CIA bionical spy devices. He was sent in to infiltrate us, part of a covert plan to put us all in those concentration camps Halliburton's building. I seen 'em, you know, they got barbed wire and spotlights up where the old World War Two POW camps was—"

"If you don't shut your trap, I'm going to kick you out of my café," Trinity heard Carlene say crossly.

"But Carlene, I'm jess saying I agree with you," Shep whined. "I'm on *your* side. I never did think he was no al Qaeda terrist. I mean, he is white, ain't he?"

"Oh, for fuck sake," Will Paterson growled. Trinity heard a scuffle and hastily stepped back, but not in time to avoid being seen as Paterson bundled Shep out the front door of the café. Shep stumbled to a halt in front of Trinity, and stared stupidly.

"Hey, he's still here!"

Paterson simply looked at Trinity, then turned on his heel, going back inside.

Shep pranced around him skittishly, wagging a finger. "I'm on to you, buddy," he said, lips pulling back in an unconvincing grin. "You ain't fooling me none . . ." Trinity stood watching warily as Shep retreated, got into his battered pickup and drove off, black smoke belching from the tailpipe. *Just great*, Trinity thought. *Half the town thinks I'm a terrorist and the other half thinks I'm an agent provocateur.*

Inside, the café had gone quiet, waiting. Trinity inhaled a deep breath and opened the screen door. No one said a word as he walked inside, a tableau of silent, pinched faces turned toward him.

Although the locals had obviously rallied round Carlene and helped to clear up the wreckage, the café still looked like the aftermath of a particularly bad Saturday night drunken brawl. And now it had the atmosphere of a war room, the committee in an obdurate mood. Trinity waited, as if standing in front of a firing squad.

"Where the *hell* have you been?" Carlene demanded, breaking the silence.

"In jail."

Carlene stared, incredulous. "In *jail!* What for?"

"Arson." He shrugged, then swallowed, his throat dry. "They thought I was someone else, mistaken identity. A computer error. It took a while to get sorted out."

Carlene went white, trembling so badly Tom Mifflin had to help her to a counter stool. "I don't believe this. I had my business and my home turned upside down because of a computer error?" she said, her voice almost inaudible with anger. "They trashed my daughter's house and confiscated her belongings for nothing? Interrogated everybody in this town and frightened the living daylights out of my friends and neighbors because some idiot made a goddamned *mistake?*"

"Ms. Ryton, I am so sorry—"

*"They took my son's letters!"*

The ferocity of her anguish left him speechless.

"They took Lonny's letters," she said more calmly, but tears had begun to pour down her face, her grief heartbreaking. "All the ones he sent me from Iraq. He wrote to me every day, and I kept them all, hundreds of them. I never threw any of them away. Now they're gone, my son's letters are gone." She doubled over, her arms clutched around her stomach as if she'd been punched. Jared Ingersoll put his arm around her, patting her back awkwardly. "I have nothing left of him, *nothing . . .*"

Trinity spun around and ran. He stumbled out of the café, nearly falling down, and staggered blindly across the parking lot, knocking into cars and setting off alarms, before his knees gave way. He collapsed, his hands sliding in the sharp-edged gravel as he struggled to keep from pitching facedown onto the ground.

He gulped his breaths like a beached fish, his lungs burning as if all the oxygen had been sucked out of the air. Slowly, he managed to sit upright, his legs folded under him. He sat on the ground for several minutes, alone, before he heard footsteps behind him. He didn't try to stand, looking up as Will Paterson and Tom Mifflin and Nick Gilman encircled him silently. Will Paterson shook a cigarette out of a pack and lit it with an old-fashioned lighter, the smell of butane sharp. He squinted at Trinity as he blew out the smoke, then sighed and looked away dispiritedly.

"I wish you people would just lynch me," Trinity murmured. "You'd be doing me a favor."

"That's too bad," Will said slowly with a tight smile. "Don't think anyone is in the mind to be doing you any favors just now."

Red Wolf hated stereotypical Indian myths, particularly the one about Indians being able to glide through the woods like silent invisible ghosts. Yes, he'd grown up hunting game, could track a deer or an antelope capably enough, knew how to stay downwind, move slowly, low to the ground. If you were as slender and as small as someone like Apanakhi, then maybe you could be a noiseless stalker. But when you're built like a goddamn bear, you're as noisy as a goddamn bear, Indian or otherwise. So he made no effort to hide his presence, had no intention sneaking up behind Trinity as he followed the trail past the fishing cabins and down to the creek.

He spotted Trinity sitting on a fallen log at a small bend in the stream. Green-gray water boiled over boulders, deep rippled pools in the center, a cloud of fat mosquitoes hovering over the water, a fine spot for fish. A tackle box full of lures stood open beside Trinity, but the fishing rod leaned against the log, the line still in the reel. Trinity sat with his head in his hands, staring across the water, oblivious to Red Wolf's approach until the Indian was nearly on him. He spun around so fast it startled Red Wolf, the naked fear in his expression shocking.

"Whoa," Red Wolf said, holding his hands up appeasingly. "Take it easy."

Trinity stood, his eyes darting around distrustfully, as spooked as any deer. "Is there a problem?"

Red Wolf wasn't even in uniform, wearing an embroidered denim shirt and well-worn jeans with a squash blossom belt buckle. "Not that I know of." Red Wolf didn't go any closer to the man, as cautious as if Trinity were standing on the ledge of a tall building. He tried to smile and adopt a relaxed posture. "Ms. Ryton said you'd likely be down here."

"Is she okay?"

"Doing better. Jack Bakker's staying with her for a few days, help her get stuff put back in order." He glanced at the fly rod. "You fishing?"

He watched Trinity's throat contract as he swallowed. "Yes, sir."

"Catch anything?"

"No."

Red Wolf raised an eyebrow. "Y'know, it kinda helps if you actually put the line in the water."

After a moment, Trinity returned his smile wanly. "Knew I had to be doing something wrong."

"What do you city boys know from fishing?" Red Wolf said genially, but still watchful. He nodded at the log. "Mind if I join you?"

In answer, Trinity shifted to the far end of the log, giving

Red Wolf as much room as he wanted. They sat for a long time without speaking, Red Wolf with his elbows on his knees, hands loosely clasped as he gazed placidly out on the water, all the while his attention focused on the man beside him.

"I owe you an apology," Red Wolf finally said.

"What for?"

"I was the one who called in Sam Delahue."

"You were just trying to help."

"Yeah," Red Wolf agreed. "Me, not you." He twisted his head to glance sidelong at Trinity. "I wanted you the hell out of Redemption."

Trinity didn't look up to meet his eyes, shrugging. "Fair enough."

"No," Red Wolf said firmly. "There was nothing fair about it. You being here was causing too much of a nuisance. Sooner or later some dickwad like Craig Bakker would go too far. You'd end up dead, we'd end up with a load of grief from DSD and Homeland Security, and nobody wins. I didn't see as I had a whole lot of options."

"How do you know Sam Delahue?" Trinity's voice was so lifeless Red Wolf wasn't sure if he was curious or just trying to be polite.

Red Wolf straightened, stretched his legs, and examined the tips of his cowboy boots. "I tried doing the right thing once before. We had a problem that couldn't be solved through normal channels. Sam fixed it." He snorted a cheerless laugh. "It came at a high price, though." He glanced at Trinity who was now watching him. "Doing the right thing can cause a lot of collateral damage to innocent people. Sometimes it just isn't worth it."

"True," Trinity agreed.

Conversation died, making Red Wolf oddly uncomfortable. Another Indian myth shattered, he thought wryly. Trinity seemed to be the one content to sit in taciturn indifference while he was ill at ease with the silence. "Why you?"

"Why me what?"

"I've read your DOJ files. You and your wife made several trips all over the Middle East—Lebanon, Jordan, Saudi Arabia, Egypt. You did business with some pretty shady characters. The financial records seemed pretty clear, your signature was on all the papers. The e-mails were sent from your company's computers. The facts are all there in black and white."

"Well, you know more than I do, then."

Trinity seemed not only unsurprised, but resigned, not even making a token protest that he'd been framed. That alone only increased Red Wolf's uncertainties.

"If you're innocent, what did you do that made them that pissed off at you?"

"A question I gave up trying to answer a long time ago." Trinity shot a peculiar glance at him. "*If* I'm innocent?"

"I read the transcripts. No one ever mentioned your son or making any deal. You confessed to funneling money to terrorists. You had nothing to gain from admitting you were guilty and everything to lose, maybe even your life. So why do it if you honestly believe you were innocent?"

Trinity laughed, a low chuckle deep in his chest, and looked back out over the creek. A smallmouth bass leapt into the air, stippled body twisting, and splashed back into the water, leaving only ripples behind. Somehow, Red Wolf suspected Trinity wasn't even aware of it.

"'Transcripts.' Interesting. I never saw a lawyer or the inside of a court. Cameras and tape recorders were banned inside the prison, not even notebooks and pens allowed in. Detainees answered to numbers, not names. I have no idea where I was held for three years, not even what country I was in. No one came to see me outside of the guards and the interrogators, *ever*. But sure, I confessed. You seriously telling me you've never beaten the crap out of someone to get him to tell what you want to hear?"

"Never," Red Wolf said. Trinity raised a skeptical eyebrow at him, irritating him. "*Never*," he repeated more forcefully. "I'm not Luke Jensen and I don't care what bullshit you see on TV, I don't need to play fast and loose with the rules. And not because it's wrong—I couldn't give a shit about half the people I arrest—but because it doesn't work. No one ever tells you their deepest secrets if you bully them; they clam up and spit in your face."

"Yeah, well," Trinity said tiredly, "I guess I'm not that much of a hardened criminal. I'm just an English teacher. I wasn't tough enough to clam up and spit in anyone's face. I got to the point pretty damned quick where I'd have confessed to shooting JFK and sinking the *Titanic* if it would make them stop." His voice had dropped to a near whisper. "Anything to make it stop."

Red Wolf was no stranger to the evil and brutality human beings could inflict on each other; he'd seen it often enough. But this bothered him on a level he didn't quite understand himself.

"*We* did this to you, we tortured you?"

"You mean my fellow Americans?" Trinity shifted on the log, then grimaced with a sharp hiss, his injuries obviously still painful. "Not in the detention camps, no. Maybe I was a shade too white, American, and Christian for them to cross that line. I was interrogated by people who told me they were FBI or CIA or MI6. Maybe they were, I don't know. But they got other people to do the dirty work for them while they watched, all hands-off. After a while, no one even bothered with the questions anymore, they didn't want to know anything. Besides, it's not considered torture if it doesn't kill you." He closed his eyes, his head bowed. "Can we not talk about this anymore?"

"No problem," Red Wolf said with some relief. Even this much had left him with a disturbing sense of voyeurism, feeling vaguely dirty and ashamed. He slapped at a mosquito on his neck, wiped the body off on his jeans, and glanced at Trinity, wondering why he wasn't bothered by the damned little bloodsuckers. His skin looked pallid, his face pinched with pain. "You okay?"

"Fine," was the automatic response, although the man looked anything but.

"Look, if you're still hurting, why won't you take the painkillers?"

Trinity didn't open his eyes, but smiled faintly. "I know it doesn't seem like it, but I really do try my best to avoid temptation."

Red Wolf puzzled over this for a moment, not liking what it implied. Suicide could be as problematical as murder. Then he stood up. "Anyway, I just wanted to say sorry about how things turned out. You could have been in Canada right now."

Trinity looked up, his expression hard. "Or I could be back in prison or dead, while you and Sam Delahue and the others ended up being indicted with aiding and abetting a terrorist to escape."

"Yeah," Red Wolf agreed uneasily. "Maybe." He started to walk back up the trail, then stopped with an afterthought, Trinity's remark about temptation nagging him. "Could I ask you one more thing?" When Trinity didn't react, he said, "You and George Jenson . . . you two haven't . . . ?"

"No," Trinity said flatly.

"It's none of my business, but it might be a good idea to keep it that way."

When Trinity nodded, Red Wolf turned to leave.

"A prison guard got a bit too creative with a Taser when I was in Tallahassee," Trinity added from behind him. "I have some trouble in that department now." He looked up with a bitter smile. "Seems they didn't have quite the same qualms in Florida with me being white, American, and Christian."

A chill shot through Red Wolf's blood.

*Doing the wrong thing could be a pain in the ass as well,* he thought.

After Dennis Red Wolf left, Trinity waited until the air became chill, the sky turning that peculiarly dark azure just before sunset, before going back up to the cabins. He replaced Lonny's fly rod from the lean-to and dealt with the mess that had been left of his cabin. While the interior didn't display quite as much damage as the café, he didn't own as much either. Clothing that had been tossed onto the floor was easily enough picked up and put away again. The kitchen cabinets had been emptied, but replacing pots and pans and dishes and tins back onto the shelves took minutes. He swept up flour and sugar and instant coffee that had been poured out onto the counters and floor, and mopped the floor where garbage had been dumped.

It was the missing things that baffled him: the bar of used soap in the shower stall, his meager collection of paperbacks, his son's photograph, a half-empty carton of milk. The daybed had been overturned, the thin mattress slit open, handfuls of stuffing yanked out. What anyone was looking for escaped him, the vindictiveness of it all so petty.

He righted the daybed, replaced the mattress, and re-made the bed, using the sheet to hold in as much of the stuffing as he could. Then he crawled in under the quilt, his body aching, and dropped almost immediately into a dreamless sleep.

If Trinity hadn't been so exhausted, he might have woken sooner. As it was, he was only aware that the subtle noises outside his cabin had been going on for some time before he struggled his way out of sleep. He'd heard plenty of other sounds before, learned to identify most of them and filter them out of his consciousness—deer exploring the porch, squirrels pattering across the roof, the scrape of branches and trees rustling in the wind—but these were different, furtive and human.

He sat up in bed, his eyes straining to make out shadows in the gloom, his heart pounding. After a minute or two of silence, he thought he might have been dreaming it, then he sniffed the air warily.

Kerosene.

A flicker of orange light teasing between the slats of the wooden shutters told him the rest of the story. Alarmed, he threw back the quilt and leapt out of bed, at the window in two strides. But the shutters wouldn't open: wood shims shoved between shutter and sill jamming them shut. He tried the door, but couldn't pull it open more than an inch, even though it was unlocked. A sudden whoosh of air and within seconds what had began as just a few small flames licking at the windows became an impenetrable blaze surrounding him. Through the loud crackle of fire, he dimly heard the engine of a four-by-four revving loudly as it drove off.

He grabbed the quilt off the bed, ran into the bathroom and turned the shower on, soaking his hair and the quilt with water. With the drenched quilt over his head, he ran back, tipped the mattress off the daybed and tried to use the metal frame as a battering ram against the door. Smoke had filled the room now, roiling swirls of black so thick he could barely see, his eyes streaming. It ripped at his lungs, choking him like a vise around his throat.

The fire's speed appalled him, a vicious howl as it consumed the cabin around him, trapping him inside walls of flame. He dragged the bedframe back and put all his weight behind propelling it into the door. This time, something gave, just enough to suck fresh oxygen into the room, feeding the fire, punching him like a huge fist.

He was dragging the bedframe back for another desperate attempt when he heard shouting and the crack of an axe against the door. It flew open, Jack Bakker staggering back with one arm over his face as he yelled, unheard over the roar of the fire. Trinity clenched the wet quilt around his head and staggered outside, across the porch, and down the stairs. The cold air hit his face with a shock like ice water. Jack yanked him along the ground, slapping at Trinity's head, hair smoldering, until they were both far enough away from the fire to collapse. For several minutes, Trinity sat on the ground, unable to speak, coughing helplessly as Jack thumped on his back. Heat blasted out from the cabin like a living thing, bright sparks as the resin in the cabin's timber popped and snapped. Pine needles on the nearby trees glowed as they shriveled in the heat, as if shrinking away in apprehension.

"That was just a little too close," Jack said, his voice hoarse.

Trinity tried to answer, his voice gone, lungs seared. The cabin was completely engulfed now, nothing left to save as the fire truck lumbered along the mountain trail, siren wailing thinly. Blue flashing lights slivered through the trees, casting dancing shadows. But Trinity could still make out the chain wrapped around the post by the porch steps, slack now where it had been threaded through the handle of the door—crude but effective.

Then Trinity caught Jack's look, emergency lights reflecting facets on his eyes. Trinity followed his glance to spot Carlene standing at the tree line, one hand at her neck clutching a bathrobe around her, her figure glowing in the reflected firelight. Trinity had nothing on but a now-filthy pair of boxer shorts. He pulled the quilt up around his shoulders, the wet cloth cold on his scarred skin. He felt the cut in his side twinge as he coughed, pulling the stitches, the wound still not healing properly.

Men shouted as the walls of the cabin twisted, roof caving in with a firework spray of sparks taking the front of the cabin with it. The little Franklin stove sat exposed, door hanging from one hinge and the smokestack pipe creaking as it toppled over. The daybed frame glittered, burning paint blistering.

"Come on, Ben," Jack said kindly, and helped him to his feet.

The walk up to the café was slow, his bare feet tender, every dead pine needle and stone sharp along the trail. Cars had pulled into the parking lot, neighbors drawn by the fire—some to offer help, some out of simple curiosity. Conversation died as Trinity walked past them and into the café. He kept his head down, looking at no one.

Carlene had made coffee, pouring cups for everyone, her movement mechanical. The volunteer fire crew eventually wandered back toward the café, the fire truck beeping as it reversed slowly up along the trail.

"Sorry 'bout this, Carlene," Frank Lewis, the fire chief said as he gratefully accepted a cup of coffee from her. His face was nearly black with soot. He'd loosened the front of his fireproof jacket, exposing pajama tops with tiny cartoon fish printed on the flannel. "All we can do is make sure the fire don't spread to the rest of the cabins, but that one's a goner."

"No one was hurt, Frank," Carlene said stiffly. "That's the important thing." Her words seemed ritualistic, hollow.

Lewis sipped his coffee, then sidled over to where Trinity sat staring down into a now-cold cup of his own. "You didn't see who did this?" he asked, his eyes not quite looking at Trinity. Trinity shook his head. "Well, just want you to know . . ." His voice trailed off. When Trinity glanced up, the fire chief's face was rigid, struggling with his words. "It ain't right." He turned as Dennis Red Wolf entered the café. "This just ain't *right*, Dennis," he finished his complaint, and walked away shaking his head.

Red Wolf had obviously jumped out of bed and grabbed whatever clothes were handy, his long hair pulled back in a sleep-tangled ponytail. He stood over Trinity for a long moment, saying nothing, then sat down heavily across from him and rubbed his fingers against his eyes. "Dammit."

The two men sat without speaking, not looking at one another. "Ms. Ryton," Trinity called out after a long moment. "Could I have a beer, please?"

"Sure." She moved automatically toward the bar, taking two steps before she stopped. "What?"

"I think I'll have a whiskey chaser with it as well," Trinity said. Red Wolf was watching him intently. "Make it a double."

"What are you doing?" Red Wolf asked.

"Having a beer." He smiled tightly. "Then after I drink it, I plan to punch you in the face as hard as I can."

The café had gone quiet, men frozen as if in a game of Statues, listening. Red Wolf lowered his voice to a near whisper. "That won't work."

"I have witnesses."

"I'm not going to arrest you."

"Then I'll start punching out everyone here until you do."

"Ben, just give me a couple days."

"No. I can't stay here anymore. It's *finished*."

Red Wolf sat back in the chair and sighed, his mouth working. Jack coughed gently, exchanging a glance with Carlene. "Dennis, he's right. He can't stay here."

Carlene looked away, as if ashamed of her fear.

"Shit," Red Wolf exhaled in frustration.

"But listen, I got me an idee. 'Til you can catch who did this, he's gonna need somewhere safe. There ain't nowhere safer than the ranch. Alison's got a couple million dollars' worth of racehorses, mighty protective of 'em, loves them more 'n her own kids. We got twenty-four-hour guards and a state-of-the art security system." He tried a grin at Trinity, although his eyes were hard. "And it's a hell of a lot more comfortable than prison."

"Alison won't like it, not one bit," Red Wolf warned.

Jack shrugged. "Alison's not in much of a position these days to be telling me what I can and cannot do." He gestured at Trinity. "Come on, son. Let's get you somewhere you can wash up and into some clean clothes. What do you say?"

Trinity's shoulders wilted in defeat. "Damn. I really did want that beer."

# CHAPTER TWENTY-FIVE

Alison Bakker didn't like it one bit. She'd come downstairs in a silk embroidered Japanese dressing gown, her hand trying vainly to straighten her hair as she glared at the two men in her huge sunken lounge. Her eyes were bloodshot and her face pinched with the telltale pain of a belligerent hangover.

As Jack explained the situation tersely, Craig and Sophie wandered out onto the stair landing above, drawn by angry voices disrupting the early morning.

"Someone locked him up in his cabin, then set fire to it, tried to burn him alive."

"It wasn't me, Uncle Jack!" Craig blurted out, alarmed. "I been here all night. Tell him, Mom!"

"Oh, shut up, you little moron," Alison snapped.

"No one thinks you did, son," Jack reassured his nephew.

"So then just why is this suddenly our problem?" Alison demanded.

Jack looked at his sister-in-law with badly disguised contempt. "The boy just had everything he owns gone up in flames, Allie, almost kilt him. He don't even have any clothes left. I know it's difficult for you, but if you can't muster up any genuine Christian compassion, at least try and fake it. You've had plenty of practice doing that over the years, why stop now?" When Alison Bakker scowled but didn't respond, Jack smiled at his niece. "Sophie, you want to go wake up Miss Jenifer for me? Tell her we got a guest needs a room making up?"

The housekeeper, a middle-aged Hispanic woman who barely glanced in his direction, led Trinity up another flight of stairs at the rear of the house, showing him to a room obviously reserved for visitors—antique furnishings and uninspired oil paintings that would have suited an elegant hotel. Comfortable but impersonal.

"You can shower in here," the housekeeper said, opening a door to an en suite bathroom. "I'll see if I can find you some clothes."

"Thank you."

He waited until she had gone to let the wet and dirty quilt fall from his shoulders. As he showered, he heard doors open and close. The quilt had vanished; jeans, a cambric shirt, and brand-new socks and briefs set out on the bed in its place. He moved them to a chair, crawled naked into the bed, and fell asleep.

He woke to a soft knock on the door, pulling the sheet up to cover himself as the door opened. The housekeeper backed into the room, her arms supporting a breakfast tray. She set it on the small table by the chair and turned to leave, never once having looked at him.

"Excuse me, what time is it?" Trinity asked, his voice raw.

"After ten. Mister Bakker said to let you sleep."

"Thank you."

She paused by the door, then glanced at him curiously. She was older than Trinity had first thought. "You're welcome," she said, and left.

He ate, not realizing how ravenous he was until he'd bitten into the hot buttered biscuits and a soft-boiled egg, washing it down with fresh-squeezed orange juice. Then he dressed, the jeans and shirt slightly too large, and went downstairs.

The house was huge, big enough to get lost in, which he

did before stumbling upon the main rooms by following the sound of voices. With only socks on his feet, he made little noise, not enough to alert them. He stopped, listening. Seemed he was doing quite a lot of unintentional eavesdropping these days, he thought ruefully.

"Nobody knows if Shep did it or not, you can't go around arresting someone for being a jerk and shooting his fool mouth off," he heard Jack saying, exasperated. "The fire marshal is still looking at the evidence. These things take time."

"How *much* time? I don't want him here, Jack. Do you have any idea what this *looks* like?" Alison Bakker's voice was harsh with anger but slurred with alcohol. "I am a respected member of this community and my church, and there's a damned *terrorist* in my house, for heaven's sake! What are people going to think?"

"Let 'em think what they want; they will anyways."

"That's all very well for you, it's not *your* reputation at stake here. Hasn't there been enough nasty gossip going around as it is? Not that you ever gave a damn about this family's good name!"

In the sudden uncomfortable silence, Trinity heard the tinkle of ice cubes being dropped into a glass, and considered making his presence known. A movement in the corner of his eye made him look up and spot the housekeeper, Jenifer, on the stairs. She shook her head, putting a forefinger to her lips in warning.

"I'm sorry you feel that way, Allie," Jack said. "But this gin-sodden pity-poor-me routine of yours is getting pretty damned tedious . . ."

The housekeeper motioned to him, silently urging him to follow her. He hesitated, then did. She led him away, down a long corridor and past swinging doors into the kitchen. "You wan' some coffee?"

"Please."

She poured them both a cup, the scent of fresh-ground

coffee filling his nose with an almost erotic pleasure. The Bakkers could afford the best, he thought.

"You don' want to interrupt those two when they get goin'," Jenifer said, her accent light and her sarcasm heavy. "I swear, if they didn't have each other to bicker with, they'd both shrivel up and die."

"You don't like working here?" he asked.

"It's this or Wal-Mart. At my age, I'm lucky just to have a regular paycheck. And fifteen years' experience as a certified psychiatric nurse's aide comes in handy now and then." She smiled at his raised eyebrows and sipped her coffee. "The world just sucks, dunnit? I got a ton of laundry to iron. Help yourself if you want another."

She left, and when Trinity finished his coffee, he simply sat, wondering what the hell he was supposed to do now. Jack Bakker rescued him, stomping into the kitchen with his battered Stetson jammed low on his head, his shoulders hunched.

"There y'are. Let's find you some boots that'll fit and go do something useful fer a change."

Mucking out stables and currying horses was a new experience for Trinity, but he was grateful for the work, anything to keep busy. Neither man spoke, the quiet more companionable than strained. Lean, silent ranch hands in worn jeans and plaid cotton shirts rolled up at the sleeves ambled by on occasion, the black butts of heavy pistols tucked into brown leather holsters strapped under their arms. They smiled and nodded politely, but said nothing, their eyes watchful.

A few hours later, Jack and Trinity heard the sound of a car, and walked out of the stables as a dark Ford drove down the long circular driveway and parked in front of the house. Trinity's heart sank as Lloyd Shovar got out and looked around before spotting him, the special agent's expression grim.

"Friend of yours?" Jack asked.

"Not exactly." Trinity handed him the curry brush, then crossed the expanse of horse paddock, feeling oddly exposed. Shovar waited as Trinity slipped between the fence railing and walked toward him, Jack following behind.

"We got a problem," Shovar said without preamble. "Delahue's been taken into custody."

Trinity absorbed this. "So now what?"

Shovar lifted his briefcase. "We go to Plan B. I need you to take a look at something." He glanced past Trinity at Jack. "You folks have a DVD player?"

Alison Bakker trailed after them as Jack led Shovar and Trinity toward the large sunken living room, a drink still in her hand. "Take your shoes off!" she demanded sharply. Shovar stared at her while Jack scowled. "Don't you even think about waltzing in here with horseshit on your boots, take those filthy things off your feet before you go walking on my good rugs." She was clearly drunk.

"Alison—"

"That is a twelve-thousand-dollar antique Turkmenistan carpet. Take your damned shoes off!"

The three men complied while Alison supervised triumphantly. But Shovar blocked her from the lounge. "If you don't mind, ma'am?"

Jack shut the huge French double doors and drew the curtains, shutting out his sister-in-law's sullen frown. Shovar inserted a DVD into the television's player, but didn't turn it on.

"I want to know if you can identify the woman on this video."

Suddenly Trinity's heart began to beat far too fast. "What is it?"

"It's a recording made three years ago by al-Jawasis, and it shows a man who claims to be Abdul bin Zahedan. It's not necessary to watch the whole thing."

Trinity sat down heavily on one of the leather sofas scattered around the huge room, his chest aching in dread.

Shovar glanced at Jack, and back to Trinity. "Are you ready?" When Trinity nodded, he pushed the Play button on the remote.

The video was grainy, the quality of both sound and picture poor. Two men and a woman knelt on the floor, barefoot and handcuffed, their foreheads pressed down in front of their knees. A banner with handwritten Arabic had been pinned to the wall as a backdrop. Behind the hostages, a group of armed men stood over them with AK47 rifles aimed at their heads, their faces completely masked behind black kaffiyehs, only their eyes showing. One of them held up three opened passports, which the camera had trouble focusing on for a close shot. The cloth over his mouth moved as he ranted into the camera, the venom in his tone unmistakable. A woman's voice had been dubbed over the sound, an Arabic interpreter translating his words.

"We have been merciful," the translator's voice said dispassionately. "We have again and again shown our good intentions . . . to treat all who obey the laws of Allah with compassion. But we are not fools, we are not monkeys. We are freedom fighters in a righteous cause . . . strong and powerful seeds of war who strike at all the enemies of God, wherever they hide . . . We cannot be . . . tricked by American hypocrites and liars . . . who dare to treat us with such contempt."

The kneeling woman was shaking so violently she had nearly collapsed. One of her male companions turned his head, whispering reassuringly to her in French. He was brusquely clubbed with a rifle butt for his indiscretion. Then the masked man reached down, grabbed the woman by her hair and pulled her upright. Shovar paused the DVD, freezing the frame on a shot of her terrified face, the voice cut off midsentence. Trinity breath caught in his throat.

"Is this her?" Shovar said quietly.

Unable to speak, Trinity simply nodded.

"Who is she?" Jack asked, subdued.

"Marie-Claude Deschamps," Shovar said. "She was born in Qom, not too far from Tehran. She was seventeen, a student at the Sorbonne staying with an aunt in Paris, when her parents and her brother were killed by Shi'ite extremists in Iran. Her brother was only thirteen. Her aunt was her only living relative, so she stayed in France, took French citizenship, and changed her name to Deschamps, her aunt's married name. Her brother's name was Abdul bin Zahedan. No relation; it was just an unlucky coincidence." Shovar glanced at the frozen screen. "She was also Mr. Trinity's wife. I'm very sorry."

"Show me," Trinity said hoarsely.

Shovar grimaced. "All we needed was confirmation of her identity, you don't want to see the rest of—"

"Show it to me."

After a moment, Shovar shook his head in regret and restarted the video. It lasted another agonizing fifteen minutes, a long vitriolic tirade that Trinity had trouble following, his attention completely locked on the woman at the man's feet. Then the man threw the passports onto the ground and gestured to someone off-camera.

"You Americans think you can hide behind false names, you think you can subvert Muslims to betray us?" the masked man was screaming at the camera now. "If you want proof we cannot be deceived, then you shall have it. You fear death. The true Warriors of God embrace it. God is great—" Even the interpreter's subdued voice had started to shake. "Death to America, death to the Great Satan."

The masked man didn't use anything as elegant as a scimitar. He was handed a short, square butcher's cleaver instead. Marie-Claude gasped in disbelief before it thudded into the hollow between her neck and shoulder. It didn't cut deeply enough, sticking into bone. The masked man jerked it out, held her head up by her hair and raised the cleaver again. She was still alive, her lips moving without a sound.

"Oh my God," Jack Bakker whispered. Shovar had looked away, his face white, flinching at the sound of the second blow. And the third. The fourth finished the job, the masked man holding up her severed head for the camera, shrieking in incoherent triumph. The two other hostages had scuttled away as far as they could, blood-splattered and sobbing with rictus horror. The two armed men standing behind them hoisted their rifles as they chanted "Zahedan! Zahedan! Zahedan!" Then the camera was switched off, the video ending unexpectedly.

Trinity sat staring blindly at the television screen, his shallow breath sour in his dry mouth. Shovar opened the DVD player and removed the disk.

"Mr. Trinity?" he said gently. "Are you going to be okay?"

Trinity nodded, then placed his palms on his knees. He bent nearly double, head between his legs, and threw up all over Alison Bakker's twelve-thousand-dollar Turkmenistan carpet.

# CHAPTER TWENTY-SIX

Lucas Jensen hadn't even had his first cup of coffee of the weekend when Undersheriff Ensler called him on a Saturday morning and told him not to bother to come in on Monday. Sheriff Holbrook followed that call up with one of his own an hour later.

"I want you to take time off, Luke," Holbrook had started out gently enough.

"What for?" Lucas was in no mood to be mollycoddled.

"Go fishing. Go hunting. Go to church, whatever you need to do to get your head back on straight."

"There's nothing wrong—"

"I know what happened over at George's place, Luke. I understand your situation, but you went too far this time."

"I had authority—"

"Not from me, you didn't. So take some time off and cool down, or you'll end up officially suspended, permanently. You hear me?"

So Lucas poured himself the last of the tequila instead of coffee at eight o'clock in the morning. He didn't go fishing, he didn't go hunting. He went to the liquor store instead to stock up on as much cheap bourbon as he could find with what money he had left in his wallet. On Sunday morning, he didn't go to church for the first time in years, spending the weekend drinking steadily and brooding in the dark with the curtains shut and the television on, all he had for company. He let the answering machine pick up when the phone rang, not wanting to talk to anyone.

Late Sunday evening, Reverend Matt Thornton banged on his door. Rousing from his stupor, Lucas kicked over the collection of empty bottles by his feet.

"Luke? You all right? Lucas, I know you're there, your car's in the drive."

"I'm fine! Go away!" His voice sounded thick and slurred with alcohol.

After a long silence, the preacher yelled, "If you need to talk to someone, Luke, my door is always open."

When Lucas didn't answer, the preacher left. *Self-righteous little prick*, Lucas thought darkly. And poured another drink.

A few years ago, Lucas had been a hero; he practically walked on water, he'd been so golden. Then this bastard Trinity fell out of the sky and turned his life to shit. A fucking terrorist was screwing his ex-wife and making sexual advances on his fourteen-year-old daughter, and instead of backing Lucas up in trying to protect his family, his own bosses had reprimanded him. Now he was on suspension.

This was just not right, not right at all. He poured another drink.

He'd gone on weekend benders before, but had always picked himself up after, showered and shaved, and made it to work on Monday morning on time. Without the job to go to, he felt lost, his very reason for existence in question. He never opened the curtains, and ate cereal out of the box when he got hungry, washing it down with beer. He spent all Monday with the curtains drawn, dozing and drinking with the television on to keep the silence at bay.

So by Tuesday afternoon, he wasn't sure if he was awake or dreaming when he saw Ben Trinity's name flash on the news headlines. The photograph of the man showed someone far younger, smiling and happy, dressed in a sharp business suit, and shaking hands with some bearded Arab type in a doctor's white lab coat and a stethoscope around his neck. Lucas fumbled for the remote, knocking it off the arm of the chair. He scrabbled around blindly before he found it, and upped the volume. He winced, the blast of sound painful.

The photograph pulled back into a box in the corner of the screen, behind the news reporter standing outside Alison Bakker's house, Bears Paw Mountains as a backdrop behind her.

"—living in this remote community in Montana," the striking blonde was saying, smiling with perfect teeth. "We'll bring you more on this breaking story as it happens. I'm Julia O'Connor for the NBC News team. Monty?"

The screen cut to the news anchor, a beefy man with buzz-cut hair. "Thank you, Julia. In business news today, fifteen hundred workers at Ritter's Bottle Company in Missoula were told the plant will close at the end of this month, ending sixty years of making designer bottles for luxury perfume and bath oils. The company announced the decision last night to close its last remaining industrial plant in the United States and move its entire production to Bangladesh—"

Lucas slouched in the sofa and waited for the news to cycle through the usual crap—Dow Jones down, unemployment up, GNP down, gas and taxes up, another terrorist attack in some godforsaken place, another disgraced politician indicted, and on the lighter side, some idiot kid's pet Merino lamb found "sheepwalking" in a supermarket, oh, Monty, you're such a kidder, now for the weather, some cloud expected overnight but temperatures high for this time of the year, blah, blah, blah. He had to wait nearly an entire hour before Julia O'Connor reappeared and for Lucas to realize he hadn't been dreaming after all. He watched with disbelief and growing anger, and a nascent conviction in the pit of his stomach.

He knew what had to be done.

He had to be the hero again, one more time.

# CHAPTER TWENTY-SEVEN

"Look, I'm not saying terrorists *aren't* a genuine concern," Shovar was saying, squinting into the dazzling lights. "But we aren't winning the war on terror because they're not an army, and trying to fight them with ours has been point-less. A *war* against terror is as unrealistic as a war against earthquakes or hurricanes." He was talking to a woman in a sharply tailored business suit, her hair and teeth flawless. She nodded earnestly, holding up a microphone between them while several cameras from half a dozen different news stations jostled for position around them.

Outside, several television vans had pulled up in front of the house, and sprouted satellite dishes and high-powered transmitter aerials, trailing thick black cables into the house. Bright spotlights on tripods had been erected in the living room, technicians rapidly turning it into an improvised broadcast studio.

After Trinity had identified the woman in the video as Marie-Claude, Shovar had made several phone calls—as did Jack Bakker who, at Shovar's suggestion, called for an emergency town meeting. News vans arrived less than an hour later, the speed of their appearance not surprising to Trinity. They must have been waiting for Shovar's phone call, ready to move in once he'd confirmed Marie-Claude's identity.

Now Alison Bakker's huge living room was filling

quickly, both with media people and locals, nearly a quarter of the population of Redemption showing up. A private room had been set up for those who wanted to see the video, and many did; some out of morbid curiosity, some because they had no idea what to expect. Those who had seen it came out badly shaken. Some made their own phone calls after, and the gathering grew. Other film crews were busily interviewing local residents, some who were delighted for the opportunity to be on TV, others—mostly those who had seen the video—far more somber.

Alison Bakker rose to her customary role as the polite hostess, hastily organizing her kitchen staff, supervising the distribution of canapé trays while she herself made sure her uninvited guests were provided with drinks. But her smile was forced, her discomfort all too apparent.

On the flickering television, a red band at the top of the screen identified Shovar as an *FBI COUNTERTERRORISM EXPERT*, while a running ticker at the bottom carried BREAKING NEWS COMMENTARY.

The blonde reporter smiled and asked, "But you're an Iraq war vet yourself, isn't that right?"

Shovar nodded. "First Gulf War, but that's not—"

"So aren't you concerned that what you're doing here today might be seen as only encouraging terrorists who want to destroy freedom and democracy—"

Shovar cut her off. "No. *This* is about separating the truth from intentional misinformation being done for domestic purposes, for governments to assure their own people they're actively doing something."

"The feel-good factor," the reporter interjected, condensing Shovar's lecture into sound bites. Shovar looked fleetingly annoyed with her dumbing-down tactic.

"If you like. But it has no real effect in combating actual *terrorism*. We're less safe now than we've ever been. If we don't fight terrorists on their terms, not ours, we lose. Every time."

The woman in the business suit briefly dipped the microphone toward herself to ask, "And how should we do that?"

In the semi-gloom of a small room down the corridor, Ben Trinity stood looking out a window at the shadow of the Bears Paw Mountains beginning its long creep slowly down the valley. Horses wandered listlessly along the paddock fencing, nibbling at the scrub oak and weeds just out of muzzle's reach, the steady breeze ruffling through their manes. Sharp-winged swallows darted and swooped after insects, riding the currents of hot summer air.

"By first understanding what it is we're fighting. Terrorism isn't about blowing things up or killing people. It's about creating *terror*. Causing fear in as many people as you can. Generating a reaction far out of proportion to the number of victims. 'Kill one, frighten ten thousand Fox News viewers.'" The reporter flinched at the mention of a rival news network.

Behind Trinity, the only other person in the room, Jack Bakker, watched the television and chuckled. "Lenin, paraphrased," he said. "They're going to love that when they figure it out."

Trinity glanced at him, momentarily bemused, then returned to staring out the window.

Shovar continued, "News management is probably the single most contentious issue in any democracy. But I'm not in the news business—my concern is how to save lives by working with responsible folks in the media like yourselves." He smiled at the reporter, she smiled back, neither of them fooled. "Televising executions on the evening news or over the Internet has long been an integral part of the terrorist arsenal. But when publicity becomes the reward it only encourages copycat abductions and escalates hostage casualties. It's a double-edged sword . . ."

"If you don't mind my asking, sir, are you a Democrat?"

Shovar blinked his surprise at the question. "No, I'm not. What's that got to with anything?"

"I only ask because it seems surprising for someone of your background to be siding with certain members of Congress against this administration. Some people might view this as engaging in a political attack. Doesn't it worry you that you're only increasing the tension in government over this issue and dividing the country even further?" the reporter retorted, her tone cutting.

Shovar sighed. "No, it doesn't worry me. Facts never worry me. It's what people choose do with them that worries me."

"So this particular video, how did you come by it . . . ?" the female reporter said, steering the interview back.

"It was sent to the al-Jazeera news station; they get hundreds of them every year, most of which they never air—too graphic, too inflammatory. They've tended to give preferential coverage when hostages are released alive—which might not be strictly objective, but it has made an impact."

"Al-Jazeera?" Tom Mifflin said. Immediately both the woman with the microphone and the camera swiveled toward him. The lettering on the red strip was promptly amended to read, LOCAL RESIDENT, as a woman with a clipboard hastily conferred with a technician who whispered to another man. Several seconds later, the lettering changed again, to TOM MIFFAN, LOCAL RESIDENT. "They're Islamic fanatics who hate Americans. How can you trust anything you get from a bunch of goddamned liars like them?"

Mifflin had been with several other residents standing behind Shovar, listening and adding background color. Others around Mifflin murmured in unified agreement.

"We've had five different independent forensic experts examine the video; it's genuine," Shovar said mildly. The camera swiveled back onto him.

"And it shows the execution of an American citizen?"

"Yes, and no."

On the television, a few seconds of the video began to play in a corner of the screen, Marie-Claude's white face and frightened eyes staring at her tormenter, replayed over and over again. "Marie-Claude Deschamps was originally an Iranian émigré who held dual French-American passports. She and her husband, Ben Trinity, were antiwar activists who ran a charity operation in the Middle East. He was later detained on suspicion of terrorist activities, but France refused to allow his wife's extradition to the States. She became a volunteer for Médecins sans Frontières, working as an interpreter when she and the two other hostages in the video, François Brazier and Dr. Hervé Giraud, were abducted. The two men were both found shot dead a few weeks later."

"By Abdul bin Zahedan, her own brother?"

Shovar took a breath and smiled for the camera. "*That* was the problem. The French government has successfully negotiated with al-Jawasis in the past in getting their people out alive. They were close to an agreement for her release as well as the two men with her . . ."

"By paying ransoms," the reporter interjected. "It is not American policy to negotiate with terrorists."

"True," Shovar agreed calmly. "Which is why the French get their people back alive and we get ours back in boxes." O'Connor's mouth thinned into a tight line. "But in this case, someone inside the American intelligence community, whether out of ignorance or malice, leaked that Zahedan was Marie-Claude Deschamps's brother— that she was in fact an al-Jawasis terrorist herself and the hostage situation was faked, a ploy to extort more money out of the French."

"If Zahedan *was* her brother, why did he kill her?"

"To prove that he wasn't. She did have a brother by that name. He died when he was thirteen. The Abdul bin Zahedan who murdered her wasn't even born when her brother died; he was not related to her at all."

"So it wasn't true, any of it?"

"No."

"Do you know who leaked this false information?".

Shovar's professional smile widened. "Get yourself elected to Congress and I'll tell you."

"So are you saying that the trust she and her husband set up really was to help injured children; it had nothing to do with al-Jawasis terrorists, and that both she and her husband were innocent?"

"There's a probability that they very well could be."

"And our government knew this, three years ago?"

"We're looking into that allegation."

"Her husband, Ben Trinity—is he here now?"

Shovar winced, almost imperceptibly. "Mr. Trinity is here today, yes."

The reporter swung around to face the camera. "And we'll be interviewing Mr. Ben Trinity in a few moments. This is Julia O'Connor, KTGF, Channel Sixteen in Great Falls, for the NBC News Network." She kept up the professional smile until the red light went off on the camera. Then it slid from her face as she dropped the microphone down to her side and glowered at Shovar. "Damn it, we need that interview with Ben Trinity *now*. I can practically hear half our viewers switching over to get an update on the Paris Hilton divorce—you're boring the shit out of them with all this talking-head filler."

"Cut him a break, Ms. O'Connor. How would you feel if you'd just watched your husband being decapitated?"

"I'd be devastated," she retorted, sounding more impatient than empathetic. "Really. I feel for him, I do. But the clock's ticking, and if he doesn't get his goddamned butt out here and on the air before Homeland Security shows up to shut us down, this whole thing is going to be an exercise in futility. You'll have risked losing your job, and more important, *mine*, for nothing."

"Um, Jules?" the woman with the clipboard said tentatively.

"What?"

"You're still on the monitor?"

In the little room, Trinity watched the image of the reporter start. "Oh, crap," she muttered darkly, and stalked off. The woman with the clipboard grimaced a weak smile at Shovar before trotting after her.

Trinity didn't turn from the window as Shovar let himself into the small room. "Mr. Trinity?"

"No."

Shovar sighed but said nothing.

Trinity turned from the window, his face set. "I'm grateful for all your help, and I am sorry you're risking your job—"

Shovar laughed. "*What* job? FBI agents don't blow the whistle on their bosses on national television and show up for work the next day. I'll be lucky if I don't end up sharing a cell with Ms. O'Connor." He raised an eyebrow at Trinity's astonishment. He stood smiling, with his hands casually thrust in his pockets, like a man without a care in the world. "I don't have any altruistic motives about saving your ass, I'm not doing it to help you. I'm expendable, always have been. But Sam Delahue isn't."

"So who did leak the lie Zahedan was Marie-Claude's brother?" Trinity demanded, irrational anger rising under the surface. "Was it Delahue?"

Shovar seemed taken aback by the idea. "Sam never even heard of you up until a few weeks ago. He got caught getting his hands on that video, except the people holding him have no clue who they have. I'll be taking the heat for him—losing my job is the least of my worries. No, the guy behind the leak is far enough up the chain of command that he thought no one could touch him. He may still be right. But even he was just doing what he told, managing damage control."

Shovar took his hands out of his pockets and sat down on the sofa, one ankle crossed on his knee as if he had all the time in the world. "Let me lay it out for you, Mr. Trinity. See, my job used to be trying to keep the people of this country safe from bad guys. All kinds of bad guys—bank robbers, kidnappers, crooked stockbrokers, you name it. It was an honorable profession, one I was proud of. Now my job is to tell a bunch of paranoid politicians whatever they want to hear. And all they want to hear is that we're winning the war on terror."

"Even if that means putting innocent people in prison?"

"You know how to find a needle in a haystack?" Shovar retorted. "Burn down the haystack. You got *any* idea just how many people like you there are? People who've been detained because they had the wrong kind of name or the wrong kind of passport. People who had their cars serviced at the wrong garage, or pointed their cameras in the wrong direction. People who took the wrong airline so they could qualify for frequent-flier miles. Someone who had lunch with someone who did business with someone who used to live next door to someone else whose second cousin had an al Qaeda poster up on his bedroom wall." Shovar was still smiling, but his voice had turned acid. "And if you can't make that six degrees of separation, then you find gullible suckers too stupid to tie their own shoelaces, never mind construct a bomb, and set them up in so-called 'stings.' You wiretap anyone and everyone, and you don't bother with pesky little things like warrants or constitutional rights, and you ignore anyone who whines about it. Sure, if you go after enough people, you're bound to catch a few bad guys here and there. Too bad if a lot of innocent people get chewed up in the process. It's worth the cost . . . isn't it?"

Trinity didn't answer. Shovar obviously didn't expect him to. "There's not exactly a quota system," he said, still relaxed. "But those agents who toe the official policy line, uncover terrorist plots under every bed, and make lots of arrests get promoted. Those agents who question the wisdom of our superiors, who dare challenge such tactics—" Shovar snorted. "We get exiled to Bumfuck, Montana." He glanced at Jack. "No offense."

"None taken."

"There aren't too many idealistic bastards left anymore worrying themselves into ulcers over real terrorists slipping between the gaping holes in our security. If they're smart, they've already quit and taken their expertise to the private sector. If they're not, they end up sticking a gun in their ear. So let's not get too apologetic over my job, I would have jacked it in sooner or later anyway—I haven't given a shit in a long, long time."

"Not until Sam Delahue," Trinity said slowly.

"Not until Sam Delahue," Shovar affirmed. "A man who hasn't forgotten that true patriotism means having the courage to defy your own government when it lies and breaks the law. For a long time, all most of us could do is bitch. Or quit. But Sam has the ability and the connections to make a real difference. He's helping to change things, turn this country around, bring back hope. Bring back *honor*. Men like him . . ." Shovar shook his head, searching for the words. "He's worth losing a job for. And more."

A soft knock made the three men swivel their heads toward the door. It opened just wide enough for the woman with the clipboard to lean inside, silhouetted by the bright camera lights in the room behind her.

"Mr. Shovar? You asked me to let you know? They're on their way, an hour, maybe less."

"Thank you."

When she shut the door, Jack Bakker asked, "Who is?"

"Eastlake. And he's coming with a shitload of armed agents and Homeland Security legal beagles to back him up. So, Mr. Trinity, you're going to get out there in front of a camera in the next ten minutes, or I'm personally going to feed you to the wolves."

"I *can't*. I talk to reporters, and my son gets hurt."

"Bullshit. Kids and puppy dogs are the backbone of schmaltz. So go tell your story and if you can manage it, shed a few tears. Because once Eastlake gets here, he's going to shut down this little circus and take us both into custody where this time you're going to disappear for good. Unless you get out there while you still can and make an impression on what passes for the American conscience these days."

Jack had pursed his lips pensively as he listened. "You boys just carry on here," he said suddenly. "I gotta go talk to a couple folks."

They barely noticed him leave. Trinity shook his head, uncertain. "You don't understand. If you had children, you'd know why I can't—"

"I have kids, one of each," Shovar retorted, stonily. "My daughter is twelve. She's a straight-A student. Gifted. She wanted to be lawyer when she grew up. We used to live in Maryland. Two years ago her class went on a school trip to Washington to see the Lincoln Memorial and a tour of the Supreme Court. They went through the usual security check, bags searched, full body scans. Then they were marched along corridors with an armed escort the whole time, like they were criminals themselves. One of the teachers stopped to look at a painting. The guard grabbed him by the arm and shoved him, told him to keep walking. While they were in a hall waiting for their tour guide, Hannah asked to go to the bathroom. The guards told her no. They told her not to talk and not to move."

Shovar shrugged, but his anger was palpable. "They're kids. They talk. They move. One of the guards yelled at her like some sort of drill sergeant, scared her so bad she peed herself, right there, on the floor. She cried herself sick for days, wouldn't go back to school. She doesn't want to be a lawyer anymore."

A muscle in his clenched jaw twitched. "She asked if I'd ever scared anyone so bad I made them pee. She told me she hoped someone would get a bomb inside and blow them up; they deserved it. We don't have to worry about terrorists sneaking past our borders. They're already here. And they're *us*. So don't give me any sanctimonious crap about not using children—who the fuck do you think I'm doing this for?"

After a moment, Trinity nodded, unhappy. "Okay." As he took a step toward the door and the waiting reporters, Shovar put his hand on Trinity's arm.

"Here, you might want this."

Trinity looked down at the familiar photograph of Antoine, then back at Shovar, shaken.

"Good thing it was confiscated before the fire," Shovar said, his eyes like ice. "I took the liberty of having it reprinted on matte paper—doesn't reflect the light as much when you hold it up for the camera."

# CHAPTER TWENTY-EIGHT

Lucas would have preferred to have his police-issue AR-15 semiautomatic, but that was locked up in the sheriff's office, out of reach. Instead, he unlocked the gun safe in the back of his closet, surveyed the half-dozen rifles in his collection, and chose his father's Remington 700 bolt-action deer rifle with a 3-9 Leupold scope. He'd cleaned the gun just after the last time he'd used it to take down a four-point buck out near Williamson Butte. But that had been nearly three years ago.

He removed the bolt, and spent fifteen minutes obsessively cleaning and lubricating the bore, eradicating any trace of grime, before he slipped the bolt back into the gun. He tipped a circle of paste wax onto a chamois and buffed the walnut stock to a shine, the grain of the wood like swirls of rich hazelnut chocolate.

He didn't dwell on any particular plans, letting his mind empty of all doubt and worry as his hands worked methodically. He reassembled the cleaned rifle, set it on the coffee table and stared at it. Then he picked it up, stripped it down, and cleaned it again.

He took the rifle out into the hills behind his house and paced off two hundred yards. Jamming a metal target stand into the drought-hardened ground, he stripped the top sheet off of a block of paper targets and clipped it to the stand. It was one of those novelty targets he'd bought years before, Saddam Hussein's leering face centered in the red circles. It had been fun back then, shooting the eyes out of the targets. But as he methodically shot off several rounds to adjust the sights on the scope, the stock recoil tight on his shoulder, the smell of burnt gunpowder thick in the air, he felt nothing but a cold knot deep in his stomach. Finally satisfied, he refilled the magazine and slipped the rifle into its leather carrier.

He left his uniform on a hanger in the closet, next to its identical mate still swathed in dry cleaner plastic, and dressed in beige chinos and shirt and a green camouflage down jacket. But he did take his badge and ID in the worn leather case, and his duty .40 caliber Glock, tucked into a snap-on holster on his belt digging into the small of his back as he drove.

The air was cool with the promise of the fall season to come and high-altitude clouds stippled in a mackerel sky as the chilled wind moved down from the north. Lucas turned off Bullhook onto Clear Creek Road, a usually empty stretch through brown pastureland that now had more traffic on it than he had ever seen before. To his amazement, cars, dilapidated school busses, trucks, and tractors were streaming out from every farm and ranch in the hills. By the time he got as far as the Davey Road junction, traffic had come to a standstill, a few irate drivers honking in impatience. He stared in disbelief at a huge combine harvester that had lumbered out into the junction and had stopped dead center, as out of place on the road as an aircraft carrier in a child's wading pool. High up in the harvester's cab, a craggy-faced rancher grinned down on the commotion while chatting into a CB radio.

A pickup with a horse trailer maneuvered itself behind the harvester, blocking what little room there was left on the junction, obstructing traffic on both roads. Behind them, several more trucks and farm machinery had been organized into a makeshift roadblock. Barbed-wire fencing and a deep run-off ditch made driving an ordinary vehicle through the fields around the barricade unlikely.

A small group of men and women had taken up positions around the barricade, some of them drivers, but most of them demonstrators, many of them casually holding rifles and shotguns. Even some of the drivers had chosen to stay and watch with an almost carnival air rather than turning around and heading back north. Two men leaned against the pickup, arms crossed, apparently the self-appointed ringleaders. Three men in suits were yelling and gesticulating in frustration while the two men stared back impassively.

Lucas got out of his Blazer and threaded his way though the cars toward the obstruction. He had his hand in his jacket pocket, about to fish out the wallet with his shield, but he slowed as he realized he'd seen the three men in suits before, all of them with the federal agents at George's house. One of them glanced at him in irritation, dismissing him with a casual glare, no look of recognition in his eyes. Lucas felt like he'd been slapped.

"I'm *telling* you," the agent's colleague was shouting at the implacable rancher, leaning toward him menacingly. "If you don't move that goddamned thing *now*, I *am* empowered to arrest you. You'll end up in as big a trouble as *he* is. C'mon! Get real! You all willing to risk going to prison over this asshole?"

The older of the two men tipped the wide brim of his hat back from his forehead with one finger, squinting as he turned his head and spit a long squirt of brown tobacco juice onto the dusty road, missing the agent's shoes by inches. The agent danced back in annoyance.

"Le' me get this straight," the rancher drawled, his face impassive but his eyes amused. "Y'all are saying that a peaceful protest is illegal in this country now?"

"Protest all you want," the agent snapped. "But obstructing public access roads, with *guns*, I might point out, and impeding a federal officer in the performance of his duties, is in breach of the Patriot Act, which makes *this* a felony offence."

"You seriously want me to believe the Patriot Act says blocking this itty-bitty road in the middle of nowhere is a felony?"

"Damn straight." He turned to one of the suited men next to him. "Tell him."

"Under Section 802, any act committed within the United States that appears to be intended to intimidate or coerce a civilian population can be considered as domestic terrorism," the man in the suit reeled off offhandedly, obviously a lawyer. "And Section 411 defines any act in support or aid of a terrorist or any terrorist activity to be in itself a terrorist activity. There's more, but that pretty much covers the main bases."

The rancher's mouth turned down as he deliberated the idea, then turned to what Lucas was certain was his son. "Hear that, boy? We're terrorists now. Ain't that sumthin'?" His son smiled as the elder man turned to shout over his shoulder at the group behind the pickup. "Hey, Jasper! Guess this makes you and your old lady there both terrorists, too!"

Muted laughter rippled through the crowd as a hunchbacked old man and the white-haired crone next to him grinned toothlessly, both trembling with palsy as they clutched antique Browning rifles even older than themselves.

"Well, now, while I can't quote the Patriot Act chapter and verse, I can tell you that a well-regulated militia, being necessary to the security of a free state, the right of the people to bear and keep arms shall not be infringed. That's Article Two from the Bill of Rights, in case you didn't recognize it. Which I think trumps your Section Eight-oh-whatever," the rancher said laconically. "So I suggest if you plan on arrestin' us all, you better go get some more backup. You're gonna need it, 'cause we won't be going without a fight."

"This isn't a joke," the agent said, red-faced.

"No, sir," the rancher retorted, his humor gone. "It sure isn't."

The agent turned away, heading back for his car. "Redneck dumbshits," he muttered to the others as he passed Lucas. He didn't even look up—Lucas might as well have been invisible. "Let's get another SWAT team up here, see how mouthy Li'l Abner feels like being then. And find me another way in."

Lucas could have told him. Lucas knew these hills as well as any other local, having hunted deer and antelope in these mountains with Lonny Ryton and Will Paterson for years. But they didn't want his help anymore, and he wouldn't stoop to offering, not this time. This time, he was going to do what they should and couldn't.

The police scanner in the Blazer told him every road into Redemption was blocked in every direction. Somehow, that bastard Trinity had managed to twist the entire town's sense of right and wrong and persuade them to shield him from the law. But he wasn't going to get away with it; Trinity couldn't convince everyone the sun shone out his ass.

There were plenty of small deer trails and dry coulee beds passable with a decent four-wheel drive that weren't listed on any map, and Lucas had little problem bouncing along them until he had reached the limit of how far he could go in any vehicle. He got out and left the Blazer unlocked, no one for miles to worry about. Shouldering the rifle, he began hiking up through the fir trees on the other side of the foothills, following the familiar winding trail leading to the back of George's property line, the boundary she shared with the Bakker estate.

He shouldn't have gone on a bender, he realized quickly enough, his head pounding, stomach queasy. Sweat ran down his ribs, his breath acid as he climbed. He felt a little better after he reached the summit of the trail, the breeze rolling across the peaks bracing. Rocky slabs of naked granite still towered above him as he began the descent into the valley beyond. He reached the corner of a barbed-wire fence, the border of the Bakkers' land with George's, and slowed, more cautious now as he worked his way through the trees and brush. The tree line ended some two-hundred-plus yards from the back of the Bakkers' house.

Lucas stopped, squatting down into the undergrowth, scanning for a clear view, then worked his way quietly several hundred feet to his left, keeping just inside the tree line for cover. Below, he could make out the drive, crowded with television vans, strangers wandering around either bored or self-important. In the distance, he observed a barricade of trucks and cars, and heard the sound of many people chanting over the honking of cars, like this was some sort of county fair, idiots amusing themselves. The Bakkers' pack of mongrel dogs barked and growled and strained at their leashes, but thankfully not in his direction; he was downwind of them, his scent carried off in the sharp breeze.

He spotted several official-looking cars, and a dozen men and women in quasi-military outfits, FBI and DHS in bright yellow letters on their navy windbreakers. They stood idly around a man talking to Jack Bakker, the old rancher's beard waggling as he spoke. One of the feds gestured brusquely to a camera crew, waving them back like recalcitrant sheep, her irritation plain even at this distance. The cameraman stepped backward but didn't stop filming, the woman in front of him doggedly poking her microphone in the agent's face.

Negotiations, Lucas thought wryly. Waste of time. This was as good a position as any, he decided, and hunkered down deeper into the brush, trying to get comfortable.

He unzipped the rifle carrier and hauled out the Remington and settled it across his knees.

That bastard would have to come out sooner or later, and when he did, Lucas would be waiting for him.

"I had this boss who was always saying stuff like, 'Never underestimate the power of stupid people in large groups,'" a cameraman remarked to Lloyd Shovar. "I always thought he was talking about, y'know, the French Revolution or hippy protests in the sixties—ancient history, man, y'know what I mean?" He grinned, hitching the bulky camera slightly higher on his shoulder, and looked around at the standoff in the Bakkers' long drive that, in Shovar's cynical opinion, hardly came up to the same order of magnitude as the French Revolution. "But this is so cool. Like, it's fucking Montana, dude, who'da thought? *Way* cool."

"Yeah," Shovar said indifferently, not paying the cameraman much attention. "Way cool. John!" He raised his hand as a balding man in an FBI windbreaker tried to elbow his way through the rowdy local residence keeping the feds at bay. The big Indian deputy whose name Shovar couldn't immediately recall stepped through the crowd as if it wasn't even there, sucking the FBI special agent along with him in the vacuum of his wake. Shovar walked away from the cameraman, meeting John Langdon halfway, one arm extended. They shook hands as they met.

"You two already know each other?" Shovar asked his station chief, hoping he wouldn't have to make introductions.

"Yep," Langdon said, to Shovar's relief. "I met Dennis a couple years back."

*Red Wolf*, Shovar suddenly remembered. "Good, good." He nibbled his upper lip uneasily, then asked, "Any news?" Meaning Sam.

Langdon shrugged, which was his answer, then said, "Your roadblocks aren't going to stop anyone for long, y'know. They're coming."

"Not my idea," Shovar said. "But it *has* bought us time." He canted his head toward the house to indicate Trinity. "He's been in front of the cameras now over two hours, still talking. How's it playing out there in civilization as we know it?"

"Well, you're pissing some people off," Langdon commented. "And you're making others sit up and pay attention. There's one hellacious scramble going on in Washington. But Joe Couch-Potato seems entertained enough. Good call on the kiddie angle, woulda been better if he'd been blond, of course. Phones have been ringing off the hook all over the country, it's hitting the Internet blogs big-time. So this thing isn't going to go away quietly—your boy in there is *not* going to disappear into thin air." He grinned fleetingly. "Mission accomplished. Now it's time to talk about our exit strategy. We got way too many guns being waved around this place right now, and no one wants to see this turn into a mini-Waco."

"Guess we'd better go have a chat with him, then," Shovar said, and eyed the Indian deputy. "You coming?"

Red Wolf grimaced but followed as they started toward the house.

"Oh, by the way, Lloyd," Langdon said casually, "you're fired."

Shovar laughed quietly.

"It is a dog-eat-dog world where only the strong will survive," the man in a stars-and-stripes USA baseball cap jabbered into a camera. He stood in the midst of a group all dressed in patriotic red, white, and blue shirts, and waving small American flags zealously. "And now you're seeing what happens when you got Congress pulling us all one way and a President pulling us the other, a disaster, total disaster."

Trinity sat on the edge of the sofa in the small room down the corridor, cordoned off as both a green room and a refuge for the family, away from the media. He had his head bowed over a glass of water, his throat sore, his mouth dry from talking for so long, uninterested in the television. Alison Bakker had switched the channels and stood leaning in the doorway, watching it with another drink in hand, her expression set into one of disgruntled defiance. On one side of the room, the FBI agents and Red Wolf stood with arms crossed over their chests as they conferred quietly, while on the other side, Jack Bakker talked on a cell phone. Craig and his sister slumped in chairs as far away from Trinity as they could manage, the boy sullen, the girl tearful.

The man being interviewed was no one Trinity recognized despite the LOCAL RESIDENT tag on the television screen, the street in the background unfamiliar. Nor was the network one of those who had reached the Bakker estate before the blockade, or been welcomed if it had; notorious within the industry—if not with the general public—as more a propaganda machine for the White House than a news station, well stocked with "reporters" loyally following official scripts.

"There's no smoke without fire, so if that man was arrested as a terrorist, I have no doubt in my mind there must have been a damned good reason why," the man on the television declared. "They should never have let him out."

"He's right about that," Alison Bakker grumbled, rattling the ice around the glass of gin and tonic in her hand. "I can't *believe* this is happening in my own home. My home, Jack . . ." She glared at her brother-in-law poisonously. He barely glanced in her direction, still talking on his cell phone.

"But surely you would agree with those in Congress who demand such reasons should be a matter of public record, wouldn't you?" the polished-looking interviewer asked in a mocking tone, implying exactly the opposite.

Taking his cue, the "local resident" snorted his disgust, backed up by his allies behind him. "Exactly the sort of traitorous, anti-Christian, bleeding-heart attitude that got us into this mess in the first place. And that woman who took him in, harbored a terrorist? Her son gave his *life* for this country! She should be ashamed of herself, kick her unpatriotic ass out of the country, somebody oughta *lynch* that bi—"

The interviewer quickly switched to another "local," camera swinging away abruptly. "And you, ma'am? How do you feel about the public's right to know?"

"Jesus, Allie, don't you ever watch any real news?" Jack muttered, then said, "Yeah, I'm still here," to whoever was on the other end of the phone.

"I think our President has a duty to keep America safe and fight terrorism by any means necessary, and making everything public could be used to aid and abet the terrorists. So don't blame it on him; blame it on this Congress who are on the side of the terrorists out to destroy us. America is the greatest nation on earth and the whole world owes us their freedom. They may not like us but no one else is doing what needs to be done to keep these terrible forces of darkness underfoot . . ."

"'No people are more hopelessly enslaved than those who falsely think they are free,'" Jack said suddenly, flipping his cell phone shut and slipping it into his shirt pocket.

Trinity smiled at the floor. "Goethe," he said quietly without lifting his head.

Craig looked from one to the other, mystified. "Gerta? Who's she?"

Jack chuckled wryly. "This house is full of books, boy. I know your mother thinks they're just for decoration, but try reading a few sometime."

"Screw you," Alison snapped, pushing off from the doorframe, wobbling. "I'm sick of you spouting that intellectual garbage. Leave my son the hell alone . . ."

The three men at the other end of the room ignored the family bickering. Red Wolf said nothing as the two FBI agents debated Trinity's future.

"Canada is still an open option," Shovar was saying. "We've still got everything set in place—"

"Not for the moment. The state governor has gotten himself involved, already talking about calling for a congressional hearing."

Shovar frowned. "He's running for reelection already, is he?"

Langdon shook his head. "You've gotten too cynical. In any case, it doesn't matter—this stays an in-house problem for now."

"So who's got jurisdiction?"

"I suppose that will depend on who yells the loudest . . ."

Trinity glanced up as Craig slowly raised a hand, as if he were in a classroom.

"Um?" Craig said, when no one paid any attention.

"You got a question, son?" Langdon said irritably.

"Kinda." Craig's eyes darted between Trinity and his uncle uncertainly. "I'm just sorta wondering why nobody's asked him what *he* wants to do?"

In the silence that followed, Langdon canted his head and stared at Trinity. "Well?" he said finally. "You have any thoughts on this?"

"I've spent a few years thinking about it," Trinity said softly, his throat hoarse from the hours of unaccustomed talking. "I want you to arrest me."

Langdon smiled dryly. "That rather defeats the purpose of this whole exercise, Mr. Trinity. You might have noticed we've all been busting our balls here trying to keep you *out* of prison—"

"I know. But I want you to arrest me for the bombing of the Amtrak train in California. I want you to charge me with providing money to the al-Jawasis. I want a lawyer and a trial with a judge and a jury of my peers. I want to face my accusers and see the evidence they have against me. I want to be convicted or acquitted, one way or the other. And I want it in an open court, in public."

Langdon studied him for a long moment. "You serious?"

"Very."

"You've got no money, Mr. Trinity. Not many defense lawyers willing to represent terrorists pro bono these days, or risk ending up sharing a prison cell with their own clients," Langdon said. "The people you'd be taking on don't fight fair, and while they've taken a few body blows, they've still got powerful friends behind them. The game is rigged. Even if you win, you'll lose."

Trinity shrugged. "I don't care. Proving my innocence isn't what this is about anymore, anyway. Is it?"

Shovar and Langdon exchanged looks. "Live, on camera?" Shovar said. He was asking his former boss, not Trinity. "Before Eastlake gets here?"

Langdon nodded. "And he's ours. We keep him."

"You do. I've been kicked off the team."

From where Lucas crouched in the scrub bushes above the house, he had a good view overlooking the area below, even without scanning through the riflescope. He settled in patiently, but hadn't waited long before the situation abruptly changed.

He didn't see Trinity standing between Red Wolf and Langdon, squinting in the bright camera lights and a forest of microphones shoved in their faces. He didn't hear the short statement Langdon made to the journalists, or his formal recital of the Miranda rights as he officially took Trinity into FBI custody. He didn't see the slight embarrassed smile on Trinity's face as his wrists were cuffed behind his back to the applause of the media witnessing the event on live national television.

What he did see was four dark police vans forcing their way slowly through the crowd, disgorging several dozen police in riot gear, armed to the teeth. He watched as the makeshift security team made up of locals with rifles and the Bakkers' bodyguards faced off, cameramen and journalists scuttling behind them like unruly schoolchildren, filming everything in sight as if their cameras could intimidate their adversaries. The cops simply took up positions and waited with an air of bored contempt, no hostility in their manner at all. He spotted a few more circumspect armed police who were quietly working their way to points around the house, well below him, as unaware of his presence as the locals were of theirs.

He saw the DSD man, Eastlake, get out of a car to confront that asshole Shovar who had strode out of the house and started flapping his hand to signal one of his own people to drive up to the front door, ignoring the DSD guy yelling angrily in his face. Lucas was too far away to make out the words, but he knew there was a change in the air, an excitement quickening through the crowd.

The time was close; he felt it rising in his chest, pressing on his heart. He sat on the ground, knees bent with his heels digging into the sloping hillside, his legs trembling slightly with adrenaline and tension. He settled the rifle butt into his shoulder, cheek resting on the warm walnut, the rifle sling pulling his forearm to steady his aim. Through the scope, he watched reporters and cameramen retreating backwards out of the house, babbling as they filmed a small cluster of people walking down the Bakkers' white colonnaded stairs into the sunlight. Leaves cast trembling shadows on the scope, the breeze rustling through the bushes where he hid. He swung his rifle slightly back and forth, searching for his target in the bobbing mass of heads and bodies below.

He spotted Dennis Red Wolf, the tall Indian towering over the rest, and Shovar following behind him. Then, his heart leaping, he found Trinity, and panted shallowly, openmouthed, trying to calm the pounding in his ears.

For a moment, Lucas was confused—Trinity's arms were behind his back, obviously in handcuffs, as a balding man in an FBI jacket led him down the stairs. But the son-of-a-bitch was smiling, and any indecision Lucas might have had was vaporized in his hatred.

Trinity slipped in and out of the crosshairs elusively, other bodies blocking him as they steered him toward the waiting car. In a few more seconds, Lucas knew, they'd reach the car and be out of range. His face ached, his teeth clenched together so tightly. He was going to lose this shot, he would never have another chance again, and he nearly wept in his frustration.

Then, like a miracle, like the Red Sea parting, the crowd split open and the sun illuminated his target, crosshairs on his chest as plain as a crucifix. Trinity waited as Red Wolf opened the back passenger door of the car for him to get in. Time seemed to slow as Lucas gently, very gently, squeezed the trigger. The striker detonated the round in the chamber, the rifle's recoil against his shoulder solid. The brass case glittered as it was ejected, tumbling end over end.

As the scope came back into alignment, he saw the shock in Trinity's eyes and a spray of bright red on his face as he stumbled backward, Red Wolf shying away from him in surprise. For one brief moment, Lucas felt the thrill of exultation flood through him.

But then the realization something had gone terribly wrong sank in. He watched in dismay as Trinity remained on his feet while Red Wolf slid down the side of the car, slowly going to one knee as if he were proposing marriage, his chest a mass of blood. Then he pitched forward on his face at Trinity's feet.

A sea of blanched faces turned up toward him, following the sound of the gunshot still ringing in Luke's ears. Several hundred yards downhill, a SWAT officer stood up from his hiding place and turned, searching, his own rifle ready. Then the sound of screaming began to echo in the hills, the people below frantically scurrying for cover.

Lucas dropped the rifle and scrambled on his hands and knees in panic up the hill, well back into the sanctuary of the trees before he stood and ran. He plowed blindly through the undergrowth and collided into tree trunks, branches whipping at his face as he sobbed for breath. He tripped and fell, but rather than getting up, he rolled onto his back and stared up at the canopy of green above him. He could hear the shouting of crisp, purposeful voices calling urgently to one another as they hunted him down. The distant thrum of a helicopter vibrated in the air, and Lucas knew he had no possibility of escape.

He saw his future in the space of a heartbeat—the disgrace of arrest, the agony of a court trial, the humiliation of his family, the hatred of the children of a man he'd murdered in error, and he knew he couldn't face it. The image of his daughter, still angry with him, floated in front of him. He'd lost her forever, but he could still give her one last gift, one final penance to redeem his soul. She would never have to be ashamed of him.

He struggled to sit upright against a tree, the bark scraping against his jacket, as he unsnapped the holster and took out the Glock. The metal barrel was cold, clicking against his teeth. The smell of gun oil filled his nostrils as he closed his eyes.

*Oh, Amy. Forgive me.*

He pulled the trigger.

# CHAPTER TWENTY-NINE

The funeral had been well attended, Lucas buried in his uniform, with full honors. A piper from the Havre Police Department played "Amazing Grace" and someone from the Hill County Sheriff's Department blew taps on a bugle as men and women in various law enforcement came in their formal best. George and Amy stood side by side, dressed in black as the coffin was lowered. Behind them, Carlene leaned her head on Jack Bakker's shoulder, the only member of the Bakker family to show up. It was obvious to everyone but Carlene and Jack how much they loved each other.

Sheriff Holbrook presented Luke's daughter with the American flag that had draped her father's coffin, now folded into a neat triangle. She took it gravely and hugged it to her chest, her eyes red and moist. A lone photographer, the only member of the press that had been allowed to be present, snapped pictures for the *Havre Daily News*. Then, in unison, the men and women in uniform saluted.

One of their own had fallen. The circumstances didn't matter, no one said a word about why Lucas had done what he had, no one speculated about what must have been going on in his mind, what drove him over the edge. Not to George.

Once it was over, they stood in a line to shake George's hand and murmur consoling words to Amy and Carlene before everyone went their separate ways.

The first snowfall came early, although there wasn't much of it, just enough of a dusting of white to obscure the realtor's number on the FOR SALE sign tacked to the front gates of the Bakkers' ranch. Sophie and Craig moved away with their mother, back to some place near Alison's family in Texas. Sophie sent Amy a couple of cheerful postcards with horses on them. Amy read them before she threw them away, but she never answered and they stopped coming after a while.

The calm after Trinity had gone was almost abnormal, although George knew Redemption hadn't been any less peaceful before he'd shown up. The quiet was in some ways worse. Although Amy didn't smile much anymore, remaining withdrawn and surly, her grades curiously improved. She threw herself into her schoolwork, and spent her spare time either endlessly on the Internet or wandering through the woods by herself. George cried when Amy wasn't looking, feeling helpless and guilty.

The café was eventually refurbished, and weekend country and western bands returned to cycle through regularly. The locals sat in the same place as they always did, drinking the same beers, and arguing heatedly over the same topics, as if the world gave a damn about their opinions. Winter came and went.

In early spring, snow patches still on the ground, George was outside, replanting tulip and crocus in the big timber planters to replace those bulbs the deer and the squirrels had eaten over the winter, when Nick Gilman pulled his pickup into the parking lot and shut off the engine. She returned his smile automatically as he got out and headed for the front door.

He stopped. "Hey, there, George, how y'doing?"

"Just fine, Nick, thanks." She would have said the same if her hair was on fire, and kept her attention on planting the bulbs, shivering in her down vest. But when he didn't move, she looked up, one hand shading her eyes as she squinted.

"You ever hear from him?"

She honestly couldn't think of whom he meant. "Hear from who?"

"Ben. Trinity," he added as if there might have been two and she didn't know which Ben he meant.

She turned back to the bulbs so he wouldn't see the heat climb into her face, her trowel stabbing into the compost determinedly. "No. Why?"

"No reason. Saw him on the TV last night. Bess and me decided to get a better satellite dish; had a devil of a time tuning in all the different channels." George didn't look up as his jean-clad legs shifted beside her. "Anyway, we got C-Span on and there he was, in front of that congressional hearing, answering questions. Looks mighty different in a suit and tie, fancy haircut an' all. Seemed pretty relaxed in front of all them senators and congressmen and folks; don't think I'd be so calm, no, sir."

When George didn't answer, Nick scuffed his boots for a moment, then said in a subdued tone, "Just sort of strange, seeing someone you know on the television. Guess he's famous now."

"Looks like," George agreed noncommittally.

"Just wonderin' if, y'know, you two kept in touch at all . . ."

"I expect he's far too busy these days." She looked up, trying not to sound judgmental. "And it's not like a lot of folks made him feel all that welcome when he was here."

Nick at least had the grace to look abashed. "Reckon so." Then he went inside, out of the cold. George planted the rest of the bulbs, her head down and an ache in her throat.

Ben Trinity never did get his trial. A grand jury decided the government hadn't sufficient evidence to indict, and all the charges against him were thrown out. But there had been enough evidence of government misconduct for a federal prosecutor to call for an investigation into exactly what had happened to the doomed Amtrak Coast Starlight, and where all the money from the Triad Medical Supply Company had gone, both before and after Trinity's three years in custody.

The timing of the Amtrak bombing had provided intransigent hardliners an invaluable opportunity to deflect the tide of criticism against an increasingly beleaguered White House. But it hadn't been perfect, so the circumstances were simply tweaked to fit the need: Joel Allan Rodrigues had indeed packed explosives into the SUV and driven onto the tracks to detonate his homemade suicide bomb. He'd been on his way to downtown Sacramento when he'd become stuck on the tracks, blowing himself up early in error. He'd had no way of knowing about the chlorine and liquefied ammonia gas tankers; the explosion that mixed the chemicals into a toxic cloud simply a horrendous twist of fate. But Joel Allan Rodrigues was not and had never been an Islamic terrorist; he'd been a depressed young engineering student with huge debts, a pregnant girlfriend, and was embroiled in a bitter legal battle after he'd been diagnosed with a particularly malignant form of bowel cancer. His insurance company had refused to pay for exorbitantly expensive medical treatment and was dragging out the case in the hope he would die before the courts could rule. His only link to the Triad Trust was an application as a volunteer, an application that had been gently turned down ten months previously with the suggestion he try again after he'd graduated.

The suicide note had been faked. The Homeland Security experts who had authenticated it were exposed as the experts who had forged it in the first place. Now it appeared that while the similarity in names between Abdul bin Zahedan and Marie-Claude's dead brother had indeed been a tragic coincidence, leaking the false story that led to her murder had been yet another cynical and malevolent scheme to cover up the Amtrak conspiracy—kill the truth. Literally.

And as one thread unraveled, it revealed even more of the tangled web of lies and deception. Trinity very quickly became just a minor player, dwarfed in the aftermath, swept up in the avalanche of vicious partisan politics.

But this was all a world far away from the small town of Redemption, Ben Trinity briefly elevated to the iconic status of a movie star. Those who had known him now spoke of him as if he were someone not quite real, a mythology unconnected to their ordinary lives.

When the phone rang while George and Amy sat in the kitchen eating their dinner, George picked it up, trying to swallow a mouthful of macaroni and cheese before she said, "Hello?"

"George?"

She didn't recognize the voice. "Yes?"

"Hi. It's me, Ben."

"Ben?" Amy's head shot up like a startled colt's, her eyes wide. "Wow." George couldn't think of anything to say without it seeming inane. "How *are* you?"

He laughed, sounding oddly happy. But then George realized she'd never known him happy. "Not bad, all things considered. I have to stay a few more days here in Washington, but I should be done soon. They don't need me for much of anything else anymore." He laughed again. "Guess what? I'm calling you on my cell phone." He sounded like a child. "I can use a cell phone again, isn't that great?"

She grinned, his joy at small pleasures infectious. "Yeah, that's really great. So what are you going to do now?"

"I'm not sure yet. My teaching credentials have been reinstated, so I was considering going back to teaching."

"In California?" George watched her daughter's head duck back down toward her plate, Amy trying to seem nonchalant although she was listening intently.

"Probably not California, no. The company's gone, all the property was sold at auction, and I doubt I'm ever going to be able to recover much. And it's not like I've got any family left. There's nothing for me there anymore. Anyway . . . that's not what I was thinking." She heard him inhale, then hold his breath for a moment before he said diffidently, "Do you think Mary Magdalene's could use an English teacher? They'd also get a French teacher thrown into the bargain and I'd be happy with minimum wage. I mean, if you think there's anyone in Redemption who would even want me back . . ." His voice trailed off.

George swallowed the lump in her throat, her eyes smarting.

"Ben?"

"Yes?"

"Come home."

# EPILOGUE

Trinity sat at his desk, leaning on his elbows with his chin on his hands, listening to the tentative voice of a fifteen-year-old girl as she stood and read out loud from the book in her hand.

" 'If you mean confessing,' she said, 'we shall do that, right enough. Everybody always confesses. You can't help it. They torture you.'

" 'I don't mean confessing. Confession is not betrayal. What you say or do doesn't matter: only feelings matter. If they could make me stop loving you—that would be the real betrayal.' "

"Thank you, Rachel." When the girl sat down, Trinity glanced up at a boy in the second row with his hand raised. "William?

"What I don't get is why Winston Smith gives in so easy, y'know? Like it's just a bunch of rats. And O'Brien doesn't even do it; he just threatens to do it. Winston Smith couldn't have loved Julia *that* much if he just caves so fast. Nobody's that much of a wimp-ass—"

The boy behind him sucked in his breath, his eyes widening, then flicked the back of William's head, hard.

"*Ow!*" William protested, turning around to glare as he rubbed his scalp.

William was new to St. Mary Magdalene's, and had no idea who Ben Trinity might have been in a former life other than just an everyday anonymous English teacher.

No doubt his ignorance would be rectified during class break.

"Keith?" Trinity said, and the boy who had rapped William's head looked up innocently. "When Winston Smith is explaining to Julia why he didn't kill his wife Katharine, he says he prefers a positive to a negative. But then he says that this is a game they can't win, that some kinds of failure are better than others. What do you think he's trying to say here—?"

Luckily, Keith was spared any public torment as Ms. Clymer opened the door to his classroom and signaled to Trinity wordlessly.

"Okay, guys, why don't you start in on chapter twenty-four. Just read quietly until I get back."

He knew that was unlikely, but they were good kids and decent students, he wasn't worried. The noise level jumped even before he had the door shut behind him.

"What's up?" he asked; then his heart lurched at the seriousness in Ms. Clymer's face. "Is it Amy? Is she okay?"

When Trinity had returned to Redemption, he had no intention to move in directly with George, being unsure how readily the locals would view his return. St. Mary Magdalene's had tiny studio apartments on the upper floor of the boarding school for transient staff, but that arrangement lasted only two months before Carlene drove the Jeep up to the school, impatiently ordered him to pack up his belongings, and carted him off to her daughter's house. Six months later, George married him in a small outdoor wedding in the backyard, attended by an astonishing number of well-wishers, and marred only by an uninvited photojournalist who was marched off the premises by Jared Ingersoll and Jack Bakker. Amy, particularly incensed by outside intrusion into a private ceremony, had none too gently wrestled the man's camera away from him and dumped it into the punchbowl. Photos of their wedding still ended up in various celebrity magazines and tabloid newspapers, but the event generally went unnoticed by the rest of the world.

The week Amy had graduated from high school, she'd tossed her backpack and sleeping bag onto a protest bus heading for Washington. Every evening Trinity and George scanned what news wasn't filtered for security, both of them proud yet worried, as the protests intensified past what even a castrated media could ignore. Placards demanding voting reform, civil rights, impeachment, and repealing the Patriot Act vied for space with signs protesting global warming, Internet restrictions, and record unemployment. Demonstrations resembled a war zone more every day with barbed wire and concrete blockades and thousands of scowling armed police. Several protesters had been killed in riots, which had only fueled the anger of the growing crowds, violent clashes escalating. The roar of a hundred thousand voices as they chanted, "*Of* the people, *by* the people, *for* the people, who the hell are *you!*" with a forest of accusing fingers thrust at both a barricaded White House and Capitol Hill was breathtaking. As well as deeply frightening.

"It's not Amy," Ms. Clymer reassured him as they walked down the corridor together. "You've got visitors."

He stopped, wary. " 'Visitors'?"

The Triad Medical Supply Company was long gone, the corpse divided up and devoured inside the first year Trinity was imprisoned. Even if he could have afforded a lawyer to sue for damages, there was nothing left to recoup. So he did what everyone in America did when they were broke—he sold his story. Three books and a very bad movie later, he'd made enough to secure Amy's college education and totally revamp George's house. But it meant tolerating the kind of endless publicity Trinity had had enough of for one lifetime.

"Not reporters," Ms. Clymer reassured him. She held open the door to her office to let him in.

Dennis Red Wolf struggled to his feet, balancing his weight on the sturdy cane Anja Apanakhi had fashioned for him from a piece of gnarled cottonwood root. The two men shook hands, Dennis's grip still frail despite the physiotherapy.

"How you doing, Dennis?"

"Gettin' there." If the big man felt any self-pity, Trinity never saw any evidence of it. "We got kind of a delicate situation."

"Okay—"

"We've found your boy."

Trinity inhaled sharply, his skin rising in goose pimples. "Antoine?"

"Yeah. Except that's not exactly his name anymore." Red Wolf winced as he shifted his weight on the cane. "He's been adopted, Ben. When his parents saw his picture being splashed all over the news, they packed up and ran. Lloyd Shovar found them. Took some talking to get them to even agree to meet with you."

"They're here? *Now?*" He looked past Red Wolf, straining to make out shapes through the milky-glass window in the door between Ms. Clymer's office and the visitor's area. "Is my son here, too?"

"Trinity?" Red Wolf said warningly. "Take it slowly, okay? They're scared to death you're gonna try to take him away from them. This isn't an easy situation for anyone."

"Nothing in my life ever is," Trinity said. "Will they let me see him?"

Red Wolf exchanged a look with Ms. Clymer, who gestured toward the visitor's door.

As Trinity entered the room, a man and woman abruptly stood up, each of them tightly holding on to the hands of a dark-haired boy. The woman looked as if she'd been crying, while the man glowered with repressed anger to mask his fear. The boy simply stared up at Trinity unsmilingly, his expression a mixture of curiosity and anxiety, but no recognition.

"Mr. and Mrs. Nessel," Red Wolf introduced them. "Martin, and his wife Tracy."

Trinity had to force himself to look away from the boy, and smile at the couple as he extended his hand. "It's a pleasure to meet you."

The man's handshake was perfunctory and a shade aggressive, while his wife's was cold.

"It's very nice . . . ," Mrs. Nessel started, then amended, "How do you do?"

"I just want to say . . ." Trinity swallowed hard. "I just want to say thank you. Thank you so much for coming."

Mr. Nessel glanced at his wife, his hostility giving way to uncertain gruffness. "You're welcome. This is our son, Tony."

"Hi, Tony," Trinity said tentatively. "How are you?"

"Okay, I guess," the boy responded gravely. He let go of his mother's hand to sweep the hair in his eyes back with his fingertips, a gesture so like Marie-Claude it made Trinity's heart ache. "Who are you?"

Trinity glanced up at Tracy Nessel's worried eyes.

"My name is Ben," he said simply.

# SANDRA
# RUTTAN

The police get the call: A four-year-old boy has been found beaten to death in the park. And almost as soon as Hart and Tain arrive at the scene, the case takes a strange turn.

They find the victim's brother hiding in the woods nearby. He says he saw the whole thing and claims his older sister is the killer. And she's missing....

When the boy's father is notified that his son is dead, his first response is to hire a high-powered attorney, who seems determined to create every legal roadblock he can for Hart and Tain. The search is on for the missing girl, and the case is about to get even stranger.

# THE
# FRAILTY
## OF FLESH

ISBN 13: 978-0-8439-6075-4

# HOW MUCH DO YOU OWE
# A FORMER LOVE?

# WINDY CITY
# KNIGHTS

Against his better judgment, private detective
Ron Shade let Paula back into his life, but then
she left again, without so much as a good-bye
kiss. Now she's turned up dead. Paula's cousin
doesn't think her death was an accident, and she
wants Shade to find out the truth. But the truth
is hard to find, and every time he gets close to it,
someone gets killed.

# MICHAEL A. BLACK

ISBN 13: 978-0-8439-6162-1

# STACY DITTRICH

Detective CeeCee Gallagher is no stranger to high-pressure cases. But this one could easily cost her career...and her life. A macabre serial killer is on the loose, leaving the bodies of his young victims made up to resemble dolls. With only a Bible passage sent by the killer to guide her, CeeCee will have to sacrifice everything to find him and end his reign of terror before another child is murdered.

# THE DEVIL'S CLOSET

*A CeeCee Gallagher Thriller*

ISBN 13: 978-0-8439-6159-1

---

# DOUGLAS MACKINNON

President of the United States Shelby Robertson is in the third year of his second term. Four-star general Wayne Mitchell is the man in charge of the nation's land-based nuclear arsenal.

For the past few years, both men have shared a common belief—**the apocalypse in coming.**

**And they are determined to hasten the process.**

Unless someone can stop them in time, they will set in motion a chain of events that could wipe clean the face of the earth.

# THE APOCALYPSE DIRECTIVE

ISBN 13: 978–0–8439–6088–4

# PAUL CARSON

# BETRAYAL

Frank Ryan knew his position as Chief Medical Officer at high-security Harmon Penitentiary was dangerous. After all, his predecessor had been murdered. But Frank never expected what happened to him the night he got that mysterious emergency call.

As he left his apartment he was
**KIDNAPPED,**
**BEATEN,**
**DRUGGED,**
and interrogated for six days.
Then, just as suddenly, released.

Now he can't find anyone who believes him, and his girlfriend has disappeared without a trace. His desperate search to find her—and some answers—lead Frank deeper and deeper into a sea of conspiracies, lies…and danger.

ISBN 13: 978-0-8439-6145-4

# ✂ ☐ **YES!**

Sign me up for the Leisure Thriller Book Club and send my FREE BOOKS! If I choose to stay in the club, I will pay only $8.50* each month, a savings of $7.48!

NAME: _____

ADDRESS: _____

TELEPHONE: _____

EMAIL: _____

☐ I want to pay by credit card.

☐ **VISA**    ☐ **MasterCard**    ☐ **DISCOVER**

ACCOUNT #: _____

EXPIRATION DATE: _____

SIGNATURE: _____

Mail this page along with $2.00 shipping and handling to:
**Leisure Thriller Book Club**
**PO Box 6640**
**Wayne, PA 19087**
Or fax (must include credit card information) to:
**610-995-9274**

You can also sign up online at **www.dorchesterpub.com**.
*Plus $2.00 for shipping. Offer open to residents of the U.S. and Canada only. Canadian residents please call 1-800-481-9191 for pricing information.
If under 18, a parent or guardian must sign. Terms, prices and conditions subject to change. Subscription subject to acceptance. Dorchester Publishing reserves the right to reject any order or cancel any subscription.